Longer Views

Other Books by the Author

Fiction

The Jewels of Aptor
The Fall of the Towers:
    Out of the Dead City
    The Towers of Toron
    City of a Thousand Suns
The Ballad of Beta-2
Babel-17
The Einstein Intersection
Nova
Driftglass (stories)
Equinox (The Tides of Lust)
Dhalgren
Trouble on Triton (Triton)
Distant Stars (stories)
Stars in My Pockets Like Grains of Sand
Return to Nevèrÿon:
    Tales of Nevèrÿon
    Neveryóna
    Flight from Nevèrÿon
    Return to Nevèrÿon (The Bridge of Lost Desire)
Driftglass/Starshards (collected stories)
They Fly at Çiron
The Mad Man
Hogg
Atlantis: Three Tales

Nonfiction

The Jewel-Hinged Jaw
The American Shore
Heavenly Breakfast
Starboard Wine
The Motion of Light in Water
Wagner/Artaud
The Straits of Messina
Silent Interviews

Longer Views

Extended Essays

Samuel R. Delany

WITH AN INTRODUCTION

BY KEN JAMES

Wesleyan University Press

Published by University Press of New England • Hanover and London

Wesleyan University Press
Published by University Press of New England, Hanover, NH 03755
Copyright © 1996 by Samuel R. Delany
Introduction copyright © 1996 by Ken James
All rights reserved
Printed in the United States of America 5 4 3 2 1
CIP data appear at the end of the book

"Wagner/Artaud" was first published by Ansatz Press (New York, 1988). Copyright ©
1988 by Samuel R. Delany.
"Aversion/Perversion/Diversion" was first published in *Negotiating Lesbian and Gay Subjects*,
ed. Monica Dorenkamp and Richard Henke (New York and London: Routledge, 1995).
"Shadows" was published in *The Jewel-Hinged Jaw*, by Samuel R. Delany (New York: Dragon
Press, 1977). Copyright © 1977 by Samuel R. Delany.

For

Henry Finder and

Kwame Anthony Appiah

Contents

Preface

In a critical epoch that has privileged, for twenty years or more, differ-ence, decantering, discontinuity, diversity, and pluralism over the elder gods of Unity, Totality, and Mastery, so much American nonfiction still finds itself attempting to appease those elder gods and their former conventions. Those of us who read regularly in criticism often find "books" whose "chapters" are, it's clear once we read two, three, or four of them, disconnected occasional essays. Often the "Introduction" that claims the remainder of the study will not attempt to negotiate its topic with systematic rigor actually introduces a collection of considerations simply of different topics. At the editorial level, forces (usually called "commercial"—though sometimes even more mystified than that) mili-tate to present collections and chrestomathies as concentrated studies.

The fiction writer is used to the same forces at work in the contour-ing of books: "Novels sell better than collections of short stories," we are told. "It's a truism of almost any fictive practice—mysteries, westerns, science fiction, or naturalistic fiction."

Most of my life my own preferred field has been science fiction; and because that field fosters so many series stories sharing characters and backgrounds, publishers and editors for many years took such stories and put them in books they called "novels," while renaming the indi-vidual stories "chapters"—largely at the behest of those forces.

The one form that—in science fiction, at any rate—tends to resist such handling is the long story (or novella). And in the range of literary criticism, it is the long essay—the essay too lengthy to be delivered comfortably as a fifty-minute lecture—that offers similar resistance to such totalizing conventions. What this tends to mean is that the collec-tion of longer essays—or, indeed, science fiction novellas—is treated as the *least* commercial of all works.

When publishers are brave enough to undertake such collections, readers, support them both!

I'm particularly grateful, then, to my editors, Terry Cochran and Suzanna Tamminen, and to my publisher, Wesleyan University Press and their editorial director, Eileen McWilliam, for accepting this book for what it is and for not suggesting I "wait till some of the pieces mature" (read: till I become tired of seeing them lie unpublished and eventually pad them out to book-length). Various readers have made wonderfully useful suggestions here and there during the composition process of these essays, including Don Eric Levine, Gordon Tapper, James Sallis, Ron Drummond, and all the editors just mentioned.

This book contains six moderately long essays with five distinct topics.

The first, "Wagner/Artaud: A Play of 19th and 20th Century Critical Fictions," has been published as a separate monograph by feisty little Ansatz Press (New York, 1988), that wonderful creation of Patrick Nielsen Hayden, Teresa Nielsen Hayden, and Tom Weber. Its topic is precisely its twain eponymous subjects—and the relationship between them as dramaturges and esthetic theoreticians. Three paragraphs have been added or expanded since the '88 edition; the diligent literary detective should be able to spot at least two of them.

"Reading at Work, and Other Activities Frowned on by Authority—A Reading of Donna Haraway's 'Manifesto for Cyborgs: Science, Technology, and Socialist Feminism in the 1980s'"—has, in pieces, provided me with various lectures since it was first written in 1985. It tries to give an account of that exciting and influential essay and at the same time tries to examine what the giving of such an account entails and, yes, means. At its center it contains a brief overview of the cyborg as a science fiction image in film, as well as a discussion of metaphor that seems to me necessarily anterior to any discussion of how *any* metaphor, such as the "cyborg," can work in the radical directions Haraway's manifesto proposes for it.

On the evening of November 1, 1991, "Aversion/Perversion/Diversion" was delivered as the Keynote Lecture at the Fifth Annual Lesbian and Gay Conference on Gay Studies, held that year at Rutgers University. It takes an anecdotal tour through some marginal tracks of contemporary (and, at that, largely queer) sexuality, even as its topic is the concept of discourse and its necessity for any sophisticated historical understanding.

This is also the topic of "Shadow and Ash"—an intellectual chrestomathy whose fragmentary method *is* finally its content. For me it is the most important essay here—and the one that needs the least prefatory matter.

"Atlantis Rose . . ." is a study of the poetry of Hart Crane, with an emphasis on Crane's wonderfully rich poetic series, *The Bridge.* Though

I hope this essay can be enjoyed without Crane's text to hand, I would urge readers to procure a copy of that wonderfully rich poem, and—in fact—to read *The Bridge* through at least once just before beginning the essay, to pause now and again to reread various sections of it on their first trip through my essay, and to read Crane's poem once more on finishing my notes here. (Poet James Tate suggests at least one of those readings be out loud.) Though I understand most of us—even most professional critics—don't have time for such elaborate undertakings, that's still the *ideal* reading my study presupposes.

As an appendix I have included another long essay that first appeared in two installments in *Foundation* 6 (London, May 1974) and the double issue *Foundation* 7/8 (London, November 1975), though it was first drafted in 1973 while I lived in England. (I revised it heavily in '74 for the *Foundation* publication; then again in '78 and again in '79.) I can't believe anyone, in considering the hard-edged language games around which so much Anglo-American philosophy is constituted, would not find the margins of their thought occasionally troubled by the illusory quality of those edges that recontextualization is constantly and playfully suggesting. Such games are predicated on the idea that certain words have their meanings because certain other meanings are rigorously excluded from ever occupying the same semantic space, e.g., whatever "blue" means, it can never mean "red." But recontextualization always presents, at least as a sort of limit case, possibilities of the following order: "Whenever I hold up the placard with the word 'blue' on it, I want you to hold up the placard in front of you colored red—rather than the one colored green, blue, yellow, or purple." If we assent to such a request, then—in such a context, however rarely it might arise in life—the word "blue" there "means" the color red. One might point out that, in such a context, the word "means" does not mean precisely what it usually means—to which one can only nod agreement: that's true. Still, that meaning of "means" is a recognizable meaning, controlled by the context. But this and many other observations make the hard-edged boundaries of meaning that control the speculations of natural language philosophers and speech act theorists so problematic.

The work of continental philosophers like Derrida has not explained away such problems. But it has demonstrated why such problems are not some marginal impediment to a more mathematically solid model of language but are rather inescapable and fundamental to what language is and how it functions, i.e., that a word is *never* out of a specific context limiting its meaning, even when it is isolated by a line of white paper above and below it, or when it is beside its definition on the dictionary page, or when it is cited as a general instance of meaning in a philosophy paper (i.e., that the absolute and unlimited Word-with-its-meaning—the transcendental Logos—is an illusion).

"Shadows," then, represents what I hope some readers will find an interesting piece of transitional thinking between the two traditions. And it prefigures much of the later work. If "Shadow and Ash" is the most important essay here, then "Shadows" is *its* lengthy, chrestomathic preface.

The excuse for such a collection is not to provide "a good read" but—indeed—to provide several, some sequential, others simultaneous. For reading is a many-layered process—like writing. The different forms, such as the long essay *vis-à-vis* the short, all have their separate excellences and pleasures. I hope this collection presents a rich field in which to look for—if not to find—them.

— New York
21 October 1993

Extensions

An Introduction to the Longer Views of Samuel R. Delany

BY KEN JAMES

> There is here a problem of framing, of bordering and delimitation, whose analysis must be very finely detailed if it wishes to ascertain the effects of fiction.
>
> — Jacques Derrida

I

The term "extended essay," in its very articulation, seems to presuppose a norm which is somehow being supplemented, exceeded, transgressed. Certainly the long pieces in the remarkable collection to follow do not fit the form of the essay we have been led (by whom? by what? for what purpose?) to expect; nor does the experience of reading them *feel* like the experience of reading a traditional essay. To better understand what these pieces are up to, then, we might want to consider the form against which they position themselves.

What constitutes a "traditional" essay, and what is the experience of reading one like? Obviously to make generalizations about a form with such a wide range of possible topics (i.e., just about anything) and possible writerly approaches is to construct something of a fiction; nevertheless, generalizations about normative trends—generalizations about what we have come to expect from an essay—are possible. Lydia Fakundiny characterizes the essay in passing as a "short, independent, self-contained prose discourse."[1] Fair enough. But as has been noted by Fakundiny and many other scholars of the history of the essay, there are other, more specific traits which have characterized the essay since the traditionally posited birth of its modern form in the sixteenth-century writings of Michel de Montaigne and Francis Bacon. From

Montaigne, for example, we inherit (among other things) a focus on the personal, on the authorial subject as the ground and goal of analytical inquiry. Montaigne prefaced his epoch-making *Essais* with a warning to the reader that, whatever the ostensible subject-matter of the pieces to follow, "I myself am the subject of my book."[2] Ever since then, essayists have, with varying degrees of intensity, been committed to presenting "the spectacle of a single consciousness making sense of a part of the chaos" of life.[3] From Bacon, we get a writerly stance that tends towards didacticism, in the specifically aphoristic mode. Bacon's *Essays*, which appeared 17 years after the publication of the first edition of Montaigne's collection, are written in a terse, pithy, authoritarian style: they do not so much analyze topics as list epigrams. Here is a well-known example of typical Baconian prose:

> Crafty men condemn studies; simple men admire them; and wise men use them . . . Some books are to be tasted, others to be swallowed, and some few to be chewed and digested: that is, some books are to be read only in parts; others to be read but not curiously; and some few to be read wholly, and with diligence and attention . . . Reading maketh a full man; conference a ready man; and writing an exact man.[4]

In Bacon we find the seeds of what the essay was to become a little over a century later in the hands of Joseph Addison and Richard Steele— a specifically *urban* mode of writing, offering an authoritarian moral compass for those who would live in the city. (At the same time, a critical tradition was developing from the essay's classical roots, giving rise to the "impersonal" form which constitutes most academic writing today.)

What often seems to characterize the works of the most popular contemporary essayists is a combination of the didactic tone of Bacon *with* the self-presentational obsessions of Montaigne—a conflation of the authorial and the authoritarian. Consider the following passage from *The Writing Life*, in which Annie Dillard compares the experience of essay-writing to a kind of path-finding:

> You make the path boldly and follow it fearfully. You go where the path leads. At the end of the path, you find a box canyon. You hammer out reports, dispatch bulletins.
>
> The writing has changed, in your hands, and in a twinkling, from an expression of your notions to an epistemological tool. The new place interests you because it is not clear. You attend. In your humility, you lay down the words carefully, watching all the angles. Now the earlier writing looks soft and careless. Process is nothing; erase your tracks. The path is not the work.[5]

Note how Dillard's use of the second-person pronoun causes the sentences in this passage to waver between description and injunction; note too how the passage gathers rhetorical energy as its sentences approach the aphoristic. I would argue that the personal focus of this passage and its epigrammatic style are typical-unto-defining traits of the contemporary essay. Certainly they are traits which, knowingly or unknowingly, we *expect* of it.

But as Roland Barthes—one of the great essayists of the twentieth century and possibly the first great theorist of the form—has persuasively argued, spectacle (even the spectacle of self-portraiture) and aphorism are two major rhetorical modes of conservative discourse—the discourse of the status quo. According to Barthes, spectacle discourages critical consideration of "motives" and "consequences"[6] as it treats the spectator to the brief illusion of a "univocal" moral order (M 25). Aphorisms, similarly, derive much of their authoritative force from their implicit affirmation of such an order, such an "unalterable hierarchy of the world" (M 154). Aphorisms serve the purposes of the status quo precisely because their seemingly "pithy" declarations discourage further inquiry into their authorizing context. The root-meaning of the word gives it away: *apo-horizein*—to delimit, to mark off boundaries, to circumscribe a horizon. Edward Hoagland has commented on the complicity of the essay with the preservation of the status quo:

> The essay is a vulnerable form. Rooted in middle-class civility, it presupposes not only that the essayist himself be demonstrably sane, but that his readers also operate upon a set of widely held assumptions. Fiction can be hallucinatory if it wishes, and journalism impassive, and so each continues through thick and thin, but essays presuppose a certain standard of education in the reader, a world ruled by some sort of order—where government is constitutional, or at least monarchical, perhaps where sex hasn't wandered too far from its home base . . .[7]

Clearly, the essay is ripe for a radical rhetorical intervention.

Samuel R. Delany was born in 1942 and raised in New York City's Harlem. Something of a prodigy, he published his first novel at age 20, and has made radical interventions in various literary and paraliterary practices for over thirty years now. In the science fiction field, he is a renowned novelist and critic, having garnered four Nebula Awards and a Hugo Award for his fiction, as well as the nonfiction Hugo for his autobiography, *The Motion of Light in Water*. His numerous studies of the history and rhetoric of science fiction have moved his colleague Ursula K. Le Guin to call him "our best in-house critic."[8] Delany has also written for comic books, and has produced a remarkable trio of pornographic novels (or "anti-pornographies," as his critical alter-ego, K. Leslie Steiner, calls them): *Equinox, Hogg,* and *The Mad Man.* And he has recently made a foray into historical fiction with the short novel *Atlantis: Model 1924,* which details a meeting between characters modeled after Delany's own father as a young man and the poet Hart Crane, on the Brooklyn Bridge one bright afternoon in, yes, 1924. Over the course of his career, Delany has again and again thrown into question the world-models that all too many of us unknowingly live by—particularly, but certainly not restricted to, those models which relate to sexual identity and practice. For this aspect of his work, in 1993 he was given the fifth William Whitehead Memorial Award for Lifetime Contribution to Gay and Lesbian Literature, an honor he shares with Edmund White, Audre Lorde, Adrienne Rich, and James Purdy.

These accolades have not come without controversy. Examples: in 1974, Delany published an 879-page novel, *Dhalgren,* which—with its story of a bisexual amnesiac's rise to fame in a mysteriously burned-out midwestern city, its frank depictions of marginal sexual practices and the social forces surrounding and pervading them, and its notoriously complex formal structure—inspired a heated discussion within the sf community about, among many other things, the very nature of science fiction, which continues in various circles to this day; and in 1979, Delany published the first of what would become four volumes of interlocking narratives collectively known as Return to Nevèrÿon, an experiment in paraliterary form which—with its unlikely combination of the hoary formulas of sword-and-sorcery fantasy with the sophisticated rhetoric of structuralist and post-structuralist theory, as well as its exploration of marginal sexuality—inaugurated a spirited debate over the question of what sort of rhetoric is "proper" to the paraliterary fields of science fiction and academic criticism. Over the course of these ongoing genre-bending interventions, Delany has had a huge influence over a whole generation of writers and thinkers: he is regularly cited as arguably *the* major sf influence, in both style and subject matter, on the cyberpunk movement, and is cited with equal regularity as a major force behind the current academic recognition of science fiction as one of the most vital and innovative fields of contemporary American writing.

In his previous critical work—collected in *The Jewel-Hinged Jaw, Starboard Wine,* and *The Straits of Messina*—Delany has more or less restricted himself to the expository form of the "standard" critical essay. (Exceptions to this restriction are "Shadows" from *The Jewel-Hinged Jaw*—included as an Appendix to this collection—and *The American Shore,* a book-length, microscopically detailed "meditation" on the sf short story "Angouleme" by Thomas M. Disch.) In the present collection, Delany turns his considerable creative and analytical energies toward a radical reworking of the essay form. He does this in part by combining, at various strategic points, the "impersonal" rhetoric of literary analysis with the "personal" voice of the Montaignean essay—a mixing of rhetorical modes which has attracted increasing interest over the years, in light of the critiques of the Western discourse of the sign and the subject put forward variously by post-structuralist, feminist, and Frankfurt School critics, among others. Delany also deploys formal tropes which he has developed and refined in his own fiction over the past two decades or so—particularly in *Dhalgren, Triton,* and that undecidable hybrid of theory and fiction, Return to Nevèr̈yon: dialectical framing structures, short textual units numbered in Wittgensteinian fashion, multiply-intersecting stories, and so on. By deploying those tropes here, Delany produces essays which, in their complexity of form and richness of resonance, resemble novels—and postmodernist novels to boot. The result for the reader is an experience which simply cannot be found anywhere else on the current American literary landscape.

It has often been observed that Delany's work is deeply concerned with myth. Specifically, as Delany himself has pointed out, it is concerned with myth-*making*—with the social, material, and historical forces that generate cultural myths.[9] The essays to follow share this concern. But they are also equally concerned with myth-*breaking*—with the analytical practices required to discern, interrogate, and dissolve myths. Nothing if not ambitious, these essays tackle the myths of High Art vs. Low, of Sanity vs. Madness, of Theater-As-We-Know-It, of castration as the Freudian and Lacanian model of socialization, of transcendent sexual difference, of biography, of the canon, and indeed of the very concept of "literature."

But these essays also interrogate a myth of the essay itself: specifically, the traditional perception of the essay as a "shapeless" form of writing. Critics, reacting to this perceived shapelessness, have for a long time called the essay a "degenerate" and even "impossible" genre, and it has never had a firm foothold in the canon of English literature—a state of affairs which once led the great American essayist E. B. White, only half-jokingly, to call essay-writers second-class citizens. Critics of a more recent generation have tried to recuperate the essay by turning this shapelessness into a plus-value, positing it as the ideal (non-)form with which to critique totalizing systems, or, more radically, as "the moment of writing *before* the genre, before genericness—or as the matrix of all generic possibilities."[10] But it is the underlying ideas of both these critical positions—that there can be such a thing as a "shapeless" discourse unfixed by pre-existing rhetorical practices, or that any single rhetorical mode could serve as the "primitive calculus" underlying everything subsequent to it—which Delany has called into question time and time again in his work.[11]

With this collection, Delany continues his critique. As I've noted, at certain points along the way he deploys formal tropes which his long-time readers may find familiar. But whether previously acquainted with Delany's work or not, readers expecting the short, monologic prose discourse that is the currently dominant form of the essay are in for a surprise—for these essays are not like other essays.

They are huge, sprawling works, encompassing an enormous range of topics and disciplines—from the origins of modern theater to the vagaries of radical feminist scholarship, from mathematical logic to the most marginal of sexual practices, from the photographs of Robert Mapplethorpe to the intricacies of literary historical sleuthing, and much, much more—and they combine these topics in interlocking narratives of madmen and burning cities, prodigies and poets, cyborgs, street-hustlers, and the author's own life, in language that is sometimes light and anecdotal, sometimes vertiginously self-reflexive, but always lucid, luminous and exuberant. "Chrestomathies," Delany calls some of the pieces to come: collections of textual fragments whose numerous interrelations the reader must actively trace out in order to gather them up into a resonant whole. In their encouragement of active reading, these essays resemble what Barthes has called the "writerly" text, the text "produced" as much by the reader as by the writer:

> This text is a galaxy of signifiers, not a structure of signifieds; it is reversible; we gain access to it by several entrances, none of which can be authoritatively declared to be the main one; the codes it mobilizes extend *as far as the eye can reach.*[12]

If any single idea can be said to fuel the fires of all these essays, it is the Foucauldian notion of discourse—the notion of the socially sanctioned systems of perception and practice that hold us all in their thrall, the "structuring and structurating" forces which keep myths alive and preserve the status quo[13]—forces which can only be countered by a "violent rhetorical shift" somewhere in the discursive space (RS 235). And herein lies the relevance, the urgency of these essays. As intellectual entertainments, they make great demands on the reader—and offer unprecedented rewards. But they are more than just entertainments: they are radical rhetorical interventions in the discourse of reading itself. And their radicalism resides precisely in their acknowledgment of the existence of the radical reader: the reader who thinks, who writes, who intervenes.

In the discussion to follow, I shall very briefly review some concepts from Delany's earlier nonfiction works about the language of science fiction which have a bearing on the analyses Delany carries out here. I will then try to suggest how the formal strategies Delany deploys in these essays both illuminate and are illuminated by the formal strategies of his fiction, as well as how they reflect the theoretical framework which surrounds and informs so much of Delany's recent fiction and nonfiction. If (to paraphrase Delany) my informal, idiosyncratic, and indeed fragmentary remarks initiate dialogue, so much the better; if they close dialogue off, so much the worse. I hope only to provide a provisional analytical frame to assist the radical reader in her further explorations of the rich and complex universes of discourse which these essays both describe and generate.

II

Science fiction, like the essay, is a form which, in its more popular incarnations, has often tended toward the didactic, in the mode of the aphoristic. Robert Heinlein and Frank Herbert, to name two examples, have actually published the "collected sayings" of their best-known fictive protagonists, Lazarus Long and Paul Atreides. Ursula Le Guin's fiction also leans toward aphorism, her essays doubly so; the list could go on. In his earlier critical work, Delany has discussed in some detail the problem of didacticism in Heinlein and Le Guin specifically and in science fiction and literature in general. (The long interpolated monologues in Return to Nevèrÿon could be read as attempts to suggest some aesthetic solutions to the problem.) Paradoxically, however, Delany has also argued that despite its flirtation with the authoritarian mode, science fiction may still be *the* privileged genre for writing against what constitutes a significant aspect of today's status quo.

To understand Delany's argument we need to recall Barthes's assertion that conservative discourse tends to de-historicize phenomena which are historically specific. In the rhetoric of this discourse, "things lose the memory that they once were made" (M 142). Both the aphoristic style and the spectacle work to reinforce this confounding of the historical and the natural. In viewing spectacle, "all that is left for one to do is to enjoy this beautiful object without wondering where it comes from" (M 151). Likewise, the aphorism is "no longer directed towards

a world to be made; it must overlay one which is already made, bury
the traces of this production under a self-evident appearance of eternity" (M 155). Delany argues that the rhetoric of science fiction foregrounds precisely the historical, social, and technological constitution
of human landscapes which conservative rhetoric tends to obscure. In
this way the rhetoric of sf differs fundamentally from the rhetoric of
"literature," the conventions and tropes of which are organized around
an entirely different focus:

> Despite the many meaningful differences in the ways of reading that consti-
> tute the specifically literary modes, they are all characterized—now, today—
> by a priority of the subject, i.e., of the self, of human consciousness. To a
> greater or lesser extent, the subject can be read as the organizational center
> of all the literary categories' many, many differing expectations . . .
>
>   Answering its own expectations as a paraliterary mode, science fiction is
> far more concerned with the organization (and reorganization) of the ob-
> ject, i.e., the world, or the institutions through which we perceive it. It is
> concerned with the subject, certainly, but concerned with those aspects of it
> that are closer to the object: How is the subject excited, impinged on, con-
> toured and constituted by the object?[14]

The point is not merely that sf tends to be "about" the object in the
sense of taking the object as its main topic of interest; it is, rather, that
all of the conventions, tropes, and reading protocols that mark science
fiction as science fiction are organized around a revelation of the object and its constituting context. And herein lies the potentially radical
force of the genre:

> . . . even the most passing mention by an sf writer of, say, ". . . the monopole
> magnet mining operations in the outer asteroid belt of Delta Cygni," begins
> as a simple way of saying that, while the concept of mines may persist, their
> object, their organization, their technology, their locations, and their very
> form can change—and it says it directly and clearly and well before it offers
> any metaphor for any psychic mystery or psychological state. Not to under-
> stand this object-critique, on whatever intuitive level, is to misread the
> phrase . . . (SW 188)

By this rhetorical model, we can see that even the most conservatively inclined science fiction, if it is in any way sophisticated *as* science fiction,
must keep a certain margin of imaginative space open for an apprehension of the historicity of objects, landscapes, and social institutions. By
this model we can also see that science fiction differs from the essay in

at least one of the same ways that it differs from literary fiction: for like literary fiction, the essay is rhetorically oriented toward a revelation of the subject, toward the presentation of a "spectacle of a single consciousness trying to make sense of the chaos." The problem for both literary fiction and the essay is that the "chaos" of the modern world originates primarily as a chaos of the object, not the subject (SW 158)—which renders these forms, at least vis-à-vis the manifold problems of the object, conservative by default.

Bearing in mind the notion of science fiction as object-critique, we can begin to see why a radical practitioner of the genre such as Delany might take an interest in such recondite analytical practices as Marxian critique, deconstructive criticism, and discourse analysis. All offer sophisticated ways of considering the relations of objects, texts, and social practices to their ideological, linguistic, and socio-historical surrounds, and all are in one way or another committed to the exploration of the *social* constitution of the individual subject, that is, "those aspects of the self that are closer to the object." All, in sum, are ways of breaking myths—ways of scrutinizing things which may seem eternal, totalized, and systemic, and questioning their totality, interrogating their systematicity.

The obstacle to such analysis, on the one hand, is the pervasive influence of the discursive surround, the interpretive context "by which we register a text well-formed or ill-formed" (RS 235). Only vigilant analytical attention can tease out the myths that discourse has embedded in any given text, precisely because discourse determines the attentional norm:

> For what discourse does above all things is to assign import. Discourse, remember, is what allows us to make sense of what we see, and hear, and experience . . . Discourse is what tells us what is central and what is peripheral— what is a mistake, an anomaly, an accident, a joke. It tells us what to pay attention to and what to ignore. It tells us what sort of attention to pay. (RS 239)

The possibility of such analysis, on the other hand, resides in language's tendency towards "unlimited semiosis"—the tendency of linguistic signs and sign-arrangements to carry connotations in excess of the normative meanings to which the discourse is perpetually working to restrict them. Deconstruction and discourse analysis exploit this inherent richness of language by evoking those meanings which the given discourse has systematically relegated to the margins of consideration, thus problematizing the meanings which would at first seem unproblematically and eternally lodged in the discourse's rhetorical center. Characterized in this way, theory begins to look like more than just a range of analytical methodologies to be applied *to* a science fiction text, or a set of rhetorical tools to apply *within* a science fiction text, but rather like a case of convergent evolution with science fiction in general. If we view them both as ways of reading and writing the silences of objects, texts, and discursive landscapes, then theory and science fiction begin to look like two very closely related modes of inquiry.

The term "unlimited semiosis" comes from the American philosopher Charles Saunders Peirce, but the idea as Delany deploys it comes from the post-structuralist critique of the Western discourse of the sign. In that discourse, the relation between linguistic signifier and nonlinguistic ("objective") signified is presumed to be clear, direct, and unproblematic; by extension, texts are presumed to have clearly delineated, finite, and masterable meanings derivable from their concatenation of signs. In post-structuralist discourse, on the other hand, linguistic signifiers do not point towards a transparently clear objective reality (what Derrida calls the "transcendental signified"), but rather towards one another in a dynamic interrelational process occurring within a larger linguistic/discursive system ("The signified," explains Delany, "is therefore always a web of signifiers"[15]).

By this argument, a "theme"—conceived in traditional discourse as an object-like "thing" which one "finds" in a given text—is actually an artifact of a readerly predisposition to order textual signs in a certain way. It marks a preconception, an effect of discourse; it has, in Delany's words, "the same political structure as a prejudice."[16] In order to get around such prejudicial reading, Delany argues, we have to stop seeing the text as a linguistic construct with object-like, synchronic referents or themes hovering "behind" it, to be systematically uncovered in a hermeneutical reading process, and start seeing the text as "a space of discourse—the space in which, at various points and along various loci, discourses (of whatever rhetorical expressions the reader is led to make) may be organized in relation to one another" (AS 174). That is, we must see the text as a contestatory site where various discursive relations are transformed by the reader in an ongoing, diachronic process of reconceptualization and revision.

(It should be noted here that Delany, like certain post-structuralists, has observed in Barthes a tendency to discuss texts in thematic terms: "Even the plural text of Barthes is a synchronic plurality" (SW 205). Delany's answer to Barthes can be found in *The American Shore*, which formally resembles Barthes's *S/Z* but differs from it theoretically in many significant respects. More on this ambiguity in Barthes's work later.)

The diachronic, discourse-space model of writing and reading has the obvious virtue of being empirically more compelling than the synchronic-thematic model: it describes a situation that *feels* more like what we do when we read and write. It also has the more subtle virtue of reminding us that discourses are not monolithic structures, despite their pervasive and seemingly systemic influence; it shows, rather, that they arise from and are subject to the rhetorical interventions of the conscientious writer and the sensitive reader. In other words, it reminds us (to paraphrase ethnographer Stephen Tyler) that discourse can always be relativized to rhetoric.[17]

For a gay black man such as Delany—or for anyone of whatever social position committed to a critique of or intervention in a status quo which seems to derive much of its strength from a whole series of discursive and coercive exclusions and oppressions—the recognition of the relativization of discourse to rhetoric is a tremendously empowering political truth. It is empowering in one sense because it reminds us that the pretense to universal authority which Barthes has shown to be the hallmark of the rhetoric of the status quo is just that, a pretense: every utterance, no matter how much it evokes a transcendental system of authority to legitimate itself, can always be traced back to an individual or group with a historically, socially, and materially specific position. It is empowering in another sense because it places the power to revise a discourse back into our hands, with whatever personal or collective energy we can bring to our revisionary project:

> Discourse says, "You are."
> Rhetoric preserves the freedom to say, "I am not." (AS 172)

Delany's own creative output can be read as a rigorous analysis of the implications of this freedom, as well as an exercising—through the production of radical paraliterary works—of this same freedom. It remains for us to look at the fallout of this prior creative work in the essays to follow.

III

The moment we turn to consider the essays in this collection, we are faced with a choice: the choice of where to begin. In his Preface, Delany informs us that the essay in the Appendix to this collection, "Shadows," was actually the first essay to be published, and is itself a preface to "Shadow and Ash," one of the essays in the collection "proper." Do we prioritize chronology of publication, then, and read "Shadows" before the rest? (But then we would also want to read "Reading at Work" before "Wagner/Artaud" . . .) Do we wait until we are about to commence "Shadow and Ash," and then read "Shadows" as a preface to that essay only? Or do we hold to the reading protocol that says an Appendix is only a marginal supplement to a main text—and defer reading "Shadows" until the very end, if we read it at all?

While we ponder our options, we might want to consider a passage from an essay completely outside this collection (except of course by citing it here I am bringing it part-way in . . .), in which Delany discusses the post-structuralist project of writing against the discourse of unity and totality:

> Under such an analytic program, the beginnings and ends of critical argu-
> ments and essays grow particularly difficult. The "natural" sense of com-
> mencement and sense of closure the thematic critics consider appropriate
> to, and imminently allied throughout, the "naturally" bounded topic of his
> or her concern now is revealed to be largely artificial and overwhelmingly
> ideological.
>
> Thus the beginnings and endings (as well as the easier middle argu-
> ments, once we are aboard) of our criticisms must embody conscientiously
> creative and political strategies. (NFW 23–4)

In the case of the work at hand, we are given a text with several possible "proper" beginnings, the choice of which involves conscious (as well as conscientiously creative and political) reflection on the reader's part over where in the discursive space she wants to position herself. Delany has used this strategic deployment of central and marginal texts extensively in Return to Nevèrÿon, each volume of which has its share of "proper" and "supplemental" tales. This strategy made its first overt appearance, however, in Delany's 1976 novel *Triton* (written concurrently with "Shadows"), which consists of a main text and two Appendices. (*Dhalgren* is similarly structured, but there the central/marginal relation is more subtle.)

Let us say, purely for the sake of argument, that we have chosen to read "Shadows" first.

The first thing we notice about "Shadows" is its unusual structure. A description of this structure can be found in "Appendix B" of *Triton*, in which "Shadows" makes a metafictional cameo appearance as the historical antecedent to the "modular calculus," an invention of the 22nd-century philosopher Ashima Slade ("Slade," says the unnamed scholarly "author" of the text of "Appendix B," "took the title for his

first lecture, "Shadows," from a nonfiction piece written in the twentieth century by a writer of light, popular fictions. . . ."[18] Here is a description of Slade's "Shadows":

> A difficulty with "Shadows," besides its incompleteness, is that Slade chose
> to present his ideas not as a continuous argument, but rather as a series of
> separate, numbered notes, each more or less a complete idea—the whole a
> galaxy of ideas that interrelate and interilluminate each other, not necessar-
> ily in linear form. (T 356)

Cross-checking confirms that this is indeed an accurate description of
the formal structure of Delany's "Shadows"—as well as clearly recalling
Barthes's characterization of the "writerly" text as a "galaxy of signifiers."
  However, our scholar also observes that if certain numbered notes
in (Slade's) "Shadows" are considered in isolation from their surrounding text, they seem to resemble nothing more than "a few more
or less interesting aphorisms" (T 357). Cross-checking again confirms
this aphoristic pattern in Delany's "Shadows." Given what we have
come to know about aphorisms, their appearance in this essay may
seem problematic.
  But consider: through their nonlinear relational logic, the sixty
numbered notes that make up the body of "Shadows" evoke a complex
discursive space with many dimensions. One could say that each of the
notes corresponds not just to a different coordinate position in that
space, but to a different dimensional axis in it: to read the essay is both
to construct that space and trace a vector path through it. To read any
given note as though this multidimensional framing context did not
exist, then, is essentially to misread it. As Slade himself comments
(and, ironically, this is the one statement we are told Slade has "lifted"
from Delany's text): "I distrust separating facts too far from the landscape that produced them" (T 357). This suggests that an aphorism
can be as much a product of reading as writing: if we, as readers, omit
enough of the descriptive context, we can reduce the potentially rich
information-value of a complex statement down to the degenerate information-value of an aphorism.
  "Shadows" explores the problematic relation between model and
context through personal anecdotes, speculative fictions, strategically
placed "aphorisms," and critical meditations on the works of Wittgenstein, Quine, Chomsky, and other such system-builders. The reader can
find in this exploration an early articulation of the problem of "empirical resolution" that provides the epistemological "arc" for the entire
Return to Nevèrÿon series (in which what seems to be a revelatory

process of mirroring or echoing in the early volumes—a proliferation of metaphorical correspondences between objects, events, and situations—shades over into an oppressive process of mistaken identity and confounding doubling in the later ones). The reader can also find an early articulation of Delany's concern with the relation of biography to form and context, which he explores in greater detail in the other essays of this collection, as well as in his own autobiography, *The Motion of Light in Water* (which, along with "The Tale of Plagues and Carnivals" in *Flight from Nevèrÿon*, and "The Tale of Rumor and Desire" in *Return to Nevèrÿon*, displays the same chrestomathic organization as "Shadows").

"Shadows" commences with an announcement that it was written "in lieu of the personal article requested on the development of a science-fiction writer."[19] After fifty-two notes, we do eventually reach the personal article in question. But by the time we get there, the autobiographical sketch seems to be less "about" its ostensible topic—the teleological development of the self, which the discourse of biography teaches us to expect—and more "about" its own enunciative context, within the greater text, discourse, and world at large. In the absence of a definitive referential center, the act of interpretation then becomes a task of "locating the play in the interpretive space, rather than positing a unitary or hierarchical explanation" (SW 95). It is in this frame of mind that we might want to approach the sixty notes—the sixty axes that make up the referential space—of "Shadows."

The formal structure of "Wagner/Artaud: A Play of 19th and 20th Century Critical Fictions" begins to suggest what an argument framed within such a multidimensional space would have to be shaped like—and the sort of reading that would be required to follow such an argument. At first glance, the essay appears to be structured like a conventional literary analysis. But once we begin, we quickly find that the text does not proceed in the linear manner we expect of such an analysis: in place of an unfolding linear argument, we are instead given a series of intersecting stories (and the fictive antecedent to this is once again Return to Nevèrÿon). As the text alights variously on Antonin Artaud's life, works, and correspondences, Richard Wagner's memoirs, and Delany's own autobiographical reminiscences, we are forced again and again to ask, "*What* is the unifying thread or argument holding these tales together? *Why*, if there is an argument, is it being presented in this way?" To pull order and pattern out of the essay, we must do a fair amount of mental work in holding these tales together in memory: in this sense, the act of reading "Wagner/Artaud" becomes something of a sustained performance.

The essay's ostensible analytical goal is to read the fragmentary aesthetic of Artaud against the discourse of "High Art" as embodied in the theatrical practices institutionalized by Wagner. To carry out this reading, Delany reconstructs events in Wagner's life which have either been suppressed by Wagner himself or, when brought to the surface and analyzed by others, have been misinterpreted due to the predispositions imposed by subsequent discursive practices. Delany thus takes biographical elements which have proved most susceptible to the colorings of discourse—to mythopoesis—and renders them vivid, concrete, and contextually specific. As we've noted earlier, this is a key move in discourse analysis. In place of a pervasive set of artistic practices which are usually accepted without question or even notice, Delany substitutes a life, its socioeconomic context, and the materially specific foundations of those artistic practices—which *can* be noticed and questioned.

The strategic placement of the two autobiographical passages near the beginning and end of "Wagner/Artaud" creates a conceptual frame within which the transformation of the myth of Wagnerian discourse can be observed. In the first passage, we are given a vivid account of the chaotic goings-on backstage during a Wagner performance at the newly opened Metropolitan Opera House at Lincoln Center:

> The proscenium is not before you to frame what you see: costumed chorus members in their intense make-up mingle with workmen in their greens and blues and technicians in sweaters and jeans, with metal scaffolding all around (invisible from the seats), lights hung every which where, and music always playing through the lights and motion and general hubbub, so that the effect is more like watching a circus rehearsal scattered about the floor of some vast hangar than an artistic performance.[20]

We are then immediately given a metaphorical reading of this episode:

> . . . one reason it is sometimes so hard to evaluate Wagner's influence is because we are always within it. We can never get outside it, never see it as an organized stage picture. There is no vantage from which we can slip into the audience and look at it objectively. (W/A 21)

By this reading, the all-engulfing backstage experience becomes an image of the ubiquity of Wagnerian aesthetic practices—in ironic contrast to the spectacle of transcendence which those practices strive to generate onstage. Yet there seems to be more to this anecdote than a metaphor for pervasiveness—the images are *too* vivid, *too* concrete. There is an excess of signification.

In the second passage near the essay's close, Delany considers Walter Benjamin's notion of the "aura" of the work of art. Arguing (contra Benjamin) that the aura is precisely what is *preserved* in the mechanical reproduction of art, rather than what is lost, Delany shows how a biographical account of a direct encounter with a work of art—such as his own with Picasso's *Guernica*—can serve as an empirical counter to the mythic "aura" that Wagnerian discourse places around reproductions (W/A 78). This conception of biography as empirical counter provides a second reading for the backstage passage: what stands out now is less the all-engulfing quality of the space than its intense material specificity. Backstage at the Met now looks less like an image of all-encompassing Wagnerism and more like an inadvertent manifestation of Artaud's insistently corporeal Theater of Cruelty. The guiding metaphor—theater as discourse—has, by its own signifying excess, overturned and revealed its subversive underside.

The deployment of a self-deconstructing framing structure here recalls the beginnings-and-endings of several of Delany's novels, most notably *Dhalgren* and *Neverýona*. Like the framing structures of those earlier works, the theater-metaphor framing "Wagner/Artaud" yields up two equally viable yet mutually subversive readings, neither of which can crystallize out into "the" definitive interpretation. Moreover, the closer we look at these two readings individually, the richer and more complex they seem to become within themselves. This self-complexifying quality suggests an explanation for the intriguing pile-up of ironies and subversions in the essay's closing pages: the simple thematic opposition of Wagner as the Elder God of the discourse of "High Art" to Artaud as the deranged Trickster God of postmodernism has begun to crumble under the weight of the analytical pressure Delany has applied to it. In its form, then, "Wagner/Artaud" is a classic deconstruction—an analysis which "dissolves the borders that allow us to recognize [a theme] in the first place" (NFW 8).

The notion of reading a metaphor or theme into its own radicalness is given its most explicit consideration in "Reading at Work, and Other Activities Frowned on by Authority: A Reading of Donna Haraway's 'Manifesto for Cyborgs.'" As in "Wagner/Artaud," the privileged critical method is the argument from empirical evidence—and as in "Wagner/Artaud," the steady accumulation of evidence leads to an overturning or inversion of the guiding theme: through an extended consideration of Haraway's notion of cyborg-as-metaphor, Delany arrives at the notion of metaphor-as-cyborg. A significant distinction between the two essays is that in "Wagner/Artaud," Delany supplies the guiding metaphor, whereas in "Reading at Work," the guiding metaphor in question is Haraway's, which Delany proceeds to re-frame. This process of re-framing continues on many levels throughout the essay: over its course, we are given a reading of Haraway's essay, and a reading of that reading; we are given a Lacanian reading of castration imagery in pop culture, and a reading of Lacanian readings in general; we are given an explication of the notion of radical metaphor, even as the form of the explication is revealed to follow from the conclusion it itself yields up. In terms of sheer economy of means, the number of simultaneous readings Delany manages to orchestrate in this 32-page essay is a bit dizzying. And as with "Wagner/Artaud," the vertiginousness of our experience is in direct proportion to the rigor of our own reading—a reading which reveals, once again, the cohering and dissolution of a rhetorical object (in this case, the traditional conception of metaphor itself) within a posited discursive space.

But beyond the textual transformations going on inside "Reading at Work," there are texts outside the essay with which it is clearly engaged as well. Readers familiar with contemporary theory will recognize in the discussion of castration and the images of theft and reciprocity clear references to the "Purloined Letter" debate, inaugurated by the French psychoanalyst Jacques Lacan's analysis of Poe's short story. Although it is in no way necessary to be familiar with this debate to follow Delany's argument, we might nevertheless want to consider the relation between them. In Lacan's conception, the paralysis that seems to fall upon each character in "The Purloined Letter" after he or she gains knowledge of possession of the letter is an image of the "truth of castration," a metaphor for the subject's entry into the Symbolic realm. "The letter," says Lacan, "always arrives at its destination": castration is inevitable.[21] Jacques Derrida counters that this image of inevitability is an artifact of the phallocentrism underlying psychoanalytic thought—an artifact conjured up by the surrounding discourse in order to ensure its own stability. Against this image Derrida posits the notion of the material contingency of society, which the image of castration exists specifically to conceal and contain. By this conception, the "truth of castration" is not that "the letter always arrives at its destination," but rather that

> . . . a letter can always not arrive at its destination. Its "materiality" and "topology" are due to its divisibility, its always possible partition. It can always be fragmented without return, and the system of the symbolic, of castration, of the signifier, of the truth, of the contract, etc., always attempts to protect the letter from this fragmentation. (PP 187)

Delany redeploys this insight for his own purposes: "Perhaps phallo-centric civilization *has* to construct image after image of castration—such as the cyborg."[22] This in turn implies a state of affairs which Delany expresses baldly and boldly: "For the record . . . I do not believe castration as Freud and Lacan have described it even exists." (RW 105)

We find a hint of what this state of affairs itself implies—for both reader and writer—in "The Tale of Plagues and Carnivals" from *Flight from Nevèrÿon*. In that tale, Delany presents us with two more parallel, dialogical texts: one a fantasy unfolding in the world of Nevèrÿon, one a tale of 1983 Manhattan. In the latter, Delany "himself" appears, hard at work drafting the manuscript of the tale we are now reading. At one point, Delany comments:

> By now I'm willing to admit that perhaps narrative fiction, in neither its liter-ary nor its paraliterary mode, can propose the *radically* successful metaphor. At best, what both modes can do is break up, analyze, and dialogize the con-servative, the historically sedimented, letting the fragments argue with one another, letting each display its own obsolescence, suggesting (not stating) where still another retains the possibility of vivid, radical development. But responding to those suggestions is, of course, the job of the radical reader. (The 'radical metaphor' is, after all, only an interpretation of pre-extant words.) Creators, whatever their politics, only provide raw material—docu-ments, if you will.[23]

Re-reading the above passage, this reader is reminded of the words of the best known avant-pop, feminist cyborg in America, the perfor-mance artist Laurie Anderson—who, in her performance pieces and albums (which are usually made up of mutually interilluminating col-lections of songs, anecdotes, and audiovisual fragments) has repeat-edly admonished her audiences: "Hey, sport. *You* connect the dots. *You* pick up the pieces."

In "Aversion/Perversion/Diversion," as in "Wagner/Artaud," we are again given a series of stories, this time of some of Delany's own sexual experiences—stories which both evoke and subvert prevailing sexual myths. The discursive object against which Delany deploys these stories is, perhaps somewhat surprisingly, the concept of Gay Identity itself—or rather, the more conservative concept of transcendent sexual differ-ence which lies latent in the use of "Gay Identity" as a catch-all label for a diverse political constituency (another manifestation of the problem of "empirical resolution" explored in "Shadows"). Once again, Delany uses these autobiographical tales as empirical counters to the reduc-tions of discursive myths: they remind us that for every individual, sex-ual preference and practice are irrefutably idiosyncratic and eccentric, always-already marginal—and that any unified political project set in opposition to the sexual status quo must be founded on an affirmation of the irreducible plurality of sexual experiences and practices.

Delany affirms the truth of these experiences, and the right to speak of them openly, simply by telling them where and when he does: "Aversion/Perversion/Diversion" was originally presented as the Keynote Address at the Fifth Annual Lesbian and Gay Conference on Gay Studies at Rutgers University in 1991. Given that context, we can see how Delany both affirms the liberatory project of Gay Studies, while at the same time placing a critical frame around it. The tales are, after all, cautionary: in their evocation and problematization of all-too-recognizable myths, they remind us that such myths *are* all-too-recognizable—that even (or especially) those engaged in Gay Studies must be constantly vigilant against the pervasive influence of such myths.

But there is perhaps a more immediate justification for strategies of analytic vigilance and empirical inclusiveness in Gay Studies than the accurate reconstruction of lost histories and the retrieval of suppressed voices. As Delany has said several times in other works and mentions in passing here, the ongoing devastation of the AIDS virus makes "absolutely imperative" such vigilance and inclusiveness.[24] At one point in *The Motion of Light in Water,* Delany indulges in a utopian fantasy that the "inflated sexual honesty" necessitated by the AIDS crisis will, once the virus is brought under control, bring about "a sexual revolution to make a laughing stock of any social movement that till now has borne the name."[25] Yet Delany is well aware of the almost fiendish tendency discourses have of "healing themselves across such rhetorical violences" (RS 235) and reifying their own conservative imperatives. The reader is urged to review Delany's discussion, in "Appendix B" of *Flight from Nevèrÿon* and in "The Rhetoric of Sex, the Discourse of Desire" (another extended essay, collected in *Heterotopia,* ed. Tobin Siebers [Ann Arbor: University of Michigan Press, 1995]), of the truly sinister ways in which prevailing sexual discursive codes have sabotaged the effective scientific study of HIV transmission vectors. In the context of such a colossal health crisis, the muddying and mystifying effects of discourse begin to shade over into near-genocidal disinformation.

"Shadow and Ash" takes up many of the images of its "preface" as well as those of the immediately preceding essays and works transformations on them. The logic of these transformations is suggested in "Appendix B" of *Triton,* in which our fictive scholar notes that, in regard to the relation between Delany's "Shadows" and Slade's, "for Slade the concept of landscape is far more political than it was for the author of the older work." (T 357) Now certainly that "older work" displays a sophisticated political sensibility; one of the chief transformations we experience in reading it is the unfolding of political significance out of such seemingly abstract topics as Quine's exploration of the "movable predicate" in philosophical logic. But in the present work, we see a whole series of transformations take place according to an algorithm of politicization: over the course of the essay, we trace a shift of attention from subject-oriented autobiography to context-oriented literary biography, from the exclusionary allusiveness of modernism to the inclusive dialogizing of postmodernism, from the "modular calculus" to "theory"—in general (to quote Hal Foster), from formal filiations to social affiliations.[26]

By focusing our attention on individual "thematic" threads running through "Shadow and Ash," we can begin to discern the micro-effects of the essay's larger conceptual transformation. For example: scattered throughout the piece we find a series of meditations on aging and mortality—typical concerns of the subject-oriented personal essay. What fascinates about these meditations, however, is how the politicization of subject and landscape wrought by the *rest* of the essay—by the context—begins to transform the status of death itself, even as Delany takes it up as a topic of personal concern. Delany sets up this transformation in note 8—a consideration of Joanna Russ' sf novel *We Who Are About To . . .* in which, according to Delany's reading, death serves as an "allegorical stand-in for whatever degree of social-political un-freedom the reader's society has reached."[27] Delany then moves elsewhere, exploring the problem of discourse in a number of realms. Midway through, though, Delany returns to the subject of actual physical death with this note:

> 26. The desire to be conscious of the process of losing consciousness, of having no consciousness at all—this paradox is source and kernel of the anxiety over dying and death. (SA 157)

But by this point in the essay, we are well aware of the degree to which discourse analysis is itself "about" our relation to the things we are least conscious of—the things we are blind or "dead" to. As we read on, death and aging seem less and less problems to be solved at the individual existential level, and more problems which are intimately tied to politics and constituencies. Here is note 9 in its entirety:

> 9. "What shall I do with this body I've been given?" asks Mandelstam. When, one wonders, was the last time he asked it? In his cramped Petersberg apartment? or in the death camp where, near mad, the elements and ideology killed him . . . ? (SA 149)

Delany seems to be suggesting a radical interpretation of the motto, "the personal is the political"—an interpretation which implodes "the political" directly into the material ground of "the personal" with the corporeal body at their interface (this in turn recalls and revalues the notion of the "absolute and indisseverable interface" of object and process explored in "Shadows"). On a human landscape defined in these terms, discourse and death become "problems of consciousness" of similar (or identical) ontological orders. For Delany, to recognize *their* interface is to gain both insight into the grounds for meaningful political action, and access, perhaps, to a very real personal solace.

Notice that our own recognition of the above transformations arises not from any overt argument on Delany's part but rather from the organization of the discursive space of the essay as a whole. Each numbered fragment, because it functions as a different coordinate axis within that space, can be said to frame, and be framed by, all the others. The complex mutuality of these framing-relations allows Delany to effect conceptual transformations without resorting to outright assertion within any single fragment. This dynamic, in which what is outside a given text-unit strongly determines what is perceived to be inside it, resembles what Derrida calls a transgressive rhetoric, in which "by means of the work done on one side and the other of the limit the field inside is modified, and a transgression is produced that consequently is nowhere present as a *fait accompli.*"[28] By evoking such a rhetoric through the deployment of an intricate arrangement of frames—and this formal strategy is at the heart of just about everything he has written from *Dhalgren* on—Delany is able to effectively sidestep spectacle. Because the essay is organized around a play of absences, because it is fundamentally *reticent* at the moment of revelation, "Shadow and Ash," like all the works in this collection, discourages the passivity engendered by spectacle in favor of the active tracing out of discursive parameters and possibilities—the reading of the *un*-said, whose shadowy presence on the offstage margins renders the *said* intelligible.

The topic of literary biography—alluded to in the closing argument in "Aversion/Perversion/Diversion" and expanded upon in one of the marginal arguments in "Shadow and Ash"—takes up the whole of "Atlantis Rose . . ." Here we are given a close reading of Hart Crane's 1930 poem *The Bridge*, in which, with almost microscopic meticulousness, Delany weaves together the textual artifacts surrounding the poem's composition into a hybrid form of multiple biography, close textual analysis, and even—in a fascinating reconstruction of an evening between Crane and his friend Samuel Loveman—speculative literary history. Along the way—as in "Shadow and Ash"—we are given an image of literary practice as a fundamentally social and dialogical activity, in which canons are made and unmade, and discourses reified and subverted, by the rhetorical interventions of individual writers. We see, for example, numerous instances of discursive "normalization" as poetry editors and critics analyze and actually revise the works of various poets according to then-prevailing discursive imperatives.

Against the rhetorical interventions of their editors Delany positions the writing protocols of the poets themselves—protocols which are also shown to both arise from and inform (depending on the case) the protocols of "homosexual genres." These genres—which use conventionalized patterns of ambiguous language to indicate, by indirection, homosexual content—call for reading protocols which privilege form and context over content. A poem deploying such conventions would thus be subject to a double reading:

> . . . while a heterosexual reading may find the poem just as beautiful and just as lyrical (that's, after all, what the poet wanted), it will not find the poem anywhere near as poignant as the homosexual reading does—because the heterosexual reading specifically erases all reference to the silence surrounding homosexuality for which the heterosexual reading's existence, within the homosexual reading, is the positive sign.[29]

Such protocols allow communication to pass across discursively and coercively enforced silence by exploiting the possibilities of excess signification immanent in the sign—by side-stepping direct reference to socially proscribed content and making language itself speak. But this notion—of speaking across the gap, of communicating across time, space, and death—is, of course, at the heart of *The Bridge*. Delany recalls reading Crane at an early age, and perceiving in his a-referential lyricism an evocation of a utopian discursive space, "a world where meaning and mystery were one, indisseverable, and ubiquitous, but at the same time a world where everything spoke (or sang or whispered or shouted) to everything else . . ." (AR 197). But of this evocation there are two readings, one indicating a presumably universal yearning for communion, the other indicating a historically and contextually specific silence all around.

For Delany, the resolution to such oppressions resides in the actions of those who elect to participate in the ongoing evolution of the discourse. Delany's call, near the essay's end, for literary anthologies edited with greater attention to compositional context can be read as an attempt to foster and encourage such participation. According to Delany, most collections are edited under the general assumption that "there exists a Common Reader of poetry who comes from no place—and is going nowhere" (AR 240). But as Delany says in "Shadow and Ash"—specifically in response to the critical work of Language Poet Ron Silliman—there need be "nothing passive" about such a reader (SA 171). Silliman himself has put it this way:

> Here the question is not whether a poet will be read in five or fifty or five hundred years, but whether that poet can and will be read by individuals *able and willing to act* on their increased understanding of the world as a result of the communication.[30]

"Atlantis Rose . . ." ends with an intriguing coda. The whole essay, we learn, was written at least partly in parallel with Delany's historical novel *Atlantis: Model 1924*—their composition dates overlap. In *Atlantis: Model 1924*, as I mentioned earlier, we are shown a fictive—though possible—meeting between Hart Crane and Delany's own father on Brooklyn Bridge in 1924. Yet what transpires in this meeting between a young heterosexual black man and a slightly older homosexual white man is only a brief and fragmentary communion, ending in comic miscommunication and misinterpretation. What is revealed is the discursive form of the two characters' mutual misunderstanding, the structure of their inability truly to meet. True, we do get a vision from the fictive Crane of that utopian space where complete communication can occur. But what we are left with, finally, is a vision of two men who communicate only imperfectly and incompletely, who quickly retreat to opposite sides of the bridge—all on an achingly beautiful day charged with subversive possibilities, but pervaded by the tragicomic order of discourse.

IV

For the reader positioned comfortably within the traditional discourse of the modern essay, the origins of which I began this Introduction by positing, it may come as a surprise to learn that the earliest essay Montaigne wrote which would eventually appear in the *Essais* was, in fact, an extended essay, entitled "An Apology for Raymond Sebond." Sebond had written a *Natural Theology* whose principal thesis is that the natural landscape is one gigantic text—literally a second book of God, which Man in his post-lapsarian state has lost the ability to read. Montaigne attempted to defend Sebond's thesis by doing an extended close reading of both Sebond's text and those of its detractors. Over the course of that extended reading, however, Montaigne manages to argue himself into a state of near-total skepticism: by the end of the "Apology," Montaigne has arrived at an image of a landscape-text that is opaque to analysis and in constant flux.[31]

After that first, long work, Montaigne's remaining essays generally restrict their focus to the concerns of the subject. We no longer see extended analytical attention paid to texts. We no longer see the topics under consideration dissolve into indeterminacy and undecidability. Instead we see meditations in which the sovereign self is the authoritative ground for analytical inquiry. Does this shift in focus trace the inevitable course toward the subject which any work aspiring toward "universality" must take? Or is this shift to be read as a restricting of horizons—a retreat from the vagaries of a mysterious reality, a mysterious play of language, towards seemingly more stable certainties?

Yet when Montaigne occasionally contemplates the effectiveness of using his own self as an anchor for his meditations, he finds that it, too, begins to dissolve under extended scrutiny: "I am unable to stabilize my subject: it staggers confusedly along with a natural drunkenness . . . I am not portraying being but becoming . . . If my soul could only find a footing I would not be assaying myself but resolving myself" (CE 907–8).

Even at the origin we have posited for it, then, the essay is a contestatory site, a turbulent confluence of—at the very least—the medieval Book of Nature and the more-recently-emerged Renaissance Book of the Self.

With this point in mind, let us return to Barthes for a moment.

In her Introduction to the essay collection *A Barthes Reader*, Susan Sontag notes that a major feature of Barthes's prose is its "irrepressibly aphoristic" quality.[32] She goes on to say: "It is in the nature of aphoristic thinking to be always in a state of concluding; a bid to have the final word is inherent in all powerful phrase-making" (BR xii). Yet doesn't this characterization of the aphoristic style—not far, after all, from Barthes's own characterization, or indeed from the root meaning of the word—suggest that Barthes's style is at odds with his message?

It would seem to depend on where we posit the metaphysical ground of our argument. For Sontag, looking specifically at his later, more autobiographical work, "Barthes is the latest major participant in the great national literary project, inaugurated by Montaigne: the self as vocation, life as a reading of the self" (BR xxxiii). If we posit the self as the metaphysical ground—and this places us squarely within the discourse of the transcendental subject—then we must agree with Sontag that Barthes was not fundamentally a political writer, that he merely "put on the armor of postwar debate about the responsibility of literature," only to take it off again later; that he was "the opposite of an activist . . . one of the great modern refusers of history" (BR xix, xxii); that in his later work he systematically "divested himself of theories," presumably to leave the unadorned, central, transcendent self open for all to view (BR xxxv). From this interpretation of Barthes arises "the awareness that confers upon his large, chronically mutating body of writing, as on all major work, its retroactive completeness" (BR ii).

A compelling reading. And, in its striving for closure, for centrality, for the transcendence of the historical, an all-too-familiar one—as Barthes himself has shown us so convincingly. Such "retroactive completeness" is surely the retroactive imposition of precisely the discursive imperatives that so much of Barthes's work was clearly positioned against. No, Barthes's life and work did not end with the neat, closed parenthesis of the final revelation of his transhistorical self: he was, after all, struck down by a laundry van—a sign of the object-world of our industrial culture if there ever was one.

Yet Sontag is indubitably right about Barthes's style—it *is* irrepressibly aphoristic. Moreover, Barthes's privileging of thematic/synchronic readings, which we noted earlier, would seem to be an emblem of the very discursive imperatives which so many other components of his work were contrived to contest. How are we to view Barthes, then? What are we to do with him? Are we to bracket all that was radical in him and place him on the altar of the sovereign self? Or does another, longer view suggest itself—and another course of action?

Here we might do well to recall Delany's words near the end of "Reading at Work":

> As I conclude this minimal bit of work—of interpretive vigilance, of hermeneutic violence, of pleasure, of aggression—my eye lifts from the text and again strays, glances about, snags a moment at a horizon, a boundary that does not so much contain a self, an identity, a unity, a center and origin which gazes out and *defines* that horizon as the horizon is defined *by* it; rather that horizon suggests a plurality of possible positions within it, positions which allow a number of events to transpire, move near, pass through, impinge on each other, take off from one another, some of which events are that an eye looks, a voice speaks, a hand writes. (RW 117)

In this ontology of the open horizon—which relativizes discourse to rhetoric, refuses closure and the transcendence of history, places the subject back into its object-context, and privileges the active, social self over the passive sovereign self—surely the proper response to Barthes would be to carry Barthes's project forward. But that project is not the "national literary project, inaugurated by Montaigne" of making self-consolidation into public spectacle. It is, rather, Montaigne's other project, marginalized by subsequent discursive practices but in fact preceding the rest of Montaigne's work: the project of reading texts into their own radicalism, of writing the extended essay. It is that project, abandoned by Montaigne, which Barthes and the post-structuralists have begun to take up again—and which Delany carries significantly forward here.

By ordinary standards—by ordinary readerly expectations—these essays, with their intricate formal strategies, their remarkable erudition, and their sheer length, may seem daunting, intimidating, "forbidding." Yet far more so than the seemingly more "accessible," monologic works which currently dominate the literary landscape, these essays are, fundamentally, invitations. As we begin them—and indeed as we finish them—we must hold in our minds one of the closing comments of "Reading at Work," which suggests our place within the discursive space Delany is exploring:

> Clearly, there is no survival *here* unless the reader turn to Haraway's manifesto, to do her or his own work, which alone can restructure mine. (RW 118)

The universe of discourse these essays begin to map out is not monolithic, eternal, always-already complete. It is evolving, historical, subject to dialogue and revision. We can revise it ourselves, with our own creative and critical work. All we need to do is enter it—with all the analytic vigilance (and sense of play) we can muster.

The universe of discourse is an open universe. With these essays, Delany invites us in.

NOTES

1. Lydia Fakundiny, *The Art of the Essay* (Boston: Houghton Mifflin Company, 1991), p. xv.

2. Michel de Montaigne, *The Complete Essays*, trans. M. A. Screech (New York: Penguin Books, 1993). (Hereafter referred to as CE.)

3. Scott Russell Sanders, "The Singular First Person," from *Secrets of the Universe* (Boston: Beacon Press, 1991), p. 190.

4. Francis Bacon, "Of Studies," from *The Essays* (New York: Penguin Books, 1985), p. 209.

5. Annie Dillard, *The Writing Life* (New York: Harper & Row, 1989), pp. 3–4.

6. Roland Barthes, *Mythologies*, trans. Annette Lavers (New York: Farrar, Straus, & Giroux, 1972), p. 15. (Hereafter referred to as M.)

7. Edward Hoagland, "That Gorgeous Great Novelist," from *Red Wolves and Black Bears* (New York: Random House, 1976), p. 176.

8. Ursula K. Le Guin, "Introduction," from *The Norton Book of Science Fiction*, ed. Ursula K. Le Guin and Brian Attebery (New York: W. W. Norton, 1993), p. 27.

9. Samuel R. Delany, "'The Scorpion Garden' Revisited," from *The Straits of Messina* (Seattle: Serconia Press, 1989), p. 29.

10. Bensmaia, Reda, *The Barthes Effect* (Minneapolis: University of Minnesota Press, 1987), p. 92.

11. See my own "Subverted Equations: G. Spencer Brown's *Laws of Form* and Samuel R. Delany's Analytics of Attention," in *Ash of Stars*, ed. Jim Sallis (Jackson: University Press of Mississippi) for a more detailed discussion of the problem of "primitive calculi" in Delany's work.

12. Barthes, *S/Z* (New York: Farrar, Straus, & Giroux, 1974), pp. 5–6.

13. Delany, "The Rhetoric of Sex, the Discourse of Desire," from *Heterotopia*, ed. Tobin Siebers (Ann Arbor: The University of Michigan Press, 1995), p. 232. (Hereafter referred to as RS.)

14. Delany, *Starboard Wine* (Pleasantville, N.Y.: Dragon Press, 1984), p. 188. (Hereafter referred to as SW.)

15. Delany, *The American Shore* (Elizabethtown, N.Y.: Dragon Press, 1978), p. ii. (Hereafter referred to as AS.)

16. Delany, "Neither the First Word nor the Last on Structuralism, Post-structuralism, Semiotics, and Deconstruction for SF Readers: An Introduction" [Original title: "Neither the Beginning nor the End . . ."], *The New York Review of Science Fiction*, Number Six (February 1989), p. 1. (Hereafter referred to as NFW.)

17. Stephen Tyler, *The Unspeakable* (Madison: University of Wisconsin Press, 1987), pp. 16–17.

18. Delany, *Triton* (New York: Bantam Books, 1976), p. 357. (Hereafter referred to as T.)

19. Delany, "Shadows," p. 252 of this volume.

20. Delany, "Wagner/Artaud," p. 20 of this volume. (Hereafter referred to as W/A.)

21. Jacques Lacan, "Seminar on 'The Purloined Letter,'" trans. Jeffrey Mehlman, from *The Purloined Poe*, ed. John P. Muller and William J. Richardson (Baltimore: Johns Hopkins University Press, 1988), p. 53. (Hereafter referred to as PP.)

22. Delany, "Reading at Work, and Other Activities Frowned on by Authority: A Reading of Donna Haraway's 'Manifesto for Cyborgs,'" p. 104 of this volume. (Hereafter referred to as RW.)

23. Delany, "The Tale of Plagues and Carnivals," from *Flight from Nevèrÿon* (Hanover: University Press of New England, 1994), p. 348.

24. "Aversion/Perversion/Diversion," p. 141 of this volume. (Hereafter referred to as APD.)

25. Delany, *The Motion of Light in Water* (New York: Masquerade Books, 1993), p. 270.

26. Hal Foster, "Postmodernism: A Preface," from *The Anti-Aesthetic* (Seattle: Bay Press, 1983), p. xv.

27. Delany, "Shadow and Ash," p. 149 of this volume. (Hereafter referred to as SA.)

28. Jacques Derrida, *Positions*, trans. Alan Bass (Chicago: The University of Chicago Press, 1981), p. 12.

29. Delany, "Atlantis Rose . . . ," p. 202 of this volume. (Hereafter referred to as AR.)

30. Ron Silliman, *The New Sentence* (New York: Roof Books, 1989), p. 30.

31. See O. B. Hardison, Jr.'s "Binding Proteus," from *Essays on the Essay* (Athens: The University of Georgia Press, 1989), pp. 17–20, and the Translator's Introduction to Montaigne's *Complete Essays* (cited above), pp. xx–xliii for more detailed discussions of Montaigne's "Apology."

32. Susan Sontag, "Introduction," from *A Barthes Reader* (New York: Hill & Wang, 1982), p. ix. (Hereafter referred to as BR.)

Longer Views

Wagner/Artaud:

A Play of 19th and 20th Century Critical Fictions

For Cynthia Belgrave
and Ethyl Eichelberger

What follows is a work of popular cultural history, not of original research. It required not one foray into any other library save my own.
Here is its only justification:

This scholar is often chary of quoting the first-hand sources of that
one, tending to summarize rather than repeat. It waits, then, for a work
of assemblage such as this to retell the social tale with the immediacy
and richness of shared original accounts through judicious quotation.
To make points, I have put together what struck me as the most exciting
parts of the stories around Artaud's final year at Ivry (and his earlier encounter with Jacques Rivière of *La Nouvelle Revue Francaise*) and of Wagner's participation in the Dresden Uprising of 1849. Lest some scholar
chide me for ignorance or willful distortion, I state here that in neither
case have I told the whole story; there are many facts that are known
about both that do not fit into the neat and headlong narratives I have
constructed. A reader would never know, from this account (for example), that the composer's young niece, Johanna Wagner, was a singer in
Wagner's company in Dresden, who, since premiering Elizabeth in
Wagner's *Tannhäuser* in October 1845 at age nineteen, was coming to
rival Schröder-Devrient in popularity, and that from time to time
throughout the fighting Wagner was concerned for her safety; nor will
the reader find any mention of some of Artaud's more tempestuous relations with any number of fascinating figures of '30s and '40s Paris
(such as his brief, intense pursuit of Anaïs Nin) that laid another layer
of legend over an already legendary man. This work is selective, then,
not exhaustive. I urge anyone intrigued by it to pursue the stories into

the realm of detail (my briefest of bibliographies will only be a beginning) where narrative neatness crumbles and—very possibly—knowledge, with its real limitations, begins.

I

Were two men more alike in their designs on an audience, in their desire to thrust theater, even art itself, to the horizon of its time, then shatter that horizon, to call up new images, sounds, emotions at the behest of spectacle? There is at least one level where—cruel, after all (Artaud explains to us in *The Theater and Its Double*), not because of its violence or its pain but because of its rigor, its demand for committed audience attention, for complete artistic dedication—Artaud's Theater of Cruelty *is* the performance site for Wagner's Total Artwork, the *Gesamtkunstwerk*.

Here is a passage from the opening page of a biography of one of them:

> [He] was both a visionary and a mystic. He saw the theater as had the people of antiquity, a ritual able to give rise to a numinous or religious experience within the spectator. To achieve such experience theatrically, he expanded the spectator's reality by arousing the explosive and creative forces with man's unconscious in determining man's actions. By means of a theater based on *myths, symbols,* and *gestures,* the [work] . . . became a weapon to be used to whip up man's irrational forces, so that a collective theatrical event could be turned into a personal living experience.

This is Bettina L. Knapp writing about Antonin Artaud. But anyone who knows of Wagner's articulate study of German mythology, from the Eddas and the *Volsungasaga* to the German legal records edited by Grimm, of his fascination with classical Greek theater or his desire to make his "music-dramas"—the term he devised to replace "opera"—strike effects of the most basic and profound emotional sort in his hearers, akin to moments of religious ecstasy, must pause a moment to be sure which man is being talked of. It would take almost no revision to make it a perfectly accurate description of Richard Wagner.

Were two men more dissimilar in the material reality of their artistic productions, in the immediate effect of that art on the world?

In February 1883, at Venice, in his apartments at the sumptuous Palazzo Vendramin, with an international entourage in attendance and an even greater audience in awe of him, favored by a king who had funded for him a temple at Bayreuth to the art of his own creation—

yes, the "music-drama"—Wagner died in his wife's arms at age sixty-nine, of diverticular gastric complications and a ruptured heart vessel. His last words were "My watch!" It had fallen from his pocket as Cosima tried to comfort him in the terminal agony that had seized him at his work desk.

Behind him were ten major and three minor operas, a youthful symphony, various preludes and much occasional music, as well as volumes of literary and theoretical works—*Art and Revolution, The Artwork of the Future*, the notorious anti-Semitic article "Jewry in Music," and *Opera and Drama*—as well as volumes of autobiography, music reviews, essays on the organization of orchestras, music schools, and opera companies, historical speculations, political essays and pamphlets, poems, plays, and stories, as well as the thousands on thousands of letters sent throughout his life.

Artaud's death?

On the chill morning of March 4th, 1948, an old man at 52, all but toothless and emaciated as only a lifetime opium addict can be, his body eaten out by rectal cancer, his bloodstream thick with the chloral that he'd used to dampen the pain once the opium and morphine had ceased to have any effect, in a room in the small eighteenth-century pavilion without heating or water at the Ivry-sur-Seine clinic on the outskirts of Paris, seated at the foot of his bed not far from a fireplace filled with the ashes from the previous day against winter's ending cold, Artaud was found dead by the gardener who was, as he had been doing for some months now, bringing Artaud his breakfast. Ivry had been Artaud's home for two years since his release from his most recent confinement at the Rodez Asylum. The walls of his room, in which the mad poet Gérard de Nerval had once been confined, were covered with Artaud's drawings. A stout wooden block, which sometimes served as a table, and which a few months before Dr. Delmas had put in his room, telling him to hammer or stab it with a knife in order to take out his hostile feelings, was chopped nearly to bits. But almost a third of Artaud's life had been passed in one mental hospital or another.

Thirteen months prior to his death, Artaud may have had his best hours. *The Theater and Its Double* (1938)—Artaud's finest book and his greatest claim to our attention—had been reprinted in 1944. His essays from the '30s on the Tarahumara Indians had been gathered into a book, *A Voyage to the Land of the Tarahumara* (republished in the U.S. as *The Peyote Dance*), at the end of 1945. The previous spring, the five long letters he had written to Henri Parisot about his drug addiction, language, poetry, and art, *Letters from Rodez* (1946), had appeared. And in June, after nine years, he had been released from Rodez and had moved into the comparatively benign Ivry-sur-Seine clinic, where he shortly was allowed to take up residence in the pavilion at the edge of the property, apart from the main building. Artaud had been released on condition that his livelihood would be taken care of; and a group of leading painters—among them Picasso, Braque, Arp, Léger, Duchamp, and Giacometti—had donated paintings for a benefit to raise the money; Gide, Sartre, René Char, Tristan Tzara, and more had given manuscripts and autographs that were also sold; and France's theater community staged another benefit on Artaud's behalf at the Théâtre Sarah-Bernhardt, at which various writers delivered appreciations of Artaud, Artaud's works were read, and where Jean-Louis Barrault took part in a forty-minute reading from *The Cenci*, Artaud's single full-length play—while Artaud himself waited, nervously, happily, in a cafe with a friend a few streets away. Interest in the haggard but brilliant man was, at this point, higher than ever before.

Artaud wanted to give a public reading of his new works—for since his release he was writing incessantly. A reading was arranged at the Théâtre du Vieux Colombier for January 13, 1947, as part of a series of poetry readings billed as *Tête-à-Têtes*. The rush on tickets was astonishing—most of them bought just before curtain time, as though the rumor of Artaud's talk had just gone around in the last hours. There were a hundred standees in the five-hundred-seat theater. The audience waiting for the curtain to open at nine included Gide, Breton, Arthur Adamov, and Albert Camus, as well as Artaud's close friends Roger Blin and Jean Paulhan—along with a host of actors, producers, directors, journalists, and students.

Shabby, dishevelled, like a zombie with overlong hair, Artaud walked on stage. He began to read from his work. He read from his recent poem "The Return of Artaud, le Mômo" (mômo is Marseillaise slang for fool; Araud had been born in Marseille):

> . . . o kaya
> o kaya pontoura
> o pontoura
> a pena
> poni
>   . . .

Not the membrane of the vault,
not the omitted member of this fuck,
born of devastation,
but meat gone bad,
beyond membrane,
beyond where it's hard or soft.

. . .
And if you don't understand the image,
—and this is what I hear you say
in a circle,
that you don't understand the image
which is at the bottom
of my cunt's hole,—

it's because you don't know the bottom,
not of things,
but of my cunt
mine,
although from the bottom of time
you all plashed there in a circle
the way one slanders a madman,
plots to death an incarceration

>**ge re ghi**
>**regheghi**
>**geghena**
>**e reghena**
>**a gegha**
>**riri** . . .

He read from another poem that night, "Centre-Mére et Patron-Minet" ("Center-Mother and Boss-Puss"):

>**. . . cunta-mite and boss-puss**
>are the shit vocables
>**that father and mother**
>   **invented**

in order to enjoy him to the utmost.

Who is that, him?

Strangled totem.

like a member in a pocket
that life *frockets*
           from so close,

that the walled-in totem will finally
burst the belly to be born . . .

And from still another, "La Culture Indienne":

> . . . Caffre of urine from the slope of a hard vagina,
> which resists when one takes it.
> Urinary camphor from the mound of a dead vagina,
> which slaps you when you stretch it . . .
> Which two, and which of the two?
> Who, both?
> in the time
> seventy times accursed
> when man
> > crossing himself
> was born son
> of his sodomy
> on his own ass
> grown hard.
> Why two of them,
> and why born of **TWO**? . . .

If the poems were opaque, the night's performance must have been stunning—in both good and bad ways: Soon, Artaud dropped his prepared papers on the stage and began to extemporize on his treatment by psychiatrists at Rodez, where he had almost died of malnutrition, and on the terrors of the shock treatments he had endured there. By midnight, when he had gone on for more than two hours, finally not to conclude but rather to flee the stage in a state of emotional distress—it was finally over!—the audience was devastated. Here are two many-times-reprinted responses by men who attended that night's "lecture." The first is from the journalist Maurice Saillet on the first prepared hour of the performance:

> . . . when his impetuous hands fluttered like a pair of birds around his face; when his raucous voice, broken by sobs and stumbling tragically, began to declaim his splendid—but practically inaudible—poems, it was as if we were drawn into a danger zone, sucked up by that black sun, consumed by the "overall combustion" of a body that was itself a victim of the flames of the spirit.

About the latter impromptu part of the night, we have a letter from André Gide, who felt that Artaud's exit was among the most moving moments of his life:

> Artaud's lecture was more extraordinary than one could have supposed: it's

something which has never been heard before, never seen, and which one will never again see. My memory of it is indelible—atrocious, painful, almost sublime at moments, revolting also, and quasi-intolerable.

To get some insight into Artaud's raillery against psychiatrists, note that, in the same month as his "lecture," one day he left Ivry to see the van Gogh (1853–1890) exhibit at the Orangerie. Returning from the exhibit, Artaud visited his art dealer friend Pierre Loeb (who had arranged the benefit sale of paintings for Artaud's welfare), excited and exalted by the paintings he'd just seen.

"Why couldn't you write a book on van Gogh?" Loeb suggested, against the rush of Artaud's enthusiasm—at which point Artaud marched upstairs to the first floor of Loeb's house, sat down, and began to write—rapidly, nervously—his impressions.

Following up his eccentric friend's interest in the exhibition, a few days later Loeb sent Artaud a letter and some newspaper clippings about the exhibit. One of the articles, written by a psychiatrist, referred to van Gogh as a "degenerate of the Magnon type." Artaud was incensed. Over five or six more days, along with the written impressions of that first afternoon, he produced an impassioned panegyric (and one of his most influential essays), "Van Gogh, the Man Suicided by Society" (1947).

Loeb once wrote that the piece was written over two afternoons, the first of them spent at Loeb's upstairs writing desk. But this is unlikely, given the essay's length—thirty printed pages. The essay has six titled sections, which have the feel of at least six sittings about them—and possibly more. One is formed of a mosaic of paragraphs, carefully assembled from van Gogh's letter to his beloved brother Theo. It is simply not the sort of thing one dashes off in an hour—even under the most manic expressive impulse. Also there is at least one reference in the text to "this month of February, 1947," which would suggest work on the piece was going on at least two weeks beyond mid-January. Still, most likely, some of what Artaud said the night of the 13th, from the Vieux Columbier stage, about psychiatry, about himself, and/or about van Gogh, became the substance for what he wrote in his essay—if not vice versa.

Artaud had written art reviews before and always had strong opinions. Delacroix, Giotto, Brueghel, Modigliani, Picasso, Klee—these were among his enthusiasms. On the other hand, for Artaud Matisse was only a "trickster" and Picabia merely "amusing." But these opinions dated from before the last nine years' internment at Rodez. Also Artaud himself was drawing and painting constantly these days.

Artaud's van Gogh essay is a perverse combination of madness and insight. Psychiatrists in general—and van Gogh's psychiatrist in particular, Dr. Gachet—are the villains of the piece. Though the essay does not survey the paintings in any particular specificity, *Wheatfield with Crows,* the painting van Gogh worked on two days before his suicide, clearly fascinated Artaud. The introduction, however, begins as close to madness as any writer might want to stray:

> One can speak of the good mental health of van Gogh who, in his whole life, cooked only one of his hands and did nothing else except once to cut off his left ear,
>
> in a world in which every day one eats vagina cooked in green sauce or penis of newborn child whipped and beaten to a pulp,
>
> just as it is when plucked from the sex of its mother.
>
> And this is not an image, but a fact abundantly and daily repeated and cultivated throughout the world . . .

Soon, however, after a foray against a psychiatrist, Dr. L., it moves on to lyrical insights into the paintings:

> Pure linear painting had been driving me mad for a long time when I encountered van Gogh, who painted neither line nor forms but things of inert nature as if in the throes of convulsions.
>
> And inert.
>
> . . . The latest van Gogh exhibit at the Orangerie does not have all the very great paintings of the unfortunate painter. But among those that are there, there are enough rotating processions studded with clumps of carmine plants, enough sunken roads with overhanging yews, enough violet suns whirling over haystacks of pure gold, enough *Père Tranquille* and enough self-portraits,
>
> to remind us what a sordid simplicity of objects, peoples, materials, elements,
>
> van Gogh drew on for these kinds of organ peals, these fireworks, these atmospheric epiphanies . . .
>
> The crows painted two days before his death did not, anymore than his other paintings, open the door for him to a certain posthumous glory, but they do open to painterly painting, or rather to unpainted nature, the secret door to a possible beyond, to a possible permanent reality, through the door opened by van Gogh to a possible and sinister beyond.
>
> It is not unusual to see a man, with the shot that killed him already in his belly, crowding black crows onto a canvas, and under them a kind of meadow—perhaps livid, at any rate empty—in which the wine color of the earth is juxtaposed wildly with the dirty yellow of the wheat.

But no other painter besides van Gogh would have known how to find, as he did in order to paint his crows, that truffle black, that "rich banquet" black which is at the same time, as it were, excremental, of the wings of the crows surprised in the fading gleam of evening . . .

For no one until then had turned the earth into that dirty linen twisted with wine and wet blood.

The sky in the painting is very low, bruised,

violet, like the lower edges of lightning.

The strange shadowy fringe of the void rising after the flash.

Van Gogh loosed his crows like the black microbes of his suicide's spleen a few centimeters from the top *as if from the bottom of the canvas,*

following the black slash of that line where the beating of their rich plumage adds to the swirling of the terrestrial storm the heavy menace of a suffocation from above.

And yet the whole painting is rich.

Rich, sumptuous, and calm.

Worthy accompaniment to the death of a man who during his life set so many drunken suns swirling above so many unruly haystacks and who, desperate, with a bullet in his belly, had no other choice but to flood a landscape with blood and wine, to drench the earth with a final emulsion, both dark and joyous, with a taste of bitter wine and spoiled vinegar. . . . I am returning [Artaud writes, in the midst of one of the essay's three rather arbitrarily-arranged postscripts, eighteen pages later] to the painting of the crows.

Who has already seen, as in this painting, the earth become equivalent to the sea?

In the eighteen-page ellipsis, and again after it, the essay plunges into a jeremiad against psychiatry and society, studded with references to Artaud's own stay at Rodez. When the essay ends, we are back in something akin to madness—if not within madness itself. On the closing page, Artaud reviles the bourgeois Parisian public who filed past van Gogh's paintings at the Orangerie, oblivious to "the hate" with which, in the winter evenings of 1946, they or "their fathers and mothers" so "effectively strangled" the self-slaughtered artist.

The essay ends:

But did there not fall, on one of the evenings I speak of, at the Boulevard de la Madeleine, at the corner of the rue des Mathurins, an enormous white rock that might have come from a recent eruption of the volcano Popocatépetl?

And it is over.

But I suspect the only responsible answer we can give to Artaud's terminal rhetorical question is: Probably not.

Still, when part of the van Gogh essay was translated and appeared in *Horizon* magazine in 1948, the young R. D. Laing read it while still a student. He claims that its discussion of psychiatry (which I have not quoted) was a decisive influence in his later thinking about the relationship between psychiatrists and the mad.

During his last year, Artaud was in great demand.

But there is a certain machinery of defeat built into the celebrity of the deranged—who are often wanted for the show they put on, more than for the substance of their work.

On February 1, 1948, Artaud's last piece, a radio play for four voices, xylophone, gongs, other percussion instruments, and sound effects, *To Have Done with the Judgment of God (Pour en finir avec le jugement de Dieu)*, commissioned from Artaud for the series *Les Voix des poètes,* was finally banned by station manager Wladimir Porché, only a day before its announced public broadcast time of February 2 over Radiodiffusion Française. The recording had been made in November, between the 22nd and the 29th. The "play" contained some older poems by Artaud, as well as a majority of new sections, written for the occasion and dictated to Paule Thévenin, a young actress who was at once Artaud's private acting student, his secretary, the wife of his medical doctor, and—after his death—the editor of his complete works.

Artaud had heard (or thought he had heard; or made it up on his own as an extended metaphor) that, in order to be admitted to public schools in the United States, American schoolboys were forced to give sperm samples that were later stored for artificial insemination in order to swell the ranks of the U.S. military. Artaud's play begins (and ends) with an outraged protest against this practice in particular and America in general. In between, it once more praises the Tarahumara Indians, excoriates the Mass, reviles sex in general, presents a hymn to shit, declares Artaud's sanity, and tells us that we must learn to "eat rat daintily."

In January, Artaud had gone to the radio studio, where he'd listened once more to the whole piece with the cast and technicians. He had made a few cuts and even re-recorded a section, to ready it for the February 2 broadcast. Porché's decision to withdraw the piece had been reached a few days before, but it was only communicated to the sickly Artaud on the first.

Throughout February, letters were written back and forth over the banning. There was a minor Parisian press war. In his outraged letter of February 4th to Porché, Artaud claimed that, after reviewing the tape himself back in January along with the rest of the show's technicians (Artaud's letter during his last two years were frequently broken up like poems), he had conscientiously let nothing "pass / that might infringe on / taste, / morals, / good manners, / *honorable intentions,* / or furthermore that might / exude / boredom, / familiarity, / routine, / I wanted a fresh work, one that would make contact with certain organic points of life, / a work / in which one feels one's whole nervous system / illuminated as if by a miner's cap-lamp / with vibrations / consonances / which invite / man / TO EMERGE / WITH / his body / to follow in the sky this new, unusual, and radiant Epiphany. . . ."

Fernand Pouey (who had commissioned the piece) scheduled a private studio broadcast, for the evening of February 5. The audience of fifty invited to the studio that night were to act as a jury and decide whether the piece merited rescheduling. Their names read like a Who's Who of the arts in '40s Paris: Raymond Queneau, Louis Jouvet, Jean Cocteau, Paul Eluard, Georges Braque, Jean-Louis Barrault . . . That night the voices of the actors, whom, three months before, Artaud had rehearsed for over two weeks in almost daily trips from Ivry into Paris—Maria Casarés, who had played Death in Cocteau's film *Orphée;* Roger Blin, who a double handful of years before had played one of the two mute assassins in *The Cenci* (Blin had also been *The Cenci's* production assistant; besides writing the play, Artaud had in 1935 starred in and directed it as well), and whose productions of Genet a handful of years hence would galvanize the French theater; Paule Thévenin; and Artaud himself—went through the howls, screams, roarings, and sobs which Artaud had interlarded throughout this agonized work. Needless to say, the audience unanimously supported the broadcast. But even the most auspicious fifty supporters, when a work has been promised to a public of thousands, must still have been distressing for the writer—who was now dying from advanced rectal cancer.

In a letter to Pouey, written from Ivry two days after the private performance, Artaud declared: ". . . I do not understand how an incompetent, scarcely out of university, like Wladimir Porché, can take it upon himself to cancel the broadcast of a document that was ANNOUNCED several weeks ago / and consequently / listened to / by dozens of technicians who judged its value / and DECIDED / that it should be broadcast. . . ." There are other letters to the press. In response to some serious comment on the piece, in still another letter to Pouey and to the technical director René Guignard, in expectation of an eventual airing, on February 17 Artaud asked for a few more cuts in the tape from the introductory section: "I think that what certain people like Georges Braque found so overwhelming and exciting about the Radio

Broadcast *To Have Done with the Judgment of God* are the parts where sound effects and xylophonics accompany the poems read by Roger Blin and Paule Thévenin. We must not spoil the effect of the xylophonics by the logical, dialectical, and argumentative quality of the opening section . . . / I beg you to make these cuts, / I beg you / *both of you* / to MAKE SURE that these cuts are carefully made. / There must be nothing left in this Radio Broadcast that might disappoint, / tire, / or bore / an enthusiastic audience which was struck by the freshness of the sound effects and xylophonics / which even Balinese, Chinese, Japanese, and Singhalese theater do not have. . . ."

Despite the jury of literary luminaries, however, station manager Porché remained adamant.

The play would not go out on the public airwaves.

Fernand Pouey resigned.

And in his last letter, to Thévenin on February 24th from his room at Ivry, a day after they had gone to dinner together at a Paris restaurant, Artaud wrote: "Paule, I am very sad and desperate, / my body hurts all over, / but above all I have the impression that people were disappointed in my radio broadcast. / Wherever the *machine* is / there is always the abyss and the void, / there is a technical intervention that distorts and annihilates what one has done. / The criticisms of M. and A. A. are unjust but they must have been based on some weakness in the transitions, / this is why I am through with Radio, / and from now on will devote myself / exclusively / to the theater / as I conceive it, / a theater of blood, / a theater which each performance will have done / something / bodily / to the one who performs as well as to the one who comes to see others perform, / but actually / the actors are not performing, / they are doing. / The theater is in reality the *genesis* of creation. / This will happen. / I had a vision this afternoon—I saw those who are going to follow me and who are still not completely embodied because pigs like those at the restaurant last night eat too much. There are some who eat too much and others like me who can no longer eat without *spitting*. / Yours, Antonin Artaud." The cancer that agonized Artaud had reached the point where his doctor simply allowed him as much chloral as he wanted. Over the nine days after that last letter (1948 was a leap year) Artaud drew or chopped at his block or dosed himself into unconsciousness—and died.

In the Ivry-sur-Seine pavilion, his friends kept vigil by the body for three days—primarily to shoo off the rats that plagued the building but also to turn away the priests they feared Artaud's family might send against the wishes of the militantly atheist blasphemer.

There is only one little point I would ask you to hold tightly to as we

move on in this discussion. Those flawed "transitions" Artaud casti-
gates himself for in this pathetic, terminal epistle are finally part of an
entire pre-Artaudian critical system—a system that, clearly, Artaud
himself was enmeshed in until he could criticize no longer, a system
whose historical constitution (not as a series of rhetorical borrowings,
which are all too easily traceable to Aristotle's *Poetics*, but rather as an
entire nineteenth-century discursive practice) is the real topic of our
essay here. A flawed "transition" is the failing traditionally invoked
when that romantic ideal, "unity of impression," was assumed not to
have been achieved: i.e., if all transitions between all the parts of an
aesthetic work are perfect, then the whole *must* appear unified, Q.E.D.
The presuppositions supporting such a critical system, however, are
myriad. They include the unproblematic transparency between life and
language, presentation and representation, intention and effect, and
our ability to locate and respond to the "parts" themselves, as well as a
psychological autonomy and a psychological malleability to the subject
represented that flies in the face of practically any materialist critique,
from the most vulgar to the most sophisticated. But more of that later.

Antonin Artaud was buried, without rites, on March 8, 1948.

Shall we look over the remainder of Artaud's work?

Most of us will be surprised that the letters, journals, poems, essays,
and various writing projects that comprise the complete works of Antonin Artaud from Gallimard, as edited by Paule Thévenin (a project
still incomplete as of this date), so far run to more than twenty-five
published volumes! (Some of these are themselves double, with an "a"
and a "b" tome.) Looking at them, one feels one is looking at the *opera
omnia* of some 19th Century literary Titan, a Balzac or, perhaps, a
Dumas. Could this really be the production of the sickly, deranged Artaud, who comes to us either as the handsome young actor of the '20s
or the frail ghoul of his final years—the '40s? Dipping here and there
among them, however, the reader soon finds that the voluminous poetry, from the 1923 pamphlet *Backgammon in the Sky* (*Tric Trac du Ciel*) to
The Return of Artaud, le Mômo (*Le Retour d'Artaud, le Mômo:* "mômo" may
also refer to the Greek god Momos, the god of raillery and satire) in
1947, is pained almost beyond endurance—and largely unreadable. In
April 1929 Artaud had registered a film script based on Robert Louis
Stevenson's *The Master of Ballantrae* and also published a book of essays,
Art and Death. In May of 1933, he'd completed a surrealistic dithyram-
bic novel, *Heliogabalus, or The Anarchist Crowned* (published 1934).
Known as a revolutionary man of the theater, Artaud nevertheless completed only a single full-length play, and that a cut-down prose adapta-
tion of a closet drama of Shelley's, by way of a translation of Stendahl's,

The Cenci. It is an interesting play, but the interest is almost entirely because Artaud wrote it. A costume historical drama, it looks and feels very similar to a number of works by Cocteau, Giraudoux, Anouilh, and Gelderhode. But it does not work anywhere near as well on stage as the best theater pieces of these other writers.

Artaud wrote some praiseful, mystical essays on Mexico's Tarahumara Indians (1937), which, for all their glorification of the primitive, are nevertheless almost wholly fascist in their presuppositions—in much the same way as Riefenstahl's photographic and textual glorifications of the African Nuba tribe are still the underside of the theory of a (if not the) "master race."

As an actor, a young Artaud had appeared in numerous plays, notably as Tiresias in the scandalous production of Cocteau's *Antigone* (1922), with its sets by Pablo Picasso, costumes by Coco Chanel, and music by Arthur Honegger. (Genica Athanasiou, Artaud's lover at the time, played the title role.) He made brief appearances in two great films: He is Marat in Abel Gance's *Napoleon* (1927) and the young monk in Carl Dreyer's *The Passion of Joan of Arc* (1928). There are numerous less distinguished screen roles—at least one of which was in a movie popular with the public for a season, Raymond Bernard's *Tarakanova* (1929); and in 1930 he had acted in the French version (unfortunately not the well-known German one with Lotte Lenya) of Pabst's film of Brecht's *Threepenny Opera,* as well as Fritz Lang's *Liliom* (1934)—in America, the Molnar play of the same name on which the film was based would become Rogers and Hammerstein's musical *Carousel.*

There are many brilliant and impassioned letters, journals, brief and luminous notes on theatrical projects, films, and what-have-you.

And there are the handful of lucid and superbly analytical essays.

The most important of these are collected in the 1938 volume *The Theater and Its Double,* the single work without which (1923–24's *Correspondence with Jacques Rivière* excepted) the encounter with Artaud would be almost entirely an encounter with a myth—rather than with a mind.

The double of the theater is, of course, life; and Artaud considered himself deliberately provocative by relegating life to the subordinate position in his title. Still, the book begins with as socially ethical a preface as any Marxist might wish:

> I must remark that the world is hungry and not concerned with culture, and that the attempt to orient toward culture thoughts turned only toward hunger is a purely artificial expedient.

But even this most lucid and socially pointed of all Artaud's works gets under way with a kind of *feuilletonage noire*, in which theater grows, somehow, mystically, out of the Plague at Marseille in 1720, and ends up in . . . acupuncture! The trip between, however, is brilliant—hugely rich in notions about theater and the general contemporary artistic condition. The wonderful central essay "No More Masterpieces" could stand (and has stood) as a manifesto for the working twentieth-century artist ever since it was written—and makes the modernist criticism of Eliot from the same period, if not Pound's, seem timid and rather trifling. Still, there is no single and entire book-length work—whether poems, drama, fiction, or, like this one, essays—from Artaud that can be securely and unquestionably accepted into the canon so cavalierly dubbed "literature." Presumably this would not have bothered him.

"All writing is garbage," Artaud had declared in his 1925 meditation-cum-prose-poem, *"Le Pèse-Nerfs"* ("The Nerve-Meter"), and went on writing poems and letters.

How, then, can we account for Artaud's extraordinary influence? In 1947, a young American, Carl Solomon, went to a reading given by Artaud on the rue Jacob. Back in the United States, ". . . in my incarceration in a psychiatric hospital in Manhattan [The Psychiatric Institute]," Solomon wrote in 1989, ". . . I encountered Allen Ginsberg, a fellow patient who was intrigued by my collection of Paris-acquired books. Among the Artaud, Genêt, Michaux, Miller, and Lautréamont was Isou's *Nouvelle Poesie et un Nouvelle Musique.* We discussed all of these things by way of layering the groundwork for Allen's eventual publication of 'Howl' in 1956." But how better to characterize "Howl" than as the textual encounter of Artaud with Whitman? And the earliest works of Artaud to be published in the United States were through City Lights and Grove Press, the two publishing outlets most closely associated with Ginsberg and the Beats. But if one can map the conduits by which Artaud arrived on the American shore, that still does not let us know the specificity of *what* arrived, besides an atmosphere, an air, a stance. Again, looking for the substance behind that influence, if one turns to the works least tainted by his inarguable dementia—his plays and his essays—the whole phenomenon simply does not make sense.

There is much in *The Cenci* at one with the wilder of Artaud's works: the interest in crime, transgression, and cruelty presented in an atmosphere dominated by aphoristic intellectual analysis. But there are works by Artaud both earlier and later (and less aesthetically satisfying overall) in which (nevertheless) it is exactly these elements, which certainly supply the energy behind Artaud, that appear so much more forcefully. Indeed, to consider Artaud's subsequent influence only in the light of this one play and the more logical and readable essays on art and theater simply will not do, for all their essayistic brilliance. It is as if Wagner had attained to his particular stature by writing only his theoretical works *Opera and Drama, Art and Revolution,* and *The Artwork of the Future*—and no other opera than *Rienzi*!

Artaud presents himself to us, then, as an aesthetic paradox—a problem. And it is as a problem that we will have to explore him to untangle his significance.

II

Richard Wagner loved the body—or certainly he loved what the body could do. Hydrotherapy was a passion with him for a season; so were silk dressing gowns and mountain hikes. *Tristan und Isolde* (1859) speaks of spiritual love, but we need listen to only a scene of it to realize this is a limpid celebration of total erotic corporeality and a dramatic exploration of its effects on body, mind, and spirit. And amidst the various scenic miscalculations, didn't that sensuous, incestuous collapse to which Patrice Chereau treated the world at the end of his *Walküre,* Act I, over PBS in 1983, seem, somehow, right?

Artaud despised and reviled the body. He hated sex and used the social horrors traditionally associated with the most vulgar language to castigate it in all forms. In what we can only call, with generosity, his less lucid periods, the bodily language he used to execrate intercourse, reproduction, even masturbation, makes the flesh crawl and the mind turn aside from an image of disease ridden with disease. The body for Artaud was only a laboratory, ill-equipped and chaotically organized before a dispersed and distracted master, in which to study, as best he could, the machinery of pain. No other dramatic theorist, including Stanislavski, has had such a sense of the actor as a body in space and time, a living gorge through which must plummet the full range of what men and women may whisper about, murmur over, shriek out, snicker at, weep, laugh or howl before. But if there was anything more cruel in Artaud's "theater of cruelty" than the unstinging rigor that gave it its name, it was the conception of a translation from mind to physicality through a fine grid of physical and mental *hurting* that was—if his writing is to be trusted—Artaud's body from adolescence through its premature senescence and death.

Susan Sontag wrote in 1973 (and has been much quoted for writing it)—

> The course of all recent serious theater in Europe and America can be divided into two periods—before Artaud and after Artaud.

—where "after Artaud" (*post hoc ergo propter hoc*) clearly means because of Artaud.

After Artaud?

Theater-in-the-round; a revival of political street theater; theater in unexpected places; multiple theaters in great centers built especially to display all of theater's myriad forms; light shows; improvisations; puppets, in all sizes and to all levels of abstraction; the interest in various traditions of Eastern theater. Both the abstract unit set and the infinite complexities of stagecraft one sees in a Broadway musical can be envisioned through Artaud; so can the idea of film as a recognized art form—if it will only consent to be film. And of course the work of such innovators as Judith Malina and Julian Beck, Charles Ludlum, María Irene Fornés, Robert Wilson, Richard Forman, and Ethyl Eichelberger in this country; while to say Brook, Grotowski, or Handke is only to make the flimsiest gesture toward European stage art. Basically, what comes after Artaud is almost anything one might call modern in the theater that does not trace directly back to Brecht—with whom, of course, Artaud overlaps anyway. Not only can all the theatrical trends listed above be traced to Artaud, but their seeds can almost all be found in that slim book of theatrical meditations already cited.

And before Artaud?

It is my intention in this inquiry to examine the fiction that before Artaud there was Richard Wagner and Wagner's theater—and that, as a paradigm for serious art, there was little else. And it is only against this titanic background that the problem Artaud presents can best be appreciated.

To make this an interesting fiction, however, and worthy of our hermeneutical energies, we must limit it in some severe, some rigorous, some cruel ways.

I do not mean that Wagner was the only artist before Artaud to produce interesting or significant art. I do not mean that Wagner was (though many have claimed it) the greatest artist who ever lived. Perhaps this is the place to mention how I came to Wagner's music. In my case, a late adolescent love of Anton von Webern developed naturally over the years to include his teacher, Arnold Schoenberg, and Webern's fellow pupil, Alban Berg. To know any of these composers in depth is to know the respect in which they held Wagner. . . .

III

My first exposure to Wagner's music-drama was in the summer of 1966. I'd just returned to New York from my first trip to Europe and was living alone in a cluttered apartment on East 6th Street in the city's Lower East Side—Marilyn had recently removed to an apartment on Henry Street and our relationship was such that I had not gone along. Among scant possibilities for making a little money, an older friend named Ed McCabe suggested to me and another friend of mine, Paul, who lived with his truck-driver lover, Joe, around on Avenue B, that we try "supering" at the Metropolitan Opera, which was about to open with its first production at its new home in the recently-completed Lincoln Center.

Far larger than the old one in the just-demolished Metropolitan Opera House, the new stage at Lincoln Center would require far more "supers" than before. And the house's opening production was to be particularly lavish.

The word "super" comes from supernumerary—often just called a "spear carrier." Supers are costumed figures in the opera who neither sing, speak, nor dance, but who fill out the stage picture in the lavish, colorful spectacles.

Supers were not paid for rehearsal.

But they were given fifteen dollars a performance. And so, one afternoon, with Ed and Paul, I reported to the stage door in the white marbled wall of the new theater building to attend the first of half a dozen rehearsals for the world premiere of Samuel Barber's *Anthony and Cleopatra*, starring Leontyne Price and directed by Franco Zeffirelli, with black dancer Alvin Ailey both as choreographer and assistant director.

The music from Barber's opera was not popular either with the singers nor—once it premiered—with the public. Largely for technical reasons the production itself was something of a fiasco. A giant turntable that was supposed to be on geared metal wheels had been put on rubber rollers instead to save money—and turned out not to be able to move under the weight of the actors and scenery. Machinery that was to roll a scenic construction from the back of the city-block-deep stage up to the footlights failed to function on opening night. But though I played an angry merchant in the first act's market scene and an Egyptian slave in Act Two (where, with Paul, under the bluest of blue lights, I carried a couch to center stage and left it there), this is not the place to detail the calamities that deviled the production from rehearsals on through its half-dozen performances. What it meant, however, was that I was allowed to super in a subsequent production of Wagner's *Die Meistersinger von Nürnberg*, which the Met mounted only a little later that same season.

I was only required in Act Three, where I was one of the burghers who gathers with the others to hear Hans Sachs's "prize song." My part was quintessentially simple, and so required that I attend only two re-hearsals—one of which I believe I missed. At the cue, I entered with a dozen other black-costumed burghers to stand at one side of a small bridge. We waited through the prize song. At a certain point, drummers entered over the same bridge and stood beside us, while the chorus sang the finale.

Very simple.

The production's opening night, however, was as dramatic and even more fraught than the Barber. I lingered in the wings, looking out on the broad stage all through Act One. Twenty minutes into it, Justino Diaz, who sang Hans Sachs, developed an extraordinary bloody nose. One of the technicians, lounging beside a TV monitor flickering beside me, commented that Diaz was singing with his face staring almost straight into the flies. Minutes later, in an unscheduled exit, he rushed off, leaving Walter and Beckmesser to sing on alone, and practically bumped into me. I looked around as he grabbed a towel from a dis-traught dresser, dropped his head, and seemed to spew out mouthfuls of blood! Smearing his face with gore, he spat out more blood; blood ran in cascades from his nose, while the whole, huge backstage area went into spreading chaos among the dozens of technicians, stagehands, administrators, friends—and supers—who fill the cavernous wings of such a theater at any moment in a performance. There were whispers of halting the production, of bringing in the understudy—all of which Diaz protested, vehemently, hoarsely, quietly. A few minutes later, he rushed back out on the stage to sing again.

It went on this way, with exits every five or ten minutes to unload the blood that had collected in the back of his throat: he still sang with his face up, each time more and more streaked with red. In the intermis-sion between Acts One and Two, the bleeding was finally stopped. But all through Act Two, a doctor and nurses waited with us, on the chance that it might start up again, under the part's considerable physical strain.

Hearing an opera from backstage, especially in a house the size of the Met, is almost a wholly vacuous experience—even when there is no medical emergency. No meaningful stage picture is visible from the wings. The performance is not directed toward you. And there are a lot of ugly sounds—gasped breaths, rough attacks, and what-have-you—that ordinarily do not make it past the footlights over the orchestra pit but which become egregiously noticeable from so near. Even though various assistants and technical directors are constantly shushing stagehands and technicians, there is so much extraneous noise from the setting of props and the moving of scenery that from so close it is impossible really to hear—or to concentrate on what you hear. The balance between orchestra and principals is so far off as to be ludicrous. The proscenium is not before you to frame what you see: costumed chorus members in their intense make-up mingle with workmen in their greens and blues and technicians in sweaters and jeans, with metal scaffolding all around (invisible from the seats), lights hung every which where, and music always playing through the lights and motion and general hubbub, so that the effect is more like watching a circus rehearsal scattered about the floor of some vast hangar than an artistic performance.

The lights from the flies and from the balconies completely blind anyone out on the stage to the audience. From the center, gazing out into the auditorium, you seem to look only at a dead-black curtain, hung just beyond the apron. Blazing about in it, here and there, are blinding white magnesium flares—so that, in the third act, after I'd filed out to stand on our little bridge, I wasn't sure, for the first minute or so, if the curtain were open or closed—if, indeed, the music I heard were from the Act Three prelude (outside the curtain) or from the act proper. Were the characters moving around below me getting in place for the act's beginning, I wondered, or, indeed, had the curtain opened already with the act already in progress . . . ?

It was, of course.

But from inside such a production is simply not the way to experience an opera—especially one new to you; even if, as I had, you've read the libretto in preparation.

Now the drummers came out to stand beside us. In rehearsal everyone had been in street clothes. Nor had they carried any actual drums. The great bass instruments they hauled out on their bellies now were streaked with paint to dull their stretched skins. Their rims were blotched with brown and gilt. One of the drummers stood no more than eighteen inches from me.

Diaz rendered the prize song.

Eva presented him with the medallion.

There was a terrifying roar—

Because of the paint, I'd assumed the drums were props (to the extent I'd thought of it at all)—and that any actual drumming would occur down in the percussion section of the orchestra pit. But, no. These drums were real; they were played by on-stage costumed musicians!

The sound of six bass drums in a *fortissimo* roll, starting all at once, no more than two feet from your ear, is louder than any cannon-shot or thunderclap!

I nearly vaulted over the edge of the bridge in heart-thudding astonishment, sure that something huge had fallen onto the stage. I lost my
balance, staggered from one of the bridge's steps to the step below,
and had to be steadied by the burgher behind me.

The chorus began its joyful "*Ehrt eure deutschen Meister* . . ." and soon
the real curtain closed, its inner lining for the first few feet of its journey
before us looking no different from the black into which I'd been staring
and at which, since the drum roll, I'd been blinking and panting—till
suddenly it swung into the light and turned gold.

It was my last Met production.

But how can one really speak of one's first exposure to Wagner's
music? How can one speak of a first exposure to "Here Comes the
Bride," that, in the years since it first opened the second act of *Lohengrin* at the Weimer premiere on the 28th of August in 1850 (during
Wagner's Zurich exile after his part in the Dresden Uprising of 1849),
has wound throughout our lives, now seriously, now as parody, from
childhood on? How can one speak of a first exposure to the *Liebestod*
that has yearned throughout the three acts of *Tristan und Isolde* since its
first performance—commanded by young King Ludwig of his idol—in
1866? When I was a child, played on a diapasoned studio console it was
the radio, then television, theme song for two different soap operas! As
an adult, I've encountered its strains, uncredited, on the soundtracks
of at least three "adult" movies. How can one speak of a first exposure to
"The Ride of the Valkyries," that opens the third act of the *Ring* cycle's
second opera, *Die Walküre?* Such music is so ubiquitous that to quote it
anywhere outside a production of the opera in which it initially occurred is to lampoon it in much the same way that the opening bars of
Beethoven's *Fifth Symphony* or Rossini's William Tell Overture produce
a similar air of self-mockery.

What is being mocked in all these cases is, of course, the very concept of High Art as expressed by opera—just as the Venus de Milo or
the *Mona Lisa* are, at this point, self-parodic works, as they are brought
round to represent art itself.

Wagner's influence as a shaper of the notion of art that all these
icons both present at the level of sublime experience and re-present in
satiric self-pollution (and buxom sopranos in horned helmets—Wagner's virginal warrior goddesses—are another image from the same
gallery) is totally pervasive. Indeed, one reason it is sometimes so hard
to evaluate Wagner's influence is because we are always within it. We
can never get outside it, never see it as an organized stage picture.
There is no vantage from which we can slip into the audience and look
at it objectively. We try to contain it by saying that Wagner's legacy

(along with Baudelaire's and Flaubert's) is that which we call modernism in art. But, for better or worse, it would be more accurate to say that Wagner's legacy is that which any modern or post-modern—at the gut level—recognizes as art itself, whether our response is to go nodding off in boredom at the whole scattered operation, whether we wander about, gazing appreciatively up at this or that grandly engineered effect, or whether, now and again, some aesthetic thunderclap galvanizes us for moments, hours, or years, shaking us to our footsoles.

In 1982, I began to listen seriously to *Tristan und Isolde* and the four operas of the *Ring*. But there were (and still are) at least a dozen composers, classical and modern, who, in terms of pleasure and significance, have meant more to me for years—and will always mean more. Today, we must remember that in the marketplace of culture, all judgments of taste are personal; none are fixedly canonical, and it is only illiterates either in the synchronic array of artistic rhetorical provender or the diachronic sweep of developing cultural discursive practices, who, hoping to achieve some dubious authority if not mere momentary stability before near-chaos, let themselves think that great art and not-great art, major art and minor art, or strength and weakness in poets has any meaning outside a given community, communities which themselves are always partial, which by themselves never constitute a people: that is one of Artaud's lessons.

Listening to Wagner, I have found him instructive, definitely. He is enjoyable, certainly. His music is beautiful, undeniably—in the terms in which he chose to make it so. Yet for me he remains a kind of super kitsch, and his philosophical aspirations far outdistance any possible achievement. But of such philosophical failures our age makes heroes: that is Artaud's other lesson.

* * *

So far, in writing of Artaud, I have written only of Artaud-the-Myth. I have quoted him, synopsized him, and narrated his life only to highlight Artaud-the-Personality: the obscene, sensitive, energetic man, obsessed with the sensual, repelled by the sexual, critical, crusading, and at once hopelessly wounded, who is Artaud-le-Mômo.

But till now I have purposely avoided writing of Artaud-the-Mind—the *problem* of Artaud-the-Mind. For that problem, especially when paced at the center of such a personality, as it manifests itself (once we have located it) with each Artaudian sentence that strays to the edge of coherence to claw its way across into a derangement that, hopelessly mixed with the poetic, nevertheless signs itself as something outside of craft, consciousness, or considered reflection, that problem is what keeps Artaud outside of literature as well—hence outside of art. And, hence, allows us to use Artaud to construct a dialogue with all that is art itself, all that resides within the precincts of art, all that is Wagnerism in the broadest sense.

> . . . the whole problem: to have within oneself the inseparable reality and the physical clarity of a feeling, to have it to such a degree that it is impossible for it not to be expressed, to have a wealth of words, of acquired turns of phrase capable of joining the dance, coming into play; and the moment the soul is preparing to organize its wealth, its discoveries, this revelation, at that unconscious moment when the thing is on the point of coming forth, a superior and evil will attacks the soul like a poison, attacks the mass consisting of word and image, attacks the mass of feeling, and leaves me panting as if at the very door of life.
>
> And now suppose that I feel this will physically passing through me, that it jolts me with a sudden and unexpected electricity, a repeated electricity. Suppose that each of my thinking moments is on certain days shaken by these profound tempests which nothing outside betrays. And tell me whether any literary work whatsoever is compatible with states of this kind.

That is the twenty-seven-year-old Artaud writing to the editor of the prestigious *Nouvelle Revue Française*, the well-known poet Jacques Rivière, ten years Artaud's senior. It is also the clearest presentation of the problem's core we have from Artaud himself. The story of the *Correspondence with Jacques Rivière* (1923–24) has often been recounted. But it is necessary to review it here, in order to locate precisely how the problem it atomizes so astutely finally allows, informs, and encourages the dialogue we must trace out.

Artaud was born at Marseille in 1896, into a close family, part French but mostly Levantine Greek. He was a brilliant, energetic, and—from certain angles—demonically good-looking young man. But an attack of meningitis, when he was seven or eight, may have been the physical origin of the mental problems that were to plague him throughout his life. Five years after starting a literary review at the Collège du Sacré Coeur and publishing his first poems in 1910, Artaud had his first breakdown and in his nineteenth year entered the first of the several mental asylums in which he would spend his early twenties. Between bouts of confinement, he spent nine months in the military, but was released on medical grounds. By twenty-four he'd begun to take laudanum. Still, by twenty-five, he had left the asylums to establish himself as an actor, both in plays and in films.

Artaud was talented, intelligent, good-looking, and luck broke in his favor on several occasions. While he never became an overwhelmingly popular public acting success, still his early theatrical years—now with Lugné Poe, now with Cocteau—were the stuff of legend. And he was also, now, writing and publishing poems and articles in various periodicals. Toward the end of April 1923, Artaud sent a small group of poems to Rivière at the *NRF.*

On May 1st, Rivière rejected them. "But," Rivière wrote, generously and encouragingly, in his rejection note, "I am interested enough in them to want to make the acquaintance of their author. If it were possible for you to stop by the review some Friday between four and six, I would be happy to see you." A month later, on June 5th, Artaud dropped in for a late Friday afternoon visit and chat. That same evening, Artaud composed a letter to Rivière, asking him to reconsider his rejection of the poems. His reasoning was most unusual.

"You must believe, sir, that I have in mind no immediate or selfish goal; I wish only to settle a desperate problem." The problem that Artaud spelled out is the one with which we began this section. But that more articulate expression of it that we've already quoted is from later on in the correspondence. Here is Artaud's first elaboration of it from his first letter to Rivière:

I suffer from a horrible sickness of the mind. My thought abandons me at every level. From the simple fact of thought to the external fact of its materialization in words. Words, shapes of sentences, internal directions of thought, simple reactions of the mind—I am in constant pursuit of my intellectual being. Thus as soon as *I can grasp a form,* however imperfect, I pin it down, for a fear of losing the whole thought. I lower myself, I know, and I suffer from it, but I consent to it for fear of dying altogether. . . .

This is why, out of respect for the central feeling which dictates my poems to me and for those strong images or figures of speech which I have been able to find, in spite of everything I propose these poems for existence [i.e., that Rivière reconsider taking them for the *NRF*]. These figures of speech, these awkward expressions for which you reproach me, I have noticed and accepted. Remember: I did not contest them. They stem from the profound uncertainty of my thought. . . .

In showing you the poems, it seemed to me that their faults, their unevennesses were not sufficiently flagrant to destroy the overall impression of each poem. . . .

I cannot hope that time or effort will remedy these obscurities or these failings. . . . And the question I would like to have answered is this: Do you think that one can allow less literary authenticity and effectiveness to a poem which is imperfect but filled with powerful and beautiful things than to a poem which is perfect but without much internal reverberation? . . . The question for me is nothing less than knowing whether or not I have the right to continue to think, in verse or in prose.

Artaud concluded with a promise to drop by on another Friday and bring Rivière the two small booklets of poems of his that had just been published, *Tric Trac du Ciel* and *Douze Chansons*.

Rivière's answer—a reconfirmation of the rejection—was still generous in tone: But ". . . what prevents me for the moment from publishing any of your poems in *La Nouvelle Revue Française* [is that] . . . you do not usually succeed in creating a sufficient unity of impression."

This "unity of impression" has been, of course, the smokescreen against just this problem at least since Poe pulled the phrase "unity of effect" out of Aristotle's classical constraints on tragedy and put it into his review of Hawthorne's *Twice-Told Tales*, in 1842. We are directly within that critical system for which flawed transitions are the privileged error.

Seven months passed.

The correspondence did not resume until the last days of January, 1924. In a new and sudden letter, Artaud confesses that he'd resented Rivière's last answer. Artaud more or less says: I came to you as a mental case looking for sympathy. You answered with a literary judgement on "some poems which I did not value, which I could not value. I flattered myself that you had not understood me." But, he goes on, "I see today that I may not have been sufficiently explicit, and for this too I ask your forgiveness." He then proceeds "to finish that confession" which he had begun about his "distressing state of mind."

He explains to Rivière:

This scattered quality of my poems, these defects of form, the constant sagging of my thought, must be attributed not to a lack of practice, a lack of control of the instrument I was handling, a lack of *intellectual development,* but to a central collapse of the soul, to a kind of erosion, both essential and fleeting, of the thought, to a temporary non-possession of the material benefits of my development, to an abnormal separation of the benefits of thought (the impulse to think, at each of the terminal stratifications of thought, passing through all the stages, all the bifurcations of thought and of form). . . .

I only want to say enough about it to be at last understood and believed by you.

Artaud concludes by telling Rivière he is sending along "the latest product of my mind," i.e., another poem.

The poem in question, "*Cri*" ("Cry"), is in quatrains that link a series of surreal images, in which skies collide, a stable boy is ordered to guard wolves instead of horses, stars eat, slugs walk, angels return, and the sea boils. It begins and ends with "the little celestial poet," who opens the shutters of his heart, and, at the end of it all, "Leaves his celestial place / With an idea from beyond the earth / Pressed to his long-haired heart." There is an asterisk, then; and the terminal quatrain reads:

> Two traditions met.
> But our padlocked thoughts
> Did not have room:
> Experiment to be repeated.

It would be very hard, I suspect, for anyone to take "*Cri*" other than as a self-conscious embodiment of just the "awkwardnesses," "oddities," and "divergent images" Rivière had chided Artaud for in his response to the first submission. As such, there is something disconcerting and rather undergraduate about this second. It's certainly not a poem that the editor of the *NRF* would be likely to have published in 1924—if only because of its fairly clear intention to ridicule, however ironically and by example, Rivière's well-meant—and well-put—criticism.

Rivière did not get around to answering this one. I think it's understandable why. He had rejected Artaud's poems. And because he had presented himself as accessible and open on a personal level, he was being badgered to change his mind and take them anyway. There is one level where Artaud's argument, no matter how intriguing, parallels one that anybody who has ever taught creative writing has gotten at least once from the belligerent student who has had his (it is almost always a he) work criticized and is unhappy about it: "What you call my mistakes aren't that at all. They're exactly what I intended to do. The uncomfortable and awkward effects they produce *were* what I wanted. They document how I was feeling about it all when I wrote it. You just didn't understand that. But now that you do, don't you think it's better than you did?"

Indeed, the only thing that separates Artaud's argument from that of the wounded student defending his run-on and fragmentary sentences, protesting that his misplaced modifiers, clichés, and wrongly used words are exactly what he meant to write, is the language Artaud uses to detail his position, the energy with which he expresses his ideas, and the general insight, acuity, and level of abstraction at which he pitches his argument. Artaud was canny enough not to say that he placed flaws in his work intentionally. Rather, he argues, because of his mental condition, he could not avoid flaws. Nevertheless, once they'd been committed, he recognized them as signs—documents—of that condition, and decided—intentionally and for aesthetic reasons—to let them stand because that's what they were.

The problem that Artaud brings us to the edge of (and that the contemporary philosopher Derrida pulls out of Artaud's arguments in two brilliant essays on the French poet and dramaturge) is whether or not we ever really think—and, by extension, whether or not we ever really create—*anything* "intentionally." We create things that bear signs of order or disorder. We say, "I'm going to write a novel or a poem about X," and then we go on to write a novel or a poem that may turn out to be about X or about something entirely other. Or we may not write anything at all. As the language centers of the brain offer up words to put down on paper, we decide to accept those words, or we decide to reject them and wait for others with which to replace them. But in terms of the offering-up itself, does intention *really* have anything to do with it? The blocked writer can *intend* to write until the cows come home; but he or she sits before the blank page and the wells yield no language.

Isn't writing, finally, a responsive and non-understood process as opaque in its workings as life itself, which consciousness only oversees, overhears, and which the fiction of intention only tries to tame?

Perhaps intention is an empty philosophical category to mask this profound split in the consciousness of all speaking and writing subjects, a split where language never really cleaves to intention but is always in excess of it, or escapes it entirely, or contravenes it openly, or even fails to come near it.

Perhaps it is just this split that poets from Dante Alighieri to Yeats and Jack Spicer (not omitting Artaud) have dealt with by talking of their work as given to them, as dictated to them, as originating somewhere on the other side of a profound gap in the self, where intention has no sway.

And what happens to art if that is, indeed, the case?

But if Artaud's psychological analysis is more precise—or even more honest—than that of the protesting student writer, the underlying emotional belligerence and the immaturity that propel them both are all too clearly the same. The most generous interpretation we can put on that aspect of Artaud's argument is that this emotional morass may just *be* the "collapse of the soul" Artaud is writing of. Nevertheless that aspect was probably what made Artaud's argument, no matter how astute, difficult to respond to.

A week shy of two months later, when he had still received no answer, Artaud sent a brief, curt note to Rivière:

> My letter deserved at least a reply. Return, sir, my letters and manuscripts.
>   I would like to have found something intelligent to say to you to indicate clearly what divides us, but it is useless. I am a mind not yet formed, an idiot: think of me what you will.

It was hectoring. It was belligerent. It was disingenuously self-pitying ("... a mind not yet formed, an idiot ..." indeed!). But three days later, on March 25th, Rivière returned an answer. In spite of everything, he had come to appreciate just those qualities of energy, acuity, and living language in Artaud's letters. He wrote, "One thing strikes me: the contrast between the extraordinary precision of your self-diagnosis and the vagueness, or at least the formlessness, of your creative efforts." Rivière went on, in his longest letter to date, to try to discuss Artaud's problem at the same level of analysis that Artaud had.

I do not think Rivière's analytical passages strike most readers today as very strong.

Thus it is even more to his credit that he could recognize (in the face of all Artaud's emotional theatrics so transparently trying to mask simple, badgering rudeness) an impassioned and subtle analytical writer when Rivière could not offer an analysis of his own to equal it. Still, Rivière's letter broached at least one important idea that Freud had put forth twenty-five years before, which seems germane:

> You speak somewhere in your letter of the "fragility of the mind." This fragility is superabundantly borne out by the mental disorders studied and catalogued by psychiatry. But it has not, perhaps, been sufficiently shown to what degree so-called normal thought is the product of chance mechanisms.

The suggestion here is, of course, that abnormal thought processes may provide insight into normal thinking. If you want to learn about the psychological mechanics of falling asleep, do you ask the exhausted quarryman whose eyes seal nightly within the minute his head hits the pillow—or do you ask the insomniac who has examined in anxious anticipation every instant of the painfully protracted process of dozing off? If you are seeking an anatomy of the creative impulse, do you ask the titanic artist who belches forth a rich and sumptuous novel in a week or six—or do you ask the hesitant, all-but-blocked poet, for whom each word is a travail and a gamble with an endless, obliterating silence? If you want to know the workings of the normal mind, do you ask the clearly, the smugly, the certainly and safely sane—or do you turn to those for whom "normal behavior" is only a fleetingly-arrived-at state, unretainable despite all effort, a state that tears itself to pieces between passages of derangement?

"I am keeping your poem," Rivière concluded his letter; and added, perhaps more rashly than generously, "Send me everything you write." Enthusiastically, Artaud returned to the discussion they had already begun. ("One thing in your letter remains a little unclear to me," he broke down to include toward the end, "and that is the use that you intend to make of the poem I sent you." Anyone else, I suspect, would have realized Rivière had meant "I'm keeping the poem for my personal pleasure—but I'm still not publishing it.") And in his answering letter of May 24th, Rivière begins:

> An idea has occurred to me which I have resisted for some time but which I find extremely attractive. . . . Why shouldn't we publish the letter, or rather letters that you have written me? I have just reread again the one you wrote on the 29th of January. It is really altogether remarkable.

Rivière went on to suggest that "a little work of transposition" might make it easier on readers, turning the whole into a kind of "epistolary novel." Artaud had already taken advantage of Rivière's request to send more work. One of the things sent, besides more poems, was an essay on the painter Uccello, which showed some of the same analytic perspicacity as the best parts of his letters. Now Rivière all but recanted: "Perhaps we could also include a bit of your poetry or of your essay on Uccello?"

Artaud responded: "Why lie, why try to put on a literary level something which is the cry of life itself, why give an appearance of fiction to that which is made of the ineradicable substance of the soul . . . ?" And in a letter immediately after that, he went back to his central problem: "My mental life is shot through with petty doubts and peremptory certainties which express themselves in lucid and coherent words. And my weaknesses are of a more precarious structure, they are themselves nebulous and badly formulated . . ." A final, lengthy, sympathetic letter from Rivière concludes the exchange. Towards the end of it, Rivière again quotes Artaud back at himself:

> You wrote me: "I have, to cure me of the judgment of others, the whole of the distance that separates me from myself." Here is the function of this "distance": it "cures us of the judgment of others"; it prevents us from doing anything to bribe this judgement, or accommodate ourselves to it; it keeps

us pure, and in spite of the variations in our reality, it assures us a greater degree of identity . . . There is no absolute danger except for him who abandons himself; there is no complete death except for him who acquires a taste for dying.

Affectionately,
Jacques Rivière

It was decided to publish, in addition to the letters, only "*Cri*"—as it was really a part of one of them—and not the Uccello essay or anything else. The correspondence appeared in the September 1, 1924 issue of the *NRF*. Shortly afterwards, it was released as a small book. Certainly, more than any of his poems, it laid the base for Artaud's literary reputation. It also defined, both for Artaud and for his early readers, what was to become—apart from the theater as a paradigm for art—Artaud's overriding theme: his own ever-inwardly-collapsing creative condition. But even more importantly, what the correspondence did and still does—in exactly the way the belligerent creative writing student's protests would, if we took them seriously—is throw into question all the underlying precepts of artistic craft, content, reference, and communication that, unspoken, nevertheless and always underlie, support, and allow any location of artistic value in its connotations, suggestions, and resonances.

For connotations, suggestions, and resonances must be organized around denotations, statements, and clearly defined objects or they are connotations, suggestions, and resonances of nothing. The whole notion of art as we know it demands something immediate, meaningful, and made or chosen with some sort of conscientious skill. It is not that the work of art must be a representation. Rather the work of art must be, somehow, a manifestation of an intention—and readable as such from the signs it displays. This is true even when the intention is specifically (as it is in many modernist pieces) to create something that bypasses one, another, or a whole group of intentions usually associated with the art of a previous era. If the work is not a manifestation of an intention (is not a representation in signs of a certain psychology), then— and this is the danger that Artaud's "problem" opens us to—it can be anything and everything. Not only do all classical standards vanish, but there is no way to distinguish between art and anything else, from found objects and scenes in nature . . . to the maunderings of the mad—or of the bourgeois banal.

This is precisely the situation Artaud would go on to explore—joyously, polemically—in what is perhaps his most concentrated intellectual performance, the central essay of *The Theater and Its Double*, "No More

Masterpieces." He would even, in that essay, suggest some solutions to the dilemma. But this problem of intention, which Artaud highlights in such an intriguing way, is why it is so hard to read signs of [a] failure of execution or [b] lack of intention (and we must remember that [a] is just a subset of [b]) as signs of an *alternate* intention—whether the justification put for that reading is the creative writing student's clumsy self-defense or Artaud's far more refined one. Yet this is the problem various formalisms invariably leave us with—precisely as they try to avoid what they call the intentional, or the referential, or the communicational fallacy. And that is why Artaud's argument—as well as his seemingly formless, extravagant works, in which madness and the unconscious clearly and constantly triumph over reason and conscious thought—is particularly important to the contemporary, post-modern formalists which, more or less, we have all become . . . especially as it prompts "intentional" readings of the sort Derrida has made of it.

The Theater and Its Double would appear fourteen years later in February 1938, just after Artaud returned from a trip to Ireland—in a straitjacket, to be handed over to the French authorities, thirteen years after Rivière's death in 1925.

For now, however, we can only ask if, when, at fifty-two, his looks (and teeth) gone, his demeanor changed from that of a handsome devil to that of an emaciated ghoul, Artaud chose the title for what was to be his last work, *To Have Done with the Judgment of God,* did he recognize it—did he take the title intentionally—as a posthumous gift from Rivière, who had picked out the phrase "to cure us of the judgment of others" from those early letters and re-presented it to Artaud in Rivière's own slightly varied context?

* * *

In terms of an attitude toward art, in terms of art's very definition, the organization of its entification inscribed within the discourse of those generations that, since the middle of the nineteenth century, have called themselves modern—in terms of those gut responses all of us are still constantly arguing with as to what is and what is not art—in terms of art's hidden, inner-dimensional matrix and its external mythical and social moorings, Wagner may well have been the largest influence on Western culture we have yet known. Nor am I talking about a few phrases or paragraphs in his work that can be seen to embody, after the fact, the seeds of future trends. (For that, finally, is much the way Artaud works on us—nor would he, mystic that he was, have had it otherwise.) I am talking about the massive imposition of theatrical practices, supported by the state, coupled with a public fascination so great that, for nearly fifty years after his death, practically any European who aspired to any level of culture had in some way to be molded by the Wagner phenomenon. How intense was this phenomenon? Recall Proust's Mme. Verdurin, who, still at the turn of the century, would not allow Wagner to be played at her soirées, as the music was too exciting to her nerves. Whether one was for him or against him, the nerves that shivered and quivered under the Wagnerian onslaught were those of the entire European bourgeoisie. Wagner represented the birth of "the modern" in art, not as a fashion, but as a program, a practice, and a philosophy. That is how artists from Baudelaire and Berlioz up through T. S. Eliot, D. H. Lawrence, and James Joyce heard him.

Even with the early nineteen-eighties' resurgence of interest (1983 marked the centennial of Wagner's death), it is still hard for many of us to imagine the extent of Wagner's influence. But we get some inkling of it when we remember that by World War I, the three human beings about whom more books, more monographs, and more articles had been written than any others in history were Jesus Christ, Napoleon Bonaparte, and Richard Wagner.

IV

"We have no artists today whose nobility, stature, and greatness of spirit equal that of Lord Byron, George Sand, Richard Wagner . . ."

Considering herself or himself more or less in touch with the evanescent shifting of late modernist and postmodern aesthetic values, the contemporary listener must smile at such a statement. I resuscitate it here to invoke what we might call today, somewhat clumsily, the establishment aesthetic of the last decades of the Victorian age, when such a sentence (yes, it is part of my fiction) might have been uttered. Certainly this particular galaxy of judgments (which probably would have been momentarily extended to include Victor Hugo and, as it turned to England, would have looked with almost equal favor on Edward FitzGerald's *Rubá'iyát* and Tennyson's *Idylls of the King*, and would have turned expectantly to Swinburne well before Yeats) becomes rarer and rarer through the Edwardian coda to the nineteenth century until, by Edward VII's actual death in 1910 (when, wrote Virginia Woolf, human nature changed), such pronouncements either cease or at least come to take on some of the connotations of a certain mental fossilization that this value matrix, once so quintessentially European, has for us today.

For us, that thirty years from 1880 to 1910 is a rather bleak period in, say, English poetry. Yeats and Hardy are its high points. The first of these decades includes some of Hopkins's working period, but that work will not be discovered until later. Rudyard Kipling, A. C. Swinburne, Robert Bridges, George Meredith, Alice Meynell, Francis Thompson, Oscar Wilde, Ernest Dowson, Lionel Johnson—and A. E. Housman was read so ubiquitously, of course, as to make him a kind of misanthropic Rod McKuen of minuscule output—do not mark out for most a major poetic epoch.

Yeats aside, whatever one's personal enthusiasms for the English poets of this period, one has the feeling that they are just that: personal. And this is, of course, the period to which my reconstructed pronouncement belongs, even more so than it belongs to the years contemporaneous with the artists it evokes.

"The nineteenth century," as Auden tells us, "is the European century. Insofar as neither England nor America is part of Europe . . . [they] can be called provincial." And it is the provincials' justly-awed view of Europe, a view that took a while to filter down and become commonplace, that our "Bryon/Sand/Wagner" pronouncement reflects. Europe herself was busy during this same time inventing the avant-garde. But that had not yet come across the various waters.

What kind of world was it for, say, an Englishman concerned with art? For one thing—and it is perhaps the most surprising thing for us today—during this period there was no course in any English university called "English Literature."

The populations of the industrial nations, like England, were rising—doubling, tripling, quadrupling. Religion simply could not constrain the actions of the swollen urban laboring class in the way it had served as a sanctioned set of guiding superstitions for a rural peasantry.

Try to imagine a great city without written signs!

A minimum level of literacy is an urban necessity for maintaining minimal order. Add to that the necessary socialization that schools provide in that most anti-social construct, the big city, and we begin to understand the necessary rise in public education that accompanied the rise in urban populations.

Walter Benjamin notes in his work on nineteenth-century Paris that, with the new size of cities and the advent of public transportation necessary to get about in them, for the first time in history a sizable number of people were now spending comparatively long periods of time every day in horse-drawn trolleys and rattling trains, sitting across from and surreptitiously looking at people they did not know and to whom they were not going to speak. From this new, unnatural, and (at first) wholly urban experience, Benjamin speculated, the whole air of social mystery and the resultant hunger for social analysis grew up that was answered first by a now-long-vanished genre of writing called "physiologies." These were collections of literary sketches—not quite short stories, not quite essays—that simply described or analyzed the various types you might see moving about in the city. They were extraordinarily popular in the mid-years of the nineteenth century, until the novel, under the pressure of Thackeray, Brontë, Dickens, Eliot, and Wilkie Collins, adjusted its great and generous chambers to include an equal range of character types in even more interesting and mysterious interplay—thus satisfying that hunger even more (and making obsolete the physiologies). The urban crowd itself became a kind of mythic phenomenon, hiding within it mystery, crime, romance, desire . . . Again and again in those nineteenth-century novels, menacing or desirable (or simply ambiguous) characters emerge from it, or turn to become lost in it.

The crowd of strangers was a wall of mystery. News from its *far* side was available only through the papers, which reported from a world of melodrama, where upstanding fathers and husbands could be beset by calamities, so that in a single year's time they would turn into drunkards, thieves, murderers, rapists or suicides; where chaste and filial maidens could be disappointed in love so that they fell into a swoon or bad company or prostitution or tuberculosis or death overnight; or where the most dissolute and depraved of criminals might be touched by grace, whereupon they would be transformed, in a moment, into *bona fide* saints (if *only* one could get those *transitions* right between those autonomous/malleable subject states)—whereas on *our* side, the evil were stigmatized before their births by the misdeeds of their families and the good were equally well-marked; where nothing ever happened and transition itself was impossible, save that purely economic shift in monetary status—up or down—that always presupposed some violent bodily wrenching away from the endlessly stagnant social reality to begin it.

But that's because the relentlessly repeated experience of a crowd of strangers was itself historically new, and had to be imaginatively explored—a crowd that the other giant of nineteenth-century opera, Verdi, gave voice to again and again in his works, and that Wagner felt—hopelessly, desperately, stridently—should be only his audience and given as little voice as possible in his music dramas, which were, after all, relentlessly about the individual, the heroic, the will.

Those wise and willful Victorians had a remarkably clear view of the job education had to do in their new, mysterious city, in promoting the values of tolerance, acquiescence, and obedience (the three coming together under the name of responsibility) among the working classes who went each day into the dark Satanic mills, either in the inner city or or on the outskirts—since religion was (in the age where sexuality seemed to extend from Krafft-Ebing at one end to Jack the Ripper at the other) clearly no longer effective.

In 1850, the year of Wordsworth's death (on April 23rd, the traditional date of Shakespeare's birth), twenty-seven-year-old Matthew Arnold stood looking out a window in the moonlight at the full, calm tide of Dover Beach (with or without a young woman, we are not sure). Four years before (while, in America, Poe was busy reinventing the unities in his defence of "The Raven"), Arnold had been to France to visit with George Sand herself, a guest at her Nohant estate. Now she was the French revolutionary government's Minister of Culture. With their smashing of the old order and the undermining of all traditional relationships between God and man, mediated by a king, republican revolutions had raged on the continent for half a decade now, and would go on raging. That night in 1850 the English cliffs glimmered vastly, out in the water. ("—on the French coast, the light / Gleams and is gone . . .") Arnold stood listening to "the grating roar / Of pebbles which the waves draw back, and fling, / At their return, up the high strand, / Begin, and cease, and then again begin . . ." After a sestet's musing on the perfect civilization of Greece, Arnold's thoughts returned to the problems of the present:

> The Sea of Faith
> Was once, too, at the full, and round earth's shore
> Lay like the folds of a bright girdle furl'd.
> But now I only hear
> Its melancholy, long, withdrawing roar,
> Retreating, to the breath
> Of the night-wind, down the vast edges drear
> And naked shingles of the world.

Swept with its confused alarms, the darkling plain where ignorant armies clashed was a nightmare Arnold feared lay under the dream the English could still see the world as, a world "so various, so beautiful, so new"—a nightmare that was already manifest in France and Germany, a nightmare that was uneasily feared for England herself.

This was his great poem, "Dover Beach."

Seventeen years later in 1867, as his last lecture as Professor of Poetry at Oxford, Arnold delivered what was to become the first chapter of his book *Culture and Anarchy* (1869)—and in it, it is all there. The study of Latin and Greek had promoted the necessary civilized values in the upper middle classes. But it was quite another thing to make Latin and Greek the basis of mass education for the proletariat.

Why not use imaginative works, in a language the masses already spoke, to accomplish for the working classes what disciplines such as philology and the "Greats" had done for their rulers? And thus educational crusaders fought to make English literature an academic discipline. Here is Professor George Gordon—among the first professors of English Literature at Oxford—in his inaugural lecture just on the near side of the Great War (as quoted by Terry Eagleton in his *Literary Theory: An Introduction*):

> England is sick, and . . . English literature must save it. The Church (as I understand) having failed, and social remedies being slow, English Literature has now a triple function: still, I suppose, to delight and instruct us, but also, and above all, to save our souls and heal the State.

No doubt when, within hailing distance of World War I, Professor Gordon made his statement, "healing the State" meant making sure there was no workers' revolution—since Arnold's Sea of Faith was generally acknowledged by now to have dried wholly up.

Most of us here are, today, more or less the products of that Edwardian discovery, English Literature.

Paradoxically, one of the most important people in its establishment as an academic discipline was a brilliant and erudite Frenchman, Hippolyte Adolphe Taine, whose *Histoire de la littérature anglaise* was announced in Paris in 1856, was published there in 1863, and was followed by a supplementary volume on modern authors in 1867—modern meaning Dickens and Thackeray for the novel, Macauley, Carlyle, and John Stuart Mill for criticism, philosophy, and history, and Tennyson for poetry. It is certainly the work we turn to today in order to find what was by 1900 considered the most intelligent European view on any of its topics.

That French invention, *La Littérature anglaise*—or English literature—came across the Channel in the last third of the nineteenth century along with what we traditionally call "British spelling," which was not British at all but rather "provincial" England's attempt to Frankify its language, leaving the old Saxonate forms such as "labor," "color," "honor," and "theater," the spellings that appear in the manuscripts (as well as the first editions) of Dickens and George Eliot, to even more provincial America.

What does Taine have to say on such a notorious figure as Lord Byron, with whom he closes the main portion of his *Histoire?*

I have reserved for the last the greatest and most English of these artists; he is so great and so English that from him alone we shall learn more truths of his country and his age than from all the rest together.

Byron, the most English of English artists . . . ? Was Taine ignorant of the most un-English scandal of the sometimes handsome, sometimes obese, social and literary lion's "incestuous" affair with his half-sister Augusta, of his atrocious treatment of his mathematician wife Annabella, and of his most un-English flight from England during the last eight years of his life? No, it too is there in Taine. Rather, what constituted nobility, grandeur, and greatness of spirit—national spirit—for Taine in particular and Europe in general was far richer and more complex than the stereotyped prejudices such notions become in most of our minds once we pass World War II. After all, as Byron embodied the spirit of England more than any other English writer, the woman who embodied the spirit of France, if not that of Europe, was a woman who was believed by most of the public to smoke cigars and appear in public in men's clothing—which, indeed, on a number of occasions in her younger days George Sand actually did.

But Sand was the writer of over a hundred volumes; she was the great friend of Balzac's and confidante of Flaubert's; she was a correspondent of Manzoni, Gutzkow, and of the anarchist Bakúnin—Gutzkow one of the greater thorns in Wagner's side at the Dresden Opera house, and Bakúnin Wagner's most radical friend during the Dresden Uprising of 1849; Sand was the European champion of Stowe's *Uncle Tom's Cabin*; and she was inspiration to Dostoyevski, Elizabeth Barrett Browning, and George Eliot, among her immediate contemporaries. Among her immediate successors, Proust loved her pastoral novels and Henry James wrote ten review-essays praising her art. ". . . [S]uch a colossal nature in every way . . ." wrote Barrett to Browning in the summer of 1845, a year before her fervent admirer the young Arnold visited Nohant. But was that nature conceived then as something personal? I think not. For she was often called "The Spirit of Europe."

To get some idea of the awe in which a people and a nation could hold its national artists in the nineteenth century, read the description of Victor Hugo's 1885 state funeral (two years after the death of Wagner), which opens Roger Shattuck's study, *The Banquet Years*. The great writer's remains stood for four days in an immense urn beneath the Arc de Triomphe, guarded by children in togas, endless brass bands, dignitaries, speeches, crowds, while, apparently, some of the frenzied populace balled in the bushes, yards away in the underbrush flanking the Champs Elysées (then a public bridle path), in hopes of producing, or so they said when apprehended, their own little immortal. The point is not that today we have no artists of such stature. Rather it is that the particular social configuration, vouchsafed in the public psyche, the conception of the nation's greatest artist as the greatest of its civil servants, equal to its greatest generals and its grandest industrial tycoons, is simply no longer there. That, today, is no longer *what* the artist *is*. Even a Spielberg, Lucas, or Coppola—the distribution conduit of twenty to fifty million dollars with each new film, which then brings in a hundred-million-plus and feeds a gallery of images into the general cultural consciousness, images that may persist for years—is still not socially revered in the same manner and mode.

It is tempting to speculate on the machinery of such fame. In material terms, the greatest factor was doubtless the size of the literate population: in 1814, after a series of moody, speculative and narrative poems (*Childe Harold's Pilgrimage* [1812], *The Giaour* [1813], *The Bride of Abydos* [1813]) had catapulted him to astonishing literary fame, Lord Byron's narrative poem *The Corsair, A Tale* went on sale and sold ten thousand copies on the first day of publication, with lines outside London's bookstores waiting hours for the doors to open. But the entire literate population of England at that time was slightly *under* five hundred thousand! The book went on to sell over a hundred thousand copies in the next year or so of its initial life. Ten thousand copies on the first day of publication would be an impressive first-day sale for a best-selling novel in America today. Such a book might well go on to sell a million or two million copies, in a literate field that is currently over fifty times the size of England's in 1814. But Byron's sales are even more impressive when we restate the Byron phenomenon in relative terms: Byron's work was purchased by two per cent of the entire English reading population on the first day of sales and, in the first year, went on to be owned by almost twenty per cent of that population. For a book—be it a poem or otherwise—to achieve comparable success in the United States now, it would have to sell half a million on its first day and twenty-five million over the next year.

It is not that poetry will not sell in such figures today.

Books today simply do not sell at such figures: *Gone with the Wind*, during the whole of its phenomenal success since publication in 1936, has sold perhaps twelve million copies; in its first year, it sold no more than a million and a half.

This is the material situation against which observations such as, "Well, back then there was no radio, television, or film to compete with Byron (or Goethe, or Sand, or Hugo) . . ."—or even the more astute observation that, because *The Corsair* was not quite two thousand lines long, it could be sold at considerably less money than the novels of Jane

Austen, Sir Walter Scott, Charlotte Brontë, and William Makepeace Thackeray (who were successful novelists in the surrounding years)— become simply banal. The whole field against which such fame was constituted was so different from the contemporary that such statements do far more to mystify than they do to explain.

Goethe was, of course, the first artist to become such an international celebrity. But that celebrity was very much a function of cities and of the increased communication they fostered.

In this light, the fame of any serious artist is wholly a social construct. Keeping that in mind, we can ask: What sort of men and women were granted this celebrity? Certainly they tended to be titanic producers. At the same time, they tended to be very serious men and women about their art—and equally serious about their critiques of society. All of them were associated with some antisocial incident or action, frequently highly salacious, that tended to become a point of ethical debate around which any number of social arguments raged, so that they were figures of sexual rebellion and sexual desire. Byron loved his sister and was rumored to carry a great and melancholy curse—about as close as those days could come to admitting his bisexuality. Sand had appeared in public in men's clothing and smoked cigars in her youth, and had left her legal husband, first to live with the poet Alfred de Musset, then with the Polish musician Chopin; Wagner lived in sin with Cosima (Liszt's daughter and von Bülow's wife). Goethe before and Hugo later had long and notorious affairs with . . . actresses! In the field in which their fame was constituted, this combination of massive work, high seriousness, and scandal was a terribly effective configuration. Needless to say, in a field differently constituted—such as the contemporary one—fame must work, both materially and psychologically, differently; and the conscious or unconscious efforts of the media to make these nineteenth-century parameters function to produce fame today is one of our greatest current comedies. In the end, it was not that such artists achieved mass fame to a degree that does not happen today. Rather, they achieved their relatively greater proportional fame before there was, in today's terms, any mass audience at all.

The Corsair was a romantic, exotic, foreign tale—as distant from the bourgeois life of middle-class London as a poem might be. But Byron was the most English of English artists because *The Corsair* begins,

> O'er the glad waters of the dark blue sea,
> Our thoughts as boundless and our souls as free,
> Far as the breeze can bear, the billows foam,
> Survey our empire, and behold our home!

Thus he addressed ten thousand literate middle-class Englishmen on that spring day in 1814. Had he addressed fewer of them *or* had he addressed them differently, he would not have been.

To understand what art—in light of such artists—was, however, which means to understand, with more than a smile, such pronouncements about those artists with whom we began this section, we must investigatively reanimate a nineteenth-century Europe where greatness was based on a notion of character, of nobility, of spirit, a spirit that was at once both political and aesthetic.

The young Hegel had articulated the idea of a spirit for his century in 1807, with his concept of the *Zeitgeist*, the Spirit of the Times, National Character, the Soul of the Race. Today, we tend to see Nietzsche as a figure in opposition to the totalizing systematization of Hegel's sweeping reductions. But Nietzsche's concept of the *Weltanschauung*, from his inaugural lecture of 1869 at the University of Basel (only two years after Arnold had given that final lecture at Oxford, "Culture and Its Enemies"), when the twenty-five-year-old German philosopher was an intimate member of the Wagner family circle at Triebschen, seems far more in keeping with Hegel's concept than opposed to it:

> All philological activity should be embedded and enclosed in a philosophical *Weltanschauung* so that all individual or isolated details evaporate as things that can be cast away, leaving only the whole, the coherent.

For Hegel, writing in the first, glorious years of the Napoleonic onslaught, history and progress were forces that marched hand in hand. For Nietzsche, writing sixty-two years later, history was a nightmare and progress a joke. (His older friend Wagner, in his projected *Ring* cycle, through a recourse to myth, had taken on precisely the job of redeeming the historical concept without recourse to the degraded notion of progress.) But the conceptual screen both Hegel and Nietzsche worked against was one with the concept of unity put forth by Aristotle and Poe. This nineteenth-century reductionism, this plea for a unity in which all that is anomalous can be ignored, this appeal to rationalism over empiricism, is behind the whole deadly concept of race; by the end of that century we will see its fallout in the virulent anti-Semitism of the Dreyfus Affair, in what we now speak of as British imperialism, and in Rhodesian and South African racism. Such reductionism when essentialized becomes the philosophical underpinning of this century's totalitarianisms, whether Hitler's or Stalin's or, in its so much milder form, that most social of social constructs—the "human nature" which everyone seems so reluctant to do battle with in the name of pleasure in this country today.

Our current history is the history of the abuse of such reductionism and such essentialism. It is the chronicle of their genocidal failure to support humane behavior within and between nations, within and between institutions, between individuals and institutions, and between individuals of unequal power. So much is this the case that the contemporary historian Carl Schorske can write,

> What the historian must now abjure, and nowhere more so than in confronting the problem of modernity, is the positing in advance of an abstract categorical common denominator—what Hegel called the *Zeitgeist*, and Mill "the characteristic of the age." Where such an intuitive discernment of unities once served, we must now be willing to undertake the empirical pursuit of pluralities as a precondition to finding unitary patterns in culture.

But how can we truly accept such a program until we truly understand what it is we are against: the spirit of the age, the nation, the race, as it became something that might be manifested in the greatest artist of the times, the age, the nation: in a Byron, a Sand, a Hugo, a Wagner. The entire *Annales* school of history, from Lucien Febvre and Marc Bloch to Fernand Braudel and Emmanuel Le Roy Ladurie, would seem to confirm the currency of Schorske's position in the field of contemporary historical studies: that is, of analyzing great men and great events down into the socioeconomic matrix of needs, conventions, and desires that position them. This particular view of history, when transferred to art, is tantamount to a certain dismissal of the notion of "greatness" itself and fosters a movement toward the occasional/disposable poem, as in Frank O'Hara, or Ted Berrigan, or the courting of hermetic banalities carried on so luminously and daringly by W. S. Merwin in one direction and John Ashbery in another. But could anyone have better prepared us for this inevitable fallout from the continuing rise in the functionally literate population, sometimes called "the death of the author," than Artaud?

The death of the author follows, of course, on the death of God so vigorously noted by Nietzsche in *Thus Spake Zarathustra*, whose first two parts were published in the year of Wagner's death, 1883; and whether Foucault is right that the author's death precedes the death of Man, we still have some way to go before we find out for sure. My personal suspicion is that all three are pretty much aspects of the same thing.

But England's replacement of the ideology of religion with the ideology of literature was only the provincials' catching up with a process that had been going on all through the European century: the replacement of the general ideology of religion with the ideology of art. While Arnold was speculating on the religious aspects of revolution from across the moonlit channel, Wagner was a wanted political criminal with a price on his head, who had just managed to emerge from the fighting and bloodshed at the barricades. To articulate his situation is to articulate most clearly, if not most importantly, the continental manifestation of that nineteenth-century trend in art, a trend in the vision of what art was and might do, a trend that, paradoxically, went hand in hand with the rise of the ideology of science.

What Arnold and his followers wanted to do with literature, Wagner, of course, had set out to do with music. The theoretical works of 1849 and 1850, written during his exile in Zurich after the calamity of Dresden's uprising of 1849, are where Wagner formulated his attack on the future of art.

With the accomplishment of the *Ring* and the other music-dramas that followed this three-volume-plus elaboration of the social function of art in general and music in particular, Wagner came to be considered, for better or for worse, the embodiment of the spirit of his times; which is to say, at the time, the spirit of the modern—that spirit which, in the postmodern view, modernism must dismiss in order to become politically responsible.

Is the lesson we are about to abstract from Wagner, then (to anticipate ourselves just a bit), the idea that all High Art—all Great Art, all Serious Art—is necessarily conservative, or even fascist, because there is no way it can avoid reifying the anterior (and always social) system that prepares the labels "Great" or "High" in the first place? I do not believe we have to do this—not so long as we bear in mind the problematics of a figure, a mind, a creator such as Artaud.

V

If Wagner *is* kitsch, then the status we have claimed for Artaud's work should also apply to his.

But of course the operas stand there, a mosaic of one impressively telling psychological moment laid down after another, this one five seconds long, that one forty-five seconds, one lasting a whole six minutes, now another that endures thirty seconds (for Nietzsche, Wagner was finally—with no mean paradoxical intent—the "great miniaturist"), until a massive structure has been bridged, exhausting not because of its duration, which is considerable, but because of the intricacy of its articulations, which are near numberless. They were not always kitsch. And it is our critical duty to look at art that can still speak to us in, as far as possible, its historical context.

At the close of the nineteenth century, in his little book *The Perfect Wagnerite* (1898), George Bernard Shaw wanted to redeem Wagner from the endless images of buxom, bull-horned blondes with spears and shields that had already become a parodic symbol of all "serious art." To do it he took Wagner's four-paneled portrait of eternity, the *Ring* cycle—where the human, the superhuman, and the subhuman (this last in the form of giants and dwarves) lived, lusted, and battled in a world before time—and tried to read some socialist awareness into it. Was there, anywhere in that great, mythic allegory of history and psychology, some understanding—international understanding, that is—of the new currents of socialism that had blown from west to east and were now blowing back again? Shaw was certain that there were. There seemed to be everything else.

Eighty years later, in 1979 at Bayreuth, the French *enfant terrible*, then thirty-year-old Patrice Chereau, tried to do much the same.

Allegories being what they are, especially well-articulated ones, it is not too hard to read anything one wants into Wagner's panorama of the intricate and interconnected failures of gods, men, and women.

But we can reasonably ask, in historical terms, if any of these socialist ideas were, indeed, Wagner's.

It's customary to turn to the Dresden Uprising of May, 1849, as the rack on which Wagner's true political colors were displayed—or the forge at which his political convictions were hammered out. Wagner devotes considerable space to it in his autobiography *Mein Leben* (My Life). The book is a massive, colorful, sweeping account by a vigorous, inexhaustibly energetic man, as much a document of "the European century," the century of revolutions, as Hugo's *Les Misérables*.

Wagner's twentieth-century biographers have gone on endlessly about the ways Wagner suppressed, colored, or outright lied in his book. His account of the spring of '49 in Dresden, and what led up to the calamitous events there, has under particular censure. But the shortcomings of *Mein Leben* are basically two. First, Wagner wrote it at the personal request of a king, so that it is really a letter to his most powerful and influential fan. Second, he dictated it to his second wife, Cosima. The three things the book is traditionally taken to task for are, first, its incomplete coverage of Wagner's debts; second, its fragmentary account of his love affairs; and, third, its muting (and many have used much stronger words) of the active and energetic part he took at Dresden.

Feelings for his amanuensis certainly explain the second reticence. And even there, considering to whom he was dictating, I find Wagner remarkably honest: the only affair he wholly represses (and he had many), so that one cannot even read it between the lines, was his most recent one (at the time of the writing) with Mathilde von Wesendonk. But that, of course, is the one we are most interested in, since it so deeply influenced the writing of *Tristan und Isolde*, the opera of Wagner's that, today, we are most ready to concede greatness to in purely musical terms.

Also missing is, of course, the alleged affair with the young Judith Gautier. But Cosima, who is supposed to have known of it, kept up a warm correspondence with Judith through the whole of it till well after Wagner's death. I suspect this was more likely one of Wagner's intense friendships that he instituted with young men and, more and more frequently as he grew older, young women all through his life.

If one reads only his biographers, however, one can get the notion that Wagner never once, in *Mein Leben*, mentions debt at all. Or one begins to assume that, indeed, by 1865 (when, at the request of young King Ludwig II, who had rescued Wagner and Cosima from Wagner's creditors in a move that was quite like something out of a fairy tale, Wagner began these memoirs) Wagner was presenting himself merely as a spectator to the 1849 events at Dresden. I have seen the whole book dismissed as an unreadable tissue of fabrications. But while, in his theoretical writings, Wagner's style takes on a Germanic academic recomplication that veers toward the incomprehensible, if not the meaningless, the king *Mein Leben* was written for was not yet twenty-one; and while he was "artistically sensitive" enough, he was not, in Wagner's private estimation, overly bright. Wagner was, by this time, a comparatively experienced journalist as well as a musician, and the account is straightforward and (at least in its current Andrew Gray translation— Cambridge University Press: 1983) reads far more easily today than, say, any number of Dickens's novels.

In *Mein Leben* hardly a year goes by in which Wagner does not recount some creditor or other harassing him with a bill for one or another loan. The agony of financial embarrassment seems to be his constant companion. His most famous biographer, Ernest Newman (who most rigorously and famously challenged this aspect of *Mein Leben*), seems to be trying to say that, with all the debts Wagner recounts, there were simply dozens more left unmentioned—and, frequently, unpaid. My own estimation, on considering both Newman's and Wagner's versions, is that if Wagner was not accurate to the letter in his autobiographical tally of his financial extravagances, he certainly gave the feel of his debts and doubtless recounted, if not the largest ones, the ones he remembered suffering over most.

There are, of course, numerous inaccuracies all through Wagner's account of his life. Toward the beginning of autumn in 1847 Wagner left Dresden, the capital of Saxony, where he had been Second Royal Kapellmeister since 1843, to visit Berlin, where he had been asked to conduct several performances of his early and (moderately) popular opera *Rienzi*. The invitation had come as a result of an audience with the Queen. Wagner felt the trip would further his career and that he might even meet with the King and thus interest Friedrich August II and other powerful people in supporting performances of his newer works, *Tannhäuser* (which had already had some success in Dresden) and *Lohengrin* (on which he was still working). Though Wagner liked the man personally well enough, the Berlin tenor, around whom *Rienzi* turned, was simply inadequate—in an otherwise passable production. But King Friedrich did not attend any of the performances he himself had, at the Queen's request, commanded. Wagner was obliged to borrow money against his Kapellmeister salary to get back to Dresden, and the trip had to be written off largely as a failure—and a dismal one, given the financial considerations. Wagner came back to his Kapellmeister job that Christmas season deeply dejected. Within days of his return, he learned that his mother had died in Leipzig.

We know Wagner's mother died on January 9, 1848.

But Wagner recounts making the comparatively brief rail journey to the funeral, in time to view her remains and see her buried, as taking place in February. Doubtless he is a couple of weeks off. But the feel of the winter funeral is still there:

> It was a bitingly cold morning when we lowered the casket into the grave in the churchyard; the frozen clumps of earth, which we scattered on the lid of the casket instead of the customary handfuls of loose soil, frightened me by their ferocious clatter. On the way back to the house of my brother-in-law Hermann Brockhaus, where the family got together for an hour, my sole companion . . . Heinrich Laube . . . expressed anxiety about my unusually exhausted appearance. Then he accompanied me to the railway station . . . On the short trip back to Dresden the realization of my complete loneliness came over me for the first time with full clarity, as I could not help recognizing that the death of my mother had severed all the natural ties with my family, whose members were all preoccupied with their own special affairs. So I went coldly and gloomily about the sole task that could warm and cheer me: the orchestration of my *Lohengrin* score . . .

This seems to be the sort of mistake that abounds in *Mein Leben*. Dates are off here and there. Sometimes Wagner misremembers names. Occasionally events are out of order. But save for those discretionary omissions and a sense of occasion that are the prerogative of any auto-biographer, I don't find examples of rank lies or outright prevarication. Indeed, Wagner expends considerable energy and narrative ingenuity to achieve the proper tone and feel for complexes of occurrences that even the most exhaustive memoirist would have had to abridge in order to remain readable.

In his account of the calamities in Dresden in the spring of 1849, Wagner describes his actions of early May—the decisive period—with dates and days of the week. Researchers have ascertained he was off as much as two days in some of the early events and a steady day off in his account of what occurred on May 6th, 7th, 8th, and 9th. Biographers have since tried to document this period in Wagner's life day by day and, in some cases, hour by hour. The import of these times is easy enough to understand simply by the cataclysmic devastation they encompassed:

On Palm Sunday of spring 1849, Second Royal Kapellmeister Richard Wagner conducted a triumphant concert of Beethoven's *Ninth Symphony* at the Dresden Royal Opera House, to a sold-out audience in a benefit performance for the orchestra's pension fund, recreating for the second time his triumphant Palm Sunday concert of 1846, when he first performed the same work for the skeptical Dresden public. In '46, through careful placement of articles on the difficult symphony in local papers, an imaginatively written program for the concert, and meticulous rehearsals for the orchestra (and an intelligent rearrangement of the usual orchestra placement into a form we are all familiar with today but which in 1846 was novel) and the chorus of three hundred, Wagner achieved a great success with what had been considered till then a difficult and inaccessible work, which had, when it had been conducted by First Kapellmeister Reissiger a few years before, left the Dresden audience bewildered and unenthusiastic.

By mid-May, some six weeks after this third Palm Sunday benefit performance of the *Ninth*, which, over three years (missing only 1848), Wagner had made into a Dresden tradition, thousands of men, many of them miners, were dead in the Dresden streets. The Dresden Opera House, where the concert had taken place, had been burned to the ground and was now a charred foundation. And Richard Wagner was in flight from Germany, under an assumed name ("Professor Werder") and with a false passport, for Paris and finally Zurich.

Three of his friends, the Russian anarchist Mikhail Bakúnin, the head of the Dresden Provisional Government, Otto Heubner, and the publisher of the radical newspaper, *Die Volksblätter* (which Wagner himself had edited for a while and written for extensively), August Röckel, had already been arrested, to be sentenced to life imprisonment or death for treason.

Wagner had ridden with Bakúnin and Heubner to Freiberg. A newspaper editor from Rochlitz named Semming, with them in the coach, years later gave this account:

> Conversation . . . was out of the question: before us, around us, behind us, was nothing but a crowd of armed men in great agitation. But all the din, all the shouting and rattling of arms, was drowned by the flaming talk of Wagner. Never have I seen a man so excited. . . . "War!" he kept shouting. This was all he had on his lips and his mind: he poured out such a flood of words that it is impossible for me now to remember it all. . . . The paroxysm lasted perhaps more than half an hour: and so overwhelmed was I by the storm of words of this man sitting next to me—shall I call him Wotan or Siegried?—that I could not address a single word to him. This scene remains with me as one of the most thrilling of my memories of those terrible, stormy days.

Soldiers had climbed on the back of the coach, and the vehicle was loaded down. The coachman complained that the carriage had very delicate springs and was likely to break under the weight; he begged people to dismount, and at one point even broke out sobbing. Bakúnin thought this viciously funny. ("The tears of the philistine," he whispered to Wagner, "are the nectar of the gods," and continued by telling how, earlier, when he'd had to order trees along the Maximilians-Allee in Dresden cut down, so as not to provide shelter for the Prussian invaders, the people who lived on the street had complained volubly of the fate of their "bee-yoo-ti-ful trees.") But finally Wagner and Heubner dismounted and continued together on foot, while Bakúnin stayed in the coach. While they were walking, some messengers from a group of soldiers the two men spotted on a hill extended an invitation to Heubner to come to Chemnitz and set up his provisional government there. (Wagner was on his way to Chemnitz because his wife had already gone there to be with brother-in-law Brockhaus, and Wagner was going to rejoin her.) When they reached Heubner's Freiberg home, Wagner ate with Bakúnin, Heubner, and Heubner's family, and rested there a while. The exhausted Bakúnin went to sleep sitting on the living room couch, his huge, bearded head falling on Wagner's shoulder.

As Wagner recounts in *Mein Leben*, it was only a mix-up, due to a delayed mailcoach from Freiberg to Chemnitz, on May 9th, that prevented Wagner from ending up again in the same carriage with Heubner and the Russian, who had already ridden on to Chemnitz; when they announced themselves come to set up the provisional government, they were arrested at their inn.

The invitation from the soldiers to establish the new government there had been a lure and trap set by the opposition officers.

In the course of Wagner's flight, on May 10th, he stopped to attend a rehearsal of *Tannhäuser* his friend Liszt was conducting in Weimar. From there, on the 14th, he wrote to his wife Minna of revolution:

> [P]eople of our sort are not destined for this terrible task. We are revolutionaries only in order to *build* on fresh soil; it is *re-creation* that attracts us, not *destruction*, which is why we are not the people whom fate requires. These will arise from the very lowest dregs of society; we and our hearts can have nothing in common with them. You see? *Thus do I bid farewell to revolution. . . .*

I think it's to Wagner's credit that, while he did send the above to Minna, he neither quotes it in *Mein Leben* nor does he express any similar sentiment there. By 1865 he was willing to take responsibility for what he had done—at least for what of it he was willing to admit to. But despite any personal regrets he had at the time, by the 19th of May a Wanted notice appeared in the *Dresdner Anzeiger*:

> *Warrant.* The Royal Kapellmeister Richard Wagner, of this place, being somewhat more closely described below, is wanted for questioning on account of his material participation in the rebellious activities that took place in this city, but has not so far been found . . . Wagner is 37 or 38 years old [Actually he was three days shy of 36], of medium height, has brown hair and a high forehead.

. . . And an unpublished personal description (quoted in his biography by Martin Gregor-Dellin) goes on: "Eyebrows: brown. Eyes: gray-blue. Nose and mouth: well proportioned. Chin: rounded. Wears glasses. Special characteristics: *movements and speech abrupt and rapid.* Clothing: overcoat of dark green buckskin, trousers of dark cloth, velvet waistcoat, silk cravat, ordinary felt hat and boots."

But Wagner was now more or less safe in Zurich, where he began writing what turned out to be nearly 700 pages in his collected works: *Art and Revolution, The Artwork of the Future,* the notorious anti-Semitic article "Jewry in Music," and *Opera and Drama,* a theoretical outpouring which was apparently necessary before he could move onward with the music of the *Ring.* There is a great deal of social observation in all of these works, much of it very modern. All of it has been commented on, at length.

But we must examine the Dresden events and what led up to them if we really are to learn of Wagner's politics. We must also examine them because in the year that preceded them and, arguably, during the Dresden Uprising itself, the ideas that shaped the *Ring* were fired, forged, and annealed.

VI

With all the criticism that has fallen on *Mein Leben*'s account of Dresden, I can find only three places where Wagner has inarguably omitted pertinent facts.

His most eyebrow-raising abridgement is this: Wagner and Röckel ordered a large number of hand grenades from a brass founder, Karl Oehme, and on May 4th (so Oehme claimed at Röckel's trial for treason) Wagner placed an order for them to be filled with gunpowder.

This is *not* mentioned in *Mein Leben*.

Whether the grenades were used in the Dresden fighting at all is not, in fact, known. One theory is that the men placed the order for their friend Bakúnin and that the grenades ultimately went to Prague, where Bakúnin also had his finger in the fighting. While such an interpretation may be bending over backwards to exonerate Wagner, what I think we can be sure of is that, even if he ordered them, whether subsequently they went off in the streets of Dresden or in the streets of Prague, he did not throw them. And if, by some chance, during the fighting he did, while it pertains to whether, at the time, he did or did not commit a criminal act during the fighting that warranted his imprisonment, in terms of what we are interested in today—the political ideas behind his involvement in the uprising as they were to be expressed in his later work, particularly the *Ring*—, it only makes the extremity of his beliefs that much more intense (and Wagner was nothing if not intense). But it does not change their basic nature.

Wagner's second suppression in *Mein Leben* is not so cataclysmic.

Days after the *second* Palm Sunday concert, on April 8th, 1847, Wagner and his wife, the former actress Minna Planer, with Minna's illegitimate daughter from an adolescent liaison, Natalie (who was raised all her life to believe she was Minna's younger sister), a parrot, and a dog, moved into their new quarters in the second floor apartments of Dresden's beautiful Palais Marcolini, upstairs from a sculptor named Hänel. The palace's spacious French-style gardens were at their disposal, where Wagner would sometimes go out to sit on the Triton in one of the dried-up fountains, orchestrating. The rent was low. The only drawback to the location, Wagner writes, was its inordinate distance from the theater, where he had to go to rehearse the orchestra and conduct performances.

". . . I often found the cabfare," Wagner remarks in *Mein Leben,* "a serious problem."

Just after Wagner returned from his mother's funeral in Leipzig, the news of Louis Philippe's flight and the proclamation of a Republic in France (February 24, 1848) reached Dresden. February gave way to March, and with it came Germany's March Revolution. King Friedrich August was besieged with petitions to recreate Germany's government structure in a more liberal form, on the French model, while he stubbornly withstood all such demands. "On the evening of one of these really anxious days," writes Wagner, "when the very air seemed heavy and full of thunderclouds, we gave our third big concert, which was attended, like the first two, by the King and his court." The program was Mendelssohn's *A-minor Symphony* (Mendelssohn had died that past November while Wagner was in Berlin and the choice was commemorative) and Beethoven's *Fifth.* Just before the concert, Wagner wondered out loud if two such pieces, both in minor keys, might not seem too grim to the audience. His first-chair violinist and concertmaster, Lipinski, quipped to him, however, that after the two opening bars (it was already a performance warhorse), no one ever heard the rest of the *Fifth Symphony* anyway.

Minutes later, Wagner ascended the podium.

As the eighth note of the Fifth rang through the house, someone from the balcony shouted down, "Long live the king!" and the rest of the audience (bourgeois, paying) seemed to hear the remainder of the rich and sprightly music as a paean to, and an expression of, the unified German spirit—breaking into spontaneous and vociferous applause at every stirring passage! What did the thirty-four-year-old conductor actually think of the audience's response, so clear in the house behind him—other than that he was off the hook of having to please them with two major works in minor keys? Was he amused at their simple-minded chauvinism? Was he repelled by the anti-republican sentiments their response was clearly based on? Was he annoyed at the interruptions? Did his own spirits, at the same time (politically? aestheticically?), soar along with theirs? Was he pleased with his own powers, in such a charged field, to move his hearers so? In *Mein Leben* he is, of course, writing *for* Ludwig. I think we can read his silence on the topic, there—as well as the fact that the incident stayed vividly enough in his memory for him to recount it at all—as a sign that his feelings, as he conducted that evening, probably contained elements of all, and were more complex than any, of these.

Between Leap Day and March 13, Saxony found herself in a sort of mini-revolution, which ended with Friedrich August II, self-styled "the Beloved," dismissing his cabinet and calling in the opposition. Government censorship was relaxed in the city of Dresden. Trial by jury was introduced there. Electoral reforms were guaranteed, and feudal rights and tithes were abolished. It wasn't a republic, but it was a step in the republican direction.

The night of the 13th, lights burned late in the Dresden streets, and the king was cheered and applauded by the crowds as he moved about the city that evening. One of the most vociferous cheerers was Second Royal Kapellmeister Richard Wagner, who moved through the crowds to catch yet another glimpse of the king and shout his approbation of the new freedoms.

But while this was going on, the Paris situation was producing even more reactions throughout Europe. Only five days after that exciting Dresden night of March 13, Metternich was thrown out in Leipzig; barricades had gone up in Frankfurt and Berlin, and the fighting there, so ran the reports back in Dresden, was vicious and bloody.

Meanwhile the Dresden newspapers urged the city's citizens to eat stale bread and make chicken soup with particularly old and tough fowl. For despite the new political freedoms, economically these months were hard.

Though Dresden was the Saxon capital and the seat of King Friedrich August, it was a small city of only 70,000. Many of the laboring men in the vicinity worked in the mines. Now two parties formed in Dresden, the comparatively conservative Deutsches-Verein (The German Association) and the more radical Vaterlands-Verein (The Fatherland Association—which Gray translates, somewhat disingenuously, as "The Patriotic Union"). Wagner makes no secret that his good friend August Röckel was the head of the Vaterlands-Verein. Wagner attended Vaterlands-Verein meetings, made speeches, published articles in Röckel's newspaper, *Die Volksblätter*, and, toward the end, took over the editorship of the paper, when Röckel was put out of commission. All this is in *Mein Leben*. Wagner mentions that he attended "some" of the meetings when they were held in "a public garden." What he does not mention is that the particular public garden was the French garden behind the Marcolini palace, with its non-working fountain and its Triton, and that Wagner himself had invited them to meet there. What does not come across at all is that Wagner was, for all practical purposes, the host for at least *some* of these meetings.

The third omission concerns Wagner's publications during these heated and, finally, violent times; it is the most important in terms of our concern here, though it is also the one where he may be least accused of outright prevarication, as it is the one that most clearly segues into matters of tone and interpretation.

In *Mein Leben* Wagner quotes four lines from a poem he sent off to be published in a Berlin paper in support of the rebels. He does not say, however, that on May 15th, when fighting again broke out in Vienna, Wagner responded with a poem, "Greetings from Saxony to the Viennese," which was imprudently published in the *Allgemeine Oesterreichische Zeitung* on June 1st.

In *Mein Leben* Wagner synopsizes—accurately—a speech he delivered on June 12 to a rally at Röckel's Vaterlands-Verein (in the Marcolini gardens?),—a speech that went on to appear as a newspaper article which, indeed, attracted quite a bit of public attention—to the effect that he was for the establishment of a republic, but that he wanted the king to remain the first citizen of that republic. While he dismissed communism, i.e., ". . . the equal distribution of property and earnings . . . ," as ". . . that most fatuous and senseless doctrine . . ." (no, it is fairly certain that he had not read Marx and Engels's *Communist Manifesto* published a few months before; but he had read Proudhon and may have discussed some of Marx's ideas with Bakúnin, who was certainly familiar with Marx's writings), he called on His Majesty to do the right thing by his people and on the people to march towards light and freedom. At least one of the lines amidst his inflated rhetoric, however, scored a hit. He accused his fellow Saxons of having "a standing army—and a recumbent militia." A day later the speech appeared in the *Dresdner Anzeiger*. In the various papers of the politically super-charged city, the general response of commentators, after the ire over Wagner's insult to the local armed forces, seems to have been pretty much what such a harangue might be expected to yield today. In trying to appease all sides, Wagner, said everyone else, while stirring up already uneasy waters with his rhetoric, had said nothing of much usefulness. In one commentator's words, from another newspaper, Wagner's speech was far more "full of problems than of solutions." But as fiery as his speech was, unless one can conceive of a Marxist who is also a Monarchist, however parliamentary, there was nothing of socialism in it.

In Röckel's *Volksblätter*'s October 15th issue, an anonymous article by Wagner, "Germany and its Princes," appeared. It took the court to task for its indolence and irresponsibility and declared: "Awake! . . . the eleventh hour has struck! Abandon your impotent and futile resistance. It can only visit suffering and ruin upon you!"

In April of '49, three of his poems appeared in Röckel's paper, one of which was called "*An einen Staatsanwalt*" ("To a State Attorney"), another, "*Die Noth*" (which means, in German: *Need, crisis, desperation*, or any number of other such concepts): the first heaped scorn on state officials and the second pictured the miseries of the German people while inviting them, only somewhat metaphorically, to take up arms. It is significant, because Siegfried's reforged sword, in the *Ring*, was eventually named *Nothung*—though it started out as *Balmung*. The third was a prose poem called simply "Revolution," which is embodied as a goddess, who declares to the people that, among other things: "I shall destroy the dominion of the one over the many, of the dead over the living, of matter over mind. I shall shatter the power of the mighty, of law and of property . . . destroy the order of things that divorces enjoyment from labor, makes labor a burden and enjoyment a vice . . ."

In *Mein Leben* only the rally speech of June 12 (and the article that appeared from it) is mentioned. What Wagner does not say in *Mein Leben* is that he published numerous other articles (and poems), some signed, some unsigned, and some of which were far more vehement.

What Wagner does give us in *Mein Leben*, however, is a portrait of himself at the center of the organization of Dresden's republican rebels. His advice is sought and he advises. He edits the radical newspaper. He prints posters to propagandize the royalist soldiers and hangs them up. He runs information and goes on missions for Heubner and Bakúnin. Once the open fighting starts he stands guard in the Kreuzkirche Tower all night. And when Dresden has to be abandoned because of the bloodshed, he accompanies Bakúnin and Heubner on their trip to establish a provisory republican government for Saxony at Chemnitz. Though he does not come out and say it in so many words, he leaves a strong impression with the reader that if, indeed, the new government had *been* established at Chemnitz, Wagner himself would probably have been third or fourth down on the new totem pole. (If anything, one suspects he is exaggerating his importance, influence, and position!) But while he is clearly not anxious to rehearse the fiery extremes his republican rhetoric reached under military fire from the Prussians, I don't see how he could have presented himself as *more* involved in the Dresden Uprising if he'd tried. What I think has been missed in his Dresden account is that Wagner was not trying to exonerate himself from involvement with the republican cause so much as he was trying to make the republican cause, in which he was clearly and centrally involved, appear as rational, logical, and civilized as possible to his young, royal patron. And he does not, of course, admit to any crimes. But we must remember, besides being the century of romanticism and revolution, the nineteenth century was also the century of euphemism and decorum. No one aspired to the late twentieth century's ideals of radical honesty on all fronts.

If Wagner failed to mention the odd grenade or a slew of over-vehement poems and articles, it is because he wanted the republican cause to look rational to the young king and not seem a criminal enterprise; it is not because he wants to make himself appear any less involved *in* it or less sympathetic *to* it.

In his study of 1897, *The Perfect Wagnerite*, George Bernard Shaw saw the *Ring* as a clear allegory of the proto-Marxist ideas Wagner received from the anarchist Bakúnin. I think Shaw overstates the case. The question at Dresden was Monarchy or Republic, not Monarchy or Marxism. Still, it would be hard for any reader of *Mein Leben* not to feel that Wagner wants us—or King Ludwig—to attribute at least one of the important ideas of the *Ring* cycle to the Russian anarchist, still serving a prison term for his various activities at the time Wagner was writing.

Wagner had already conceived of his Nibelung project when he met Bakúnin. He had written a strangely confused essay, "The Wibelungs: World History as Revealed in Saga," in which he played with spurious etymologies of the word *Nibelung*, deriving from it everything from the Wibelungen ancestors of Frederick Barbarossa, or as we are more likely to know them today, the Ghibellines in the Ghibelline/Guelph conflict of Dante's era, to "Nabelon"—Napoleon! (And, of course, the Gibichungs of the *Ring*.) It was mystical nonsense, but it fascinated Wagner.

Bakúnin arrived in Dresden in the high summer of 1848.

Because there was so definitely an influence on Wagner from the brilliant, burly, bearded Russian, even if it did not extend as far as Shaw thought it did, it's instructive to look at Wagner's portrait of him.

> When I now met him, under the humble shelter of Röckel's roof, I was at first truly amazed by the strangely imposing personality of this man, who was then in the prime of his life, aged somewhere between thirty and forty. Everything about him was on a colossal scale, and he had a strength suggestive of primitive exuberance. I never got the impression that he set much store by my acquaintance, for by then he appeared to be basically indifferent to spiritually gifted people, perferring on the contrary ruthless men of action exclusively; as occurred to me later, he was more profoundly dominated in such things by abstract theory than by personal feelings, and could expatiate on these matters at great length: . . . He argued that the only thing necessary to conjure up a world-wide movement was to convince the Russian peasant, in whom the natural goodness of oppressed human nature had survived in its most childlike form, that the incineration of the castles of his masters, together with everything in them, was entirely just and pleasing in the eyes of God, and that the least to be expected from such a movement would be the destruction of all those things which, deeply considered, must appear even to Europe's most philosophical thinkers as the real cause

of all the miseries of the whole modern world. To set this destructive force in motion seemed to him the only goal worthy of a reasonable person. (While Bakúnin was preaching these horrendous doctrines at me, he noticed that my eyes were troubling me as a result of the bright light, and despite my protests, held his hand before it to shield me for a full hour.) The annihilation of all civilization was the objective on which he had set his heart; to use all political levers at hand as a means to this end was his current preoccupation, and it often served him as a pretext for ironic merriment. . . . [But] Bakúnin offered the consolatory thought that the builders of the new world would turn up of their own accord; we, on the other hand, would have to worry only about where to find the power to destroy. Was any of us insane enough to believe that he would survive after the goal of annihilation had been reached? It was necessary, he said, to picture the whole of the European world, with Petersburg, Paris, and London, transformed into a pile of rubble: how could we expect the arsonists themselves to survey these ruins with the faculty of reason intact?

What Wagner has recounted Bakúnin describing is, of course, the ending of *Götterdämmerung*, the final opera in Wagner's four-part Festival Play, with both the earthly city and the heavenly city in ruins. I think Wagner wanted his readers, royal or otherwise, to know this was where the notion came from. But what has to be stressed here is that the idea that an effective revolution required an absolutely clean slate and the violent destruction of all previous civilization was not Bakúnin's personal property—any more than it was Wagner's. It was, indeed, an idea—or at least an image—widely abroad in the European imagination.

In France at about the same time, Baudelaire was writing, "I say, 'Long live the revolution!' as I would say, 'Long live destruction! Long live penance! Long live chastisement! Long live death!' I would be happy not only as a victim; it would not displease me to play the hangman as well—so as to feel the revolution from both sides! All of us have the republican spirit in our blood as we have syphilis in our bones . . ."

In the iconography of the Romantic period, the ruin was a backward-looking and melancholy image because it spoke of vanished glories. But it was also a spiritual, uplifting, and sublime image because it alone on the crowded European landscape, in that age of science and industry, vouchsafed the possibility of progress, of building anew, of greater glories to come. (The terrifying ruin, the ruin of ghosts and unspeakable horrors, was the isolated ruin, the forgotten ruin, the ruin where the modern scientific and industrial spirit had not yet come to gaze, and, after gazing, establish its reassuring and progressive erections in the shadow of the old: the materialist reading of that horror is an unsettling projection of wasted real estate without any "spirit" of potential.) The destruction of the Great War of 1914 obliterated this positive reading of the ruin—by saturating the landscape with so many of them, all associated with real and recent death, that we can hardly see the ruin today as the nineteenth century saw it, as redolent of potential as it was of mystery. Similarly, it is only the twentieth century's critique of so many revolutions accomplished and revolutions failed that makes this demand for a totally clean slate, which the ruin represented, seem like the ultimate in political naïveté—rather than the ultimate modern image, as it marked a locus where new building might begin, absorbing as it did so the spirit of the old.

By October '48, in addition to his political articles and speeches for the *Voksblätter* and the Vaterlands-Verein, Wagner had also completed his "Prose Sketch" for the *Ring*. Commentators have seen that practically everything we can find in the finished *Ring* is there in one form or another in the "Prose Sketch." What they have not stressed quite as much is to what extent we can find the situation of Saxony in general and Dresden in particular in the same essay. The Nibelungs of the "Prose Sketch" are laborers and miners, as were many of the working class of Dresden and many of the other small towns in Saxony.

The "Prose Sketch" begins:

> Out of the Womb of Night and Death there came into being a race dwelling in Nibelheim (Nebelheim) [Home—or Place—of Mist, Fog, or Obscurity], i.e., in gloomy subterranean clefts and caverns. They are known as the Nibelungs: feverishly, unrestingly, they burrow through the bowels of the earth like worms in a dead body: they anneal and smelt and smith hard metals . . .

The last day of October brought news of the murder of the revolutionaries Blum, Becher, Jellinek, and Messenhauer in Vienna, and of the bombardment there. Robert Blum was a Saxon, and his body was returned to Dresden for a funeral where liberal cabinet members joined the funeral procession, fearful of both the people on the one side and the king on the other.

There were more clashes in Berlin in November, and the Prussian National Assembly was finally dissolved. Now, just before beginning the libretto, *Siegfrieds Tod* ("Siegfried's Death," the first version of what was to become the last of the four operas in the *Ring* cycle), Wagner received the news that the promised *Lohengrin* premiere had been officially canceled at the Opera, even though the sets had been begun.

No doubt the conservative theater management felt that the more and more radical Kapellmeister had to be disciplined; besides, there were not enough royal funds for producing new operas. Only four new operas were produced in all of Germany that year. Everyone involved had read the libretto and certainly no conservative official wanted to chance King Heinrich's exhortation, from the opening minutes of the opera, "Let all who are German be prepared to fight / That none will ever again affront German soil," going out to an audience that might take it as a rebel call to arms.

Siegfrieds Tod was finished, and—along with fifty-odd pages of a sketch of another drama based on the life of Jesus, in which Jesus is presented as a property-despising revolutionary—was read to an otherwise sympathetic group of republicans, though it did not get much sympathy from Bakúnin, who was among the hearers.

No doubt the Kapellmeister's political interests were also causing rifts at home. It's highly possible that at this time Wagner also wrote an article that may have been an early version of "*Das Judentum in der Musik*," of which Minna was to write two years later, "you defame[d] an entire race." Minna would not read it—or, at least, was highly unhappy with it. The article was not published—at least in that form. But from that time on, Minna later chided her husband, Wagner would neither show her nor play for her any more of his creative works. While our reconstruction of the reasons for his behavior towards her is largely supposition, we do know that at some point in the midst of all this, at least momentarily, Wagner decided to break with her: there is a journal entry to that effect from this date. But apparently he decided not to act on it.

The general rehearsals for the annual Palm Sunday benefit concert were opened to those of the Dresden public who could not afford the expensive tickets to the actual performance.

Wagner recounts:

> The general rehearsal had been attended, in secret and without the knowledge of the police, by Michael Bakúnin; after it was all over he came up to me unabashedly in the orchestra in order to call out to me that, if all music were lost in the coming world-conflagration, we should risk our own lives to preserve this symphony.

If, of all people, Bakúnin could declare such a grand and noble musical work as the *Ninth* worth preserving, then it might also be worth writing such a work, especially if it dramatized the way in which world civilization, both the noble and the base in their intricate relation, came to destroy itself to make way for the new order. Some vision of that task was what I feel Wagner, in the year covering '48 and '49, was forming for the *Ring*. But the new order was, at least as far as we can tell from what Wagner had been proclaiming for most of a year now, basically the old order with free elections, trial by jury, and a much stronger parliament.

Röckel had temporarily fled; so Wagner took over the *Volksblätter* editorship. On May 3, 1849, writes Wagner,

> . . .the appearance of the crowds streaming through our streets made clear enough that what everybody undoubtedly wanted was going to happen, for all petitions to obtain recognition of the German constitution, the main bone of contention, had been rejected by the government with a firmness it had heretofore failed to show.

Wagner attended a particularly unruly Vaterlands-Verein meeting the next morning. The workers at the meeting were angry and talked of arms and preparation for invasion, while the more theoretically-inclined middle-class members seemed indecisive. When it was decided to end the meeting, Wagner's impression was one of "utter chaos."

He goes on:

> I departed with the painter Kaufman, a young artist whose work I had observed in the Dresden art exhibition, where he had shown a series of drawings illustrating the "History of the Human Spirit." I had seen the King of Saxony pause in front of those drawings, which represented the torture of a heretic by the Spanish Inquisition, and had noticed him turn away from this abstruse subject, shaking his head in disapproval. I was on my way home in conversation with this man, whose pale and troubled countenance reflected his realization of the coming events, when, just as we reached the Postplatz in the vicinity of the recently erected fountain designed by Semper, the bells in the nearby tower of St. Ann's Church suddenly began to clash out the signal for revolt. "My God, it has begun!" my companion shouted, and vanished from my side forthwith. . . . I never saw him again. . . . It was a very sunny afternoon. . . . The whole square before me seemed bathed in a dark yellow, almost brown light, similar to a color I had once experienced at Magdeburg during a solar eclipse. My most pronounced sensation was one of great, almost extravagant well-being.

Wagner's first act was to run to the nearby house of the tenor Tichatschek and requisition the singer's sporting guns from his wife. (Tichatschek was out.) Leaving her a receipt for them, he went to park them at the Vaterlands-Verein headquarters. He claimed he was afraid that the general rabble in the street might rush in and seize them—or that the excitable tenor might do something silly with them. At any rate, this is another claim often taken by his later biographers to be disingenuous. And when the warrant was issued for him later, it was listed as among his crimes.

Then Wagner went out to explore what was happening in the city—and at some point wrote out an order for the powder to be packed into those grenades.

About fifty years after the fact, that indefatigable English collector of Wagneriana, Mrs. Burrell, transcribed an eyewitness report from a daughter of one of Wagner's Dresden friends, who recalled the first day of violence in the city, when, as a young girl, she sat watching and listening from her third story window, as first a young miner, then an older one, harangued the crowd, which later marched off looking for arms. After the first shots, a bit later she saw the corpse of the older of the two miners wheeled by her house in an open van, surrounded by the people, the body half naked now and lying on its belly, displaying a bloody back wound—the first casualty, or one of the first, in a list that was to swell, over the next days, to thousands. Wagner's favorite soprano at the Dresden opera, Wilhelmine Schröder-Devrient, saw them pass from her second floor window in the same block of flats and shrieked out, "*Rächt Euch an der Reaction!*" ("Revenge yourselves upon the reactionaries!") which, misinterpreted by the people, started a round of merchandise looting from the ground floor apothecary, which was used as a barricade in a nearby street.

Wagner also encountered the soprano. Either it was earlier that day, or possibly the account above comes from a day later. At any rate, Wagner writes:

> I now descended again into the streets to see what was going on in the city, apart from the clangor of the tocsin and the yellowish solar eclipse. I first reached the old market square and noticed a group there in the midst of which someone was making an animated speech. To my almost delighted astonishment, I beheld Frau Schröder-Devrient, who had just come back from Berlin, and was standing in front of a hotel evincing tremendous excitement at the news immediately communicated to her that the populace had already been fired upon. She had just seen an attempted revolt crushed by force of arms in Berlin, and she now was highly indignant to see the same thing happening in what she regarded as her peaceful Dresden. . . . I met her again the following day at the home of my old friend, Heine [the recently dismissed set-designer for *Lohengrin*], where she had taken refuge; there she once again implored me, inasmuch as she attributed to me the requisite *sang-froid*, to make every effort to stop the senseless and murderous struggle.

Shots had been fired; men had been killed; there were barricades in the streets; and Wagner was at the city hall in the thick of meetings and conversations and arguments. The King by now had quit Dresden proper, for Konigstein on the Elbe. Saxon royalist troops were in the city; but Prussians had been called in.

The next day, Wagner, who had been editing the *Volksblätter* himself for the past few weeks, had the paper's printer run off handbills to win over the royalist soldiers. The boys who put up the bills ("Are You With Us Against Foreign Troops?") inadvertently pasted them up on the rebels' side of the barricades where the Saxon soldiers couldn't see them. So Wagner had another 200 printed up, carried them through the barricades, and handed them out among the King's soldiers himself.

Mein Leben tells the story of the handbills; but it does not go into the details of their incorrect placement or what Wagner did about it.

On the following night, with a Döbeln schoolmaster and a Reichenbach professor, Wagner stood watch atop the 300-foot Kreuzkirche Tower, where, under fire from the royalist soldiers, bullets splattered against the back wall now and again through the night. Between discussions of the Christian philosophy of life, the men observed and wrote down the movements of the royalist troops, tying the messages to rocks and tossing them over into the square below to be run to General Heubner and Bakúnin at the city hall, who were trying to maintain some organizational efficiency among the volunteer rebels.

On the floor of the tower, Wagner finally slept. Just before daylight, he records:

> I was awakened by the song of the nightingale wafting up from the Shutze garden close beneath us; a sacred calm and tranquility lay over the city and the broad expanse of its surroundings I could see from my vantage point: toward dawn a light fog settled on the outskirts: penetrating through it we suddenly heard, from the area of the Tharandt road, the music of the Marseillaise clearly and distinctly; as the source of the sound came closer, the mists dispersed and the blood-red rising sun glittered upon the guns of a long column marching into the city. It was impossible to resist the impression of this unfolding sight; suddenly that element I had long missed in the German people, the absence of any evidence of which had contributed in no small part to the mood which had dominated me until then, now pressed in upon me in the freshest and most palpable colors; these were no fewer than several thousand well-armed and organized men from the Erzgebirge, mostly miners, who had arrived to help in the defence of Dresden. Soon we saw them march into the old market square, outside the city

hall and, after a jubilant greeting by the people, encamp there to rest after their march. Similar contingents kept arriving throughout the day.

One can only remember here the miners in the opening paragraph of the "Prose Sketch."

Sometime before noon, someone spotted flames springing up from the old Dresden Opera House.

Always a firetrap, it had been torched by the insurgents while the fire could be controlled, to prevent its going up accidentally in the bombardment, where it might destroy the whole neighborhood. Wagner had come to loathe his Kapellmeister job. The *Ninth Symphony* aside, his attempts at theater reform had been stymied at every turn. And there was the canceled *Lohengrin* premiere . . .

Wagner sent down from the tower for wine and snuff in honor of the theater's destruction; they arrived with a message from Minna to please return home. And the lookout tower was now filling up with armed men, sent there to fire upon the approach to the old market square as soon as the expected attack on it from the Kreuzgasse began. At last Wagner descended from his outpost and philosophical eyrie.

At the Marcolini, he found his apartment full of his wife's excited friends, including Röckel's wife, who was particularly upset. Two of his young nieces had arrived. Their exuberant mood over the shooting and excitement even infected Minna, who was much relieved to see her husband back safe. Downstairs, the sculptor Hänel had wanted to shut up the whole palace "so that no revolutionaries might get in," which had angered the women. Now everyone enjoyed making fun of his terror.

The next day, when Wagner was passing St. Ann's church, a member of the Communal Guard called out to him, "Herr Kapellmeister, the spark of divine joy—" quoting from Schiller's "Ode to Joy"—"has certainly ignited everything; the rotten building has burned to the ground."

"Obviously this enthusiast had attended the last performance of the *Ninth*," Wagner comments wryly in his journal. (The "Ode" is, of course, the choral text for the *Ninth*'s final movement.) Later, when he had a moment to note the conflagration, Wagner (again in his journal) wrote: "Opera house now burned down; strangely contented."

After meeting with Bakúnin, Wagner got Minna and Natalie (and the parrot and the dog) off to Chemnitz, after taking a last walk along where he had done much of his thinking, talking with friends, and composing, while the sounds of gunfire rattled through the melancholy spring morning. Leaving Minna and her little "sister" with his own married sister, Klara, he returned to Dresden on May 8th (Wagner writes May 9th):

. . . the only safe way to advance was through shattered buildings, making my way toward the city hall on the old market place. It was already evening; what I saw offered a truly horrible picture, for I was passing through those parts of the city where everyone was prepared for house-to-house fighting. The unceasing roar of big and small arms fire made the other sounds of the armed men calling to one another from barricade to barricade, or from one shattered house to another, seem merely an uncanny murmur. Torches burned here and there, and pale exhausted figures lay about close to the guardposts, while stern challenges met the unarmed intruder.

At the city hall, everyone was exhausted. People's voices croaked or were hoarse. The old city council clerks stood around, cutting up sausages and spreading butter on slices of bread, while others distributed provisions to the hungry.

Heubner alone seemed to have retained his energy, though his eyes flickered with an "unearthly fire"; he had not really slept for seven nights. He was glad to see Wagner, and the two men conversed.

Bakúnin . . . received me on one of the mattresses which had been spread out in the city hall council chamber, a cigar in his mouth and at his side a very young Galician Pole, by the name of Haimberger, a young violinist whom he had referred to me recently for recommendation to Lipinsky for further training on his instrument . . . Bakúnin had made a place for him on the mattress, and gave him a vigorous slap on the back whenever he twitched at the sound of a heavy cannonfire. "You're a long way from your violin here," he called out to him. "You should have stayed with it, musician."

Bakúnin brought Wagner up to date. No one had seen the recently returned Röckel since the previous evening. He had probably been caught. Wagner told of the troops he'd seen between Chemnitz and Dresden, including several thousand reinforcements. Bakúnin and Heubner sent Wagner off to drum up more vehicles for the rebels, along with Wagner's old friend Marschall von Bieberstein, which the two men did, going to Freiberg and, after various adventures and some success, returning.

The retreat from Dresden had already begun before Wagner quite reached the city. Someone pointed out the coach carrying "the provisional government," and Wagner flagged it down to join Heubner, Bakúnin, and the Rochlitz editor (remember Wagner's arguments for war) in the overloaded carriage on the trip to Erzgebirge—which is where we started our story in the previous section.

All that lay ahead was the dismounting, the trap, the missed coach, the arrest of Heubner and Bakúnin—and Wagner's flight.

* * *

Again, we must ask: Is there anything in all this *Sturm und Drang* that is in any way radical as we understand the word in its political sense today?

Certainly Wagner was aware of oppression. Shortly he was to write in his book, *Art and Revolution:* "Our modern factories present a wretched picture of utter human degradation: ceaseless exertion, destructive of mind and body, devoid of love and enjoyment—often, too, almost devoid of purpose."

His answer to these ills, however, was neither a major redistribution of wealth nor any basic reorganization of society: what he proposed was to reinsert some enjoyment into the worker's lives, and that via music—Wagner's music.

The air of a socialist critique hovers about the *Ring* for the same reason that the air of a socialist revolution hovers about the incidents at Dresden—which is to say, because it *was* a revolution, complete with guns (and grenades), we associate it with the twentieth-century revolutions that we are more familiar with. Because the *Ring* grew out of a real revolutionary critique of society, we associate that critique with the most radical critiques of today, starting from *them* as we begin to unwind its allegorical threads. But though what the Dresdeners rebelled against was real enough, what it was a rebellion *for* simply could not be called in any way, by today's standards, radical.

In reviewing the words of Wagner's fiery prose poem "Revolution"—the Goddess of Revolution will come and destroy "the order of things that divorces enjoyment from labor, makes labor a burden and enjoyment a vice . . ."—one of Wagner's recent biographers, Gregor-Dellin, asks, in the midst of quoting one of Wagner's more utopian flights from another unpublished fragment of this period where Wagner is waxing euphoric over a "communism" that will bring "the full emancipation of the human race and the fulfillment of pure Christian ideals":

"Who was going to do the actual work?"

But the answer is the people who did it ordinarily; only now they would have wonderful music, composed by Wagner, to make them happy while they did it. Again, we must stress that even if it meant throwing a grenade, the conflict at Dresden was between Monarchy and Republic, not Monarchy and some form of socialism. And Wagner's rare use of the word "communism" in a positive context has to be taken as the most idealistic of metaphors, rather than any sort of materialist program. When he does use "communism" in any material sense, as we saw in the January 12th speech to the Vaterlands-Verein, it is only to execrate it as ". . . that most fatuous and senseless doctrine . . ."

Those battles were to come—and, when they came, they would obscure much of the conservative theory behind the actions of men like Wagner with a radical aura.

Wagner saw the ills of society. He had real sympathy for the oppressed. He even had some understanding of the machinery through which society replicated its oppressions. But while his answers for those ills included the range of republican rights and liberties, they involved no fundamental reorganization of the social structure.

Higher wages, better working conditions, more leisure for the working classes?

He was certainly for them all. But what they were supposed to do with that leisure was to listen to more music; and that would make them fundamentally content with their lot. His analysis in the end was far closer to Dickens's than it was to Marx's. What would end the evils of humanity was less greed, greater spirituality, stronger love. God was dead. (Wagner was an atheist.) But art in general and music-dramas in particular could disseminate these feelings of love and great-heartedness throughout the people.

Art can, of course (and especially theatrical art), move an audience to great emotion. But the nineteenth century saw this as a material force that could work throughout society for the greater social good.

We have talked about the received idea, current in the nineteenth century, of the destruction of civilization as a prerequisite for the "new order." But there was another received idea that runs through the whole of Wagner's thought and writing. That is the idea we discussed in terms of Matthew Arnold and English literature in our fourth chapter: i.e., all that reformers in England, from Arnold to Professor Gordon, believed literature would do, Wagner, among many others, believed music could do.

What probably strikes modern readers of *Mein Leben* as most odd is the tone in which Wagner, again and again, justified his activities by claiming that his only interest in the republican revolution was because of the possibility of theater reforms that it held out, the possibility of higher performance standards that could benefit, and even calm, a revolutionary populace. Wagner was certainly serious about the reality of musical performance. And it was precisely these emotions that, again and again, he wanted to appeal to—with his own work, and in his performances of the works of others.

In 1846 he had submitted a hundred-page proposal for the reorganization of the Dresden orchestra to the royal cabinet by way of the Theater Intendant, Baron August von Lüttichau, in which for all practical purposes he invented the modern orchestra as we know it. His proposal covered everything from the musicians' salaries to the placement of the players. This last is worth looking at, because, twenty years later at Bayreuth, Wagner was actually able to institute these changes; and from there they became standard orchestral practices all over the world. Till then, in most European opera houses the players sat with their backs more or less to the audience in a long line, two deep, across the theater. The conductor stood behind the orchestra, facing the stage, his back to the players and the audience, directly conducting the singers, for whom he also acted as prompter. Watching him from behind, the musicians did the best they could. Wagner suggested that the players be pulled together (much along the lines of his *Ninth Symphony* arrangement) so that they could see (and hear!) each other, and that the conductor stand in *front* of the orchestra and guide the players— and that the singers (first) learn their parts better and (second) take a cut in salary, which should be distributed among the orchestral players who more deserved it. He also suggested that the stolid wooden music stands be replaced with lightweight metal ones, which he'd designed. It is a commonsensical document with higher standards of performance as its goal, and must make anyone who has ever played in an orchestra, no matter how small, love Wagner—at least momentarily. We should remember, of course, that all through the nineteenth century such proposals for musical reform were being made by serious musicians all over Europe. Berlioz's biography abounds in such intelligent suggestions—and indeed such defeats:

Shortly after the Palm Sunday concert of 1847, right after Wagner moved into the Marcolini, his proposal had been rejected.

But it is only this belief in the possibility that art can be as great a force as religion once was that creates the grandiose potential in the artist's social position, as reflected in artists such as Hugo, Rossini, Sand, Byron, and—later, once Ludwig interfered—Wagner. And it is only this nineteeth-century belief that allows Wagner's explanation of his motivations to make sense at all and not seem a ratiocination too preposterous for any intelligent man to expect *anyone* to believe! It also explains why men like Röckel, Bakúnin, and Heubner would put such trust in an artist like Wagner in the first place or would consider having a conductor and opera composer, even if he was a Second Royal Kapellmeister, among their advisers and intimates.

Today, we might understand (though we would probably smile at, even so) an artist who threw herself or himself so actively into such a revolution to "get material" for a work. (And that smile and those quotation marks sign an even further historical displacement of the artist's social position.) But that is not Wagner. Although the republican revolution gave him a view of the world that, indeed, marked all his subsequent work almost as strongly as it did Victor Hugo's, Wagner threw himself into that revolution in order to make manifest the real possibility of using what he saw—a possibility and a use that can only be understood in nineteenth-century historical terms.

In its final tableau, the allegory or the *Ring* leaves us with a silent, awed populace, void of articulation but full of expectation, standing among the ruins of history, metaphysically freed of the chains of religion and physically released from monarchy (a monarchy that they have not overthrown but that has simply destroyed itself through its own inner corruption and collapsed), ready now not for socialism but for elected leaders, trial by a jury of one's peers, education, science, public programs for the dissemination of the arts (art that would, indeed, perform the same tasks as religion once had in strictly monarchical times), and the universal (male) vote.

VII

There are many aspects to Wagner that, if not discussed, leave our considerations radically incomplete. Yet this exploration can only be but so long. I should like here, for example, to explore Wagner's anti-Semitism.

Apologists for it, such as Bryan Magee and Martin Gregor-Dellin, to me seem to hover somewhere between troubling disingenuousness and true naïveté. Both appear wholly oblivious to the reality (and demonstrable social effects) of an active, incontrovertible, and energetically functioning social prejudice against the Jews in Germany throughout the nineteenth century, however subtle that prejudice could be or however often it was overtly denied. Even so meticulously researched a study as Jacob Katz's *The Darker Side of Genius: Richard Wagner's Anti-Semitism*, strikes me as somehow misguided. Professor Katz argues that before 1850, in the considerable documentation that exists on Wagner, there is no anti-Jewish statement from the man. During this time Wagner even championed Jewish writers, such as Heinrich Heine—and set two of Heine's poems to music. The notion that Wagner's later statements in *Mein Leben*—that, whether he said so or not, he felt repulsion against the Jews—are therefore suspect, seems to me to ignore the fact that the age under study was one in which, socially, conventions of hyperbole and hypocrisy were rampant—so much so that we can hardly give them those names today without distorting them.

Certainly anti-Semitism is there in *Mein Leben*—right before the events of the revolutionary Dresden year—in Wagner's discussion of his friendship with the Jewish writer Berthold Auerbach, whose stories he had read and been impressed by. What remains seductive about it, even today, is that Wagner can listen to the stories of the childhood oppressions of his Jewish friends, can hear of the taunts they endured from others, can learn of the ostracism they suffered, all with true sympathy; "[But] . . . one day," he tells us of Auerbach, "I turned to him in an amiable intimate way and advised him simply to let the Jewish question go hang; there were, after all, a number of other standpoints from which to judge the world. Curiously enough, he lost all his ingenuousness at that point, adopted what struck me as a not entirely authentic tone of whimpering emotion, and assured me he could never do that, as Judaism still contained too much that demanded his complete sympathy . . . When I saw him again in Dresden, I found his countenance changed in a disarming manner: he looked extraordinarily common and dirty; his former refreshing liveliness had turned into the usual Jewish fidgetiness, and every word he spoke came out in such a way that one could see he regretted not having saved it for the newspaper." (In his study, Professor Katz refers to this account as having "an undertone" of anti-Semitism about it; I can only throw up my hands.) What Wagner is totally blind to is precisely what such blindness as his will lead to historically.

The anti-Semitism is there right after the Dresden account in the odious essay he composed within a year of fleeing the devastated city, "Jewry in Music": Jews cannot write great music because their relation to culture is foreign, secondary; and because they have no usable musical culture of their own they are in an inauthentic relation to the mainstream of music tradition . . .

Anti-Semitism, indeed, so pervades *Mein Leben*, in everything from Wagner's digs at the Jewish composer Mendelssohn (whose rediscovery of Bach's music Wagner championed and at whose house Wagner was sometimes a guest) to his final repudiation of Meyerbeer, a Jew and the most popular opera composer of the day (as well as, for a period, a supporter of the young Wagner), that one only wonders how, for the length of the Dresden uprising, Wagner manages to put it aside. But what truly disarms about Wagner's anti-Semitism is just how modern—and how familiar—it sounds.

If Wagner represents the creation and the subsequent dissemination of the modern in artistic attitudes, we must remember that on several national fronts, *the* modern experience is that of the concentration camp and genocide. Wagner, his four-part Festival Play, and his philosophy are so intimately connected with one of those fronts that the question of the relationship between a national concept of art and a nation's political practice must be raised, however we decide to answer it.

I should like to take on, both for agreement and disagreement's sake, the criticisms of Wagner made by Theodor Adorno in *In Search of Wagner*, written between autumn of 1937 and spring of 1938, in London and New York. Adorno claims Wagner is an anti-intellectual composer; he is gestural, rather than developmental. Wagner intentionally abandoned the entire classical range of developmental techniques to make his music more democratic, more accessible. In place of development, Wagner substituted the insistent hearable and comparatively simple repetition of the leitmotif. This decision for simplification and democratization was made before the coming of music's mechanical reproduction would educate hundreds of thousands to a familiarity with just that classical range—the same educative process that would reduce Wagner's music to kitsch.

Adorno was not the first to voice this criticism. And Debussy had defended Wagner against it well before Adorno's book, with his observation that, indeed, *Tristan und Isolde* was nothing *but* development from one end to the other! But Wagner would probably not have said so. ("Unending melody"—the term Wagner wanted—is *not* continuous development.) While clever, Debussy's remark is finally disingenuous.

Adorno's comments mirror Nietzsche's late and somewhat disturbed quip over the already-mentioned swelling Wagnerian literature (which Nietzsche himself twice contributed books to, as well as several essays). In *The Case of Wagner*, published five years after Wagner's death, Nietzsche wrote:

> Not every music so far has required a literature: one ought to look for a sufficient reason here. Is it that Wagner's music is too difficult to understand? Or is he afraid of the opposite, that it might be understood too easily—that one will not find it difficult enough to understand?

I should like to essay my own analysis of the social allegory presented in the *Ring*. Writing *The Perfect Wagnerite* during the height of the explosive anti-Semitic feelings ignited by the Dreyfus Affair, Shaw (it would seem) felt that the anti-Semitic elements could be politely skipped over and the work could still make its point. I believe that unless we trace clearly its massively anti-Semitic strands, the work is historically unreadable. Whatever one thinks of it, or however unacceptable one finds it today, clearly the major outline of the social allegory presented in the *Ring*'s prologue, *Das Rheingold*, is that it was the Jews (Alberich) who gave up human love for wealth and power, by the initial seizure of the Rhinegold. And in *Siegfried*, the *Ring*'s third opera, clearly the allegory runs along the following lines: the heroic spirit of the West (Siegfried) grows up through being nurtured by a tradition of Jewish skepticism and social cynicism (Mime); but that heroic spirit will only come into its own when it learns to repudiate and finally throw off that tradition (Siegfried kills his foster father, Mime), because that tradition is ultimately greedy, petty, destructive and is bent on enslaving the spirit for its own ends. The point of course is that the Nibelungen are—in terms of Wagner's allegory—not *just* Jews; they are workers, they are bohemians, they are all that was considered socially marginal by the nineteenth-century Christian German middle classes. But Wagner certainly meant them to be read *largely* as Jews. And in his allegory it is, of course, the Jewish infiltration of the ruling classes (the Gibichungs) in the person of the halfling Hagen that brings about their downfall.

Indeed, the allegory may be more specific than this.

I find it incomprehensible that no one, for instance, among the biographers of Wagner I have read (and they approach a dozen) has even asked the question, if only to answer it yes or no, if any of the mine owners in the Dresden area were Jewish; or, indeed, if there were any mines owned specifically by a pair of Jewish brothers.

However unpalatable a confirmation might be, to me the four operas clamor, one way or another, for an answer.

When Wagner had completed *Parsifal*, he was set on having the Jewish conductor Hermann Levi conduct its premiere at Bayreuth. Levi was understandably dubious; Wagner's anti-Semitism was, by this time, blatant and notorious. Wagner invited Levi to Wahnfried, Wagner's home at Bayreuth, and prepared a banquet for him at which Jewish wines were served and traditional Jewish foods were prepared. Wagner's argument was great-hearted—and, ultimately, convinced the not-insensitive Levi. Given the fact that Levi was, in Wagner's estimation, the finest conductor in Europe, it was particularly important, Wagner argued, for *Parsifal*, the work of a famous and committed atheist, but nevertheless based on a Christian myth, to have a Jewish conductor. This would be a way of stressing that it was the mythic and universal significance of the story that Wagner intended to signify—and not any narrow, sectarian interpretation. It would be a gesture, declared Wagner, toward brotherhood among all peoples.

Nietzsche had already broken with Wagner. At least part of the reason was that he felt the great atheist artist, by choosing a Christian religious story, was pandering to the bourgeoisie, which Nietzsche—and, until then, Wagner—claimed to hold in contempt. Another reason for the break was that Wagner had taken an untoward—and unwanted—interest in the younger man's masturbation and campaigned to have it ended medically! Which was paramount, however, at this date it is hard to say.

Levi consented to Wagner's request. He conducted Wagner's last opera; on Wagner's death, he was one of Wagner's pallbearers—and, till his own death, one of Wagner's staunchest defenders.

Levi's defense of Wagner is precisely what one would expect of a nineteenth-century intellectual at home with the philosophy and cultural presuppositions of his time: Wagner's anti-Semitism does not represent the authentic Wagner. Anti-Semitism was not central to Wagner's being. Rather, for Levi, Wagner was still the great republican revolutionary who wished to promote universal brotherhood. Like the young Hegel, like the young Nietzsche, Levi wished to cut off all that was idiosyncratic, anomalous, and marginal about Wagner, as he saw it—unaware that such margins and such centers are wholly a product of personal perspective—which is the same as personal blindness. Indeed, it is not till Theodor Adorno's 1964 (!) study, *The Jargon of Authenticity*, that we commence a critique firmly identifying the problem to be the concept of the authentic/inauthentic as valid for the subject in the first place. It is the notion that such personal centers (one) exist and (two) are constitutive of the subject that creates the problem. This and similar critiques are what have slowly opened us up to the postmodern notion that the subject is constituted across a split (rather than around a center), a notion that begins, of course, with Freud's idea of the conscious/unconscious dichotomy in *The Interpretation of Dreams* (1900), but which has been further radicalized by thinkers such as Lacan, Barthes, Foucault, and Derrida in the 1950s and '60s.

My own feeling is that Wagner's treatment of Levi does not mitigate Wagner's anti-Semitism—from Cosima's diaries and Wagner's own late articles in his own paper, the *Bayreuther Blätter*, we know that by his last years, even after *Parsifal*, such feelings in him grew obsessive. But one could, indeed, cite Wagner's similarly warm and respectful treatment of any number of his other Jewish friends. A particular case in point is Heinrich Porges, whom Wagner asked to the rehearsals of the *Ring* at the first Bayreuth Festival in 1876 to take down those incredibly revealing notes on the production that have facilitated performances ever since.

Anyone interested in almost any aspect of mid-nineteenth century romantic art should read the "Introduction" by this earliest, erudite, and most intimate Jewish commentator on Wagner. (*Wagner Rehearsing the Ring: An Eye-Witness Account of the Stage Rehearsals of the First Bayreuth*

Festival [Die Bühnenproben zu den Bayreuther Festspielen des Jahres 1876] began to appear in sections in the *Bayreuther Blätter* in 1881.) It is a wonderful compendium of nineteenth-century critical tropes, some already sedimented for a century or more and some radically new and vibrant with mid-romantic fervor, all of them welded into a brief, impassioned defense of the Wagnerian enterprise. Indeed, Porges's whole study is equally illuminating. And though the Nazis later suppressed this "Jewish commentary" on the Master, there is no mention in it of anything overtly anti-Semitic.

What this and the case of Levi point up more than anything else is, first, how insistently modern the form of Wagner's anti-Semitism was: rationalized, depersonalized, intellectualized, with intermittent moments of liberalism, and constantly excused by what has now become a hopeless cliché: "But some of my best friends . . . !" Second, it shows ultimately how little threatened Jews such as Levi and Porges felt in the face of such ideas in those pre-Dreyfus days. We must remember, as Hannah Arendt points out in her study *The Origins of Totalitarianism,* anti-Semitism as a virulent political plank in various hard-edged political platforms did not begin till 1886—that, indeed, anti-Semitism was so violently to change its practical implementation and material extent, if not its rhetoric, in these later years of the nineteenth century that Arendt can assign its very "invention" (along with that of South African and Rhodesian racism) to that year, at the end of an explosion of printing and political pamphleteering unheard-of before in history. Presumably after that date, Porges and Levi might have felt somewhat differently.

I should also like to discuss Wagner's musical theories, which, put briefly, hold that, while the words tell the story, the singer's melody portrays the character's expressed emotions, with the orchestra painting in the same character's inner psychology, memories, and associations during the Wagnerian monologue. Wagner remained an artist, I suspect, because he specifically abjured using his orchestra to signal to the audience what *they* were supposed to be feeling (see the incident of the incidental music in Gutzkow's play at the Dresden Opera), but wanted it rather to depict meticulously, even objectively, what was happening inside the characters that could neither be said nor sung in words. The opera composer, he declared in *Opera and Drama,* was above all a psychologist.

In light of those theories I would have to mention how an editor of the French journal, *La Revue Wagnerienne,* Edouard Desjardin, a handful of years after Wagner's death, wrote a novel, *Les Lauriers sont coupés,* in which, by his own statement, he tried to do in words what Wagner had done in music. James Joyce read that novel, was impressed with the method's potential, and from it took the idea of "stream of consciousness" or what is sometimes called "silent monologue" or "*monologue intérieur.*" I would also recall for you how Joyce's Stephen, who like Wotan in the *Ring* carries an ashplant, when he raises it to strike the chandelier in the Nighttown bordello cries out, "*Nothung!*"—Siegfried's cry as he forges his sword.

At the conclusion of *A Portrait of the Artist as a Young Man,* Joyce had his young hero write in his journal:

> Welcome, O life! I go to encounter for the millionth time the reality of experience and to forge in the smithy of my soul the uncreated conscience of my race.

Well, both the sentiment *and* the metaphor were Wagner's; and that uncreated conscience was a recreation of the nineteenth-century *Zeitgeist* (now moved to Ireland), the *sine qua non* of art as religion.

I'd like to discuss the Wagnerism in which the whole of Eliot's *Waste Land,* as well as its major source, Jessie L. Weston's *From Ritual to Romance,* are sunk. Miss Weston's book on the significance of the Parsifal legend, you will recall from its preface, was inspired by her 1911 visit to Bayreuth, and is, after all, a continuation of the work begun in her first book of 1896, *The Legends of the Wagner Dramas.*

Is it wholly attributable to the political climate after the Second World War that, during the 1950s and '60s, one could sit through college class after college class dealing with *The Waste Land,* in which, while Webster and Kyd were ceaselessly discussed, Wagner, the most frequently quoted writer in the poem, was not mentioned? This suppression did nothing to diminish Wagner's influence; it only denied it its name and mystified it, making it that much harder to seize, analyze, and combat. Today there seems to be afoot a concomitant academic enterprise to find the roots of modernism in every nineteenth-century artist *except* Wagner. This is not difficult to do. The point is that most of Wagner's ideas were not his own, whether they were about the ends of art or the Jews. (Baudelaire wrote in his diary: "A fine conspiracy could be organized for the purpose of exterminating the Jewish race." And even before Wagner—under the pseudonym of K. Freigedank—published "Jewry in Music" in two parts on the 3rd and 6th September 1850 in the *Neue Zeitschrift für Musik,* Wagner's friend Heinrich Laube had written, ". . . there are only two ways to solve the Jewish question. One must either fully annihilate the Jews or completely emancipate them.") But it was through Wagner that these ideas were disseminated to become part of the very codes by which the general middle class, first of Europe, then of the United States, learned to recognize art, even if the name Wagner, over two World Wars, was erased from that recognition.

I'd also like to discuss D. H. Lawrence's 1912 novel, *The Trespasser*, called in its first draft *The Saga of Siegmund*, which is almost a panegyric to Wagner. In its first version the heroine's name was Sieglinde, before Lawrence revised it to Helena—after Helen Corke, on whom the character was modeled. She is learning German so she can better understand Wagner in the original. And the hero and heroine whistle Wagner and hear his music in every rustling tree.

But the fact is, in the post-Edwardian pantheon, any writer who took herself or himself seriously had to appeal to Wagner in some way, whether by direct reference or by implication; for by then, Wagner *was* Serious Art.

But though there may someday be an ideal version of this paper in which these topics are discussed rather than glossed, I cannot try your patience with other than glosses too much longer. We must leap, like Valkyries, ahead.

What we overleap is an occurrence that not only changed the course of Wagner's life, but absolutely changed the way we consider him and his art. Without it, we would remember Wagner's work as we do any famous nineteenth-century opera composer's—if indeed we remembered him at all. (The four new operas that *were* produced in Germany in the year *Lohengrin*'s premiere was cancelled at the Dresden Opera House are all by composers unknown today.) Wagner's technical innovations would be just that: technical. His trials and tribulations would be, at best, one with Beethoven's and Berlioz's. Thanks to this occurrence, however, Wagner's art became the exemplar of all nineteenth-century art. And more than anything else it is responsible for the pervasive Wagnerian influence, overt before World War II and covert after it, that the above galaxy suggests.

In the spring of 1864, the newly crowned eighteen-year-old king of Bavaria, Ludwig II, who, since age thirteen, had been mad over Wagner's music, sent for the composer. "I can only adore you," the young king wrote, "only praise the power that led you to me. More clearly and ever more clearly do I feel that I cannot reward you as you deserve: all I can ever do for you can be no better than stammered thanks. An earthly being cannot requite a divine spirit." Ludwig went on to bail Wagner out of copious debts, set him up in a household, and committed himself to supporting Wagner through the rest of his life (on a level that dwarfs, say, the Archduke Rudolf's support of Beethoven or the Esterhazys' support of Haydn), building for Wagner the *Festspielhaus* at

Bayreuth and funding the Wagner festivals. The relationship between Ludwig and Wagner was not easy, and problems plagued every aspect of it. Ludwig was, after all, mad.

Remember those metal music stands—and the idea of placing the conductor in *front* of the orchestra—that the Dresden cabinet rejected in 1847? Bayreuth is why almost all orchestras and musicians use them today.

Here are some more customs that Wagner established at Bayreuth. He was the first opera producer to insist that the house lights be lowered during performances. Wagner was the first person to have the audience sit in darkness with light only on the stage. In Wagner's theater, for the first time latecomers were seated only at the end of the act, or at a suitable pause between scenes. He made it clear with placards in the lobby that in his theater talking would not be tolerated during the performance. Applause was to be entirely suppressed until the act was over—and, with *Parsifal*, he stipulated that there should be no applause at all after Act I, with its pseudo-religious closing. Our current custom of not applauding between the movements of symphonies and string quartets is another of Wagner's impositions on concert audiences at Bayreuth. This is not even to mention his advances in stage-craft and general performance standards that characterized, if not the first Bayreuth Festival (where the full *Ring* premiered, somewhat rockily, in 1876), then all the many non-operatic concerts he conducted there.

Things that Wagner wanted to do? Liberal to the last, he wanted to make all the tickets in the Bayreuth *Festspielhaus* one price. (At first he'd wanted the admission to be entirely free!) And he wanted to abolish formal attire as a prerequisite for opera attendance. But because the first was financially impracticable at Bayreuth, finally he had to admit that the second was socially impracticable as well. These changes had to wait until a later epoch.

Till 1864, certain advanced intellectuals and certain enthusiastic adolescents had been fascinated by Wagner's music. Baudelaire and Berlioz represent the first; Nietzsche, Judith Gautier, and Ludwig himself represent the second. But soon the entire world was fascinated by the favor of a king; and, though the road was gravel-strewn, progress along it was nevertheless headlong: Wagner and his music swooped on, over the nineteen years that remained to him, to a celebrity that was, till then, undreamt-of: it was comparable to the Beatles' in its breadth, and surpassed the Beatles' in staying power.

Today, to get some idea of what pre-Wagnerian theater was like, you only have to read some theater scene from Balzac, or, indeed, George Sand—the endless visits from box to box, the conversations, the recognitions across the auditorium, the romances, the intrigues, now one group applauding, now another group of claquers booing and disrupting the performance. Only by reading particularly carefully can you even be sure, in those candle-lit opera houses, that a performance is indeed in full swing on the stage. (I have known readers to assume some of these scenes were taking place during some interminable intermission!)

Today, however, when we go into a theater, when we sit down and the house lights dim as we fix our silent attention on the stage, we are in Wagner's theater.

We are not in Shakespeare's.

We are not in Moliere's or Racine's.

We are not in Mozart's or Beaumarchais's.

We are not in Goethe's or even Hugo's.

We are wholly in Wagner's.

With Wagner, the proper attitude before the artwork becomes a mass of people, who, for all their physical closeness, now must consent to be more or less oblivious of one another, while each engages in the private contemplation of the object before them all. And from the *Festspielhaus* at Bayreuth, this aesthetic posture spread throughout Europe, to America and all her theaters, her museums, her galleries, and even to family readings from novels in the evening—until finally it had joined with that of the solitary reader and her novel, her poem, her text.

At this juncture, in which—throughout the nations caught up in the social and industrial situation outlined earlier—the public attitude toward the contemplation of an artwork became one with the private contemplation of a printed prayer, art finally and completely appropriated the social position of religion.

* * *

Antonin Artaud writes:

One of the reasons for the asphyxiating atmosphere in which we live without possible escape or remedy—and in which we all share—is our respect for what has been written, formulated, or painted, what has been given form, as if all expression were not at last exhausted, were not at a point where things must break apart if they are to start anew and begin afresh.

We must have done with this idea of masterpieces reserved for a self-styled elite and not understood by the general public. . . .

Masterpieces are good for the past. They are not good for us. We have the right to say what has been said and even what has not been said in a way that belongs to us, a way that is immediate and direct, corresponding to present modes of feeling, and understandable to everyone.

It is idiotic to reproach the masses for having no sense of the sublime, when the sublime is confused with one or another of its formal manifestations, which are moreover always defunct manifestations.

This is from Artaud's famous essay in *The Theater and Its Double*, "No More Masterpieces." It would be hard to find as succinct and as revolutionary a statement in all of the writings of Eliot or Pound, whose basic strategy, after all, was to resuscitate the tradition and locate themselves before and within it—suspiciously like the bogus historicism of some of Wagner's own speculative or theoretical works.

But the "Masterpiece," considered not as a particular order of object, but rather as an attitude of respect, silence, awe, and attention that certain objects are privileged to receive, *is* Wagner's. "Serious Art," seen as a type of attention and behavior in a general audience, was Wagner's invention. And it was imposed on the greater bourgeois art world of the West by the celebrity of Bayreuth. Reviews of the *Ring*'s premiere were among the first half-dozen messages broadcast on the newly laid transatlantic cable in 1876 and were published on page one of newspapers in Paris, New York, Chicago, and San Francisco, only a day or two after the performance.

In his best-known essay, "The Work of Art in the Age of Mechanical Reproduction" (1936), Walter Benjamin suggests that what will not survive photographic and other modes of mechanical reproduction is the artwork's "aura" (the quotation marks are Benjamin's), so important to serious art: an "aura" socially formed, in the case of Renaissance painting (Benjamin explains) by the spectator's knowledge or intuition of the artwork's royal commission, imperial acceptance, and aristocratic ownership over generations—an "aura" communicated for Benjamin largely by the monumental architecture of the museum halls, through which the state appropriates the range of aristocratic privileges, at least at the level of signs.

Another fifty years, however, have proved Benjamin almost a hundred-eighty degrees off in his assessment. What is lost in mechanical reproduction is, of course, the artwork's material specificity. Lines blur. Colors dim. Hues, intensities, and color relations shift. All effects dependent on absolute scale and material texture vanish. Mechanical reproduction always distorts (when it does not wholly obliterate) the dimensionality and the plasticity of the artwork. Even when reproducing a work "full size," reproduction renders that size a variable quantity rather than a fixed form. What "comes through" in a mechanical reproduction is a highly reduced range of relative relations, impoverished because deprived of so many elements, distorted because intruded on by so many others: i.e., the materiality of the reproductive medium itself, the surface of the photographic or printing paper, the register of the inks, the hiss of the tape, the dust in the groove, the grain of the film, the grid across the glass screen—materialities that constitute the grounding of the esthetic experience exactly to the extent we overlook them, either in the "original" or in the "reproduction." The *only* thing that, through reproduction, survives intact about the artwork *is* the "aura"—because it is socially constructed, because it is not *in* the work but rather is entirely around it.

When we pore over a "translation" of an ancient Greek poem that comes to us as a few English words amidst a field of lacunae and ellipses, trying to perceive its original austerity and beauty, we are wholly within the "aura" of art. When we strain to hear, through the mechanical burr, the sublimity of Enrico Caruso's voice production or the nuances of Billie Holiday's vocal interpretation, we are within the "aura." What the experience of High Modernism has made clear is that this "aura" is a far more complex semiotic structure than the mere juxtaposition of an economic provenance with a few architectural signs.

For my generation of New York children, who, during the fifties and sixties, walked into that gallery of the Museum of Modern Art displaying Picasso's monumental *Guernica* (before, in the initial years of the eighties, it was returned to its Spanish home), before any of the horrific and angular images from that night of violence during the Spanish Civil War could register as content, the first and overwhelming experience was of the sheer *amount* of paint, white and black, spread ceiling to floor, edge to edge, over an entire *wall!* There simply was no art object within the doors of any other museum in the city that used as much!

Now, after perusing the above account (its verbal reduction straining after the historical *ding an sich* with italics and exclamation points), suppose a reader (who may or may not have walked into that gallery on the second floor of the 53rd Street museum during those years) then goes on to gaze at the next three-by-five postcard of that awesome work (or, indeed, even, in Spain, at the work itself), trying to get some feel of that scale, of that material. For that reader, then, something generated by my childhood experience of the painting will have been exchanged with something of the social "aura," in all their shared semiotic complexities, repairabilities, interpenetrations, articulations, and flexibilities.

The assumption implicit in Benjamin's essay, that this "aura" is the result of a simple historic, and uncritical imposition by the powerful on the weak, is one of the places Benjamin skirts vulgar Marxism. But because they are constituted of absence/difference, signs can *only* be transformed/exchanged. It is almost impossible simply to "impose" them in an allegory of unidirectional power. The influence of royalty on the "aura" cannot be denied any more than can the influence of popular art and social poverty: in the play of fictions, in the "aura's" construction, there is as much work, both positive and negative, from below as there is from above.

This is what Benjamin (as well as Adorno!) misses. And that construction—that "aura"—is what Wagner, more than any other nineteenth-century artist, helped engineer throughout the Western bourgeoise. Against that "aura," Artaud's esthetic enterprise was to take precisely the plasticity, the dimensionality of art—all that was lost in mechanical reproduction, all that was material about any and every medium *of* reproduction, all that was in excess of the "aura"—and seize it as the domain of the theater, use it as the substance of art.

What I must leave you with is not the satisfying counter that Artaud's enterprise seems to make against what, till now, we have for the purposes of our fiction been silently considering "Wagnerism," but rather with an irresolution, an unsettling, a disturbance:

Notice, however uncomfortably, that Artaud, even as he opposes our Wagnerism, appropriates something pivotal from it, nor can he acknowledge its historical existence within that tradition. But he escapes that tradition no more than he escapes the critical system of "unity of impression"/"flawed transitions" that dogs him from his first letters from Rivière to his own last letter to Thévenin.

What he appropriates is all that, Ludwig aside, Wagner had to give up to make his work support its popularity, its pervasiveness, its ubiquitousness—all that Wagner had to put aside to accelerate the mass acceptance of his art once it was allied with the social nostalgia for royal patronage that still makes the new baby of Prince Charles and Princess Diana or the death of Princess Grace fit subject for years and years for a presumably democratic audience the size of the *National Enquirer*'s; all that is implied by Adorno's critique: for that, in terms of content, was what had contoured a "respect" (to use Artaud's word) for the "formal" even in the most revolutionary: the desire for mass acceptance in the first place.

Wagner's desire to bring beauty, pleasure, and enlightenment to the people was not very different from his contemporary Matthew Arnold's desire, as expressed in "Culture and Its Enemies," to bring to an oppressed people "sweetness and light," even with Arnold's own reminder: "I mean *real* sweetness and *real* light" (italics Arnold's).

Making it accessible, making it popular, is nowhere near as important as making it available. That, of course, is the modern problem in a world where Wagnerism creeps everywhere without its name. How to read, we are all presumably capable of learning—even a little Latin, if less Greek.

In 1948, the year of Artaud's death, Auden wrote:

> Wagner was the first, as Yeats was the latest, to create a whole cosmology out of pre-Christian myth, to come out openly for the pagan conception of the recurrent cycle as against the Christian and liberal humanist conception of historical development as an irreversible process. Though the characters of the *Ring* wear primitive trappings, they are really, as Nietzsche pointed out, contemporaries, "always five steps from the hospital," with modern problems, "problems of the big city."

Need I point out that Nietzsche did not, in 1888 when he wrote *Der Fall Wagner,* mean mental hospital, but rather that, once wounded, Wagner's warriors always acted in their death-throes as if they could at any moment get up and avail themselves of the newly antiseptic nineteenth-century medicine. But much of modernism, if not the whole romantic movement, can be written of with some analytic perspicacity as a sequence of reactions to various stages in the growth of the newer, bigger, more boisterous, more sophisticated (but also more impersonal) cities that were growing about the European landscape. Whether it is the early romantics' glorification of nature or Flaubert's attack on the narrow-mindedness of the provinces, both presuppose the city as a foil. Baudelaire attacked the urban landscape mercilessly and directly. If, in comparison, Wagner's art seems to be about not much more than some nineteenth-century urban architectural ornamentation brought to life for the evening, we must remember that, in terms of the *Zeitgeist* philosophy of unity and coherence that dominated the century Wagner's art was created in, the knowledgeable viewer was expected to be able to read in those ornaments a commentary on the trajectory and composition of every great avenue running by them, the relationship of the various neighborhoods they joined, or the varied social classes that used them, as well as of those classes' and avenues' origins and destinations. And it was this sort of allegory Wagner strove to inscribe in his Festival Play. It is the desire for a vision of history the city cedes us.

Wagner had written his four-part Festival Play, *Der Ring des Nibelungren,* for the enlightenment of the German peoples, in hopes of founding an inchoately German art. You are Christians now (he said in effect). But less than a millennium ago, *this* was our religion. Look at these gods, goddesses, heroes, heroines, dwarfs, and dragons, if you really want to see what is going on with us today. Be quiet, now, and pay attention. . . .

But the cyclic in Wagner is largely the *Ring*'s allegorical repetition of the present. The development of the story is actually dialectical—Hegel's historical dialectic. But that's another aspect that tends, today, to suggest Marx when no Marx is there—if only because of Marx's materialist revision of Hegel's historical notion.

With all respect to Auden, I wonder if it is all that easy to separate the cyclic from the progressive in "modern" thought. Each, repressed, is at play in the concept of the other. That point made, his is nevertheless another version of the observation that Wagner begins precisely what is continued in the myth of modernism.

Myths are conservative.

As Ernst Cassirer remarked so many years ago now, the committee nature of their composition assures it. And Wagner today, as more and more literature devoted to him fills the shelves, is more and more a myth—the conservative myth of nineteenth-century art.

But Robert Scholes has also remarked, more recently and possibly more to the point, that myth is the opposite of literature. It is the opposite of what is personal, persistent, and idiosyncratic. To write any myth down—even Wagner's—is immediately to subject it to ironies, to resystematize it, to make it a fiction, as dramatists as different as Shaw, Gide, Sartre, Giraudoux, and Anouilh all seemed to know as they proceeded through their own versions of early modernism. Were Shaw's *Saint Joan,* Gide's *Oedipe,* Cocteau's *Orphée,* or Sartre's *Les Mouches* (not to mention Joyce's *Ulysses*) trying to manifest something immanent in the Wagnerian enterprise? Or were they arguing against it with their own bright analytic laughter? Was Wagner himself?

We might speculate, but that is to set out on still another side-path in an exploration that already may have veered dangerously toward the diffuse.

And what of the elements in Wagner's music that, kitsch or not, clearly transcend the Wagnerian fiction we are weaving here? I mean the chromaticism that Wagner, reaching after the most emotional sounds he dared, admitted into the theater with *Tristan und Isolde,* which became the springboard, under Schoenberg's twentieth-century tutelage, for the austere and impersonal compositions of Webern, if not the richly personal and passionate atonality of Berg?

Let us return to Artaud's text:

"I think both the theater and we ourselves have had enough of psychology."

Is he addressing Wagner the operatic psychologist? Is he addressing Taine?

Taine said specifically of the novelist, almost as soon as he commenced his supplementary 1867 volume on the modern: "In my opinion he is a psychologist, who naturally and involuntarily sets psychology at work. He is nothing else, nor more. He loves to picture feelings, to perceive their connections, their precedents, their consequences . . ."

It must be said that the domain of the theater is not the psychological but the plastic and physical [Artaud wrote]. And it is not a question of whether the physical language of theater is capable of achieving the same psychological resolution as the language of words, but whether there are not attitudes in the realm of thought and intelligence that words are incapable of grasping and that gestures and everything partaking of a spatial language attain with more precision than they. . . . It is not a matter of suppressing speech in the theater but of changing its role and especially reducing its position, of considering it as something else than a means of conducting human characters to their external ends, since the theater is concerned only with feelings and passions in conflict with one another, and man with man, in life.

The way "feelings and passions conflict with one another, and man with man, in life," was, of course, as Taine told us, psychology in the nineteenth century. It was only with the dissemination of Wagnerism that it ceased being what goes on *between* subjects and, instead, became specifically what goes on *within* the individual subject; for as the solitary experience, whether in public or in private, became the model for the aesthetic experience (as with bourgeois—but *not* working-class—religion), it also became the model for all significant experience, including the psychological. In short, Artaud unwittingly asks for a return to the nineteenth-century psychology of Taine (and of the English novelists Taine examines), precisely as he demands that we *abandon* the psychology Wagner helped replace it with.

I'd also like to discuss, of course, the contemporary attempt to combine Wagner directly with a gallery of Artaudian effects in Hans-Jürgen Syberberg's film *Parsifal:* at one point Wagner seriously considered having Parsifal's part, from the young man's anointment on, sung by a woman. This androgyny, which Wagner finally abandoned, Syberberg returns to the opera, in his film, with some effect. In that discussion I'd only point out, however, that when such an aggressively avant-garde achievement is produced in Lincoln Center by as basilaic a figure as Francis Ford Coppola, it begins immediately to reify precisely the

Wagnerism the film so vigorously tries to critique—a reification that still awaits an equally vigorous deconstruction. But, then, whenever the work of an individual artist is presented by an institution, state or private, with its attendant respect, its sense of a value—even if it is assumed to be wholly aesthetic—chosen and committed to, a value sense we cannot escape in such a situation, we are reinventing, on whatever scale (a gallery exhibit, the choice of a local theater group), Wagnerism; we are reinscribing its form in contemporary society. This is indeed why, as long as art and institutions are involved with one another, this aspect of Wagnerism cannot be rescinded by post-modernism. For it is as much the institutional framing as anything that can render the most polylogically conceived work a monologue.

And even Julia Kristeva's radical question for literature, "Who speaks?" is the obvious and inevitable demand before the Wagnerian monologue, transferred directly to literature by the monologues of Joyce.

In such a light, how different her question seems from that implicit in Bakhtin, "Who contests? Who conflicts? Who is in dialogue?"—questions that can only be answered in the plural, in the social, in which the frame is always called into analytical question, rather than by individual observation of some moment of subjective individual totality in which meaning, melody, and harmony fill up the whole of the theater, the whole of consciousness, as an individual subject portrays an individual subject for an individual subject.

Is Artaud's theater really a refutation of Wagner, then? Or is it an appropriation, this time of what was artistically radical in Wagner, despite his conservative politics? Is it an appropriation in the same way that Bettina Knapp's words in the first pages of this study are ambiguous not because they *actually* describe both Wagner and Artaud, but because, however uncritically, however inevitably, Knapp has appropriated her rhetoric from the ubiquitous Wagner fiction to describe in Artaud what is in excess of a monologic Wagner?

To the extent that we see Artaud's work as a single, impassioned, and—yes—deranged monologue, then he is very much a modernist. For in order to see it that way, we must evaporate "all individual or isolated details as things that can be cast away leaving only the whole, the coherent."

That's Nietzsche, you recall, age twenty-five, in his most *un*critical, nineteenth-century mode.

The modernists—whether Joyce or James, Proust or Pound, Eliot or Stevens or Frost or Faulkner—are all basically monologuists. (Pound's purpose in his cutting and critique of the original version of Eliot's *The Waste Land* was basically to bring unity to it by turning it from a poly-

logue into a monologue.) And it is the monologue that Wagner gave to
the text of modernism as something to value, to aspire to, to seek a totality in, either in terms of execution or in terms of interpretation. To
the extent that Artaud's monologue breaks up, will not remain a single
cascading torrent, but fragments and becomes a dialogue between several voices, deranged, supremely rational, conservative or radical in
political terms, none with a complete and totalized argument but
none, at the same time, able to exist without the others, because—and
after the correspondence with Rivière, is there any other way to read
Artaud?—it is the existence of each that makes the others signify, Artaud implies what might be called, with whatever reservations and
qualifications, a post-modern aesthetic.

Certainly his significance as a writer is that there is so much in his
texts that urges us on to this sort of reading.

* * *

We critics never tire of reminding theater directors. But they nevertheless go on and, above the smoke wafting the stage at the end of *Götterdämmerung*, as they recall something of Wagner's great and noisy
"steam curtain" at Bayreuth ("which looked exactly like what it really
was and made the theater smell like a laundry," commented Shaw),
project a restored ring of light on the cyclorama, thinking, hoping it
sounds the note (as Auden says at the end of what may be the greatest
of the modernist monologues, "Caliban to the Audience," among that
most wonderful monologue collection, *The Sea and the Mirror* [1944])
of the "restored relation." Transitions are all in order. Unity is immanent. That—certainly, somehow, they believe—is what Wagner must
have meant.

How does one recall for them that at the end of the four-part Fes-
tivial Play, while the gold is restored to the Rhine, precisely its circular-
ity, its closure, its cyclic implications, its formal properties *as* a ring are
what are obliterated by the restoration? Whether one agrees either
with its analysis or with that analysis's presuppositions, the *Ring* is
about what it takes to *break out* of the cyclic, the mythic, and into history and progress. It is about what is necessary to get free of Nietzsche's eternal return. It is about a cycle at last and finally shattered.
With the "praise Brunhilde" motif, love survives the destruction,
through *Götterdämmerung*'s final diminuendo D-flat major chord (mu-
sically as *far* away from the opening E-flat major of *Das Rheingold*, at
least in terms of large, democratic whole tones, as it is possible to

get—for those searching for developmental significance); but it survives as a spirit, in, with, and purely as music, a memory of a great and heroic love, hovering above the nineteenth-century ideal image of material and spiritual ruin Wagner had been so struck with in Bakúnin—a ruin that, with its silent inhabitants, alone could allow (if we may strain Wagner's allegory; but can any contemporary reading of it be other than a misprision?), as Wagner or Bakúnin, or even the hard-headed Heubner might have seen it, Time and History to begin.

Let us see, then, destruction and ruin at the end of the Ring! (Let us, too, be content—however strangely—that the House has burned down.) Certainly not restoration!

Myself, I do not think we can "refute" Wagner's theater with any real historical understanding; we cannot deny its effect on our concept of art, or—indeed—on our Wagnerian fiction, any more than we can "redeem" it and still remain true to Wagner's political notions. It is currently too pervasive. It is historically too specific.

But I do think we can use writers like Artaud (and Kristeva and Bakhtin) to subvert it at strategic points, to interrogate it, to reveal through their own appropriations from it, appropriations both from its centralities and its marginalities, the nature of its tyrannies—just as Wagner's theater interrogated, subverted, and systemically revised the theater and the art that came before it. It is through such historical awareness that I believe we can best say "what has been said and even say what has not been said in a way that belongs to us," with whatever fictions, for whatever strategic purposes, we undertake as writer and as reader, as audience and as artist.

— *New York City*
October '83–December '87

Bibliography

Adorno, Theodor. *In Search of Wagner,* trans. Rodney Livingstone. London: NLB, 1981.

————. *The Jargon of Authenticity,* trans. Knut Tarnowski and Frederic Will. Evanston, Illinois: Northwestern University Press, 1973.

Arnold, Matthew. *Poems,* ed. Kenneth Allott. Harmondsworth, UK: Penguin, 1954.

Artaud, Antonin. *Selected Writings,* ed. with intr. by Susan Sontag; trans. Helen Weaver. New York: Farrar, Straus and Giroux, 1976.

————. *4 Texts,* trans. Clayton Eshleman and Norman Glass. Los Angeles: Panjandrum, 1986.

————. *The Theater and Its Double,* trans. Mary Caroline Richards. New York: Grove Press, 1958.

————. *The Cenci: A Play,* trans. Simon Watson Taylor. New York: Grove Press, 1969.

————. *The Peyote Dance,* trans. Helen Weaver. New York: Farrar, Straus and Giroux, 1976.

Auden, W. H. *Collected Poems,* ed. Edward Mendelson. New York: Random House, 1976.

————. "Introduction" to *Victorian and Edwardian Poets: Tennyson to Yeats,* ed. W. H. Auden and Norman Holmes Pearson. New York: Viking, 1950, pp. xv–xxiii.

Benjamin, Walter. *Charles Baudelaire: A Lyric Poet in the Era of High Capitalism,* trans. Harry Zohn. London: NLB, 1973.

————. "The Work of Art in the Age of Mechanical Reproduction," *Illuminations,* ed. Hannah Arendt; trans. Harry Zohn. New York: Schocken Books, 1969, pp. 217–51.

Blunt, Wilfrid. *The Dream King: Ludwig II of Bavaria.* London: Hamish Hamilton, 1970.

Lord Byron [George Gordon]. *Poetical Works,* ed. Frederick Page; new ed. corr. John Jump. London: Oxford University Press, 1945.

Derrida, Jacques. "La parole souflée" and "The Theater of Cruelty and the Closure of Representation," *Writing and Difference,* trans. Alan Bass. Chicago: University of Chicago Press, 1978, pp. 167–95 and 232–50.

Eagleton, Terry. *Literary Theory: An Introduction.* Minneapolis: University of Minnesota Press, 1983.

Esslin, Martin. *Antonin Artaud.* London: Fontana, 1976.

Gilbert, Stuart. *James Joyce's Ulysses.* New York: Random House, 1930.

Gregor-Dellin, Martin. *Richard Wagner: His Life, His Work, His Century.* New York: Harcourt, Brace, Jovanovich, 1980.

Hayman, Ronald. *Nietzsche: A Critical Life.* New York: Oxford University Press, 1980.

Katz, Jacob. *The Darker Side of Genius: Richard Wagner's Anti-Semitism.* Hanover, New Hampshire: University Press of New England for Brandeis University Press, 1986.

Knapp, Bettina L. *Antonin Artaud: Man of Vision.* New York: David Lewis, 1969.

Magee, Bryan. *Aspects of Wagner.* New York: Stein and Day, 1969.

Newman, Ernest. *The Life of Richard Wagner.* 4 vols. New York: Knopf, 1937–46.

———. *Wagner Nights.* New York: Putnam, 1949.

Nietzsche, Friedrich. *The Birth of Tragedy* and *The Genealogy of Morals,* trans. Francis Golffing. Garden City, N.Y.: Doubleday-Anchor, 1956.

———. *The Birth of Tragedy* and *The Case of Wagner,* trans. Walter Kaufman. New York: Vintage, 1967.

Porges, Heinrich. *Wagner Rehearsing the 'Ring': An Eye-Witness Account of the Stage Rehearsals of the First Bayreuth Festival,* trans. Robert L. Jacobs. Cambridge: Cambridge University Press, 1983.

Schorske, Carl E. *Fin-de-siècle Vienna: Politics and Culture.* New York: Knopf, 1980.

Shattuck, Roger. *The Banquet Years: The Origins of the Avant-Garde in France, 1885 to World War I.* New York: Random House, 1955.

Shaw, George Bernard. *The Perfect Wagnerite: A Commentary on the Niblung's Ring.* New York: Dover, 1967.

Taine, H[ippolyte]. A. *History of English Literature,* trans. Henri Van Laun. New York: A. L. Burt, undated.

Wagner, Richard. *My Life [Mein Leben],* trans. Andrew Gray, ed. Mary Whittall. Cambridge University Press, 1983.

———. *Letters: The Burrell Collection,* ed. John N. Burk. New York: Vienna House, 1972.

Westernhagen, Curt von. *Wagner: A Biography,* trans. Mary Whittall. 2nd ed. Cambridge University Press, 1981.

Weston, Jessie L. *From Ritual to Romance.* Cambridge: Cambridge University Press, 1920.

Reading at Work

and Other Activities Frowned on by Authority:
A Reading of Donna Haraway's
"Manifesto for Cyborgs: Science, Technology, and
Socialist Feminism in the 1980s"

> "Thank you. Would you like to see my work?" Helva asked,
> politely. She instinctively sheered away from personal discus-
> sion . . .
>> "Work?" asked the lady.
>> "I am currently reproducing the Last Supper on the head
> of a screw."
>> —Anne McCaffrey, *The Ship Who Sang*

*Isn't there something—could it really be missing from the text above—urging us
to read this passage from Anne McCaffrey's series of science fiction tales about the
young cyborg Helva as irony? Pin down (or up) that irony, and we admit at the
same time: Our laughter only checks a more violent urge to dash the screw from
Helva's metal grip, to declare: "Fool, fool! Blind metal fool! For all your microscopic vision, that is no work at all!"*

*Work? we go on, to ourselves, stalled between laughter and rage in the uncer-
tainty between responses that is irony's sign. "Work!" we do not quite ejaculate
into a silence that, for all we know, is as likely formed of Helva's ignorance (she
does not suspect the vanity of her labor) as by her terror (even at age twelve she
must know what her audience—at least the male fraction—might do or say) as by
her indifference (she is not human; she is only something we—the males among
us—make: though, in this case, she has been written by a woman). The silence,
now, is Helva's: she is doing something—work—that is, maddeningly, not responding to us. A few (of us) may even notice what we have left out—that what is
missing is our own terror at work on an historical indifference we can hardly bear*

and, therefore, will not bare . . . because it flies in the face of all (or only: male/het-erosexual) desire. (Metaphorically identifiable with any other kind? by extension of any sort of logic or psychology?) "This is work?" we go on. "Oh, no! If that is what you think—" we silently inveigh—"there is something decidedly missing." As we perceive the futility of Helva's task, our anger turns on her precisely as we would use it to unlock her silence, her ignorance, her error—this victim of an impover-ished notion of production:

Angels on a pin?

Apostles on a screw?

We want to snatch its emblem—drawn and patterned so incisively by a woman—violently from her! Certainly writer McCaffrey intended something like this . . . from us. ("I bet she loves it," grunts my grosser brother, with a snicker. "I be-lieve this was her intention," declares my more refined, with a smile.) We want to commit some violence against this deflated notion of work that will leave Helva's claw empty, will leave her lights and lenses and paint brush fixed or blinking or probing about in some brutal absence, an illuminated space from which an object has just vanished, a space that is saturated with meaning precisely because some-thing is no longer there. (Art? Labor? What confusion of boundaries between pres-ence and absence is written in that violent, violated, void locus whose legibility we would unlock—to read into it our own words, our own meanings—even as it fades to pure blankness, even as we watch, under the combined mechanical/human gaze—hers, ours—still, somewhere, backed by human brain?) Among the more ar-ticulate of us, this turn of the lock, this rape of the screw—this violence motivated wholly by a conflict of interpretation—goes on in silence even as we admit that the fictive creators of this metal and glass and nervous creature (whose genitals have already been removed, like a phrase snipped from the body of the text by the closure of parentheses) are our brothers. They exist only in the empty margin writer McCaf-frey has assigned them, yet their operations stall us—the men, that is—on some confused level between experience and myth, before a contradictory gap in the logic or poetics of bodies or machines. For the moment we do not know which . . .

As of yet we cannot name it.

Something is still missing.

Still, in excess of the silence, of the absence, of the incompleteness, don't we all understand (whether that "we" is the pathologically "socialized" few who sympa-thize with, or the morally "civilized" many who abominate) this rape fantasy by which we have just indulged in an ugly and overextended metaphor of desires we would rather not admit that we, some of us, have or admit that we, all of us, have seen rampant throughout "civilized" (read: patriarchal) society: despite whatever religious image has been incised on it by Helva's vice-like virginal grip, certainly one screw less in this collection of metal and glass and wire that is cyborg Helva (extended or, better, constituted by her technology as much as writer McCaffrey, writing in 1959, was extended or, better, constituted by typewriter, printing, etc.), in which the organic—reduced to pure subject, pure ego, pure nerve (or over-wrought nerves)—is wholly hidden behind some hard and inanimate shell, couldn't be a theft, an appropriation, a rape—could not possibly create an absence in any way missed or mourned in the face of any understanding of work, or art, or desire, or rage . . .

Well, as long as it remains only a fantasy . . . but what we all know now is that where all these ellipses, pauses, gaps hide, veil, cover, and even violently destroy the possibility of completion to the thoughts either side of them, obliterate the work that might have gone on within them, there is something wrong. For such elisions are the visible and resonant marks of an error we can all at last read: it is precisely in these moments of silence that fantasy returns to trouble—that is, to present us with the possibility of its realized fact that must, certainly, be based upon it, that must be construed, if not constructed, by it.

There, certainly, we can find—definitely—something troubling, something missing.

I

As they sit safely on the other side of the boundary between type fonts, as they hang over the border marked by our initial Roman numeral, squeezed and set off in the upper margin of our text along with the poor and prior epigraph they read with such distress, let us consider the above italics to be a bad dream—something which we would all, as would Helva, sheer away from rather than consecrate by personal discussion.

The unpleasantness will, certainly, return to trouble. (The boundary is clearly not all that secure.) But for now let us turn to Donna Haraway's "Manifesto for Cyborgs," to read, to work, to rework.

In a slow, careful, and even ponderous perusal of this 34-page text (41 with Acknowledgments and References), which first appeared in *The Socialist Review* for Summer 1985, a perusal where the labor was all in an attempt to negotiate a fixed and unitary signified (while all the interpretative work was allowed to drift lazily within the confines set out by a strongly fixed and socially commonplace ideological authority), it was fairly easy for me to read Haraway's manifesto more or less as follows:

In an introductory movement ("An Ironic Dream of a Common Language for Women in the Integrated Circuit," the title a play on a book of poems by Adrienne Rich), itself introduced by an alignment of "faithfulness," "irony," and "blasphemy," the metaphor of the cyborg was worked upon: the cyborg (the cybernetic organism of Norbert Weiner, transformed by numerous science fiction stories into any combination of organic—usually neurological—and mechanical or electronic material) was discussed as "reality," "fiction," and "lived experience," as suggesting the bisexual reproductiveness of ferns and invertebrates, as well as that eighty-four-billion-dollar item in the U.S. defense budget, C^3-I (control-command-communication-intelligence). The cyborg suggests science and politics, "partiality, irony, intimacy, and perversity." Perhaps even more important is what the cyborg avoids: it avoids "the seductions of organic wholeness" and "skips the step of original unity"; as well it escapes the polar structure of "public and private." "The cyborg does not dream of community on the model of the organic family, this time without the Oedipal project. The cyborg does not recognize the Garden of Eden; it is not made of mud and cannot dream of returning to dust (p.67), i.e., it is not subject to Freud's "death wish." For Haraway, the cyborg partakes of the delirium of the bodilessness of the miniature and post-modern silicon chip, "a surface for writing." The hardest sciences, she notes, are the places where the boundaries have become most confused. "The new machines are so clean and light" (p. 71)—and deadly. The cyborg suggests a double myth, one that courts "the final imposition of a grid of control on the planet," but, in opposition to that, courts as well the "lived social and bodily realities in which people are not afraid of their joint kinship with animals and machines, not afraid of permanently partial identities and contradictory standpoints." (p. 72)

With this account of Haraway's introductory move, I suspect at least some of her delirious striving "for pleasure in the confusion of boundaries" is a response to a "social reality" that several science fiction writers have addressed with various amounts of insight—sundry works by both Chelsea Quinn Yarbro and Joanna Russ come to mind. Only as a society becomes more and more infrastructurally stable does it permit greater and greater superstructural freedom—of expression, of action, of belief. Conversely, as soon as the society is truly menaced at the infrastructural level, then precisely those freedoms are the first to go.

The freedoms that we, in the West, are taught to think of as the foundation on which our society is built are actually—in historical terms—of recent vintage. They are very much on the surface of our culture—which is why so frequently they seem so easily threatened in less stable societies.

We must point out, then, that the two versions of Haraway's cyborg myth do not function at the same social level: "the final imposition of a grid of control on the planet" is very likely to be an infrastructural grid, which alone *allows* the superstructural freedom of (some) people to explore "their joint kinship with animals and machines" in a fearless, utopian union. What seems to be missing, at least from Haraway's introductory move, is any sense of the darker, even tragic side of this situation—a side we enter with the graffito from Joanna Russ's science fiction novel,

We Who Are About to . . . : "Money doesn't matter/When control is some-where else!" Not only does *money* not matter in such a situation, nei-ther does language or sexual freedom. To change things at the infra-structural level—to establish a *different* structure for the deployment of wealth, say—is a lot harder than the simple re-deployment of different people into the *existing* wealth structure. And in our society, the sec-ond process just cited is a self-repairing mechanism by which the exist-ing oppressive wealth structure heals any infrastructural damages done to it.

Perhaps, I remark in passing, a little more faith in a more tradition-ally socialist approach (and a little less Baudrillardian *exstase*) might turn Haraway's criticism to the larger lived realities of the vast majority of peoples in the U.S.—female and male, white, black, and Hispanic—whom the existing wealth structure wholly excludes from exploring any such utopian kinships or boundary confusions with any joy at all.

Yet, that reservation comes to me as easily as her account, so that I was not particularly troubled by it in my progress through her text.

And here, at the end of this account of her introduction, I can think of no better place to give that introduction's opening:

> This essay is an effort to built an ironic political myth faithful to feminism, socialism, and materialism. Perhaps more faithful as blasphemy is faithful . . . Blasphemy has always seemed to require taking things very seriously . . . Blasphemy protects us from the moral majority within . . . Irony is about contradictions that do not resolve into larger wholes, even dialectically, about the tension of holding incompatible things together because both or all are necessary and true. (*Socialist Review*, Summer 1985, p. 65. All quotes are from this article unless otherwise specified.)

And a page later she writes:

> This essay is an argument for *pleasure* in the confusion of boundaries and for *responsibility* in their construction. It is also an effort to contribute to so-cialist-feminist culture and theory in a post-modernist, non-naturalist mode and in the utopian tradition of imagining a world without gender, which is perhaps a world without genesis, but maybe also a world without end. The cyborg incarnation is outside salvation history. (pp. 66–67)

A world without end is, of course, a world without science—is, indeed, *the* "pre-scientific" salvationist model: for the great, scientific tragedy is the realization that everything runs down eventually, every fire burns out—the individual, the society, the species; the world, the sun, the uni-verse. But Haraway locates her myth *as* myth. As such, it functions more as a literary irony—thus, as with my first reservation, I am not much troubled by it.

A premise of this essay is that "the need for unity of people trying to resist worldwide intensification of domination has never been more acute. But—" Haraway proposes (and herein lies the energy and importance of her work)—"a slightly perverse shift of perspective might better enable us to contest for meanings, as well as for other forms of power and pleasure in technologically-mediated societies." (p. 71)

As much as she approves of "oppositional consciousness," what Haraway is proposing here is a kind of oppositional judo, a slight skewing of concepts, practices, programs, that may accomplish the same ends. Well, in a world where energy is such a threatened commodity, the suggested economy alone of her proposal privileges it in our attention.

In the section of her manifesto, "Fractured Identities," Haraway looks to the plurality of women's movements.

While the fragmentation and dissension among the various women's movements has its painful aspect, Haraway tries not so much to unify them as to unpack from the various theoretical positions an encouraging polyvocality.

She looks approvingly at Chela Sandoval's "women of color," with its insistent lack of capitalization as well as its "oppositional consciousness," which opens up, and finally deconstructs (i.e., makes radically undecidable) any hard-edged definition of what a woman of color is, save by the accrued negations of having been heretofore denied a place to speak from.

A similar approval is given to Katie King's more theoretical enterprise. King "emphasizes the limits of identification and the political/ poetic mechanics of identification built into reading 'the poem,' that generative core of cultural feminism . . ." while opposing "the persistent tendency among contemporary feminists from different 'moments' or 'conversations' in feminist practice to taxonomize the women's movement to make one's own political tendency appears to be the *telos* of the whole."

Thus, "[t]he common achievement of King and Sandoval is learning how to craft a poetic/political unity without relying on a logic of appropriation, incorporation, and taxonomic identification."

When, after another brief theoretical foray, Haraway turns to look at Catherine MacKinnon, from the first sentence of Haraway's consideration her sympathy becomes highly strained. ("Catherine MacKinnon's version of radical feminism is itself a caricature of the appropriating, incorporating, totalizing tendencies of Western theories of identity grounding action.") By the end, if any sympathy was there to start, it has vanished:

MacKinnon's radical theory of experience is totalizing in the extreme; it does not so much marginalize as obliterate the authority of any other women's political speech and action. It is a totalization producing what Western patriarchy itself never succeeded in doing—feminists' consciousness of the non-existence of women, except as products of men's desire. I think MacKinnon correctly argues that no Marxian version of identity can firmly ground women's unity. But in solving the problem of the contradictions of any Western revolutionary subject for feminist purposes, she develops an even more authoritarian doctrine of experience. If my complaint about socialist/Marxian standpoints is their unintended erasure of polyvocal, unassimilable, radical difference made visible in anti-colonial discourse and practice, MacKinnon's intentional erasure of all difference through the device of the "essential" non-existence of women is not reassuring. (p. 78)

This section of Haraway's manifesto concludes with an appeal to the strength of "partial explanations"; thus she further reinforces her support for those feminisms that do not claim to explain everything. Here, Haraway invokes the explanatory excitement of Julia Kristeva's notion that "women appeared as a historical group after World War II, along with groups like youth." Haraway goes on: "Her dates are doubtful; but we are now accustomed to remembering that as objects of knowledge and as historical actors, 'race' did not always exist, 'class' has a historical genesis, and 'homosexuals' are quite junior." Haraway could have extended this historical revisionism to include that literature does not begin till shortly after World War I (Terry Eagleton, *Literary Theory, an Introduction*) and that racism and anti-Semitism are products of 1886 (Hannah Arendt, *The Origins of Totalitarianism*).

My reservation here, in terms of Haraway's critique of MacKinnon (which Haraway uses as the springboard for this terminal exhortation for a polyvocal feminism), is that in an attempt to maintain a theoretical level, she skirts the real danger of MacKinnon's position. MacKinnon is after all a lawyer, and her enterprise is primarily a legislative one—the institution of laws against pornography and sexually explicit material that presumably degrade women. MacKinnon bases her whole program on the theoretical assumption that fantasies about actions and the actions themselves have a simple, direct, and uncritically causal relation—that, indeed, we should not consider any differences at all between them—a theoretical position that must certainly find itself hostile to, just for example, the whole complex fantasy element that motivates, controls, and that indeed represents the ends of Haraway's manifest cyborg enterprise.

This is certainly a more troubling reservation than my initial one about infrastructural and superstructural levels, because this blindness to what strikes me as a basic hostility in the two positions seems either suicidal—or profoundly manipulative. And, frankly, if it's the latter, I am not sure who or what is being manipulated nor to what end. I am still willing, however, to read an irony here.

This second section concludes:

> Some differences are playful; some are poles of world historical systems of domination. "Epistemology" is about knowing the difference. (p. 79)

The third section of the manifesto is "The Informatics of Domination." It chronicles, by means of two comparable lists, a shift in sensibility that may, indeed, represent the sort of developmental discontinuity Foucault locates at the end of French classicism in *Les Mots et les choses*, when the science of wealth, natural philosophy, and general grammar transformed into political economy, biology, and linguistics.

What sort of change is really involved, Haraway asks, when questions of "Representation" give way to practices of "Simulation," when the "Bourgeois novel" and "realism" are replaced by "science fiction" and "post-modernism," when the notion of "organism" is driven out by that of "biotic component," or when questions of "depth and integrity" become considerations of "surface and boundary"?

Her list runs on to 32 paired terms.

The first in each of her pairs (". . . Perfection . . . Hygiene . . . Reproduction . . . Microbiology, tuberculosis . . . Freud . . . Sex . . . Mind . . ."), Haraway notes, are comfortable and hierarchical. The second in each pair (". . . Optimization . . . Stress Management . . . Replication . . . Immunology, AIDS . . . Lacan . . . Genetic engineering . . . Artificial intelligence . . .") are, in her words, "scary" and "new."

"It it not just that 'god' is dead," Haraway writes out of a consideration of her lists; "so is the 'goddess.'"

Up to this point, even with my reservations, I found myself more or less comfortable with my first reading of the manifesto. And this was the point, in the midst of the third section, that I first looked ahead to note that there were, indeed, three sections to come: "The Homework Economy," "Women in the Integrated Circuit," and finally "Cyborgs: A Myth of Political Identity." But it was also at this moment, cut loose from that initial and dedicated, original and unitary reading—precisely at that moment in Haraway's argument that I, as a worker caught in the murky labor of reading, sat down on the job as it were and let my eye be tempted ahead to encompass the remaining pages of the argument—that, even before I left the still legible trace of the argument fading in my mind, I snagged on:

Any objects or persons can be reasonably thought of in terms of disassembly and reassembly . . . (p. 81)

And:

The entire universe of objects that can be known scientifically must be formulated as problems in communications engineering (for the managers) or theories of the text (for those who would resist). Both are cyborg semiologies. (p. 81)

Certainly my own ear, here, was shut down to any play of irony that might have informed this particular section—here. With my ears closed to all revoicing and my eyes wide before a blankness and impersonal starkness of white page and black print, in a moment of Spenglerian vertigo I read:

Human beings, like any other component or subsystem, must be localized in a system architecture whose basic modes of operation are probabilistic, statistical. No objects, spaces, or bodies are sacred in themselves; any component can be interfaced with any other if the proper standard, the proper code, can be constructed for processing signals in a common language. Exchange in this world transcends the universal translation effected by capitalist markets that Marx analyzed so well. The privileged pathology affecting all kinds of components in this universe is stress—communications breakdown. The cyborg is not subject to Foucault's biopolitics; the cyborg simulates politics, a much more potent field of operations. (p. 82)

But as Haraway's argument recovered with, now, a borrowing from Zoë Sofoulis's notion of techno-digestion, now a reborrowing of Rachel Grossman's image of women in the integrated circuit, pouring in from a margin till now silent came a rhetorical battery of discord and aggression, to damp all play in my reading: how could such an argument fall victim to such a well-worn set of flaws as those that a retired highschool teacher laid down in total patriarchal seriousness in 1919, alone in his furnished room, to map out a path followed by so many German intellectuals toward Nazism? (*I* was the one being manipulated! The disingenuous blindness to MacKinnon's real flaw masked, of course, a secret complicity . . . !) How can this submission of the organic *to* the machine be considered in any way historically new? Isn't this just the oldest of 19th Century stances: isn't the love of science merely the manipulated expression with which we gaze at New Jerusalem when we are most insensible to the fact that it has already turned into Brave New World?

To present such an outmoded, such an inflated set of rhetorical homilies as in any way revolutionary is hopelessly inappropriate, hopelessly angering—is, indeed, a kind of political blasphemy . . .

But here, of course, my first reading had already ceased. In the very moment I had chosen to look ahead, I was already engaged in *re*-reading. I was, again and already, within a logical impasse. I had come up against something missing from my own assumptions about the argument of this text (written by a woman) so far; I had encountered an aporia that halted me, before which the notion of such a first (is it not really the notion of a final) reading could not go on. It could no longer work.

I was fixed by it, tamed before it, at least momentarily vanquished—while, in the moment of silence, all internal urges evoked in me any and every socially given fantasy as argument or as retribution or as compensation . . .

That, certainly, is only a somewhat fictive rendering of the first half of my first reading of Haraway's manifesto—indeed (and here our troubling dream has already returned), it is only another version of my initial reading, in italics, of McCaffrey's text—of which Haraway's manifesto will, after all, provide a reading, too. Doubtless more and more women must suspect mine is the reading any man must give to any women's text with which there is not total, totalized, and terrorizing agreement—so total, indeed, that there is no possibility of dialogue. And, admit it, isn't it the reading most men assume that everyone, whether male or female, gives every text that is, no matter the writer's gender, disagreed with enough to make the term 'disagreement' necessary?

Isn't this aggressiveness finally the sign of just how serious the distinctions are between the voices in Haraway's privileged, polyvocal feminisms? Will we gain anything by postulating a *fundamental* difference in the nature of men's aggression and women's aggression? What can we do with this moment of aggression, where irony closes down into monologue even as it reopens itself and—prenamed, predicted as blasphemy, as irony—only a moment on opens up the voice(s) of the text again? (For I have gone forward; I have gone back. I have reread.) Will it work *simply* to reread the text, looking for the missed phrase that will suggest yet another revoicing to what we have already heard as a political declaration?

Certainly in Haraway's text such phrases are not hard to find:

> From the seventeenth century till now, machines could be animated—given ghostly souls to make them speak or move or to account for their orderly development and mental capacities. Or organisms could be mechanized—reduced to body understood as resource of mind. *These* machine/organism relations are obsolete, unnecessary . . . (p. 97, italics Haraway's).

Certainly the Spenglerian fallacy at which I found myself stalling is part of precisely those obsolete relations Haraway has historified for us. Why not go on and construct a super-reading that merely highlights this self-criticism as contained in the manifesto, a super-reading that reduces my violent objection to a simple and controlled skewing from the main argument, the sort of reduction I had already done twice before? (What would be repressed? What would be missing?) Certainly one would then have valorized an appeal to corrections, intentions, and auctoriality through a greater and still greater exertion of lisible labor—of readerly work. Why not allow the text to oscillate, to fibrillate, to play at the plurality of polysemy?

Because, of course, if we do, we do so at the price of leaving something out. Certainly, such a revision of my own text leaves *something* missing . . .

The fantasy, the myth, the dream of aggression . . .

Yet even as we identify it, we do so with the question: can't we, in the name of dialogue, suppress this dream once and for all?

Why can't we dash it from the center of consciousness, snatch it from under the lights and lenses where it insists on engulfing, gripping, and staining (with a violence we are momentarily sure, before we act, that is greater than any we might assert against it) an innocent void, like the trace of an age-old religious rite always-already inscribed on whatever surface we gaze at long enough, a rite of both men and women, however differently and along whatever sociological trajectory it arrives there, where it insists on inserting itself (with, at this level, an equal violence, no . . . ?) into the discourse? Why can't we put it finally and fixedly beyond some marginal border, declaring it: missing in action, or permanently missing.

Why, from the moment it is snatched away, from the moment it is outlawed, abolished, declared abhorrent and marginal, does it persist in our sight, as a pulsing blot of sunlight on the water of a lake flickers in the eye for so many moments after we have turned into the cooling and comforting woods?

Why do I, with most men, assume it works as the metaphor for (if not the myth of) the truth of *reading* whenever there is dissension/conflict/contest/agony/dialogue?

A truly satisfactory answer—one that does not stall before the difficult and unindividuable social objects from which so many social constructions arise—can be teased out, I suspect, only by going down to a more operational level:

What is this "work"?

What is "reading"?

What is "metaphor" and how do we "read" it?

How does "metaphor" "work"?

Frankly, I do not see how reading can be other than a violent process. The violence of the letter *is* the violence of the reader—a reader involved in an unclear, cloudy, struggling, masochistic relationship with a text that, at any moment it would produce joy, *must* do so violently.

For without violence, all ideology—radical or conservative—is incomplete and blind to itself.

Was not that Freud's major insight in *Civilization and its Discontents?*

The thrust of what is written here will be to search out a way to reread Haraway's manifesto—and my own reactions to it—both productively and provocatively. For during that "first" reading (another fiction, certainly, because—and I am aware of it—I have let much remain missing from *all* the various fictions I've so far indulged), I find them both—my reading of Haraway and my response to that reading— "human, all too human." To mitigate their organic failures and their mechanical ellipses (my reading, my reaction, and what, rightly or wrongly, I have always-already taken to be Haraway's mistakes), I need something more rigorous, almost scientific, technical.

If I am to deal seriously with my response to this argument that Haraway proposes and that I make my own by reading, I must, myself, become something of a cyborg to critique them . . . as she, indeed, claims in her paper I must.

Isn't there an irony (as she so declares) *here?*

In the course of an "argument for *pleasure* in the confusion of boundaries and for *responsibility* in their construction" Haraway writes: "Liberation rests on the construction of the consciousness, the imaginative apprehension, of oppression, and so of possibility." For me, certainly, keeping the play between the two primary meanings of "construction" in mind in both sentences is to begin, at least, to read her argument most rigorously, richly, and usefully:

Construction: to build, to create from former materials.

And: Construction: to construe, to understand, to analyze, to tear down into its constituent parts.

If, in reading her, we privilege either meaning at the expense of the other, her argument becomes trivialized. Take "understanding/analysis" as the fixed reading, and the argument soon becomes ungrounded theoreticism at play around a rather flighty image. Take hard-headed "building/making" as the fixed reading, and the argument slides in among those endless demands for action and reformation without theoretical basis.

The boundary between them is more than confused enough today for our purposes. Pleasure? Well, perhaps.

Nevertheless, what, above all, Haraway's paper urges us to do is to construct/construe the cyborg—that unwhole and unholy amalgam. So let us turn, however tentatively, to the required work.

"We are cyborgs," she has written. She tells us as well: "Who cyborgs will be is a radical question." She says: "Cyborgs are ether, are quintessence." It is possible to read this progression as developmental. But it is also possible to read it as contradictory. ("Ether"—like "phlogiston" and the "world without end"—is something the development of science has told us does not exist. And Haraway knows it.) And I choose that reading.

In whatever understanding I pretend to, in terms of the text I question, as my lights and lenses illuminate, magnify, or as my brush reinscribes it, carefully, like a copy of a deeply venerated image ambiguously located between religion and art, there will always be something missing in my simulation to the extent that: I am not a cyborg, not a woman, not fully a man. Thus, however fleetingly, however impermanently I take on the image, however I would try to use a woman's image to speak with or through, there *will* be something missing. (Who, now, would snatch these images in anger away?) I use this troubling imagery (ceded me by the prerequisite of a dream of rape I abhor) to remind all my readers, male and female, that *any* man's argument (especially against a woman's) is always troubled by such bad dreams as were called up by the tedious, exacting, ironic, and apparently trivial work of the cyborg we began with.

Most women, certainly, know them.

For my—or any man's—argument to be useful, especially to a woman, women must not accept it whole. It must be analyzed, fragmented, sliced open, cut up, cut off, fragments of it recombined with what may at first seem wholly inappropriate technicalities, till all unity is struck from it (the very concept of unity only returns to trouble, to critique, to annoy), resembling rather some junk-lot of deformed monsters, part human, part machine, and then—perhaps—some part of it cut off or up or out for new use, while the rest is simply left missing . . .

Be assured: the process is painful, angering, violent, troubling to all involved . . .

Thus, these images of rape, dismemberment, and violence (metaphors that trouble the whole range of our language), are, in this discussion of a feminist paper, a kind of irony, a kind of blasphemy.

Why and for what reason, unify *these* images here?

Is it to reduce—or, indeed, reveal—the terroristic element that hides in the margins of all manifestos and thus invalidates a document consecrated to pleasure, to reveal a certain sadism fundamental to all pleasurable affects?

Certainly I would hope not.

What notion of unity, of totality, of power, then, do they disrupt? Once again I quote from the opening section of her manifesto: "This essay is an argument for *pleasure* in the confusion of boundaries and for *responsibility* in their construction."

Well, if such images as I have called in do, indeed, create confusion between what we would all approach as clearly defined categories of argument, ideology, and allegiance, they certainly don't bring much pleasure. Don't they place an intolerable strain on Haraway's call for negative capability under the rubric of irony? Isn't the introduction of them, here, to construct something that is the opposite of responsible argument?

Rather, I would say only this: blasphemy, as it represents just the aporia we have outlined, is—as Haraway has written—serious. And the boundary between the two meanings of construction is, clearly, nowhere near as clear as even a first deconstruction would have had us suppose: it is a truly dangerous one, and must be negotiated with great vigilance.

It is a boundary line.

It is an abyss.

Over it let us place the cyborg.

II

> . . . But complete theories do not fall from Heaven, and you would have had still greater reason to be so distrustful, had anyone offered you at the beginning of his observations a well-rounded theory without any gaps; such a theory could only be the child of his speculation and not the fruit of unprejudiced investigation of the facts.
>
> — Sigmund Freud,
> Clark University, 1910

What renders the cyborg confusing?

In recent popular imagery, the Good Cyborg is, of course, Luke Skywalker, who, at the moment of his Oedipal shock in *The Empire Strikes Back*, when his hand is cut off ("I am your father . . ." Darth Vader tells him, in the midst of the agony), takes a ritual plunge of awesome dimensions (into the mythical abyss we wrote of above?), at the end of which, negotiating the whole effect of everything that came before, he is given a mechanical prosthesis: once the imitation skin is closed over the cam-shafts and circuitry, it remains hidden, unmentioned, invisible for the remainder of the trilogy. It is only suggested, at the climax of the final film, in a moment of ' Oedipal identification, when, after "breaking training" in a paroxysm of rage initiated by the paternal revelation of incest ("She is your sister"), Luke hacks off *his* father's hand, to find Vader is already a cyborg of the same order: only wires and metal protrude from the severed wrist.

(Amidst all this extraordinary narrative closure, isn't there perhaps something missing?)

Do we believe, at the trilogy's end, the astonishing ease with which Luke not only accepts the "incest taboo" but seems to be, if anything, its walking embodiment? (*Is* there something missing . . . ?) For upon learning that Leia is his sister, once his rage at his father is spent and has been replaced by love, he does not just accept the fact that his desire for her cannot be fulfilled: rather, the desire itself seems to vanish—indeed seems never to have existed!

Isn't there *something* left out . . . ?

The quintessentially Evil Cyborg to rage across the country and its giant screens in the year before Haraway's manifesto appeared was Arnold Schwarzenegger, in *The Terminator*—certainly *his* best film. The allegory is a lot more violent, a lot less subtle, than in the *Star Wars* triptych: The Terminator has crossed time (another of those mythical abysses) in a spectacular leap, leaving him vividly naked, to attack, at the root, the seed of all possible future civilization. Here, the mechanical component begins as hidden, secret, implied within Schwarzenegger's abundant flesh. But during the film that flesh is punctured, scarred, ripped or cut away—sometimes brutally and dispassionately by Schwarzenegger himself. (The scene in which he fixes the machinery inside his own forearm is a kind of onanistic replay of the scene already cited in the Lucas film.) At the two-thirds point, what remains of the corporeal is incinerated once and for all by a gasoline explosion, and the mechanical, burned free even of tarnish, rises gleaming and clanking to dominate the film's final third, pursuing the heroine (pregnant with the superman) until she finally crushes him by making him crawl after her between the ominous and claustrophobic plates of a giant metal crusher, managing to throw the switch when she reaches the other side, creating a kind of *vagina dynama*, dangerous for her but—we all know it, and only wait for visual confirmation—fatal for him . . . making her, at least for a moment, something of a cyborg herself. He is flattened, with his bright claw out, already grasping her ankle in what, moments later, we know would have become a mortal grip.

But let's extract the mangled metal from the crusher plates, straighten the crumpled limbs, examine the remains of this gleaming monster.

On exhumation, we can see it is basically a metal skeleton. It is clean and efficient (flesh and blood, if anything, only seemed to hamper it, encumber it, make it heavy and slow); and, as we saw, it was desperately strong. Its torso was a polished barrel, most certainly hiding complexities of circuitry, as doubtless did its skull's tin egg with red lenses. (As with Lucas's C-3PO, its mother was the Maria robot from Lang's *Metropolis*.) But note: its hips are a single bar no thicker than femur or ulna.

Certainly, there, *something* is missing . . .

Such pursuits of beleaguered women in commercial films all have their sexual component, *all* have their punitive—I hesitate to say "sadistic," but there, in the hesitation, it has been said, as though it refuses to remain absent from this rhetorical galaxy—reading. Yet, as we have lavished an extra bit of attention to the physical structure of the cyborg in this film, we must pay a bit of extra attention to the narrative in which he has been so violently thrust. Unmarried, his woman adversary has had sex, and is pregnant as proof. (Everywoman, she bears the name of five others in the film—all previously "terminated" by the cyborg.) Are we mired, then, in that rape fantasy comprising the narrative genre running from *Clarissa* through *Tess of the D'Urbervilles* to *Dressed to Kill* that ordains women who do not have sex must be punished for withholding it; and women who choose to have sex with one man must be punished for not having it with another?

Probably.

There is confusion in the myth here, though, for Sara manages to escape, to triumph, to kill, to bear a son. Well, at Haraway's exhortation, let us take pleasure in it and go on with our work.

Haraway posits the cyborg as a feminist image—or at least an image useful in the pursuit of feminist goals. These two cyborgs, one a secret (and good) cyborg, the other an overt (and evil) cyborg, are both male: neither is mentioned in Haraway's manifesto. But her own attentions compel me to the following observation.

One of them—Luke—is *such* a friend to women (or, rather, to the single woman—Princess Leia—in the foreground story) that most of the audience just doesn't believe it. Indeed, his friendship to women has much the quality of Lucas's own throughout the trilogy: a kind of on-again-off-again lackluster concern with keeping Leia from becoming too much of a wimp, strongest in the first film, a left-over habit in the second, and simply missing from the third—a "feminist sympathy" that never gets as far as what, after all, must be *the* most important step: i.e., allowing Leia to know (or talk to, or be friends with, or consider the situation of) any other woman in the universe.

The other cyborg—the Terminator—is an implacable enemy of

woman (and of life and of everything else), but can, thank some Higher Power (all too easy to name in the Wagner/Bergson/Shaw vitalistic tradition that controls the plot of both *The Terminator* and *Star Wars:* the Life Force), be vanquished by one.

Is the key to the cyborg image provided in the observation by historian Louise White in the symposium *Women in Science Fiction* published in Jeff Smith's fanzine *Khatru* in 1975? Writing of Helva, that most famous cyborg in the precincts of written science fiction, White notes that she is ". . . another woman with her cunt cut out."

Written between 1961 and 1969, and collected together as *The Ship Who Sang* (New York: Ballantine Books, 1970), the McCaffrey series, which we have already tried to read, tells of a little girl who is born hopelessly deformed. But to save her life, most of her deformed body (including her genitals) is surgically removed and the rest is made the central brain in a complex mechanical body, or "shell," with many superhuman qualities—magnifying vision is the first one we see at work in the tales—that finally becomes the basis for a spaceship. Helva's foreground story is her love for her captain, his death, her mourning, her eventual revenge ("The Ship Who Mourned" and "The Ship Who Killed" are, recall, two of the story titles from within the series), and finally her happy repartnering with a new captain.

But, as White has noted, even in this most heterosexually sobrietous tale—as, hopefully, we have seen by now in all our others, however troubling—there is something missing.

III

> . . . But what in fact was this appeal from the subject beyond the void of his speech? It was an appeal to the very principle of truth . . . But first and foremost it was the appeal of the void, in the ambiguous gap of an attempted seduction of the other by the means on which the subject has come compliantly to rely, and to which he will commit the monumental construct of his narcissism.
> — Jacques Lacan,
> *The Function and Field of Speech*
> *and Language in Psychoanalysis*

Let us skip over a great deal at this point. Let us leave a gap. Let us allow whatever is missing to remain . . . missing.

(Let us hope, with the rest of civilization, that the disruptive force of the occlusion does not return to destroy us and/or our argument . . .)

Castration, Freud tells us, is the way the subject is brought to civilization. Says Lacan, castration is what ushers the subject into the Symbolic Order . . . and claims to be saying more or less the same thing.

The phallus is, unlike the penis or the clitoris (Lacan goes on to say), manifested *only* in castration. The phallus is what remains to the Imaginary when the object of desire is veiled, removed, occluded, or snatched violently away from current Symbolically mediated experience. Its Imaginary occultation alone gives it its Symbolic power. And (cutting out a great deal more) we are strongly urged by many Lacanian commentators, many of them women and feminists (from certain rhetorical turns in Haraway's text, we wonder if she wishes to be counted among their number), to take this as the inarguable reason why civilization is, and must no doubt remain, phallocentric.

Yet, as a theory, the castration explanation seems somehow incomplete.

Again something is missing.

That is to say, the lived experiences of women and men all around us are again and again in *excess* of the theory.

Again something returns to trouble.

The acceptance, the internalization, the sublimation of castration anxiety, be we male or female, is what is supposed to fit us into civilization. And yet, if that is the case, it would seem that none of us—male or female—is ever really castrated *enough*. Civilization doesn't seem anywhere near as civilized as we would like it to be. All of us, for better or for worse, can conceive of a better one.

And as for the one we have, we *don't* fit in.

Or, at least, for most of us, the fit can be described as only more or less comfortable.

To look at civilization anywhere around us is to criticize it: this civilization, for better or for worse, is just *not* civilized.

In brief, all the castration theory seems to cut us down to is the acceptance of phallocentric society. It seems to leave out what rankles and roils and complains and, more or less suppressed, carries on hysterically, like the adult "Dora," Ida Brauers, inveighing to Dr. Deutch against the strictures of married life, twenty-four years after cutting off, in 1902, her therapy with Freud.

Perhaps phallocentric civilization *has* to construct image after image of castration—such as the cyborg.

But (and this is what I shall keep on looking for in Haraway, after this account is finished) it will also have to construe them: it will have to fix clearly on the missing parts, respond to them as completely as possible, describe them, and analyze them into their constituents, if it is ever to get beyond the desperately efficient self-replicating system by which our civilization, by which castration, repairs itself in the face of almost any wound to it, almost any attempt to cut it down or up.

For the record, I might as well say it here: I do not believe castration as Freud and Lacan have described it even exists. But I do believe—and I do not know how many times I can write this in a single essay and have it remain coherent—that *something* is missing.

* * *

This is something I desire—violently—be fixed in my own argument. Yet, moments after the reader's eye has passed it, it will be gone, its "existence," around which so much of my desire is organized, remaining only as the flicker of an afterimage, a troubling absence-presence that "is" no longer "there," like the child's spool tossed over the edge of the curtained cradle before it is hauled back on the confused and knotted string connecting memory to reality.

IV

> The relation of the subject to the Other is entirely produced in the process of gap.
>
> — Jacques Lacan,
> *The Field of the Other: Alienation*

The pursuit of the radical metaphor—and the general consensus seems to be that castration (and cyborgs seem to be the figure of castration, the phallus, whether male or female) was once as radical a metaphor as any, though it is not at all one today—is a risky business; and it is arguable (indeed, it is philosophy's classical argument against metaphor) that there is something inherently reductive and, by extension, conservative, in the very metaphoric process.

As we prepare to confront our mythical, or metaphoric, cyborg, here is one model of metaphor it may be helpful to bear in mind:

Object P, with aspects (a, b, c . . . A, B, C . . . α, β, γ . . .), is compared with object Q, with aspects (1, 2, 3 . . . A, B, C. . . . □, ○, △ . . .). The metaphor is logical because aspects (A, B, C . . .) are common to both objects. Logically, the resultant metaphoric system privileges aspects (A, B, C . . .), the aspects common to both objects, and dismisses the combined set of aspects (a, b, c . . . 1, 2, 3 . . . α, β, γ . . . □, ○, △ . . .). Thus the metaphorical logic is reductive, disjunctive, and conservative in its logical privileging power.

But this model, at least at this stage of elaboration, leaves out something very important. (. . . there is something missing.) It does not explain the vividness with which, from time to time, metaphors strike us. It suggests, rather, that the experience of newness, liberation, and daring with which so many metaphors register is, at bottom, simply nostalgia, a pure reassurance, the wholly sedimented and completely safe called up in a flash so bright and brief we do not recognize it for what it is.

I don't think the suggestion corresponds to the lived experience of metaphor.

But to construe and critique our model in such a way that it yields something closer to what I believe to be the truth of metaphor, we must leave the logic of metaphor to read its murkier psychology.

Assume: We are reading.

As we move along through the text, negotiating a fairly familiar and coherent description of a scene or process, we encounter the mention of object P, whose syntagmatic placement (or paradigmatic displacement) announces it as metaphor. Immediately we are distracted from our familiar scene to consider the play of P's aspects, among which, for the moment, we are not entirely sure which will be the logically privileged ones.

With the aspects of P still at play in our mind, we move on through the text, till we encounter mention of another object, Q, which, syntax and expectation tell us, is the metaphor's referent. Now we are momentarily distracted from the play of P's aspects by the aspects of Q. But we must not let that first set go. Attention heightens, to hold the play of aspects about both objects—aspects that, indeed, constitute both objects. (It's important to note here that we have *not* yet perceived the logic of metaphor. We have perceived, rather, only the collective aspects of P and of Q.) From among the conjoined set of aspects of P and Q, the logic of metaphor must now be built up.

We set about pairing up aspects, identifying aspects from the metaphor with aspects from its referent, to create the logical link.

As these pairs (or identities) are located, they are, so to speak, psychologically set aside into that part of the mind reserved for conscious and conscientious systems; but what we are left with in the part of the mind that perceives, that visualizes, that imagines is the heightened image of many of those aspects of both P and Q that are in *excess* of those identities.

In brief, then: because of the heightened attention needed to create the logic of metaphor, it is those aspects in *excess* of the logical ones, highlighted by that attention, that constitute the metaphor's psychological vividness.

If this psychological explanation for the vividness of metaphor (or for those which register as vivid) is correct, then the psychological affect of metaphor is conjunctive, playful, and intensifying—nor does it require a terribly vast metaphoric leap to see such a process as always having something of a radical and disruptive thrust. It is only when metaphors become so overworked and familiar that no heightened attention to the combined play of aspects is needed to locate the identities in the play of similar and dissimilar aspects that they are finally reduced to nothing but their disjunctive, logical sediments.

Every fully functioning metaphor, then, is a cyborg.

A more Bakhtinian notion of metaphor might be that the function of all metaphor is to compare objects in such a way that their identical aspects are formed into a logical system while their nonidentical aspects gain in psychological intensity through the very search process by which the system was created. Thus the logical system and the extralogical play can be at once severed, systematized (into a logically closed side and a psychologically open one), and allowed to dialogize.

"Women and men are cyborgs." A metaphor.

The logic of metaphor seems to be saying here that, for better or worse, women and men can be both unbelievably good and inhumanly terrifying, but are nevertheless castrated (civilized) and vanquishable. Our concept of both must be complex. But something is missing from each.

The psychology of metaphor seems to be saying that women and men and cyborgs all have about them both metal and flesh, nerves and circuitry, parts that we understand, parts that are mysterious, parts that are impossible, parts that are there, and parts that are missing: that both exist in relation to the human and to the technical in diverse and intricate ways; that some of the things they can do are real (i.e., political) and some of the things we would like them to do, or are afraid they might do, are ridiculous, or fascinating, or wonderful, or unbelievable; metal and flesh may be, either one, hidden inside the other, where either may be, surprisingly, supportive or subversive; all subjects are split, but in endless, myriad, angular, and often irreconcilable ways; and . . . well, it says many more things besides. But each of these is in turn a metaphor, with a certain logic, a certain psychology, each of which might be radicalized by work (work is in demand), in a process of unlimited semiosis.

At this point I choose to read Haraway's own irony as applying to the conservative logic of the cyborg metaphor. The logical link is precisely what urges the totality even as the diversity of the elements compared suggests (always wrongly; never enough; something will be missing) the totality will not work. I read the blasphemy as fairly well restricted to that metaphor's psychology. And as long as we clearly and responsibly retain the two (the logic, the psychology, and the highly uneasy, easily confused boundary between), then we can see that they are engaged in a serious and intense argument with one another. Here, the intensities are partial, local. They do not, together, form some mutually safe, supportive, totalized and unitary system. All right, then: I'll go along with this cyborg metaphor and say, "Sure, in its complexity—in its dialogic conflict—it's a very good one!"

But the conclusion I've arrived at (once again) is that metaphors by themselves are, finally, neither radical nor conservative. They gain their ideological slant only as they are read. And any attempt to pose a radical metaphor is only a more or less conscientious call for some hard work at a more or less radical reading.

With any metaphor, we must read it and ourselves closely and minutely in order to reach its radical potential.

It takes both effort and skill. (Possibly more than I possess, so that at best, here, only fragments of the process may be sketched, with much too much left missing.) It often resembles counting the angels on the head of a pin, if not carefully numbering there those we would have as our apostles. At the same time we must remain articulately aware our angels (or our apostles) are by no means original; they arise, rather, each and every one, from historical conditions of production, from freedoms and oppressions that we construct.

And no construction is whole.

V

Note: In *The Language of Psychoanalysis* (Laplanche and Pontalis) the entry on the word "gap," used with some frequency by both Freud and Lacan, appears to be missing.

After this "metaphoric explosion" detonated by a mere wandering of attention, of happenstance in the midst of Haraway's manifesto, we have escaped from none of our fictions—though hopefully all of them are somewhat revalued, recontoured, restructured by it, both those before and those to come.

Let us, then, continue our reading—somewhat less blind to its unitary presumptions, somewhat more open to its polyvocality.

In commenting on her twin lists in the third section of the manifesto, "The Informatics of Domination," as she considers pairs such as "organism/biotic component" and "reproduction/replication," Haraway writes:

> Sexual reproduction is one kind of reproductive strategy among many, with costs and benefits as a function of the system environment. Ideologies of sexual reproduction can no longer reasonably call on the notions of sex and sex role as organic aspects in natural objects like organisms and families. Such reasoning will be unmasked as irrational, and ironically corporate executives reading *Playboy* and anti-porn radical feminists will make strange bedfellows in jointly unmasking the irrationalism. (p. 81)

In an argument that I otherwise agree with, I find Haraway's closing, marginal quip somewhat naive. As with her discussion of MacKinnon, that naivete involves a blindness to the fact that *Playboy* (and the "executives" who read it—though I suspect it is part of the same naivete to confuse the male executives in the advertisements *in* the magazine with the largely white- and blue-collar male readers *of* the magazine) and MacKinnon both push a world view in which fantasy and reality equal one another, an equivocation which alone justifies their respective enterprises—whereas a *distinction* between fantasy and reality is insisted on for its very survival by the commercial pornographic films and videos shown regularly in homes and sex-moviehouses in almost all medium-sized and larger cities in the country to their overwhelmingly male, working-class audience. Sympathetic (or unsympathetic) commentators on hardcore porn may well unmask some irrationalisms in our society and its sexual and/or pornographic organization. The oversimplification of the fantasy/reality relation that MacKinnon and *Playboy* finally share tries to uphold this notion: that softcore *Playboy*, in which women are *always* pictured in static photographs naked and alone, somehow says the same thing as hardcore commercial pornographic films, in which women are *always* pictured in motion, both clothed *and* naked, *always* both with *and* without men, almost always with other women and a large majority of the time *with jobs*. *Playboy*—regardless of what it claims—certainly *wants* to be read as hardcore pornography *precisely* as much as MacKinnon wants to read it that way. But the fact is, it isn't. But such an uncritical fantasy/reality relation doesn't seem a very strong position from which to unmask too much of anything.

Here is also perhaps the place to note that my metaphoric explosion/insertion occurred directly after a somewhat dubious statement on race (and I am, after all, a black commentator, for whom, in this country, metaphors of rape court their own dangers):

"Likewise for race," Haraway writes directly after the paragraph last quoted, "ideologies about human diversity have to be formulated in terms of frequencies of parameters, like blood groups or intelligence scores. It is 'irrational' to invoke concepts like primitive and civilized." (p. 81) Alas, I remain historically dubious about these particular parameters of blood and intelligence, which would seem, centered in their own mythic systems of heredity and psychology, to have been precisely the white scene of the debate at least since Louis Agassiz.

I am not sure what is new, or cyborgic, here.

This is also the moment that precedes Haraway's Spenglerian exhortation, in which "Control strategies applied to women's capacities to give birth to new human beings will be developed in the language of population control and maximization of goal achievements for individual decision-makers. Control strategies will be formulated in terms of rates, costs of constraints, degrees of freedom." (p. 81) Is it so odd, in the face of such an analysis, to wonder how the imposition of such "control strategies . . . developed in the language of population control and maximization of goal achievements" could possibly leave, say, the yes/no "degree of freedom" in the choice of, say, whether to have an abortion or not, to the women in whose bodies the fetuses happen to be growing?

To me, with such control strategies developed in terms of what I know of such language today, it doesn't seem likely.

Though I offer the suggestion with no sense of completing or finishing off Haraway's twin lists, I wonder if "castration" (on the comfortable, hierarchical side) paired with "cyborg" (or, really, any "prosthesis," on the new and scary side) might not have made a darker, more aggressive, but finally more difficult, sensitive and, possibly, self-critical array of concepts to draw from.

But the recovery of Haraway's argument comes fairly quickly, when it talks directly about what, I presume, is behind some of these assertions:

> One important route for reconstructing socialist feminist politics is through theory and practice addressed to the social relations of science and technology, including crucially the system of myth and meanings structuring our imagination. (p. 82)

Throughout Haraway's piece is the feeling the women's movement has been too reliant on notions of "the organic" and "the natural," seen in an essential opposition to the technical and the scientific. The range of feminisms, at least those most popular, Haraway suggests, give small heed to the fact that "the natural" and "the organic" are empowered by, and indeed only exist as powerful conceptual and explanatory categories because of, modern science and technology. As an aid in the recuperation of science and technology for socialist feminism, Haraway writes: "The cyborg is a kind of disassembled and reassembled, postmodern collective and personal self. This is the self feminists must code."

Haraway ends this section with a consideration (which also happens to work as a justification for her project so far) of the problem of such new coding options: "tool and myth," she writes (and by extension instrument and concept, as well as historical anatomies of possible bodies and historical systems of social relations), finally and eventually "constitute each other." In a passing move, as an ironic critique of her own formulation, she suggests that (along with a consideration of the ethical confusion around animal hearts in human babies), "Gay men, Haitian immigrants, and intravenous drug users are the 'privileged' victims of an awful immune-system disease that marks (inscribes on the body) confusion of boundaries and moral pollution.

"But these excursions into communications sciences and biology have been at a rarefied level." (p. 84) This quaint recall of a moment in the AIDS epidemic by this manifesto written when the number of people with AIDS was closer to seven thousand than to the well over eighty thousand who have died from AIDS today, may, four years later, not look so rarefied at all.

Haraway brings the section to a close with a consideration of the transformation by which the *tool* of microelectronics ("the technical basis of simulacra, i.e., copies without originals," a notion courtesy of Baudrillard) controls the conceptual shift from labor and typing into robotics and word processing; of sex into genetic engineering and reproduction technologies; of mind into artificial intelligence and decision procedure. Haraway uses Rachel Grossman's image of "women in the integrated circuit" to name women's place in this intricate technologically and scientifically restructured world—restructured at the level of mutually constituting tool and concept. Her last and modestly hopeful sentence here is:

Some of the rearrangements of race, sex, and class rooted in high-tech-facilitated social relations can make socialist feminism more relevant to effective progressive politics. (p. 85)

I suspect she is right, though I'm not sure how it's going to happen. The next section is entitled "The Homework Economy."

A new work force has been created. As a quick example, Haraway cites the women in Silicon Valley, whose work is structured around employment in electronics-dependent jobs: ". . . their intimate realities include serial heterosexual monogamy, negotiating child care, distance from extended kin or most other forms of traditional community, a high likelihood of loneliness and extreme economic vulnerability as they age." (p. 85) More to the point, Haraway explains, this new class is made up of people—mostly women but not all—whose jobs have been feminized: "To be feminized means to be made extremely vulnerable; able to be disassembled, reassembled, exploited as a reserve labor force; seen less as workers than as servers; subjected to time arrangements both on and off the paid job that make a mockery of a limited work day; leading an existence that always borders on being obscene, out of place, and reducible to sex." (p. 86) This is what Richard Gordon has called "the homework economy," wherever it takes place. Haraway goes on: "The homework economy as a world capitalist organizational structure is made possible (not caused by) the new technologies." (p. 96) We are asked to consider this situation specifically for women in terms of "the loss of the family (male) wage," "the collapse of the welfare state," "[t]he feminization of poverty," the new "integration with the overall capitalist and progressively war-based economy," and the problem (particularly in third world countries) of "access to land."

Fredric Jameson, Haraway reminds us, has suggested that, in terms of esthetics, realism goes along with commercial/early industrial capitalism and nationalism; modernism goes along with monopoly capitalism and imperialism; and post-modernism goes along with multinational capitalism and multinationalism. Haraway suggests that added to this tripartite alignment we should further align (1) the patriarchal nuclear family with the first, commercial/early industrial stage; (2) the modern family "mediated (or enforced) by the welfare state and institutions like the family wage," with a flowering of a-feminist heterosexual ideologies, include their radical versions represented in "Greenwich Village around World War I," with the second, monopoly capital stage; and (3) "the 'family' of the homework economy with its oxymoronic structure of women-headed households and its explosion of feminisms and the paradoxical intensification and erosion of gender itself" (p. 87) with the third, multinational stage.

The problem of the growing feminization of work is one Haraway sees for both developed and underdeveloped countries; she suggests that the general situation that black women have known for a century or more, vis-à-vis the *un*employment of black men, now will spread to become the general model for both men and women in the West—if not the world.

My only problem here is an historical one: the similarity of the problems of the current underclass and the problems of women is not a new analysis. It extends back before the American Civil War with the alliance of women's rightists and abolitionists—and arguably started that war.

The new thing that Haraway *is* suggesting here, which almost gets lost in the synoptic breadth of her rhetoric, is that the new technologies may be creating a new, vast underclass—and what's more, ten or fifteen years from now, many people who today would seem to have perfectly reasonable expectations of middle-class security may well (as our monumental national deficit snowballs closer and closer to home) find themselves right in the midst of that underclass with no way to break free.

Haraway glances at the relation of the feminization problem both to food production ("women produce about fifty percent of the world's subsistence food") and to leisure time activities ("the culture of video games is heavily oriented to individual competition and extraterrestrial warfare . . . More than our imaginations is miniaturized"). She cites the reification of "traditional" male/female traits performed by sociobiology, and notes that, even after the success of feminist "icons" such as the speculum (and presumably books such as *Our Bodies, Ourselves*), "Self help is not enough." The danger Haraway sees coming is "a strongly bimodal social structure, with the masses of women and men of all ethnic groups, but especially people of color, confined to a homework economy, illiteracy of several varieties," (along with the three Rs, she no doubt means "computer illiteracy" as an important one) "and general redundancy and impotence, controlled by high-tech repressive apparatuses ranging from entertainment to surveillance and disappearance." (Read: "government liquidations," as in various South American regimes.) "An adequate socialist-feminist politics," she concludes this section of her analysis, "should address women in the privileged occupational categories, and particularly in the production of science and technology that constructs scientific-technical discourses, procedures, and objects." (p. 89)

The section ends with a cascade of exhortatory questions as to how various people, from various "new groups doing science" to the "high-tech cowboys" of Silicon Valley, can help.

"Women in the Integrated Circuit" is Haraway's brief, penultimate section. In an attempt to summarize "women's historical locations in advanced industrial societies," Haraway eschews any schema appealing to notions of public and private life. "The only way to characterize the informatics of domination," Haraway finds, "is as a massive intensification of insecurity and cultural impoverishment, with common failure of subsistence networks for the most vulnerable." (p. 90)

She mentions hopefully "SEIU's District 925." Unless you know what it is, however (and I don't), the reference is opaque.

For all the work she cites being done, the hope looks rather slim.

The penultimate paragraph in this penultimate section is, however, both the most personal and the most hopeful:

> I am conscious of the odd perspective provided by my historical position—a Ph.D. in biology for an Irish Catholic girl was made possible by Sputnik's impact on U.S. national science education policy. I have a body and mind as much constructed by the post–World War II arms race and cold war as by the women's movements. There are more grounds for hope by focusing on the contradictory effects of politics designed to produce loyal American technocrats, which as well produced large numbers of dissidents, rather than by focusing on the present defeats. (p. 91)

Here is Haraway's "utopian moment," if you like. And it is deeply suggestive about much of what she has been doing in this essay: she cites forces in the "organic/technological" oppositional battery that are assumed to produce evils (e.g., "loyal American technocrats") and shows how, instead and to everyone's surprise, they produce good (e.g., a radical feminist scholar). I can remember one of the first times I encountered this particular rhetorical strategy and how impressed with it I was: in that case, it was an explanation of the uprisings in Vietnam that led to the war—astonishingly, the technophile explicator explained, the major cause for the rebellion was the importation of Western television into Southeast Asia. Knowing that the country was a political powder keg, Western capitalists introduced TV (so ran his tale) to calm the populace and distract them. Nothing even vaguely controversial was ever shown. The entire broadcast fare was American soap operas—bland enough, it was assumed, to lull anyone into general boob-tubery. What capitalism had not counted on, however, was the backgrounds and sets to these mindless domestic sagas, filled with home appliances, flocked wallpaper, fine china, and cut crystal. Tiny villages, their entire populations sitting about before the one or two TVs in the town, had their noses rubbed in the Western way of life for a couple of hours each morning at McLuhanesque intensities—and lo and behold there was an uprising and, a little later, a full-scale war.

But there is something missing from this picture, however technologically informed it is. And that is reading, aggression, critique—interpretive *work*, if you will.

Someone had to turn off the television and think hard about what she'd just seen—and had to talk, if not write, about it.

As much of a materialist as I am, I find the assumption that critique can be taken as a given, that it simply and uncritically falls out of the technology, a suspect if not an outright dangerous notion, a notion in which something crucial and distorting is always left out. Modesty perhaps prompts Haraway to leave it out of her *own* account. Nevertheless and once again: metaphors are *not* radical in themselves, whether they are delivered by TV soap operas, science education programs, science

fiction tales, or socialist feminist manifestos. Critique—critical work—
is created and constituted by people, by individuals, by individuals
speaking and writing to others, by people who are always in specific situations that are tensional as well as technological.

But—and this is Haraway's point in her concluding paragraph to
this section—we do not need a totality, a total unity, a monovocalic
feminism (or, presumably, a monolithic socialism) in *order* to work, to
get at least some of the necessary work done: "We do not need a totality in order to work well. The feminist dream of a common language,
like all dreams for a perfectly true language, of perfectly faithful naming of experience, is a totalizing and imperialistic one. In that sense,
dialectics too is a dream language, longing to resolve contradictions.
Perhaps, ironically, we can learn from our fusions with animals and
machines how not to be Man, the embodiment of Western logos."

The last and longest section of Haraway's manifesto (before the Acknowledgments and References) is "Cyborgs: A Myth of Political Identity"—a "myth about identity and boundaries." Here Haraway surveys a
range of marginal texts, science fiction and poetry. She notes that three
radical feminist poets and writers, Susan Griffin, Audre Lorde (who is
black), and Adrienne Rich, "insist on the organic, opposing it to the
technological." But she is ready to justify this in light of a general world
view in which capitalism is seen, in world terms, as controlling the general mode of production—while socialism is reread to encompass anything at all that is oppositional to the general mode. (Thus Griffin's,
Lorde's, and Rich's antitechnology stances might be seen as part of a
general oppositional activity.) There is something terribly seductive
about this position—and yet there is also much about it of the exhausted collapse into a kind of intellectual pathway of least resistance.

Why, I've wondered for a good dozen years now, shouldn't socialism
be the world mode with, now and again, moments of capitalism arising
(or even being encouraged) temporarily to combat local socialist
breakdowns?

At any rate, in Haraway's reading of science fiction writers, I feel
more conviction. In her survey Haraway shows a (at least to me) comforting sensitivity to the importance of writing in marginal literatures
and paraliteratures. She explains:

Cyborg writing must not be about the Fall, the imagination of a once-upon-a-
time wholeness before language, before writing, before Man. Cyborg writing
is about the power to survive, not on the basis of original innocence, but on
the basis of seizing the tools to mark the world that marked them as
other. . . . Writing is preeminently the technology of cyborgs [she continues
a page later], etched surfaces of the late twentieth century. Cyborg politics is

the struggle for language and the struggle against perfect communication, against the one code that translates all meaning perfectly, the central dogma of phallogocentrism. That is why cyborg politics insist on noise and advocate pollution, rejoicing in the illegitimate fusions of animals and machines. These are the couplings which make Man and Woman so problematic, subverting the structure of desire, the force imagined to generate language and gender, and so subverting the structure and modes of reproduction of "Western" identity, of nature and culture, of mirror and eye, slave and master, body and mind. . . . [And, still further on, she declares gloriously:] cyborgs are the people who refuse to disappear on cue, no matter how many times a "Western" commentator remarks on the sad passing of another primitive, another organic group done in by "Western" technology, by writing. (pp. 93–96)

It is shortly after this that we encounter Haraway's reading of Helva's story with which we began:

Anne McCaffrey's *The Ship Who Sang* explored the consciousness of a cyborg, hybrid of girl's brain and complex machinery, formed after the birth of a severely handicapped child. Gender, sexuality, embodiment, still: all were reconstituted in the story. Why should our bodies end at the skin, or include at best other beings encapsulated by skin? From the seventeenth century till now, machines could be animated—given ghostly souls to make them speak or move or to account for their orderly development and mental capacities. Or organisms could be mechanized—reduced to body understood as resource of mind. These machine/organism relationships are obsolete, unnecessary. For us, in imagination and in other practice, machines can be prosthetic devices, intimate components, friendly selves. (p. 97)

This becomes the entrance point in her consideration of a range of other science fiction texts, most importantly Joanna Russ's *The Adventures of Alyx* and *The Female Man*, most generously a work of my own, followed by discussions of Octavia Butler's *Wild Seed* and Vonda McIntyre's *Superluminal* and its rich world of "protean transformation and connection."

The conclusion of her conclusion is a meditation on monsters. "There are several consequences to taking seriously the imagery of cyborgs as other than our enemies," (p. 99) Haraway writes. True. But I hope in the central work of this consideration I've suggested some of the things we may remain blind to in their friendship if we do *not* consider what may be missing from them as enemies. In the midst of this monstrous meditation, there is an oddly satisfactory challenge to the notion of the everyday—of "dailiness"—as women's traditional preserve. And it is here that Haraway manifests—I almost want to say, at last—the bipolar meaning of "construct" I read into her text so long ago, to recomplicate that reading (if we choose to work at it) even further: "There is no drive in cyborgs to produce total theory, but there is an intimate experience of boundaries, their construction *and* deconstruction" (p. 100, italics mine: my gift to Haraway, her gift to me). Cyborgs, she goes on to say, are not about rebirth, with its originary, Edenic presuppositions, but about regeneration—with its ever-present possibility of partiality, deformation, monstrosity.

> Cyborg imagery can help express two crucial arguments in this essay: (1) the production of universal, totalizing theory is a major mistake that misses most of reality, probably always, but certainly now; (2) taking responsibility for the social relations of science and technology means refusing an anti-science metaphysics, a demonology of technology, and so means embracing the skillful task of reconstructing the boundaries of daily life, in partial connection with others, in communication with all our parts. (p. 100)

Yes—*if* we're willing to work at reading, to read at work. But cyborg imagery will not *do* the work, will not promote the necessary analytic vigilance, *for* us. And it is work that Haraway appeals to in her final cadences: "This is a dream not of a common language, but of a powerful infidel heteroglossia . . . It means both building and destroying machines, identities, categories, relationships, spaces, stories." (p. 101) In this power, in this building, in this destroying, is there pleasure? Haraway's last sentence: "Though both are bound in a spiral dance, I would rather be a cyborg than a goddess." (p. 101)
Doesn't a preference sign, at *some* level, pleasure?

Here something is missing.

*As I conclude this minimal bit of work—of interpretive vigilance, of hermeneutic violence, of pleasure, of aggression—my eye lifts from the text and again strays, glances about, snags a moment at a horizon, a boundary that does not so much contain a self, an identity, a unity, a center and origin which gazes out and de-*fines *that horizon as the horizon is defined* by *it; rather that horizon suggests a plurality of possible positions within it, positions which allow a number of events to transpire, move near, pass through, impinge on each other, take off from one another, some of which events are that an eye looks, a voice speaks, a hand writes. When I try to articulate the positions from which I write, as a male, as a black male, as a gay black male, as a gay black male whose work is the writing of para-literary fictions, of which this, as you read it, may be one—it seems only reasonable someone else might protest: "Who* else *would cite, would mark, would take on and torture so this particular text?"*
The question, then, is: How has Haraway's text survived my violence?

(I call that violence 'aggressive,' but is it oppositional? Blind, yes. Ignorant, probably. But how is that aggression positioned?)

In this consideration I have cut her text up, cut bits of it out, compressed, paraphrased, brought together dispersed bits, constrained and contorted her argument . . . to what ends?

Clearly, there is no survival here unless the reader turn to Haraway's manifesto, to do her or his own work, which alone can restructure mine.

From a position, with its rigors as well as its accidentals, I read. I write. I work.

From another position, it would seem that something is missing . . .

Thus I pass a text — a simulation of an interpretation — from one position to another, from this borrowed position it would be so inadequate to call mine (alone) to one that it is too suspicious to call yours (alone), as it was passed on to me, as it will pass on from you.

Perhaps this is only a simulation of a passage.

By reading, do we halt it?

By reading, do we move it along? Do we move along it?

But, now, we'd best let Helva have back her screw and get on with her work.
Pace, *and good luck, Ms. Haraway, with yours.*

— New York/Amherst
1985–1988

Aversion/Perversion/Diversion

After an introduction by George Cunningham, this talk was delivered at Scott Hall, Rutgers University, 8:00 p.m., Friday night, on November 1, 1991, at the Fifth Annual Lesbian and Gay Conference on Gay Studies.

Aversion, perversion, diversion—the topics of my talk—present us at the outset with their intensely overlapping euphony, their entwined etymologies—sharing much with the Latin *"proversus,"* source of "prose," "verse," "verb," and "proverb." Certainly they start with the suggestion of three very inter-confused topics. Nor is that confusion allayed by my further explaining that my talk tonight will be about neither "inversion" nor "reversion"—that is, it will not be about "homosexuality," female or male, considered as some notion either of the masculine or of the feminine inverted, negated, turned inside out or upside down to produce the "lesbian" or the "gay male," a production presumably recoupable by the simplest uncritical reversion to its former state—no matter how violent the effort needed, a violence too often justified by the very simplicity of the move.

But whatever confusions I bring you this evening, I shall assume that basically you have asked me here as a storyteller. So let me say that, true to my triplet topics—aversion, perversion, and diversion—the tales I shall tell are tales that trouble me. Something about them makes me want either to turn away from them, or to turn their telling away from the pattern the tale made when it was presented to me.

There is, of course, a tale I would very much like to tell. The protagonist of that story is without sex. He or she is wholly constituted by gender—female, male, gay male, lesbian. What's more, our protagonist is unaware of any contradictions in the constitutive process, so that his or her blissfully smooth, seamless self may be called "natural," "unalienated," "happy"—or what-you-will.

Our hero—for certainly she must be a hero—never does anything that is ego-distonic, that does not please her. All her actions—purposeful, habitual, gratuitous—are ego-tonic. They *feel* good.

The only unpleasant things that befall her inevitably originate outside the self. Whether she is defeated by them or triumphant over them, their external origin is a knowledge she is secure in. I hope we can all recognize in the basic situation here the story of that most glorious political comedy that we have yet been able to erect in the name of liberation.

I adore it as much as anyone.

But it worries me; for while it can make me thrill, rejoice, and wildly applaud, it never makes me weep—other than in joy . . . and from what I know of the world, that is something to worry about. That is *why* I'm worried.

There was a movie theater in New York once, called the Cameo, whose screen provender was heterosexual commercial porn, whose clientele was overwhelmingly male, and whose management encouraged a high level of homosexual activities in its corridors, stairwells, side seats, and—to a lesser extent—its bathrooms; and, in its upper balcony, a somewhat lower level of drug commerce and use.

Of the many hundreds of men with whom I had sex there over more than a decade, from a dozen or so regulars with whom I had a settled and comfortable routine to a cavalcade of one-, two-, or three-time-encounters, a number stand out. One such was a young man, white, with dark hair, of about twenty-five, who usually wore a suit jacket—in a population largely black and Hispanic and usually in jeans and sport shirts. Sitting on the right-hand side of the theater, a seat apart, we had exchanged some five or ten minutes of furtive eye contact, when he motioned me to sit beside him.

As we began to touch each other, he leaned toward me to whisper, in a light, working-class accent associated with the outlying boroughs of the city, "You know, I've never done anything like this before. All the other sex I've ever had has been with women. But somebody told me about this place. So I just thought . . ." He shrugged. And we continued, easily enough considering his virgin status, to some satisfaction for us both.

Three months later, visiting the theater once more, after a stroll down one aisle and up the other, I noticed the same young man, again sitting off on the side. Recalling our last encounter, I slid in immediately to sit a seat away from him, smiled, and said softly, "Hi!" This time, he motioned me to the next seat right away, grinning and saying hello. As we began to touch each other, again he bent forward to explain: "You know, I've never done this before—with a man, I mean. I've had sex with women, sure. But this is my first time doing it with a guy . . ."

I thought better of contradicting him. We went on as before—with the same results.

Some months later, when I met him there again, he actually began talking to me by saying, "Hello! Good to see you. How've you been?" quite ready to acknowledge that we knew each other. But when, in a moment, we started to touch, again he whispered: "You know, this is the first time I've ever done this—with a man, I mean . . ."

What troubles me in the memory of these encounters is, of course, how much of myself I can see in this fellow. His litany, like some glorious stutter, recalls Freud's dictum: repetition is desire.

But I have no way, at this date, to ascertain whether he experienced that desire as sexual predilection or as social fear. Was his endlessly renewed homosexual virginity (with its corresponding claim of heterosexual experience) part of the person he felt he must be to be sexually attractive? Or was that portable closet, that he was perpetually just stepping out of, merely some silly and encumbering excuse that could have been dispensed with by the proper enlightenment—the simple revelation that, other than himself, no one at the Cameo he was likely to run into really cared.

The fact that the latter represents, however, a certain level of common sense is what suggests that the fantasy itself might be part of the sexual order of his desire. But the social marginality of the situation, and the extreme behavioral range in that margin—for the breadth of human experience generally remaining outside one sub-language or another is far greater than what, from time to time, over-spills into the centers of articulation—militates for a social interpretation.

What was he averring socially?

What was he averring sexually?

And certainly it does not take much to see the two as diverging dramatically.

But it was precisely my lack of concern with these questions, plus a general sympathy for the eccentric (and he *was* good looking), that let me move with him through the labyrinths of mutual desire without questioning such contradictions.

The first time I taught for a full term at an American university, I had my thirty-second birthday while there as a Visiting Professor. As sometimes happens when a writer comes to a new school, a handful of the brighter students attached themselves to me, and soon I felt that some of those students had even become my friends. Among them was a brilliant young Hispanic woman, who, for the sake of the telling, I'll call Carla, and who, while I knew her, had her nineteenth birthday.

Full-figured, with black hair and astonishing gray-green eyes, Carla turned a questioning energy on everything about her. She was an attractive personality for anyone who enjoyed the pleasures of thinking for its own sake.

That term I came out to my students as soon as it flowed from the material we were dealing with. If it did not put them at ease, it made me feel more comfortable. But I was clear about announcing the fact that I was gay within the first two weeks of classes.

The isolation of a visiting professor moving onto a new campus—and, in my case, it was also my return to the U.S. after two years in England— can be extreme. The few people, including Carla, who helped alleviate it, I was grateful to. One day, however, when she was walking with me across the campus, she confessed, somewhat jokingly, that she was sexually interested in me and would have pursued it with some passion had I been straight. "I'm just a slave to my body," was her comment; it has remained with me for years from that afternoon. I know the feeling. But I reiterated that I wasn't straight; still I hoped we could stay friends. A notable current of my adult social education—and I feel it's very near the core of what I sometimes characterize as what it means to be a "responsible gay male"—is not to be irrationally terrified either by female anger or by female desire. I enjoyed Carla's friendship and hoped she could still enjoy mine, even if she had to suppress an overt sexual component—a relationship I have had, and have enjoyed, with many men. I decided to make no effort to distance myself from her, but give her the opportunity to reconceive the friendship in non-sexual terms—an opportunity a good number of men, both straight and gay, have given me.

Classes ended, and, about a week before I was to return to New York, Carla, an older male student (a carpenter we'll call Fred, an aspiring poet in his late twenties, whom, I confess, I was attracted to; but Fred had made it as clear to me as I had made it clear to Carla that he did not want to pursue a sexual relationship, even though, in his own words, the possibility flattered him), and another woman student who was Carla's close friend, invited me out with them for an evening. The specific suggestion came from Carla. She explained I was to be their guest for the night, and that dinner and dancing afterward were their way of showing their gratitude for my term's teaching.

A very pleasant night it started off. Somehow, however, I ended up with several more drinks than I wanted—twice when I came back to the table from a trip to the john, my half-finished drink had been replaced by a full one; and at least three other times a round I didn't really want at all was bought over my protests.

But we were dancing, having a good time—and there was much talk of "drinking up."

In Fred's van, we returned from that very loud Buffalo dance bar which, in 1975, claimed to be the original home of the Buffalo chicken wing; and when we reached the double tier of motel rooms in which the university had housed me that term, Carla announced she would give me some help upstairs to my room—I only realized, perhaps, I needed some when I was halfway there.

In my room, she pushed me backward onto the bed, grabbed my arm to keep me from falling onto the floor, and proceeded to pull off first my clothes, then hers.

She climbed on top of me.

Then, at her insistence, we made love. I had the presence to ask if she was using any birth control. She answered: "What do you think I am? Crazy?" The only other interruption was, once, when I pulled away to race into the bathroom to be messily ill in the toilet. Solicitously, she brought me back to bed. The next morning, it was a while before anyone felt like moving. And, in the haze of my hangover, I recall her rising to dress and leave.

Some time later that day, she returned. I answered the door. She entered, and immediately began to undress.

"Wait a minute," I said. "Let's talk."

And so, for a while, we did.

It seems, she confessed, her plan from the beginning had been to take me out for the evening, get me drunk, bring me home and, in her words, "Fuck your brains out."

"Yeah," said Fred on the phone a little later. "But I told her she probably wouldn't succeed. I don't think you can really *do* that kind of thing to a guy, can you . . . ?"

I pointed out to Carla that, one, this just was not what I wanted our relationship to be. Two, if I had done the same thing to her—or to any of her undergraduate friends—she would have been justifiably furious. "Didn't you just tell me, about a week ago, about some male professor here who tried something rather like this on a young woman that you knew? As I recall, you were pretty pissed off at him."

"Yes," she said. "But it worked when he did it, too."

"Carla," I said. "If we're going to be any sort of friends, you're going to stop this—*we're* going to stop this."

"Yes," she said. "I guess we are."

And she left.

And left me wondering if, indeed, we *could* be friends anymore.

I hope you find this story, so far—for it is not over—troubling in all its resonances. I certainly did.

My term was up at the university. Three years later, when I was living in New York with my then-lover, I received a call from Carla. She was now in her second year of law school, there in the city. I said, quite sincerely, that it would be nice to see her again.

I mentioned that I had been living with a lover for more than a year.

She sounded very pleased. And about a week later, she came by. Her dark hair was cut very short and she wore very tight white jeans. "I want you to know," she told me, as we sat and talked in my study, "that I took your advice."

"Advice?" I asked. "What advice?"

"I'm a lesbian now."

"This," I asked, "was advice *I* gave you? I can't imagine my advising anyone to 'become' a lesbian—or a gay man. Although I hear it happens, I wasn't particularly aware that it was any more common than becoming straight."

"Well," she said, "what I meant is that I followed your example."

"What example?" I asked, totally lost.

"You were married for thirteen years or so, weren't you, before you became gay?"

"Ah!" I said. "No, I've been pretty aware that I was gay since I was eleven or twelve—though, yes, I did get married. But now, at least, I have some idea what you're talking about. But 'advising' someone to become gay—that's like advising someone they'd be better off black than white. Sure, in anger, you could suggest someone might learn something if they experienced some oppression. But no one who's part of an oppressed group, who's really thought about the nature of that oppression, is going to *advise* someone else to join in."

Now it was her turn to say, "Ah." She went on: "Well, it's true; you never said it in so many words. But I thought that's what you were doing. Anyway, whether you gave it to me or not, it's been the best advice I've ever taken!"

"I'm very glad it was," I said. "But, next time you think I'm giving you advice, *do* ask me to tell you directly what it is. I'll feel better about it, even if you don't."

Two years later, Carla passed her bar exams. And, on another visit in which she came by to tell me both of her new job working as a civil rights lawyer and of her new and most satisfying relationship with another young woman, she said: "You must have been very angry at me, back at school. I have a very different take on all that now—we handle sexual harassment cases. That must have been quite dreadful for you."

"For whatever it's worth," I told her, "I wasn't angry. I don't know whether it has anything to do with it or not: but at least once in my life I've been held down by two men and raped. It was a lot less pleasant than what you did."

"Well," she said, "I'm glad you still let us be friends. I've gotten a lot from it."

"I'm glad too," I said. "So have I."

I have no way to be sure, of course, what that experience meant to Carla—or, indeed, how often it returned to her. Here we are speaking, and I feel it's important for me to say it clearly, of a situation where laws were violated, where the kinds of moral and ethical concerns Carla herself was now working with in her job were, on both sides, mine and hers, called sharply into question.

Were I asked what tales *were* characteristic of my young manhood as a gay male, what comes to mind are those nights circumstance put me beside some other man, peacefully asleep, whom I knew I could *not* touch—and so lay sleepless the night in a paroxysm of desire. But all the tales I have told and shall be telling tonight I've chosen precisely because they are *un*characteristic.

So, another tale—in this case of a muscular Puerto Rican, with curly black hair, whose workshirt bore a name we'll say was "Mike" in yellow stitching across the gray pocket. He wore a green jacket with a green and yellow knitted collar—to the same theater where I met the first young man I spoke of. Across the back, yellow letters spelled out "Aviation Trades High School," from which, I presume, he must have graduated sometime over the three-and-a-half years I knew him.

Mike was as regular a visitor to the theater as I was. He was handsome, in a bear-like way. From a couple of quiet approaches, however, I'd gathered he was not interested in me. From time to time, I would see him sitting in various seats in the balcony or orchestra. Nearly as frequently, as I walked up or down between the lobby and the balcony, I would pass him, sitting on the stairs toward the top, sometimes leaning forward, forearms across his knees, sometimes leaning back, elbows on the step two above and behind.

Once, after I'd stopped paying much attention to Mike, I was sitting a few seats away from another black man, in green work clothes and dilapidated basketball sneakers. Knees wide against the back of the seat in front of him, he was slouched low in his chair, watching the film.

Mike, I noticed, was slouched equally low in the row ahead, one seat to the right.

Then something moved near the floor.

I glanced down—to see a hand. Under the seat and behind the metal foot of the ancient theater chair, it looked rather disembodied. But the fingertips now and again brushed the rubber rims and black cloth uppers of the man's right sneaker. Glancing at the top of Mike's head, then down at the man's foot—the man seemed oblivious to what was happening—I realized Mike had reached down between the seats and was playing with the man's shoe.

"Ah . . . !" I thought, in all the self-presumed sophistication of my own sexual experience. "So *that* explains it!" And, four or five times over the next few months, I noticed Mike, now in the balcony, now in the orchestra, at the same practice with different men.

This was back in the years when today's ubiquitous running shoe was just emerging as *the* casual fashion choice. As is more usual than not, I was at least a year behind most other people; and it was only that week that I broke down and got my first pair—in which, I confess, I never ran in my life.

They were a conservative gray.

One day I stopped at the Cameo and, on my way to the balcony, passed Mike sitting on the steps. Several people stood near the top, watching the movie; I stopped behind them, largely to watch them.

Minutes later, I happened to glance down. Mike's hand was on the step, the edge of his palm against my shoe sole. I was surprised, because till then I had considered myself outside his interests. My first and most innocent thought was that his hand's straying to that position had been an accident, even while more worldly experience said no. Precisely because of what I knew of him already, while it might have been an accident with someone else, *his* hand's resting there could *only* have been on purpose—though his attention all seemed to be down the stairs.

I tried to appear as though I was not paying any attention to him. He continued to appear as though he was not paying any attention to me. I moved my foot—accidentally—a quarter of an inch from his hand. His hand, a half minute later, was again against my shoe. Again—accidentally—I moved my foot a quarter of an inch closer, to press against his fingers—and two of his fingers, then three—accidentally—slid to the top of my foot.

In ten minutes, Mike had turned to hold my foot with both his hands, pressing it to his face, his mouth, leaning his cheek down to rub against it.

To make the point I'm coming to in all this, I must be clear that I found his attention sexually gratifying enough so that I continued to rub his hand, his face, his chest, his groin with my shoe until, at last, genitals loose from his gray work pants, he came—and, over the next three weeks, when we had some four more of these encounters, I came as well during one of them.

We do not even have a term for the perversion complementary to fetishism. The myth of the sexual fetish is precisely that it is solitary. Its assumed pathology is the fact it is thought to be non-reciprocal. A major symptom of the general insensitivity of our extant sexual vocabulary is that as soon as fetishism is presumed to move into the realm of reciprocity, the vocabulary and analytical schema of sadomasochism takes it over; and to me this seems wholly to contravene common sense and my own experience.

Mike and I became rather friendlier now—when we were not directly engaged in sexually encountering one another. If we met outside the theater on the street, we said hello and nodded. If we passed in the theater stairwell, we might exchange brief small talk. There were no words at all, however, about what we were doing. It was clear to me that Mike did not want to flaunt his practices before the other patrons, with some of whom he was rather more friendly than he was with me. Among the theater's younger clientele were a number of hustling drag queens and pre-ops: their teasing and joking could be intense. And these were the people who, in the theater, were Mike's conversational friends.

Running shoes, at least the brand I'd bought at that time, do not last as long as they should. Soon it was time to replace them.

I thought of Mike.

By now, though, I'd glimpsed him several times get as involved with other men's running shoes or sneakers as he could from time to time with mine. I felt nothing but empathy and goodwill toward him. But clearly some excited him more than others. The specifics of his preference, however, I hadn't been able to piece together. How, I wondered, do I ask about such a thing? How do I put such a question into language?

Not much later, when I was getting up from my seat in a legitimate 42nd Street movie house where I'd gone to see some genre horror film, I saw Mike—also leaving. We smiled across the crowd and nodded to each other. I decided the best thing to do was to be as open and aboveboard about my curiosity as possible.

"You know," I said, as we joined each other, walking toward the lobby, "I've got to get a new pair of sneakers, one of these days soon. What kind do you think I should get?"

He seemed not to have heard me. So I persisted: "Is there any kind you like particularly—some kind you think are the best?"

Mike stopped, just inside the lobby door. He turned to me, a look blooming on his face that, in memory, seemed a combination of an astonishment and gratitude near terror. He leaned forward, took my arm, and whispered with an intensity that made me step back: "Blue . . . ! Please . . . *Blue!*" Then he rushed away into the street.

I'd expected an answer at the same level of fervor I'd offered my question. But, I confess, that afternoon, with an anxiety that, somehow, did

not seem all my own but borrowed, at Modell's Sporting Goods I purchased a pair of blue Adidas.

Two days later, when I wore them to the theater, however, Mike was
not there.

Nor did I see him on any of my next dozen visits.

After a few months, I realized he had dropped the place from among
his regular cruising sites. Three times over the next year I glimpsed Mike
in his green jacket with the yellow letters, now on a far corner under the
marquis at the Port Authority bus terminal, now by the subway kiosk at
72nd Street, now with his hands in his pockets, hurrying down 45th
Street toward Ninth Avenue. But I never saw him in the theater again.
I've wondered if our encounter in the second movie had something to
do with his abandonment of the first: I can only hope that, among his
friends, he might be telling *his* version of this tale—possibly somewhere
this evening—for whatever didactic purposes of his own.

A few years ago, however, when I first wrote about Mike to a straight
male friend of mine—a Pennsylvania academic—he wrote me back: "If
you can explain the fascination with licking sneakers so that I can understand it, you can probably explain anything to anybody!"

My first thought was to take up his challenge; but, as I considered it, I
realized all I could explain, of course, was *my* side of the relationship. I'd
found Mike desirable—well before I had known of his predilections. Using
some formulation by Lacan—"One desires the desire of the other"—it
seems easy enough to understand that, if Mike's desire detoured through
a particular focus on my sneakers, it was still *his* desire, and therefore exciting—perhaps not quite as much, for me, as it would have been if it had
focused on my hands, my mouth, over all my body, on some aspect of my
mind, or on my genitals; but it was exciting nevertheless.

As I thought about it, it occurred to me that, in similar environ-
ments, I'd actually observed many hours of fetishistic behavior by any
number of men over the years, though most of those had involved
work shoes or engineers' boots in specifically S&M contexts—so, therefore, I knew something quite real about that behavior. But, at the same
time, I'd spent perhaps less than a single hour talking about that behavior with any or all of the men involved—including Mike.

That meant there was a great deal I *didn't* know.

What could I explain?

What could I not explain?

Even though I'd responded sexually to Mike, I could no more speak
for him than I could speak sexually for any of the very few women (eight,
by my count) I had gone to bed with—or, indeed, for any of the many
thousands of men.

The Freudian dimorphism in the psychoanalytic discussion of fetishism is one of the empirical disaster areas in the generally brilliant superstructure of Freudian insights: men can be fetishists but women are kleptomaniacs. And within the last two years I have heard at least one psychoanalytic critic state all but categorically that no one has ever found a female fetishist.

Those of you who have read my autobiography of a few years ago (*The Motion of Light in Water* [1988], New York: A Richard Kasak Book, 1993) may remember that my own fetish is men's hands—especially the hands of men who bite their nails. Nor do I have any problem analyzing my particular perversion *as* a fetish. This critic's pronouncement put me in mind of a gathering of artists and artisans some fifteen years ago in Greenwich Village, that included a lean, good-natured redhead, who was both a carpenter and a leather craftsman and whose hands were large, work-soiled, and (to me) sexy—and his petite, blonde wife. In the course of an afternoon, where the group was jesting with one another loudly about sex, I heard the redhead's wife declare, "Someday Todd's going to wash his hands, get them completely clean—at which point I'll probably leave him forever!"

To say my ears perked up is to use a wholly inadequate metaphor for my response. At the time, I was still trying to understand my own sexuality in these matters; minutes later I'd contrived to question the young woman as to exactly what she meant. And, while the others joked on at the other side of the table, we spoke in some detail about her own attraction for men's hands soiled from work, and how this attraction had been—and currently was—constituted into the range of her sexual life: we exchanged childhood experiences, jokes, and current observations. Granted that there were idiosyncratic differences between her object and mine, nevertheless by the end of the conversation I simply had to say: if I had a fetish, then so did she.

And unless she was prevaricating, to say it is impossible that she exists simply will not do. Nor can I think that all those leather dykes have merely snitched their jackets, studded belts, wristbands, chains, and engineer's boots.

In other places I have written that singular, empirical examples—and that is all the particular orders of narrative I indulge here can give—are the place from which to start further, operationalized investigations. They are not the place to decide one has found a general fact. And I mean it—here, too. Certainly I would like to see such operationalized study begun. And my utopian hope is that in such stories as these such study might begin. That is why I've told the tales I have.

But this suggestion of an egalitarian fetishism brings us to a truism in the field of gay studies that, like any truism, it might be time to review. It is one that again and again, in other discussions, I have felt must stand at the head of any number of talks and articles on matters gay. Let me quote from the last time someone else quoted *me* on just this point.

Here is Teresa de Lauretis, writing in her introduction to a 1991 issue of a special number of *differences,* devoted to Queer Theory:

> Delany opens his introduction [to *Uranian Worlds*] with the words: "The situation of the lesbian in America is vastly different from the situation of the gay male. A clear acknowledgement of this fact, especially by male homosexuals, is almost the first requirement for any sophisticated discussion of homosexual politics in this country." [De Lauretis goes on:] And, as if he were reading my mind or telepathically sharing the thoughts I put into words in this introduction, he adds: "Gay men and gay women may well express solidarity with each other. But in the day to day working out of the reality of liberation, the biggest help we can give each other is a clear and active recognition of the extent and nature of the different contexts and a rich and working sympathy for the different priorities these contexts (for want of a better word) engender."

Then de Lauretis goes on to quote my co-introducer, Joanna Russ, in her delineation of precisely what some of those differences were in terms of literary availability.

Paradoxically, it is because I wrote that—and because I still stand by it—that I want to tell another, worrisome tale.

It is a simple one. It happened on a chill, early spring afternoon, during my middle twenties, when I sat on the rim of the fountain in Washington Square with a hefty young woman about my age, who wore glasses, black jeans, a leather jacket, and who went by the name Hank.

We talked—talked from the breeze-laced height of the day till the sky above us deepened to indigo, sharing our sexual histories. We were not talking of my adventures on the docks or in subway johns or about my frustrations at trying to establish a more lasting relationship in such a context; we did not discuss her bar life or the cycle of seemingly endless hurts that were serial monogamy.

Rather we talked about the burgeonings of our sexual awareness, in the family, in school, in the street, and in the times we moved from one to the other, now in our early summer camp experiences, now on our visits to cousins in the country, or with playmates away, at last, from overseeing adults. We talked mostly of happenings that occurred before ages thirteen and fourteen, and of experiences that certainly seemed, for both of us then, directly constitutive of who, sexually, we had become.

Both of us, again and again, were astonished at how many experiences we shared, how many of the separate lessons that we'd learned were clearly congruent, and how much of the stuff of the initial awareness of the sexual—from the body out—seemed all but identical for the two of us. But, given the time we had our conversation, no one had yet told us that we were supposed to be all that different. Hank remarked on the similarities. So did I.

For better or for worse, the solidarity I feel with many lesbians is still based on such experiences. What my understanding of that vastly differing context explains for me is why those conversations are rarer for me with women than with men. An understanding of that vastly differing context allows me to translate from women's experiences to mine—when such translation is possible. An understanding of that vastly differing context explains for me why so frequently no translation takes place at all. But what that context does not do in any way is validate the notion for me of some transcendental, irreducible sexual difference between men and women, either in terms of sex or gender, straight or gay, a difference that becomes the ground for any and every social difference one might want to elaborate from it. Indeed, it is precisely my understanding of the specific complexity of the context that makes an acceptance of that irreducible and transcendental difference impossible for me.

Certainly the identification I speak of is always partial, problematic, full of mistakes and misreadings. . . . But that is my experience with any identification I feel with *any* other, male, female, gay, straight. . . .

Thus even the similarities are finally, to the extent they are living ones, a play of differences—only specific ones, socially constituted. Not transcendental ones.

Thinking about discussing this with you tonight, I was wondering at the same time about the inside/outside metaphor that common sense so frequently asks us to use—but which has come under an intensive critique in recent years.

For, in terms of the progression of my didactic narrative argument, we are about to take up the phrases "inside language" and "outside language."

I did not tell Hank all my stories.

Doubtless, she did not tell me all hers.

I told her, for example, none of the stories I've so far told here. And the stories I did tell—it occurred to me when I was reviewing the incident for inclusion in this account tonight—were, none of them, included in the autobiography I wrote twenty years later . . . though I still remember them very well! Which is to say, they still remain largely outside language.

Diana Fuss has written, introducing the fine volume she edited, *Inside/Out: Lesbian Theories, Gay Theories* (New York: Routledge, 1991): "The figure of 'inside/outside' cannot easily or ever finally be dispensed with; it can only be worked on and worked over—itself turned inside out to expose its critical operations and internal machinery" (p. 1).

Fuss begins the argument I have quoted from the "philosophical opposition between 'heterosexual' and 'homosexual,'" heterosexuals representing the inside and homosexuals the outside. But I think there's a finer economy of inside and outside where her point is just as valid: that is the notion of sexuality itself as always occurring partly inside language and partly outside it.

I am not speaking of a hypostatized language as an unarticulated totality, beside which some sex acts occur in an ideal silence apart from the word, while others are swaddled in a constant, approved, and privileged discourse. I speak rather of language as an articulated and variegated set of discursive fields, many of them interpenetrating, but many of whose distinct levels bear a host of economic relations one to another. Some of those levels are privileged, some are not; some are notably more ephemeral than others. These levels fall into hierarchies of reproducibility, accessibility, and permanence. And some never leave that most ephemeral state—that internal speech of the individual we call unarticulated thought. In that sense, of course, all human activity is inside language. But by the very same set of distinctions, all human activity takes place inside certain orders of language and outside certain others—and that is the force of the metaphor behind what I've said about activities inside language and outside language till now, as it will be behind what I have to say in the discussion to come.

As comfortable as I am calling the tales I tell here "true," these tales are nevertheless quite coded—coded as to their selection, as to their narrative form, as to their referents, their texture, and their structures; and the conventions that code them were more or less sedimented well before the incidents that prompted the accounts took place. Despite their sedimentation, however, these codes have also shifted with history: such tales certainly could not have been told, say, thirty-five years ago at a formal, public, university gathering—inside this particular order of language.

No less coded—and no less true—is this last of my tales. Its coding today may even be the most self-evident, the most obvious.

One bright, November afternoon, as I was passing just across the street from the theater I was telling you about before, a young man in his early twenties, slight and half-a-head shorter than I, came up to me. Pretty clearly Irish American, he was wearing a jean jacket and a broad smile. His hands were in his pockets, and, in the sunny chill, he breathed out white wisps. "Hey, you want to get together with me? I seen you

comin' around here a lot. Somebody told me you write science fiction.
I like that stuff. I read it all the time. Makin' it with somebody who
writes about spaceships, and time machines, and flying saucers and
stuff, that'd be pretty cool."

I laughed. "Sorry," I told him. "Not today." And went on about my
business.

A few days later I passed him again, and again he approached me:
"Hey—when are you an' me going to get together?"

Smiling, I shook my head and walked on.

Days later—the third time I passed him—he called me over to a
doorway he was standing in and, when I came, bombarded me in an
intense whisper with a detailed and salacious account of what he could
do for me. He finished up: "And I ain't expensive either. Man, I'm a
street person. I can't afford to charge high prices—isn't that a bitch? I
just want to make enough to get high."

"Look," I said. "First of all what's your name?"

Let's say he said it was Billy.

"Billy," I said, shaking his offered hand, "I was about to get something to eat. I'll buy you a sandwich. But that's all."

"Sure," he said. "It's a start. Maybe something'll develop."

"Nothing's going to develop," I told him, "except a sandwich. But
come on."

At a hot-plate bar two blocks south on Eighth Avenue, I had a pas-
trami on rye, while Billy had a roast beef on whole wheat, which he ate
with two or three fingers of both hands pushing and working inside his
mouth, for seconds at a time, to tear the food apart. No beer; he just
wanted a soda. While he drank it, he listed the titles and summarized
the plots of the last dozen science fiction novels he'd read. I allowed as
to how he had good taste. Wiping at his mouth with his napkin, he
apologized: "You know, I used to be a pretty neat eater, would you believe it? But I guess living out here, I'm turning into kind of a pig. It's
my teeth. They give me a lot of trouble, and a lot of things I can't really
chew. How come you won't give me a tumble?"

"Do you really want to know?"

He sat back in the high, wooden booth seat and countered: "Do you
really want to tell me?"

I laughed. "You seem like a smart kid. You're actually pretty good-
looking—and you keep yourself clean. I'd never have thought you
were living rough."

"I wash in the bathroom at Port Authority every morning." He
winked at me. "I do sort of okay out here."

"Billy, the truth is, I just don't find you sexually attractive. And if I'm going to pay for it—even the price of a bottle of crack—it seems to me I should be getting something I'll enjoy."

"You'd enjoy it," Billy said, with a nod of mock smugness. "I'd see to that. But I get your point." Then he narrowed his eyes. "You say I look good; so how'd you know I was a crackhead?"

"How did you know I was a science fiction writer?" I asked. "It's a fairly small world out here."

"Mmm." Billy nodded.

But two weeks later, the next time I ran into him, Billy approached me with:

"I'm hungry. You wanna buy me a sandwich?" Which I did—the second of perhaps a dozen over that winter and into spring. During our meals I got the pieces of a story, tedious in the similarity of its details to any hundred like tales of like young men and young women: relations severed angrily and violently by a Brooklyn family because of his drug involvement; a penally checkered career throughout his late adolescence; his last two years (he was twenty-four) living on the street—most of that time, in Billy's particular case, sleeping in the upper tier of the Port Authority Bus Station's Gate 235, which, because the gate was not in service that year, became the rotational sleeping space of some dozen young people (all but Billy, in those days, black) in an uneasy and often violated truce, both with each other and the Station authorities. Some of those details bespoke a level of organization, however, notably higher than most street druggies maintained—especially those on crack. Billy always kept two shirts and a pair of pants in the dry cleaners around on Ninth Avenue, one of which he took out every three or four days. Sometimes I gave Billy science fiction novels to read.

As such friendships will, this one tapered off to where we just called hello to each other on the street when we passed; later, from time to time, we only nodded, or raised a hand. Then, one summer's day as I was walking up Eighth Avenue, I saw Billy sitting on the single step in a doorway, plaid sleeves rolled up his forearms, still neat and clean enough so that most people would not guess immediately he was homeless.

As I nodded, he looked up at me, elbows on his knees and one hand holding his other wrist. "Well," he said. "I got it."

That halted me. I searched about for a reasonable response. Billy was not above feigning illness to put the touch on you. For three months, about six months before, he'd had a low-grade ulcer which, while he'd treated it with Mylanta and Emergency Room prescriptions, he'd not been above working up into something more serious to hustle a few dollars from sympathetic passers-by. But this seemed outside Billy's usual range of fictions. I asked: "Any idea how you picked it up?"

"Oh," he said, "sure. Needles. I'd never do anything sexually that would give it to me." He nodded. "Sharin' needles."

"Well," I said, at a loss to think of an appropriate rejoinder. "You've got to take care of yourself." Then I walked on . . . while I realized the fact that Billy had *not* asked me for a handout as I moved away was probably the surest confirmation of the truth of what he'd just told me.

I saw Billy a couple of other times—even had another sandwich with him. "I had the pneumonia," was how he put it, at the hot-plate bar; he dug inside his mouth. "They said, at the hospital, if I got it again, that would be it. They also said, since they knew I had it now, if I showed up with pneumonia again, they *wouldn't* take me back. Can they do that? I guess, if you don't got any money, they can do what they want. Right?"

All I could say was that, honestly, I didn't know.

Work had already taken me out of state; the next few times I saw Billy were in my sporadic trips back to the city. October a year ago, when the weather took a final leap into Indian summer warmth, briefly I was in New York and walking up Eighth Avenue. In the same doorway where I occasionally used to find Billy sitting, I noticed a gaunt man, his shoulders near nonexistently thin. His eyes and temples were sunken. The lower part of his face was swollen so that he seemed a sort of anorexic Neanderthal. He wore a baggy blue t-shirt, and his legs came out of a pair of even baggier Bermudas like sticks. He looked up to catch me staring at him—and I thought to look away. But, slowly, he smiled and said: "What's the matter, Chip—don't you recognize me?"

"Billy . . . ?" I said. Then, because I couldn't think of anything else to say, I said: "How're you doing?"

"Pretty bad," he said, matter of factly. His voice was decidedly slurred, and I wondered if the swelling in his jaws was the packing of some internal bandage. But I don't think so.

I kept on walking, because for the last year, that's what I did when I saw Billy.

But later that evening, I was in one of the neighborhood gay bars—Cats. I'd come down to talk with a gay friend, Joe, a recent Jesuit novice, who'd left his calling and whom I'd helped get a job in publishing. We'd been catching up on his adventures and mine, when the door opened and three young men came in, Billy among them. He saw us, grinned, came over, draped one matchstick arm around Joe's neck and one arm around mine. "Hey," Billy said, with the same slur from the afternoon, "you guys know each other? Joe's my special friend here."

Which Joe confirmed by a grin and a hug.

"Just a second. I'll see you in a minute." And Billy was off to say something to the other hustlers he'd come in with.

Again, I had no idea of the protocol for such situations. "Billy's a good kid," I told Joe. "How long have you known him?"

"Oh, about three weeks."

"Mmm," I said. Then I said: "You know, of course, he's got AIDS. At least he told me he did, sometime back."

"I kind of . . ." Joe nodded. "Suspected it. He doesn't say the word. But he talks about it."

That didn't make me feel much better.

But Joe said: "We don't really do anything, anyway. We lie around and hold each other. He says he likes it and it makes him feel good. But that's all."

At which point Billy was back, arms again around our shoulders, bony head thrust between. "Joe says he'll take care of me whenever I get real sick," Billy announced, straight off. "He's a special guy. Like you."

"That's good," I said.

Joe, at any rate, was smiling. Billy reached behind him and pulled a stool up between us. As he sat, his baggy Bermudas rode up his gaunt thighs till his uncircumcised genitals hung loose. Reaching down with one finger he hooked the plaid edge back even more. "It's amazing," he said, and I realized I was getting used to his slur, "most of my johns haven't deserted me. But that's because I always gave 'em a good time, I guess." (Though I had never been his john, looking at him now it was a little hard to believe.) Gazing down, Billy apostrophized himself: "You bought me a lot of dope. Made me some money—some friends. Gave me a good time." Shifting to the side, he pulled his shorts leg down now. "Got me into a lot of trouble, too!" He looked back up, grinning at us with swollen jaw and bony face.

And, for the first time in the years I'd known him, to my distress, I felt sexual excitement rise toward Billy. I had another drink—I bought him and Joe respectively a ginger ale and a beer. I shook hands with them both, wished them well—and went home.

October's weeks of Bermuda-shorts weather are brief.

A month and a half later, when I happened to get Joe on the phone at work, I asked how Billy was. He told me: "A little while after I saw you at the bar, when it started to get cold, Billy showed up sick at my place. I kept him there for a week of *spectacular* diarrhea! Really, the guy was exploding shit—or water, mostly, after a while. Then he said he wanted to leave—I didn't think he *could* leave. But he went off somewhere. I haven't seen him since."

No one has seen Billy since—for a year now.

You and I know Billy is dead.

Nor is Billy the only one in these tales to die:

Carla was killed in an accident during a rainstorm, when a metal piece fell from a building cornice and struck her down as she was hurrying to bring her lover an umbrella in a Brooklyn subway station. While I rode the subway, I saw the *Daily News* headline across the aisle, "Lawyer Slain in Brooklyn," and only a day later learned that the lawyer was my friend—and it was as stunning, and as horrid, and certainly more tragic and interruptive in the lives of her friends than this intrusion of its awful and arbitrary fact is here.

I spoke at Carla's memorial service. And, whatever I have said of her—here—she was an easy person to praise.

Billy's death?

I called a number of hospitals—so did Joe. As far as we could learn, Billy did not die in any of them, though his name was on record at two: outpatient treatment for a junior ulcer at one and a stay for pneumocistis pneumonia in the other. But unless he went very far afield, he probably *wouldn't* have been admitted. And Billy was bonded to that central city neighborhood—sometimes called the 42nd Street Area, sometimes the theater district, and occasionally the Minnesota Strip—through his very familiarity with it, by his knowledge of the surge and ebb of its drug traffic, because so much of what he knew was how to eke from it the limited life it allowed.

Well, why, in our clean, well-lighted space this evening, do we need this story? Why do we need to add to these others this tale of a moment's fugitive desire *en route* to an untraceable death behind some burned-out building or in an out-of-service bus gate at the Port or beneath a bench in an Eighth Avenue Subway station?

It was four years ago I first realized that, among my personal friends and acquaintances, AIDS had become the biggest single killer, beating out cancer, heart disease, and suicide combined. Certainly Billy is not typical of my friends—nor is his death typical at all of theirs.

Why not, then, tell of a cleaner, more uplifting death? Well, I tell it because such deaths are *not* clean and uplifting.

I tell it because the story troubles me—the purpose of all these tales: it troubles me because it is as atypical as it is.

Understand: I recount these stories not as the "strangest" things that have ever happened to me. Purposely I am not going into particulars, here, about the well-dressed sixty-year-old gentleman in the 96th Street men's room who asked for my shit to eat, or the American tourist who picked me up in Athens who could only make love to me if I wore a wristwatch with a metal band, and that band low on the arm, or the young Italian who had me hammer his stretched scrotum to a piece of pine planking with half-a-dozen ten-penny nails.

What I'm trying to remind you is, simply enough, that these are all part of a gay experience—*my* gay experience. I can't claim them as characteristic of some hypostatized universal gay experience involving the range of gay women and gay men, black and white, middle-class and working-class. They are not even characteristic of my own. Perhaps they could occur only in the margins of the experience of one sexually active black, American, urban gay male, in the last decades of the twentieth century. But, in terms of that experience, they are a good deal more informative than Sunday brunches and Judy Garland records, in that they are parts of a sexual experience—with men and with women—which, as a gay male, I would not trade for the world with anyone else's.

You must understand, there *are* sexual experiences—with both men and women—I would happily give up. As I once told Carla, I have been held down by two men and raped. When I was seven or eight I was sexually abused, very painfully, by a girl a few years older than I at my first summer camp. Both experiences, believe me, I could easily have lived without.

The tales recounted here—as they touch on the sexual, however troublingly—belong to a *range* of sexual occurrences, the vast majority of which have never and can never make their way into language, the range that gives me my particular outlook on human sexuality, an outlook certainly different from many other people's; and those experiences have done more to dissolve any notions I ever held of normal and abnormal than all my readings on gender, perversion, and social construction put together.

But "the gay experience" has always resided largely outside of language—because all sexuality, even all experience, in part resides there. Simple aversion—at whatever social level—is enough to divert our accounts from much of what occurs. But even to seek the averse is to divert our accounts from the characteristic. And because of this economy, in anything that I can recognize as a socially and politically meaningful discussion of sex, the triplicity of aversion, perversion, and diversion cannot, as far as I know, be avoided—here, tonight, anywhere . . .

To make such a statement about the realm of sexuality is another way of saying that what has been let into language has always been highly coded. That coding represents a kind of police action that, even while it is decried in the arena of politics, often goes, among us in the academic area of Gay Studies, unnoticed.

This is why I have tried to bring up these specific and troubling tales, to help cast into the light the smallest fragment of the context of—no, not Gay Studies in general, but simply the context of the talk that I am now in the process of giving. And if, when we take as our object of study, say, some lines by Shakespeare or Whitman to a boy, citing the contestation of other, homophobic scholars, or when we examine some profession of love to another woman in a letter by Emily Dickinson or Eleanor Roosevelt or Willa Cather, contested equally by still other homophobic scholars, or the coded narratives of Melville's wide world of navigation, of Oscar Wilde's or Dorothy Strachey's London, of Thomas Mann's circumscribed tourist town of Venice, or Djuna Barnes's wonderfully sophisticated Paris—if we take these tales and assume that we are not dealing with a code that, in every case, excludes a context at least as complex and worrisome as the one I have here gone to such narrative lengths to suggest, then, I maintain, we are betraying our object of study through a misguided sense of our own freedom, by an adoration too uncritical of that wonderfully positive tale we all, perhaps, adore.

What I hope worries you, what I hope troubles your sense of the appropriateness of these tales for the here and now of what, certainly, most of us will experience as a liberating academic occasion, is what suggests that, even with the surge of linguistic freedom that has obtained since '68 and with the movement toward political freedom that has been in motion since the Stonewall riots of '69, what is accepted into language at any level is *always* a highly coded, heavily policed affair. Though strictures relax or tighten at different places and in different periods, the relaxation never means that the policing or coding has somehow been escaped.

The sexual experience is *still* largely outside language—at least as it (language) is constituted at any number of levels.

Ludmilla Jordanova's book *Sexual Visions* (University of Wisconsin, 1989) is a stunningly fine and informed study of gender images in science and medicine over the last three hundred years. It was recommended to me by a number of astute readers. I have since recommended it to a number of others perusing like topics of concern.

In its preface, however, Jordanova takes to task Paula Weideger's book, *History's Mistress* (Viking Penguin, 1985), which reprints a selection of extracts from an 1885 book by a gynecologist, Ploss, *Woman: a Historical, Gynecological and Anthropological Compendium*. Writes Jordanova of Weideger: "Her fictional scenario is supposed to make the point that the thirty-two photographs of breasts in the 1935 English edition are included for prurient reasons. Yet the way she makes the point, her chosen title, and the whole presentation of her book, serve to heighten any sense of titillation in readers and buyers."

Jordanova then goes on to advise, most wisely, a careful study of such works and their circumstances in order to understand the objects they represent.

Yes, a wise suggestion. But the problem with such a suggestion is that such works—especially in 1935, if not 1885—belonged to a category which tried as carefully and as ruthlessly as possible to exclude the specifically sexual component from all the language around them. Some years ago, I talked to a handful of men, fifteen to thirty years older than I, who recalled using such books as pornography in their youth. What made such works both accessible and pornographic was precisely that the sexual *was* excluded from any overt mention: it is not absurd to assume that art works, medical works, and legal works occupied such a position all through the nineteenth and the first three-quarters of the twentieth century—especially given that 150 years' proscription on pornography *per se*. But the problematics of dealing with sexual research in periods when much of sexual discourse was all but nonverbal is as much a problem for the historian of heterosexuality as it is for the historian of Gay Studies.

Because both today and in earlier times what of the sexual that was allowed into language is notably more than what was allowed in during that period of extraordinary official proscription any of us over forty can still remember, we must not assume that "everything" is *ever* articulated; we are still dealing with topics that were always circumscribed by a greater or lesser linguistic coding and a greater or lesser social policing. Because Alexander Kojeve and Jerome Carcopino have discussed the double writing of the Emperor Julian and Cicero, and because Robert Martin has traced a like process going on in Melville's tales of the sea, we must not forget that double codes as well as single codes still exclude, still police. They simply do it at two stages for two audiences—even if one of those audiences is gay. And what is excluded by the code, that code functions specifically *by* excluding. And because the whole analytical bastion of psychoanalysis lies there to talk about repression both in the areas of the socially articulated and the socially unarticulated, we must not fall into any easy uncritical alignment of the socially excluded with the unconscious and the socially articulated with the conscious. Repressions takes place at a wholly other economic order.

It is often hard for those of us who are historians of texts and documents to realize that there are many things that are directly important for understanding hard-edged events of history, that have simply never made it *into* texts or documents—not because of unconscious repression but because a great many people *did not want them to be known*. And this is particularly true about almost all areas of sex.

Though our academic object as textual explicators must begin with what is articulated in a given text, we must always reserve a margin to deal with what is excluded from articulation, no matter the apparent inclusiveness.

That goes just as much for my tales this evening as it does for Musil's

Young Torless or Gide's *The Immoralist.* It goes just as much for Hall's *The Well of Loneliness* or Brown's *Rubyfruit Jungle.* It goes just as much for the text collected by a sociologist from a gay informant, female or male, who is being questioned about the realities of gay history.

In 1987 I published an autobiography a good deal of whose motivation was to retrieve various historical articulations in just this context, as I had observed it between the years 1957 and 1965. The advent of AIDS made, I feel, absolutely imperative an inflated level of sexual honesty that dwarfs the therapeutic exhortations for sexual openness that can be seen as the fallout of a certain industrial progress in methods of birth control coupled with Freud's, if not Reich's, sexual ethics, and enhanced with the political strategy, dating from Stonewall, of "coming out" (a strategy devised specifically to render the sexual blackmailer without power) . . . a code, a police action if you will, that controls a good deal of what I say here.

It seems to me that when one begins to consider the range of diversities throughout the sexual landscape, then even the unquestioned "normalcy" of the heterosexual male, whose sexual fantasies are almost wholly circumscribed by photographs of . . . female movie stars! suddenly looks—well, I will not say, "less normal." But I will say that it takes on a mode of sexual and social specificity that marks it in the way every other one of these tales is marked, i.e., as perverse.

Similarly, the heterosexual woman whose fantasies entail a man who is wholly faithful to her, and whom, only while he is wholly faithful, does she find sexually attractive, but whom upon showing any sexual interest in another woman—heaven forfend that it be another man—immediately is rendered sexually unacceptable to her; well—like the male above, her sexual condition seems only a particular form of a socially prescribed perversion—one that I could even, for a while, see myself getting behind. Certainly, it would be no more difficult than getting off on someone licking my sneakers. (And it would be, for me, a lot easier than getting off on female movie stars—or most male ones, for that matter.) But both strike me, as do all the other situations I have described tonight, as socially constituted and perverse. And in this case, for all my sympathy, neither perversion happens to be mine.

Similarly, when one surveys the range of fetishes, at a certain point one begins to see that the sexualizing of a hand, a glove, a foot, a shoe, a breast, a brassiere, a buttock, a pair of panties, a jock strap, a sailor's uniform, a policeman's uniform, a riding crop, a cigar, a swastika, or the genitals themselves—whether the possessor be a man or a woman—all work essentially by the same mechanism. All are generalizable and proscribable. All, if you will, are fetishes.

But even as we recover ourselves—at this moment of general inclusiveness—I hope for at least a few moments I have been able to maneuver some of you this evening into thinking: "Is *this* what Gay Identity is supposed to be? What does all this sneaker licking, drunken undergraduate mischief, and another sob-story of a hapless drug user have to do with *my* sexuality—my gay identity?" For certainly raising that question was precisely my intention. I said these tales were to trouble. And the troubling answer I would pose is fundamentally as simple as any of the tales themselves:

Quite possibly not much.

The point to the notion of Gay Identity is that, in terms of a transcendent reality concerned with sexuality *per se* (a universal similarity, a shared necessary condition, a defining aspect, a generalizable and inescapable essence common to all men and women called "gay"), I believe Gay Identity has no more existence than a single, essential, transcendental sexual difference. Which is to say, I think the notion of Gay Identity represents the happily only partial congruence of two strategies, which have to do with a patriarchal society in which the dominant sexual ideology is heterosexist.

In terms of heterosexist oppression of gays, Gay Identity represents a strategy for tarring a whole lot of very different people with the same brush: Billy, Mike, my perpetual virgin—at least, that is, if the people with the tar believe in a transcendent difference between male and female. (For those are precisely the people who historically have contrived to keep male homosexuality not talked of and lesbianism trivial.) And if, on the other hand, they simply believe deviance is deviance, then it includes as well, you, me, Carla, and Hank. The tar is there in order to police a whole range of behaviors—not only in terms of the action that is language but also in terms of the language that human actions themselves must generate, including the language of these tales tonight.

In terms of gay rights, Gay Identity represents one strategy by which some of the people oppressed by heterosexism may come together, talk, and join forces to fight for the equality that certain egalitarian philosophies claim is due us all. In those terms, what we need these stories for is so that we don't get too surprised when we look at—or start to listen to—the person sitting next to us. That person, after all, might be me, or Hank, or Mike—or anyone else I've spoken of this evening. In those terms, Gay Identity is a strategy I approve of wholly, even if, at a theoretical level, I question the existence of that identity as having anything beyond a provisional or strategic reality. Nor do I seek what Jane Gallup has written of so forcefully as some sort of liberation from identity itself that would lead only to another form of paralysis—"the oceanic passivity of undifferentiation" (*The Daughter's Seduction*, Ithaca: Cornell, 1982, p.xii). For me, Gay Identity—like the joys of Gay Pride Day, weekends on Fire Island, and the delight of tickets to the opera— is an object of the context, not of the self—which means, like the rest of the context, it requires analysis, understanding, interrogation, even sympathy, but never an easy and uncritical acceptance.

That is to say, its place is precisely in the politically positivist comedy of liberation we began with—but probably nowhere else. But the reason why that partial congruence between the two strategies is finally happy, is because it alone allows one group to speak, however inexactly, with the other. It allows those who have joined together in solidarity to speak to those who have been excluded; and, to me even more important, it allows the excluded to speak back. That very partial congruence is the linguistic element of the conduit through which any change, as it manifests a response by a vigorous and meaningful activism, will transpire.

Again: in a field of heterosexist dominance and homophobic oppression, however much the policing of what is allowed into language has broadened since the late sixties, the bulk of the extraordinarily rich, frightening, and complex sexual landscape has been—and remains— outside of language. Most of it *will* remain there for quite some time. It is precisely because I have talked of it as much as I have that I am so hugely aware of how little of it I have actually spoken. But because that sexual landscape is not articulated in certain orders of language—written language, say, of a certain formality—does not mean it doesn't exist. Nor does it mean that its effects as a pervasive context do not inform other articulations, that either do not reflect it directly or that reflect only a highly coded, heavily policed portion of it.

From time to time I have been accused—I have always taken it as praise—of trying to put the sex back in homosexuality. Here, not as a matter of nostalgia, but to facilitate an analytical and theoretical precision, I am trying to trouble the notion both of what we aver and what we are averse to, in its perversity and its diversity—or, if you will, through occasional appeals to the averse, I am trying to put a bit of the perversity back into perversion.

I hope many of you so inclined will welcome it. And to all of you tonight: Love, luxury, justice, and joy.

Thank you.

— *Amherst*
30 October 1991

Shadow and Ash

1. Rhetoric is the ash of discourse.

2. Probably in the winter of 1797–98, in what has become known as *The Gutch Memorandum Notebook*, Samuel Taylor Coleridge jotted down the sweepingly sonorous verses:

> the prophetic soul
> of the wide world dreaming on things to come—

In those 95 sheets that served him over some three years as commonplace book, journal, and project notebook, after a few more entries, including some odd lines from Shakespeare's sonnets and a tercet that grew into the third verse paragraph of "Christobel," Coleridge copied out a glorious description of alligators from a travel book by one William Bartram with the sesquipedalian title *Travels through North and South Carolina, Georgia, East and West Florida, the Cherokee Country, the Extensive Territories of the Muscogulges, or Creek Confederacy, and the Country of the Chactaws; containing an Account of the Soil and Natural Production of these Regions, together with Observations on the Manners of the Indians*. After about a page, the transcription is interrupted by a paragraph-long entry on an accident with Coleridge's infant son:

> —Hartley fell down & hurt himself—I caught him up crying & screaming—& ran out of doors with him.—The Moon caught his eye—he ceased crying immediately—& his eyes & the tears in them, how they glittered in the Moonlight!

Then, after the mention of a "wilderness plot, green & fountainous & unviolated by man" (an image that perhaps helped to hold the winter at bay), Coleridge goes back to transcribing Bartram on alligators; followed by Bartram on the flowering Gordonia Lasianthus; followed by Bartram on the snake-bird . . .

In his magisterial study *The Road to Xanadu* (1927), John Livingston Lowes suggests that these New World alligators are the Ur-versions of the archaic sea monsters that would wriggle and slither over the waters of "The Rime of the Ancyent Marinere, in Seven Parts," as it would be titled when, just after the famous "Preface," it opens *Lyrical Ballads* (printed by Biggs and Cottle for T. N. Longman, Paternoster-Row, London) in 1798. Certainly Bartram's and Coleridge's water beasts share, as Lowes points out, both aspects and adjectives.

At the end of his cadenza ("Chaos") on the riches of the *Gutch* (the notebook eventually passed into the hands of Coleridge's schoolmate, John Matthew Gutch, from whom it was purchased by the British Museum in 1868: hence the name), Lowes mentions half a dozen Coleridge poems with germs lying among the fragments he has exegeted: "Christobel," "The Wanderings of Cain," "The Nightingale," "Kubla Khan," "Lewti," "Love," "Fears in Solitude," "The Rime of the Ancient Mariner" (the revised title that would eventually head the poem, along with the addition of the marginal rubrics), and even Wordsworth's "Ruth."

But one poem, whose germ is clearly here and, to a modern ear, most obviously so, is absent from Lowes's list. Lowes knew everything Coleridge wrote, phrase by phrase, and mentions the poem near half a dozen times in the course of his monumental exploration of the range of Coleridge's reading. But nowhere along the road to Xanadu does he explicitly connect it to the first lines he quotes from the *Gutch*. Was the connection too obvious? Or too banal? I mean, of course, Coleridge's meditation—written as little Hartley slept in his cradle, while the fire in the grate burned low that winter—"Frost at Midnight."

> The frost performs its secret ministry,
> Unhelped by any wind. . . .

the poem begins. In the second of its four verse paragraphs, Coleridge's thought retreats from the dark night by the barely glimmering fire and his sleeping child's cradle to his own school days. There he recalls the bells on a hot Fair Day that rang from morn till evening

> So sweetly that they stirred and haunted me
> With a wild pleasure falling on my ear
> Most like articulate sounds of things to come.

In the next verse paragraph Coleridge is back at the cradle, apostrophizing the sleeping Hartley. And in the last, his thoughts go out to all the year's seasons, hot and cold. But surely in the lines cited, we have a strangely reduced version of what the prophetic soul of the wide world had been dreaming on, now articulated in the bells.

What prompts me to all this speculation? Doubtless it is only because I am a science fiction writer. And in 1939, a dozen years after Lowes first published his wondrously thorough book, noting the *Gutch* line in Lowes, H. G. Wells was prompted to entitle his first and only film script—and certainly one of the finest science fiction films ever made—*Things to Come.*

3. The initial question in discussing the cascade of inventive and almost always beautiful sentences making up the corpus of Ron Silliman's poems and prose poems is whether or not a discussion of work that so rigorously eschews argument is betrayed by an argumentatively coherent exposition.

Silliman's poems side-step argument; but they do not—at least the early pieces that make up the major series, The Alphabet (*ABC,* its first volume, appeared in '83)—avoid situation. "Albany" really *is* about impressions of the Bay Area as contemplated from that West Coast suburb of Berkeley. And "Blue," announced by its feminization of the famous line by Valéry ("The Marchioness went out . . ."), meditates on literary effects.

In the later poems, however, each sentence becomes its own situation. A fine sense of this is perhaps the best thing to bring to a reading of Silliman's texts.

While for most of us so much of the impulse to write grows from a desire to capture something of the subject, to stabilize passages of lived experience in the headlong career toward death, what strikes me most about Silliman and, by extension, those poets who work in the abstract, is that these poets' almost complete abandonment of the subject as narrative topic seems so staggeringly brave!

4. The only thing untoward about my April visit to Swarthmore was that, during my afternoon reading, while I was sitting in the red wing chair in the richly paneled room of a Sunday noon, with the students in shorts and t-shirts, cross-legged on the rug, and the sportily dressed faculty in chairs behind them (while dragons careered Nevèrÿon's night), a fly lacrosse ball smashed an oval hole through a hand-sized pane beside me, strewing glass bits on the blue carpet—to worry about a third of the youngsters, who'd come barefoot.

5. A thought on the day after my 49th birthday: We move through life's second half with scrumbling joint and grinding gristle.

6. The high modernist prejudice against biography is, of course, an acknowledgement of the fact that, since most biographies are not good ones, to have no biography is better than having a bad one. But what would the ideal biography be? To me, Richard Aldington's biography of Lawrence, *Portrait of a Genius, But* . . . is a more interesting book than any of Lawrence's novels. (This marks me as a certain type of vulgarian, I realize. Still, what interests is what interests.) Sections of life are, I suspect, governed by tone. A good biography should catch that. (But those sections are not exhausted by tone; and Aldington manages to relate dissonant details to the broader tone—one reason his book works so well.) I wonder, however, if you had a subject who actually thought, rather than a subject such as Lawrence who simply acted forcefully on feelings (or prejudices—and when that action involved writing, mistook them for thinking), how the intellectual development of a man or woman ought to be attended to. The one thing I'm sure of is that the development of ideas does not proceed in the lucid order in which it is presented in, say, most biographies of Freud, be it Jones's, Gay's, Rozzen's, or even Manonni's.

Could anyone actually like *both* Lawrence and Nabokov? To me that seems an exercise in negative capability beyond human accomplishment—or, at any rate, beyond mine.

7. I never thought of myself when young as someone who, someday, would have "quite a collection of old moustache-wax brushes." But I do . . . simply because I now have quite a moustache!

8. Thoughts on Joanna Russ's achingly fine sf novel, *We Who Are About to* . . . :

In Tom Godwin's science fiction short story, "The Cold Equations," during the early days of space flight an eighteen-year-old girl stows away on a moon-bound spaceship. Because the fuel is portioned out in exact accord with the payload, her extra weight has not been taken into account. If she stays on board, the ship will not be able to make the return trip to earth, and all of the five-man crew will perish. Thus, there is no option but to jettison her to her death— which, tearfully, she acquiesces to.* The equations which govern Russ's *We Who Are About to* . . . are just as cold; but they are more complex.

---

* Kathryn Cramer points out that if three or four of the men (and, to be fair, the young woman herself) each had been willing to have a leg amputated at the hip, they might easily have compensated for the hundred-ten, hundred-twenty pounds involved. But this, she goes on to point out, would amount to symbolic castration and thus be far too distressing within the story's symbolic framework.

At the height of the New Wave, an sf convention that particularly exercised editor Moorcock at *New Worlds* was what Kurt Vonnegut had already characterized as "the impossibly generous universe" of sf: When, in the real world, 95 percent of all commercial jet crashes are 100 percent fatal and we live in a solar system in which presumably only one planet can support any life at all, science fiction is nevertheless full of spaceship crashes (!) in which everyone gets up and walks away from the wreckage unscathed—and usually out onto a planet with breathable atmosphere, amenable weather, and a high-tech civilization in wait near-by to provide interesting twists in subsequent adventures.

This is the convention that Russ's novel takes to task. She does it, however, by making it seem, in the first few entries of her tale, that this is precisely the convention she is bowing to. But at the start only a few phrases of a tell-tale harshness suggest how cold her equations are:

> About to die. And so on . . . The light of our dying may not reach you for a thousand million years . . . We're a handful of persons in a metal bungalow: five women, three men, bedding, chemical toilet, simple tools, an even simpler pocket laboratory, freeze-dried food for six months, and a water distiller with its own sealed powerpack, good for six months (and cast as a unit, unusable for anything else).
>
> Good-bye everybody.
>
> At dawn I held hands with the other passengers, we all huddled together under that brilliant flash, although I hate them.
>
> O God, I miss my music.

For the flash of the exploding spaceship above them is the light of their dying—though the working out of the tortuous and protracted deaths lingers on another few months, in terms of the single natural death, five murders, and two suicides which comprise the actual plot.

With its cast of a child and seven socially functional adults—all but the narrator, in effect, in thrall to just that notion of an impossibly generous universe—*We Who Are About to . . .* functions as the bad conscience of Golding's *Lord of the Flies*.

The revelation of the temperature at which these equations work is what sets Russ's gelid vision: L.B. has only to be annoyed *enough* at the screech of the baby sparrows to kill them. The polite and well-bred Alan-Bobby has only to wake up to the fact that he is stronger than anyone else for civilization to slide back three thousand years.

Radically, Russ suggests that the quality of life is the purpose of living, and reproduction only a reparative process to extend that quality—and not the point of life at all. (Only feudal societies can really believe wholly that reproduction—i.e., the manufacture of cannon fodder—is life's real point.)

The narrator herself—certainly the most "civilized" person among the passengers—both recalls and re-voices Walter Benjamin's famous observation: "Every act of civilization is also an act of barbarism."

We Who Are About to . . . is a dangerous book because it is readable as allegory, though not an allegory about death: rather, death in this novel is the allegorical stand-in for whatever degree of social-political un-freedom the reader's society has reached. For a long time the book will remain a damningly fine analysis of the mechanics of political and social decay we have undergone to arrive at "this point," however "this point" changes.

Can I think of half a dozen works written in this century of the same length that are as brilliantly structured? Camus's *La Chute*, Davenport's *The Dawn in Erewhon* . . .

But these are Russ's esthetic peers.

9. "What shall I do with this body I've been given?" asks Mandelstam. When, one wonders, was the last time he asked it? In his cramped Petersberg apartment? or in the death camp where, near mad, the elements and ideology killed him . . . ?

10. At 1:45, just before we were ready to go down to Port Authority to catch the 2:45 bus up to Amherst, Dennis stood at our New York kitchen window, looking out at the snow dropping toward Amsterdam Avenue, five stories below. "To think, I used to sleep outside in that shit."

Me: "That must have been fun."

Dennis: "Yeah, it was so much fun, I'm gonna get a snow-making machine for my room."

How much context is needed to make sense of such ironies?

11. A poetic bestiary: Rilke's swan and panther, Moore's buffalo, moose, snail, fish, and jellyfish; Bishop's fish, rooster, and moose; and Davenport's medusa. To read them all one after another is to reinvest with energy and incision the range of sensual relations between the animal and the natural.

12. "Public life on television is more real than private life in the flesh," explains a character from the sound track of Cronenberg's unsettlingly astute *Videodrome*, shortly before he undergoes a negative industrial birth in which his belly swallows a gun. But the fact is, public life—the life known, understood, and finally constituted by society—has always felt

more satisfying than private life. That's what lies behind the conflict thrashing at the center of Romanticism to render private life public.

13. The decade of the eighteen-sixties gave us three extraordinary novels. All of them could be described as turning on a single theme—the republican revolutions that had wracked the century so far in France, Germany, and Italy:

Hugo's *Les Misérables.*
Flaubert's *L'Education Sentimentale.*
Verne's *20,000 lieues sous la mer.*

All read in the same month—what a dialogue they construct with one another!

14. I am the sweeping tapestry of my sensory and bodily perceptions. I am their linguistic reduction and abstraction, delayed and deferred till they form a wholly different order, called my thought. I am, at the behest and prompting of all these, my memory—which forms still another order. I am the emotions that hold them together. Webbing the four, and finally, I am the flux and filigree of desire around them all.

Perhaps, though, I am only the interpretation of all of them—that I call reality. (Do I write with my pen? Does another daemon hold the pen and write with it?) Am I the sexual surge and ebb that cannot quite be covered by any of the above, but that impinge on all the others and often drown them? What of the bodily apparati in general, as they fall, pleasingly or painfully, into the net of myself? I am always an animal excess to the intellectual system that tries to construct me. I am always a conscious sensibility in excess of the animal construction that is I. And that is why I am another, why my identity is always other than I.

15. "Things are more like they are today than they have ever been before," announced American President Dwight D. Eisenhower during one of his '50s terms of office. And in 1989, on first reaching the Peruvian Altoplano, American artist Gregory William Frux remarked: "Sure is alto. Sure is plano." Reams have been written explicating the remark of German philosopher Martin Heidegger: "Nothing nothings." And on more than one occasion I have been known to remind my daughter: "Remember, no matter where you go, there you are."

16. Laura Bohannan's delightful 1966 essay, "Shakespeare in the Bush," while it makes some interesting cross-cultural points, seems to me to work even better as a kind of sf parable about discourse and rhetoric—specifically what happens when certain rhetorical figures are moved from one discursive field to be read within another.

The parable dramatizes what happens to the "universal appeal" of *Hamlet* when its plot is retold in a culture in which the sort of border-line sibling incest Claudius and Gertrude indulge is not only acceptable, but *de rigueur*, where, though magic is quite real, the concept of a ghost is unknown, and where there is no distinction between a scholar and a witch; where strict moral proscriptions preclude all intergenerational violence—and madness is always the result of witchcraft.

Even a cursory review of the plot will reveal that *Hamlet,* retold within such a discursive matrix, is a very different story from the one told in Anglo-European culture. In fact it is arguable that, within such a discursive matrix, the story we know as Hamlet cannot be told at all.

The question becomes interesting, however, when we start to explore the metalanguage necessary to begin translating one set of discursive assumptions, codes, and expectations into another. Such language is "theory." And, generally speaking, theory must proceed with extreme care, at great slowness, and must risk being rhetorically, at least at the beginning, even more incomprehensible than the rhetoric it is being used to explain.

17.   . . . Every day I read a little French because it is such a pretty language. Does that make me a rascal? and then I can't help walking around every day, a bit, in the winter countryside. Does that prove I am indifferent to a great deal of suffering?   —Robert Walser, Letter to Hesse, November 15, 1917.

The sheer bulk of John Addington Symonds's letters—three eight-hundred-fifty-plus-page volumes—suggests a totality they do not, alas, possess. While it's true that scarcely a month goes by, between Symonds's 14th year (1854) and his death from tuberculosis at his home in the Zauberberg country of Devos at age fifty-three (1893), that is not represented by two, three, or more substantial epistles, the totality of his life is still not to be had from these often informative, deeply moving, and frequently brilliant missives—if only because letters do not provide such totality.

The editors seem to have been taken in by the illusion of that totality as much as anyone. One senses it all through their astute and often revealing commentary. In the "Biographical Introduction" we find them writing, "Gustavus Bosanquet [Symonds's adolescent playmate] readily saw the humorous and the comic in life, a capacity which in Symonds seems deficient in his published work no matter how often personal accounts in other people's (like H. G. Dakyns's and T. E. Brown's) letters have stressed it" (p. 31) . . . as though a man may not be jolly in person and serious when he writes—even letters.

Or, again, when pooh-poohing Symonds's later protestations that he was miserable during his school days at Harrow because "[t]he letters to

his family written during this period contain fewer complaints than letters written by most adolescents away from home for the first time,"
and thus (they decide) it was only in retrospect that Symonds's Harrow
days seemed miserable to him (p. 32) . . . as though a brilliant, sensitive, gay child must of necessity commit all the details of his misery to
the letters he writes to his father and sister at home.

As a child, I went to a summer camp where all outgoing letters were
read by the camp director and all incoming letters were read to the
campers by this same tyrannical woman—which simply made it impossible to communicate to parents about either the emotional or the material horrors of the place; and I can recall as an adult in my thirties
writing a letter to a very good friend, while a somewhat deranged lover
of mine wandered about the apartment wrapped in a sheet and threatening suicide—I had to stop writing to argue a knife out of his hand.
But, when, a day later, I resumed the letter, the incident did not go into
it, because the letter had begun—and therefore, even though I was
writing to a very good friend, was obliged to end—concerned with
other things. The incident of the sheet and the knife never made it
into my most personal journal, either—because the same lover had a
habit of browsing through those notebooks and, if he found any reference to himself, became furiously angry.

The incident has never ended up, through any transformation, in
my fiction—because the man dreaded both the publicity and the distortion such a transformation represented as much as he dreaded anything else in the world, and he repeatedly drew promises from me that
I would never use anything in his unhappy life in a fictive rendering.

But the conversations we had that day shook me to the bottom of my
being; and they informed me about depths of human misery I have
never been able to forget; and that meant that I who finished that letter
was not I who had begun it. But though it was a most personal letter, I
doubt any of what I learned in the midst of writing it showed in its
text—although what I learned of personal despair and fear that day
still informs the whole of my life, more than a decade on.

This is as close as the incident has gotten—or will ever get—to becoming a text . . . far closer than it ever got to any text written at the time.

The larger point is, however, that letters—especially the letters of
someone who writes a great many of them—only play in one section of
the personal spectrum (different, of course, for each of us).

But when they play there as deftly and articulately as Symonds's letters
play, perhaps the editors can be forgiven for feeling they have been privy
to the range, harmonies, and scale of the "whole" man, and that all
claims that he was other than the letters present him (even at the very

hour of their writing) must be taken as errors—rather than as additions or expansions.

As letters play in one range, journals and diaries play in another; and the material of fiction plays in another still. It is hard to explain to any researcher—whose relation to writing is often very different from the titanic relations to the written held by the researched subject—that precisely in the real and obsessive writer, none of these ranges is privileged.

To be sure, overlaps between ranges occur.

But even that does not mean the whole scale is ever completely—is ever any more than partially—filled in.

For even with the most assiduous practitioner of all the intra- and extra-literary genres (letters, journals, memoirs), he or she still experiences the vast majority of her or his life outside language written to friends, spoken to friends, to the self, or to the public. Thus the researcher must never forget that the researcher's purpose, no matter how much material present itself, must always lean toward an understanding of something in excess of the material.

Should we call it discourse . . . ?

18. Yesterday, to make sense of a Sherlock Holmes story, my daughter had to look up the word "beeswing" in the OED, and discovered it meant the film forming on wine after it's stood out a goodly while.

19. Essex Hemphill notes (in *Ceremonies,* p. 39) that when viewing Mapplethorpe's "Man in Polyester Suit," it is impossible "to avoid confronting issues of exploitation and objectification." That body without a head, in which the hands alone tell us the body is black, with its big, flaccid cock loose from its fly, masked in a suit that, through the title, carries the connotations of white working class tackiness, if it cannot call up such questions, is just not doing its job. The disingenuously cool, racially neutral title works to that end: *You* bring up the racial questions, it all but instructs the viewer. Some thoughts, however, after reading Kobena Mercer on Mapplethorpe in *Transition* 51: what Mercer misses (or doesn't quite hold on to) is that Mapplethorpe's photos, especially in *The Black Book,* sit on a particularly troublesome border. They are art photographs. But they are saturated with the visual rhetoric—smooth studio backgrounds, high contrast lighting, and compositional fragmentation—of advertising photographs. Much of the disturbing quality of these erotic images comes from their generic ambiguity.

The advertising photograph always makes a coherent statement: "I've got it. You want it," it says. But the rhetorical configuration by which it says it renders such a message completely different from, say, the message of Walker Evans's and Dorothea Lange's photographs of rural Depression men and women.

The art photograph says merely: "Look at this carefully—for its esthetic aspects." And, so, Mapplethorpe . . . ?

To place the erotic into the frame of art is a standard Western move that goes back to the very beginnings of representational art, if not before. Precisely to the extent we are familiar with the tradition, Mapplethorpe's photographs, both in *The Black Book* and in his other homoerotic collections, shift between these twin, insistent statements, to all their viewers, male, female, gay, straight, black, and white. The problem is: What does such an interplay of messages mean, when the speaker of the messages is a white southern gay photographer, dead of AIDS, and the objects advertised/presented are a series of beautiful and intensely phallocised black male bodies?

The picture is ironic, outrageous—shocking? It is that last alone that renders it banal. It is only there that, as a black viewer (and a black gay viewer at that), I am back at the realization that white artists constantly use blacks to represent the extremes they refuse to picture about themselves, i.e., to invent their own normalcy. Whether it is black singer Jennifer Holliday's over-the-top performance of "And I Am Telling You" under white director Michael Bennett in *Dreamgirls,* or the jaw-dropping violence of the forced separation scene of the two black sisters in white director Spielberg's *Color Purple;* whether it is the black female nudity that the white producers of *Les Ballets Africains* wanted to (but were not allowed to) put on Broadway in the fifties, or indeed "Man in Polyester Suit": all suggest the oddly childish scenario of the white kid urging the black kid to go a little further, to violate expectations, to break accepted boundaries just a bit more than any comparable white singer/actor/ model has done till now. Is it collaboration? Is it exploitation? The effects are indisputably powerful for both white and black audiences. At the same time one notes that it is not what black directors Isaac Julian or Spike Lee are doing with *their* white actors—pushing them to outrageous, electric, audience-paralyzing depictions of whatever.

At some point, through the same mechanism by which the picture initiates its dialogue on objectification (whether one takes it as a picture of a biological lie, a statistical leaning, or a visual truth), someone has to ask: What would the picture be saying if the body in polyester was white and male—or a white female body with the fly a-gape around some hefty labia? Or a black female body? Or with a small dick, small cunt, etc.?

They would all be shocking. But what would the different trajectories of that shock be? Only such questions can sketch out the nature of what the picture-as-is is doing.

Without its schlong a-dangle, "Man in Polyester Suit" could be a sales photo for a late '70s issue of *GQ Magazine*. It is, after all, a funny picture. (It's the visual inverse of a joke people, black and white, have been telling for years: What's ten inches long, three inches around, and white? The white answer, straight and gay, male and female, is: "Nothin'!" The straight black male answer just removes the exclamation point. And the black gay answer is: "Not a thing, honey!") Its laughter is directed, however tastelessly, at straight white males—but desire (would you like to suck or fuck one? Would you like to have one?) implicates all persuasions in its dialogic thrust. Hemphill, Mercer, and Julian all ask sensibly: "What do [Mapplethorpe's images] say to our wants and desires as black, gay men?" As a black gay man, I'd suggest—sensibly—the answer starts with what one feels about big black cocks, and only point out that that answer is not necessarily conditioned one way or the other by being black alone. The larger question is, however, how predictable does the picture appear to presume the answer to be?

Just how old is the joke? And how new does dressing it up in polyester make it?

To engage these questions at all is to risk becoming the butt (as it were) of the joke. But clearly that goes for Mapplethorpe as well.

A suggestive historical note to close with: Within six weeks of the October 1839 date Louis Daguerre took out his patent on the Daguerreotype, the first man was arrested on the steps of the Louvre for selling pornographic photographs: naked women against backgrounds and in poses suggesting the most famous nudes on the museum walls within—putting high art, pornography, and photography into a contestatory wrangle that has not silenced since.

20. "Novelists ought not to be deaf," write Disch and Naylor on page 59 of their wondrous historical reconstruction *Neighboring Lives*. But, for better or no, I am losing my hearing.

21. *The Twin Cities:* One is made of polished sewer grills, violet neon tubes, and twelve-foot mosaic panes reflecting other mosaics.

The other is made of words: "tenebrose," "ineluctable," and "abrogation"—but not "sybaritic," "nilotic," or "alpine." (They cleave to other geographies, urban, agric, or mountainous, all together.) The second, like the first, has a history. The first, unlike the second, has only associations.

The first is populated by tall women in translucent plastic raincoats, short, muscular men in tanktops and loose camouflage fatigue pants, one out of thirteen of whom has a walrus moustache and is hung like a buffalo. The Japanese population is on the rise; and Native Americans have, recently, been migrating here from the west.

The second has a free public transportation system of pneumatic capsules, is cut by a river of No. 3 watch oil, and crouches in the shadow of the first. There are more animals in it than people—most of them with silver fur, ebon scales, or scarlet feathers. What human inhabitants stroll its streets tend to have hair the hue and crispness of rusted Brillo. They speak in gnomic phrases, punctuated by silences during which they examine their pocket calculators, the bolts on their roller blades, their antique calipers and circular slide rules.

The cities share, however, a dump.

And when the garbagemen from one poke pitch forks into the black sacks deposited there from the other, they step back, breathe in sharply—one or two brave ones scream—while still another stands there, eyes closed, the green canvas of his right pantsleg trembling.

22. Title for a Lacanian paper on heterosexuality: "A Lass and a Lack."

23. *The Palace and the Sea:* Late that night in the palace of Alcinous, the Traveler regaled the king and his courtiers with tales of the storm-bound, sun-shot sea. As the fire burned in the walk-in fireplace and serving women moved among the guests, refilling goblets with wine, he told of mast-high waves, rafts of ice, ropes of white fire that netted the winter waters, and the slow metamorphosis of the periplus, from split cliffs a-glitter in dawn sun to the black lace of forests under indigo evening; and of how his ship had sailed through mayhem and magic to the gate of hell.

But the little princess, whom almost everyone had forgotten by now, thought to herself as she heard him: Where is this fabulous sea? Isn't it all in the wash and wonder of his words, brought here, safe within the palace stones, made tame as a summer's pool beside which one picnics with the other girls, off in the forest . . . ?

For outside she could hear the rhetoric of the ocean, as it crashed at the foot of her home, yowling and growling around the rocks, leaping and hissing as high as her father's anciently laid foundations.

In the roaring fireplace a moist log at last took flame and—*cracked,* spouting sparks toward blackened chimney stones, sifting more ash onto the hearth and, for a moment, interrupting the flow and weave of the Traveler's cunning discourse on (his understanding of) the sea.

As if having heard his daughter's thought, King Alcinous now asked: "Say, once again, Traveler, where is that sea . . . ?"

23. "To Newton and to Newton's dog Diamond," Carlyle reminds us in

the second chapter of *The French Revolution*, "what a different pair of universes . . ."

24. "Man," says Dennis in the half-dark, "I'll fuck you up the ass so much the cum'll be runnin' out your nose—you won't need any moustache wax!" Odd how affection manifests itself in various ages and epochs, in various social niches.

25. If rhetoric is ash, discourse is fire . . .

26. The desire to be conscious of the process of losing consciousness, of having no consciousness at all—this paradox is source and kernel of the anxiety over dying and death.

27. I am awed, and just a bit terrified, at the mystery of my own existence. That something so rich and wonder-filled as fifty years or more of living should be given to someone as fallible and unimportant in the universe's larger scheme and just plain ordinary as I is astonishing.

28. The twin cities are, of course, Xanadu and Wagadu. Telemachus awaits his father's return in one; Telegonus, Odysseus's son by Circe (who, according to Eugammon of Cyrene, eventually slew his father by a spear tipped with fish bone, during Odysseus's shadowy second voyage), lurks in the other, waiting for the wanderer who, after divorcing Penelope and marrying Collidice, Queen of Thesprotia, took off on that mysterious second journey Dante, Tennyson, and Kazantzakis all write of.

Coleridge gave us the first city, while Leo Frobenius (the turn of the century's Robert Ardrey) and, more recently, Neil Gaiman in his Sandman comic, *The Doll's House: Prologue—Tales in the Sand*, brings the second to our attention.

29. Jabès's *Book of Questions,* Calvino's *If on a Winter's Night a Traveler . . .* , and Silliman's *The Alphabet* all seem to share something. The Silliman, by keeping the furthest from argument, seems the most radical to me right now. (I have moments when reading the fragments that compose *The Book* seem all too much like reading *The Journal of Albion Moonlight*—which unfortunately is not to praise either.)

30. In human society, there are two forces constantly in conflict: One always moves to socialize the sexually acceptable. The other moves to sexualize the socially unacceptable. Over any length of time, these two forces are always at play, revising the contours of the socio-sexual map.

31. Quasimodo's tercet,

> *Ognuno sta solo sul cuor della terra*
> *trafitto da in raggio di sole:*
> *ed è subito sera.*

> [Each alone at the earth's heart,
> fixed there on a sun ray:
> and it's suddenly evening.]

seemed to describe a romantic stance when I first read it at age 19 or so. Here, weeks before my 50th birthday, it seems a harsh metaphor for an all too hard-edged situation.

"And it's suddenly evening" has the same number of syllables as "ed è subito sera." But the English has more than twice the number of consonants and takes almost twice as long to say.

32. Here in Amherst, the present slides between the leafy and layered fact of immediacy and the drowsy retreat through darkness.

33. What does it mean, now that it takes me so much longer to remember things than it did even five years ago? I ask my mind to call up facts; where once they were yielded up to me in two, three seconds, today it's ten, fifteen, eighteen seconds before thought arrives in the brain, words mount the tongue. And occasionally they will not come at all without prompting—recently: the last name of the late actress Ruth Gordon; the term "certified" for a letter. When I was thirty-five, I recall noting that my dyslexia was substantially worse than it had been at 25. Is the memory situation a continuation of the same phenomenon—or is it some other development entirely?

And will I ever know?

What about the malaise, the extra weight, the free floating anxiety, all of which have their current forms in my life—if I'm honest—as much as they did when they last put me in the hospital at 22?

34. "Well, you can't see the sex / for the heterosexuality," writes Isaac Jackson in his poem "The Birds and Bees (Blues Poem)." How pleasant, a year after I read it, to run into the poet at MIT working as a computer jockey!

35. Four writers who, each reaching in an entirely different direction, achieve a sentence perfection that dazzles, chills, and—sometimes—frightens: William Gass, Joanna Russ, Guy Davenport, and Ethan Canin.

36. The poet sees two things: the world's absolute wonder and beauty in the way its edges and surfaces almost fit together in a purified geometry of desire appeased; and, at the same time, the poet sees through the world's interstices the banalities and uncomprehending stupidities with which its subjects constantly blat out what it's constituted of. Language—in its blather and breathless suspension—is at once villain and hero. Perhaps this is why reticence is such an overarching element of modernist esthetics.

37. The unarticulated myth of the American poet currently controlling so many American poetic non-careers is that anyone who has it together enough to teach regularly, edit anthologies, and write criticism cannot possibly live passionately enough to write a truly interesting poem—a good deal of this, doubtless, a holdover from the personal catastrophes of the once popular "confessional poets."

But even as "confessional" works grow less and less interesting with time, what sediments in the literary psyche still drags and dredges our ideas through its flour and egg.

As someone who has taught for four years now, there's something to the argument: only I would like to see it leave the realm of unspeakable myth and enter the pinball-courts of articulation: certainly I've never been happier that I'm not a poet since I've been a professor . . . !

Silliman is the first poet I know who really breaks through these constraints. He does it, basically, by writing such impassioned—and intelligent—criticism. He does it by embracing—passionately—the insights of contemporary literary theory and difficult discourse. He does it by eschewing as intellectually wimpy the notion that criticism itself is not as potentially passionate as poetry. What he convinces us of, in his criticism, is—quite apart from its relevance and rightness—he lives the most passionate life of the mind in America today!

He is a political poet par excellence.

At the same time, he takes the poet niche shaped by Valéry and lurches with it to the American coast.

Poets I read for pleasure: Auden, Van Duyn, Howard, Hacker, Heany, Neidecker, Bernstein, Hudgins, Levine, Cummins, Ashbery, Michael Dennis Browne . . .

But Silliman is a poet I read to break through into new halls and colonnades of verbal richness that, before, I simply didn't know were sealed up behind those walls and dead ends in the palace of art. His work must be studied, lived with. Its pleasures cannot be simply lapped up off its surfaces. But they are the subtler, sharper, and more resonant for the time they take to taste.

I wonder if I shall ever actually meet the man . . . ?

38. Too developed a sense of the usefulness of things militates against the preservation (rather paradoxically) of bourgeois order.

The sock lies in the middle of the rug. It's easy to say that the slob who's left it there simply wasn't thinking. But much more likely some nether thought of the following order did, indeed, occur: I don't know where the mate is. If I put it away, i.e., out of sight, if the mate turns up they will never get back together! Leave it lie there, then, and if, in an hour or a day or a week, the mate comes to light, I can put them together and then put the pair away. And sometimes—in an hour, or a day, or a week—that's what happens.

The problem is that, at such a tempo, the forces of disorder will simply swamp the forces of order.

The person maintaining neatness, however, must constantly go through some version of the following: That sock has no mate. Out it goes. Now I shall forget it. And if—in an hour or a day or week—the other turns up, out it goes too! And I shall forget it, too!

It is worth remembering that bourgeois order is only maintained at the expense of a ruthless, if not outright violent, attitude toward the objects—if not the people—which deviate from it.

To the extent that history is basically written in the detritus of things, maintenance of bourgeois order represents a constant and unflagging, if relatively low-level, destruction of history.

That is where the barbarism, as Benjamin originally spoke of it, comes from.

39. There are three things writers do not write about.

First, what everybody knows.

We all know fire engines are red. Thus, it is the mark of a bad writer to write "the red fire engine." Should a green fire engine come by, then the writer might be justified in remarking it. But not otherwise. With this in mind, at London University (back in the midst of writing "Shadows"), I once got into an after-lecture argument with Saul Kripke, who maintained that we could know things for certain about imaginary objects. Kripke's cited example came from Lewis Carroll's "Jabberwocky." Carroll had written:

> Beware the jub-jub bird and shun
> The frumious bandersnatch.

Claimed Kripke: We can know, therefrom, that "bandersnatches" are all, or are mostly, "frumious."

Claimed I: We can assume it only if we decide Carroll was a bad writer.

If all, or even most, bandersnatches are frumious, then there is no need for the writer to say so. If we assume Carroll was a good writer, however, frumious bandersnatches are likely as rare as green fire engines.

What possibly neither of us realized at the time was that Kripke's argument really hinged on the previous line: The verbs "beware" and "shun," set as they are in regular meter, evoke a discourse (and thus suggest a reading of the following line and its diction) that comes from an epoch before the modernist writing discourse my initial argument calls up, when, indeed, certain nouns were allowed "epithets"—an epithet being an adjective or set of modifiers that underline a self-evident quality that all acknowledge: the noble Brutus, the shining sun, the pitch-black night . . . Set by the formality of the diction of "beware," "shun," and the regularity of the meter, Kripke read "frumious" as an epithet for bandersnatch—whereas I chose to read it as an ordinary adjective. But "Jabberwocky" is a humorous poem. Who is to say where bathos, irony, and anachronism might not be read into its lines?

We can surmise many things about imaginary objects—more or less intelligently. But we can't *know* anything about them.

There is, indeed, an equally interesting argument to be formulated about imaginary aspects of actual objects. Are, for example, all birds "jub-jub". . . ?

The second thing that is not written about is that which we consider personally unimportant: for example, the true amount of muddle in the world. It was the Great God Muddle that some critic cited as the titular deity of Sterne's *Tristram Shandy*. But even there the fictive expression of muddle in no way reflects its real prevalence: this morning I got up and, still in my underwear, walked four times back and forth between the bedroom and the kitchen, looking for my coffee cup from yesterday, till, on a whim, I went into the study to find the cup sitting, where I had left it, beside my word processor. Yesterday, before going to my office at the university, I purchased a bagel and cream cheese, a glass bottle of cranberry juice, and a pecan square from the local bakery. Once in my office, I sat all the breakfast items on the edge of my crowded desk. Reaching for a pencil, I knocked the bottle of juice off the edge of the desk. Fortunately it hit the leg of my computer table, was deflected, so landed rolling and did not break. I dived to retrieve it, but the hand I grabbed the edge of the desk with moved a piece of paper, which the still paper-wrapped bagel was sitting on, so that it now fell to the floor. I put the juice on the desk and hurriedly turned to pick up the bagel, and my hand knocked the pecan square onto the floor—

All of them came up, went back on the desk, and I proceeded to eat my breakfast, trying not to dwell on the fact that I'd managed to knock every bit of it over. In the course of working on the revisions to this piece here, this afternoon I consumed most of a meal in eight or nine desultory trips to the refrigerator, most to get a single salami slice from the brown rumple of butcher paper wedged on the side of the second shelf—and, in one case, a spoonful from the container of cottage cheese—each trip immediately all-but-forgotten once it was over and I'd returned to the word processor here, to continue typing.

The conceit of the literary is that such things happen only in comedy, and are otherwise rare. But the truth is, they make up a disturbing percentage of our lives. We choose to look at them only through the esthetic framing of the comedic, which, by that framing, reassures us such happenings are not of major import. The truth is, however, that a good percentage of our lives is not just comic; it's slapstick.

The third area that is not written about is simply the socially proscribed: To what great period of literary achievement could an alien turn to learn of the workings of human life and society—the age of Greek tragedy, Japanese Haiku, the 19th Century Russian Novel, Medieval Chinese court poetry, High Modernism, the Victorian Novel, or the English Romantic Poets?—to discover that, say, human beings are creatures who, all of them, male, female, and child, have to void their bowels once or twice a day and empty their bladders between three and ten times in every twenty-four-hour period?

What poems or stories tell us that, in any random American crowd, about a third, between once and three times a week, take a small wad of wet toilet paper or cleaning rag and vigorously and carefully wipe away the hair, body scalings, and dust from the porcelain span between the back of the commode seat and the flush tank—while the other two-thirds are largely oblivious that such a job ever has to be done at all?

Neither Swift's exclamations over Celia's excretory functions nor Joyce's narration of Bloom's bath conveys such fundamental human facts.

Speaking of Joyce, how many readers of *Ulysses* today, I wonder, recall that the center of the controversy over the novel's supposed obscenity was the end of the Lotus-Eaters (section five), in which Bloom, by himself, takes a bath and observes his own pubic hair and genitals breaking the surface of the soapy water (". . . a languid, floating flower")—a scene, that, when I first read it at sixteen, I found jarringly erotic?

40. A memory remains with me from a winter visit, some twenty-five or more years ago, to the reading room of the New York Public Library. The late afternoon dimmed outside the high windows above the wrought iron balcony circling the hall, while yellow light puddled the long wooden tables under the reading lamps' green glass shades. After wait-

ing on the pew-like bench before the barred window under the me-
chanical-electric call board, with its black frame and red numbers
aglow behind the ground glass, I went to the wooden window when my
red number lit to receive my volumes. Minutes later, at one of the tables, my coat shrugged over the chair-back behind me, I began reading
over the works in various pamphlets and books of the poet Samuel
Bernhard Greenberg (1893–1917), copying out vivid lines or striking
stanzas into my spiral notebook, as, up in the little town of Woodstock,
New York, in the last, chilly weeks of 1923, Hart Crane had made similar copies from the Greenberg manuscripts, then in the possession of
William Murrell Fisher. My visit produced an epigraph to a chapter in a
novel I finished perhaps two years later.

But a return visit to the library only this past June—the same mechanical callboard, though it may have been repaired, has not been replaced—netted me an interesting revelation. In the novel, where I
quoted him at the head of the seventh chapter, Greenberg's name, I
now find, was inadvertently spelled "Greenburg." And in none of the
books currently among the Public Library stacks can I find the poem I
quoted a quarter of a century ago.

It's tempting, then, to imagine all these vanished texts, along with
their writers, if not the libraries in which the texts are on store, as inhabiting an alternate city, distinctly separate from ours, yes—yet closer,
distressingly closer, than any of us has hitherto imagined.

41. If rhetoric is ash, discourse is water . . .

42.   And then went down to the chips, set wheel to gambit,
            forth on the Reno night.
                —Ron Silliman, "Carbon," from The Alphabet

After Odysseus recounts to Naussica's father King Alcinous how the
crow-queen Circe, "dread goddess of human speech," exhorted him to
leave her isle of Aeaea—palindromal in English and near so (Aiaien)
in Greek—to visit Theben Tiresias in hell to receive wisdom, Odysseus
goes on to explain at the opening of book "Lambda" (that is, Book XI):

> *Autar epei r'epi katelthomen ede thalassan*
> *nea men ar tamproton erussamen eis ala dian,*
> *en d'iston tithemestha kai histia nei melainie,*
> *en de ta mela labontes ebesamen, an de kai autoi*
> *bainomen achnumenoi thaleron kata dakru cheontes.*

["But when we had come down to the ship and to the sea, first of all we drew
the ship down to the bright sea, and set the mast and the sail in the black

ship, and took the sheep and put them aboard, and ourselves embarked, sorrowing, and shedding big tears," in A. T. Murray's translation.]

In 1900, Samuel Butler rendered this, "When we had got down to the seashore we drew our ship into the water and got her mast and sails into her; we also put the sheep on board and took our places, weeping and in great distress of mind . . ." three years after he published *The Authoress of the Odyssey* (1897), a book that influenced Joyce, and that Pound was likely familiar with. The opening of "Lambda" (often called The Book of the Dead) gives rise to two modernist traditions. For at the beginning of "Lambda"'s second verse paragraph, Odysseus tells how soon his ship

> *He d'es peirath' hikane bathurroou Okeanoio.*
> *entha de Kimmerion andron demos te*
> *polis te, eeri kai nephele kekalummenoi . . .*

[". . . came to the deep-flowing Oceanus, that bounds the Earth, where is the land and city of the Cimmerians, wrapped in mist and cloud . . ."—Murray.]

The story is well known how in 1906 (or '08, or '10), Ezra Pound, browsing through the book stalls along the Seine's quay, purchased in an octavo volume Andreas Divus Justinopolitano's *"ad verbum translata"*—word for word translation—of *The Odyssey,* published in Paris in 1538, as part of the rebirth of interest in classical learning that gave the Renaissance its name.

Likely following notions that went back at least to those F. A. Woolf had put forward in 1795 (*Prolegomena ad Homerum*), Pound saw "Homer" as an amalgam of tales from different times, cobbled together more or less elegantly, more or less invisibly, somewhere before the classical age. Among that varied material, Pound was fairly sure that "Lambda," with its account of the calling up the dead, who come to drink the blood of the sacrifice—Elpinor, Anticleia, Tiresias, and high born Tyro—before speaking, followed by the parade of ghostly queens—Antiope, Alcmene, Megare, Jocasta, Chloris, Lede, Iphimedeia, Phaedra, Procris, Ariadne, Maera, Clymene, and Eriphyle . . .— represented the oldest material in *The Odyssey*. Using a set of principles for translation that sound like nothing so much as those Nabokov formulated to bring off his *Onegin*, certainly Divus had translated the opening more literally than most:

> *Ad postquam ad navem desaendimus, et mare,*
> *Navem quidem primum deduximus in mare divum,*
> *Et malu posuims et vela in navi nigra . . .*

Where the Greek begins "*Autar epei* . . ." (literally "But then," instead of the "But when . . ." that A. T. Murray settled on for the 1919 standard Loeb translation [quoted below the Greek], or the "At length we were at the shore . . ." that T. E. Lawrence gives us in his 1935 translation), Divus wrote "*Ad postquam* . . ."— literally "But after-that . . ." The problem with the English is that "*Autar*" is not just any old "But." For that, the Greeks used "*alla.*" Rather it is an emphatic "but"—a bit more like "but also." Also, it has a bit of the thrust of the Italian "*pertanto*" (literally "but-so-much," which usually comes out in English as "But of course"). This accounts for the "But's," the "At long last's," and the "Finally's" various translators have used to commence this passage.

Nevertheless, Pound was intrigued by the notion that what he took to be the most ancient poetic material in the poem (and thus some of the most ancient literary material in the West) began with a connective— and an emphatic connective at that—which might well be taken as joining it to prior material even older still, though now lost.

This, at any rate, was the spirit in which Pound began his own great serial composition poem, *The Cantos*, with his own translation of Divus's translation of Homer's account of Odysseus's trip to northern Cimmeria, where gaped the gate of hell:

> And then went down to the ship,
> Set keel to breakers, forth on the godly sea, and
> We set up mast and sail on that swart ship,
> Bore sheep aboard her, and our own bodies also,
> Heavy with weeping . . .

But T. E. Lawrence had a different and deprecating view of "Lambda": "Book XI, the Underworld, verges toward 'terribilitá'—yet runs instead to the seed of pathos, that feeblest mode of writing. The author misses his every chance of greatness, as must all his faithful translators." Yet Lawrence's Homer is one that most of us, scholar or general reader, probably have a bit of trouble recognizing, at least in some of its aspects: "a bookworm, no longer young, living far from home, a mainlander, city-bred and domestic. Married but not exclusively, a dog-lover, often hungry and thirsty, dark-haired. Fond of poetry, a great if uncritical reader of *The Iliad,* with limited sensuous range but an exact eyesight which gave him all his pictures. A lover of old bric-a-brac, though as muddled an antiquary as Walter Scott . . . He is all adrift when it comes to fighting and had not seen deaths in battle." El 'Awrence had, of course, both seen and dealt out many.

But it's probable that a young rural Texan, reading in *The Odyssey* as a teenager, sometime during the mid-twenties, had very much the same feelings about "Lambda" that Pound had picked up; for it was frozen, ice-and fog-bound Cimmeria that young Robert E. Howard, in the tiny town of Cross Plains, Texas, chose to make the home of his barbarian hero, Conan—who through his adventures is tormented by various and sundry supernatural escapees from just those gaping gates near Conan's place of birth.

And the same emphatic copula which, for Pound, connected *The Cantos* to something even more primal and proto- than the oldest poetic stuff of the Greeks, still, today, provides the various practitioners of the genre Howard initiated, "sword and sorcery" (Fritz Leiber's term for it), with a connection between the prehistoric and history itself.

43. The discursive model through which we perceive the characteristic works of High Modernism—from *The Waste Land* and *Ulysses* to *The Cantos* and Zukofsky's *"A"* and H. D.'s *Helen in Egypt*, from David Jones's *In Parentheses* and *The Anathēmata* to Charles Olson's *Maximus Poems* and Robert Duncan's *The Structure of Rime* and *Passages*—is that of a foreground work of more or less surface incoherence—narrative, rhetorical, and thematic—behind which stands a huge, and hugely unified, background armamentarium of esoteric historical and esthetic knowledge, which the text connects with through a series of allusions and relations that organize that armamentarium as well as give it its unity.

The educated reading such texts request is always a virtual one. Even somebody who is richly familiar with the commentaries and who has studied both sources and text can only hold onto fragments of both background and foreground, and then only for a more or less limited time.

What has happened, of course, is that eventually poets—if not other readers as well—have noted that, with or without access to the background armamentarium, there is nevertheless an *experience* of reading these texts. And numerous poets of the last forty years—if not, indeed, the last hundred—have tried to estheticize this affect directly.

Their forebear is Gertrude Stein—rather than Pound or Eliot. (The esoteric armamentarium model does not control the way we read, say, the prose in *The Making of Americans* or *Lucy Church Amiably*—not to mention in Burroughs's *Naked Lunch* or in William T. Vollmann's *You Bright and Risen Angels*.) The representational task of such poets, as it is with Stein's prose, was to generate a representation of thinking, rather than a specific and elaborated intellectual signified—as it still is, largely, in the poets who estheticize the affect without trying to pull together the intellectual background.

"Obscure" was the word applied to the hugely different Stein and Pound/Eliot/Joyce enterprises—though that Twentieth Century usage marks a major shift in the meaning of the word from its literary usage in the 19th Century.

A major 19th Century text to be labeled (perjoratively) obscure was Robert Browning's poem in six Books, *Sordello*, that figures at the start of Pound's "Canto II," much as "Lambda" figures at the start of "Canto I."

Sordello is the story of the poetic education of a 13th Century poet (Sordello) who begins as a page in a Mantua castle (with its ". . . maze of corridors contrived for sin, / Dusk-winding stairs, dim galleries . . ."). Some of its lessons parallel the young Browning's own poetic growth. The situation the poem describes is the Guelph/Ghibellin conflict (Browning's spelling) between Verona and Ferrara, the Pope and the House of Este (as well as the odd mountain bandit—or "Hill-cat," Browning's term), familiar to students of Dante. Today one makes one's way fairly comfortably through the poem with the footnotes of Pettigrew and Collins in the Penguin edition—footnotes of the sort that one might expect for a well-edited historical reconstruction first published (March 7th) in 1840. The problem is that, to follow the surface story, one needs to know a fair bit of history. (The current Penguin *Robert Browning, The Poems* goes a good way toward providing us with it.) The problem with the problem, however (and what makes for the poem's "obscurity"), is that, as one pursues the history on one's own (as one would have had to do as a contemporary reader of the poem), one discovers now that this character whom history records as a Guelph, Browning portrays as a Ghibellin. Others whom history records as bitterest enemies, Browning portrays as fast friends. And still others who were dead by the time of the events, Browning shows us as alive and kicking. Grandson becomes son. And important historical characters, such as the real Sordello's light o' love, Cunizza ("a lusty lady, married five times," notes editor Pettigrew), get squeezed out of the tale entirely.

A contemporary audience is likely to read this, in a young poet of 28, as simply his desire to tell whatever he wants to tell—letting history go hang, with perhaps a faint suspicion that a certain laziness as far as keeping on top of such research lies at the bottom of it all. But we would hardly conceive it as a major flaw: certainly it's offset by the poet's imagination. But though Pettigrew remarks, ". . . Ezra Pound, who found the poem a model of lucidity, is probably the only person who has ever seriously claimed to have understood *Sordello*," the poem's surface is no more confusing to the contemporary reader than, say, the surface of Keats's *Endymion*—and is often a good deal less so. Though what this judgment reflects more than anything, I suspect, is the kind of understanding a contemporary reader, brought up on Milton and Spenser on the one hand, and *The Cantos* and *Maximus Poems* on the other, now look for, i.e., a discursive difference the beginning of which Pound's early claim for comprehension signs.

Victorian readers felt, however, that if you bothered at all with a poem based on history, you should stick to the facts—or, that the alteration of facts should be meaningful, serving lucid, moral, or at any rate clear didactic, ends.

For the Victorians, *Sordello*'s obscurity lay not in its surface difficulty, but rather in the impossibility of justifying Browning's historical deviance. Browning's obscurity is the opposite of the High Modernists'. His surface is coherent. It was the organization of his intellectual armamentarium that was unbearably murky.

Although only 157 copies of *Sordello* were actually sold in the first ten years of the poem's life, the charge of obscurity—the moral obscurity the clearing up of which would have justified Browning's historical revisionism—besmirched Browning's reputation for twenty-odd years after the poem appeared.

When, with the popularity of his later poetic collections, such as *Dramatis Personae* (1864) and the four-volume *Ring and the Book* (1868–69: i.e., the same years as *Les Misérables* and *20,000 lieues sous la mer . . .*), attention turned back to Browning's earlier work and "what it meant." At that point, Browning made the famous quip that eventually would become enough a part of general literary folklore so that, some years before I entered high school, my father (no great reader, he) would quote it regularly and repeatedly to me, with a chuckle, as a warning against esthetic obscurity of any sort—and its wages—in the usual, if, in his case, gentle, bourgeois attack on abstraction in art and poetic difficulty (which for him included e. e. cummings just as much as T. S. Eliot). Browning had said: "When I first wrote *Sordello*, only God and I knew what it meant. Today, only God knows"—a judgment most late Twentieth-Century readers find wildly over the mark, unless we reawaken a fine understanding of the Victorian context.

"Sordello" (with quotes, i.e., the poem's title) is a metonym for its topic: "the education of a poet." And Sordello (without the quotes, i.e., the character) is a metonym for the character of the poet so educated. Read in this way, the obscurity (in the contemporary sense) of the opening tercet of Pound's "Canto II" diminishes significantly:

> Hang it all, Robert Browning,
> There can be but one "Sordello."
> But Sordello, and my Sordello?

Hang it all, Robert Browning, there can be but one "poetic education." But what about the poetic character so educated—and my poetic character so educated? Certainly this is a reasonable enough question for a poet who's just finished contemplating the "most ancient poetic material" in the West—before Pound (who allegedly began writing this Canto sitting on the steps of a Venice Cathedral, looking out over the waters) let his thoughts return by way of the historical Sordels and the Chinese artist So-shu and Helen/Eleanor/eleptolis (destroyer of cities) back to Odysseus and the hell-spawned tale of high-born Tyro, the first queen the Traveler spoke with after receiving a truly extraordinary guilt trip from his mother, Anticleia.

Queen Tyro loved the river god of the Enipus, till the ocean god Poseidon grew jealous, disguised himself as the lesser god, her lover, and struck her with a tidal wave while he held her in his arms: and she bore him two sons, Pelias and Nelias . . .

Most poets who write what can be called by today's meaning "obscure poems" are generally still in thrall to the subject. The problem with such poetry—the currently "obscure," as it clings to the subject—is that much of it, beyond a certain level, is unjudgeable as well as dull.

A poet such as Silliman, however, beginning with his commitment to the sentence/writing/prose, as well as to what he calls "the materiality of the signifier," manages to put a torque on a good deal of his work that orients it toward the object—which, for me as an sf writer, committed to my own object critique, reinvests it with a whole range of interest and intensity.

44. Often it's been observed: Writing is largely habit. Paradoxically, not writing can also be a habit. The writer who, again and again, must defer or delay getting to pen, paper, or processor finally develops mental habits of deferment and delay. A good percent of what passes for "writer's block" is simply the habit of not writing, gotten out of hand and reaching the level of addiction—possibly because of pleasurable feedback, such as concern and attention from others over the problem or even through good feelings about the things accomplished instead.

Thomas Disch's cure for writer's block at the Clarion Workshop was simply to insist that no other student communicate with the "blocked" student in any way, or even acknowledge his/her existence, until she or he had written a story.

As a technique, it was devastatingly effective—usually succeeding within twenty-four hours.

45. *ABC,* the first, gray, paper-covered chapbook of The Alphabet, was

published by Tuumba Press in October, 1983. It consists of three parts, "Albany," "Blue," and "Carbon."

"Albany"'s opening evokes a verbal arena between essay and narrative; yet the fragmentedness of the first sentence with the third's non-sequitur creates narrative and argumentative dislocations—even if sentences two, four, and five alone almost cohere:

> If the function of writing is "to express the world." My father withheld child support, forcing my mother to live with her parents, my brother and I to be raised together in a small room. Grandfather called them niggers. I can't afford an automobile. Far across the calm bay stood a complex of long yellow buildings, a prison . . .

Anyone who has passed through the Bay Area is likely to think of Alcatraz, sitting out in San Francisco Bay—and someone more familiar with the detailed geography of the environs will know that, from Albany, San Quentin is visible across the water (The "yellow" specifies it; Alcatraz is green) and connect it geographically with Silliman's title. Readers of Silliman's *Ketjak* and *Tjanting* will also suspect that some formal pattern governs the progression of sentences, even if it is not immediately visible. But even while the reader ponders on formal possibilities, the first sentence-fragment becomes the opening proposition of a grand syllogism, for which every subsequent sentence in the work serves in turn, through an initial implied "Then . . . ," as its inference.

The Alphabet's next volume to reach print was *Paradise* (Burning Deck, Providence, in 1985—the first of Silliman's poems I read. Its Library of Congress Catalogue Information erroneously gives Silliman's birth date as 1935; actually he was born in '46). Then came *Lit* (Poets and Poets Press, Elmwood, Connecticut, 1987), *What* (Figures, 1988), and *Manifest* (Zarstele Press, Leguna, 1990). The sixth volume to appear, *Demo to Ink* (Chax Press, Tucson, 1992), is relatively thick, the heftiest yet published. With its appearance, the whole *Alphabet* gains a structural clarity. *Demo to Ink* contains six parts, "Demo," "Engines" (in collaboration with Rae Armantraut—joint authorship explaining, perhaps, the single plural among the alphabetic progression of part titles so far), "Force," "Garfield," "Hidden," and "Ink," continuing and defining the progression begun in the first volume, "Albany," "Blue," "Carbon" . . .

The alphabet is, above all things, an incrementally, incredibly, dazzlingly inventive exploration of possible sentence forms; questions, exhortations, fragments, run-ons . . .

Its first-level pleasure lies in the energy and inventiveness of precisely that array, stitched through the shocks and thrills of its equally interesting juxtapositions—suggesting a Rhetoric of near-all possible sentential collisions. Nor do the collisions really occur between sentences: most of the time, rather, they occur somewhere in the middle of the next sentence, when, no matter how prepared we are, its first few words have already established continuity with the sentence before: thus, because we cannot predict where semantic dislocation will manifest (and when it happens, it is always already, as it were, over), these juxtapositions remain fresh and are always and endlessly surprising. But it is these connections—and connections shattered—that are the contemplative objects of Silliman's work; and it is these objects among the sentential cascade, in their rhythmic explosions across whatever generative structure we can pick up, that make the work more than, and more important than, a simple lyric rhapsody of discrete and sensuous sentences. For a reader open to them, such pleasures are like those of a day at the world's largest and most exotic zoo, as we move, not from peacock to koala to python to three-toed sloth, but between animals that are always a hybrid of some two.

Poems suggest a vision of the world. And finally that vision turns around to place its own analytical grid before an image of the self that perceives.

The world of The Alphabet has a surprising material specificity, a social saturation, and an observational intelligence that is as concerned with the world as it is with the word.

And the poetic subject of The Alphabet?

It is not the subject unified by consistent and coherent narrative strategies. It is a subject that is, one suspects in those moments where formal patterns are intuitable, obsessively intrigued by system; but it is still a poetic subject who refuses to present him- or herself as outside history via the move of closing or completing an easily masterable system that, through the obvious gesture of closure, steps beyond historical consideration. It is a subject whose units both of perception and action are perceived as no larger than single sentences—axioms, grasps, insights, seizures, exhortations, visions.

Silliman's criticism (e.g., *The New Sentence*, Roof Books, New York, 1989; or "Canons and Institutions: New Hope for the Disappeared," in *The Politics of Poetic Form: Poetry and Public Policy*, Charles Bernstein, ed., Roof Books, New York, 1990) tells us that there is nothing passive about such a poetic subject. Indeed, Silliman is the most passionate and persuasive polemicist I know of writing today. If anything, the rigorous an-argumentative limits he has set on his poetic enterprise, most forcefully dramatized throughout the thirteen sections I have so far seen of The Alphabet, seems to have provided him with an explosively political arsenal of argumentative material.

Certainly the most systematic of poets (the sentence collections in succeeding sections of *Ketjak,* for example, expand by a strict Fibonacci series), Silliman is nevertheless a systematician of a very different sort from the ones modernism taught us how to read.

Most sensitive poetry readers would probably consider it near-sacrilege, say, to juggle significantly the order of *The Cantos,* the variously dated sections of *"A",* or the sub-poems that make up *Passages.* But while, at the level of system, *Demo to Ink* is clearly the "second" book of The Alphabet and "follows" *ABC,* an actual reader of the poem, even while he or she might idly wonder if the exigencies of small press poetry publishing were such that the *Demo to Ink* parts were, indeed, written right after "Albany," "Blue," and "Carbon," and simply had to wait this long to see print, will still probably not sense any loss of enjoyment from the fact that she or he read other sections first; and that is specifically because we are not excluded from Silliman's system, even when we're not sure what it is—not in the same way that even the momentary inability to access some part of the background intellectual armamenterium of the great high modernist monologues, no matter how much we're impressed by them, still excludes us; and that exclusion, absent in Silliman, is still the esthetic aspect of the process by which an establishment excludes the oppressed from history.

This is not poetry as personal adventure made public. Rather this is poetry as what civilized people do—and what civilized people interested in the language of the tribe ought from time to time to take a look at, get interested in, and enjoy. But the cumulative effect of thirty, forty, seventy-five pages of Silliman's work communicates a passion in his exploration/construction of the labyrinths of language as great as—if not greater than—any personal adventure I know of in our epoch.

46. Coleridge begins Chapter Five of his 1817 *Biographia Literaria* with this observation: "There have been men in all ages who have been impelled as by an instinct to propose their own nature as a problem, and who devote their attempts to its solution. The first step was to construct a table of distinctions, which they seemed to have formed on the principal of the absence or presence of the will." One must smile as one sees Coleridge himself eminently characterizable in such a way. Whether it is a universal trait or not, certainly it is a Romantic one. And a hundred-ten years later, in his famous *Correspondence with Jacques Rivière,* Antonin Artaud might easily have gone to school at Coleridge's feet, anent precisely this point, as he demands that Rivière enlighten him as to whether or not Artaud's own form of madness—a collapsing will that prevents him from ever bringing a poem to the perfection demanded

by the esthetic of the "unified impression"—can consort with valid, literary creativity.

Is it too gross an observation that writers who are likely to make their personality problems a center for their writerly investigations are the ones whose problem impedes their writing? Certainly there are other writers who are not about to make their own personality problems the center of their intellectual delving. I mean those of us who, in spite of good intentions and common sense, must write. I mean those of us who, sunk in myriad hypochondriachal anxieties and a-swirl in cosmi-comical doubts, move to the typewriter to record a few and by so doing escape so many more. I mean those of us who, when all logic, all our friends, and all the circumstances of our person and the world say (and say truly), you would be a lot better off if you didn't write but rather did X, Y, or Z, find ourselves picking up a notebook and starting to put down words—and keep at it for hours, for days on end . . . It still can make me cry to remember my daughter, aged three, running up to me at my desk, tugging at my knee to entreat me, "Daddy! Daddy, don't write!"—or can simply embarrass me to recall wife one year or lover another passing through the next room with angry steps, while, for the tenth hour of the third day, I sat at the typewriter. This, at any rate, is a problem the contemporary writer is going to hide, going to hope at worst is ignored or at best turned into a virtue by those who come after; but it's the last problem the writer is going to probe, interrogate, and whose solution he or she will seek to turn into a carefully articulated field for philosophical adventure. But, with its attendant absent-mindedness, preoccupation, and chronic personality absence, this problem causes far more pain, I'm sure, than the other—whether or not it is connected in any way to talent.

47. Certainly I would like it said of me, as it was once said of Maurice Ravel: He had no secret except the secret of his genius. But what we all fear is that time's judgment will turn out to be: He had no secrets at all.

— *Amherst/New York*
March/April 1992

Atlantis Rose . . .

Some Notes on Hart Crane

> He is a great average man; one who, to the best thinking, adds
> a proportion and equality in his faculties, so that men see in
> him their own dreams and glimpses made available and made
> to pass for what they are. A great common-sense is his warrant
> and qualification to be the world's interpreter. He has reason,
> as all the philosophic and poetic class have: but he has also
> what they have not,—this strong, solving sense to reconcile his
> poetry with the appearances of the world, and build a bridge
> from the streets of the cities to the Atlantis . . . He never writes
> in ecstasy, or catches us up into poetic raptures.
>
> —Emerson, "Plato"

I

A reading at once sophisticated and rich—of a poem as complex as *The Bridge*—must start with details and distinctions: the realization, perhaps, that, in Crane's case, even if they started off one, by the end of his poem, Cathay and Atlantis do not allegorize the same notion: Cathay was the mistaken goal from which Columbus, on his first voyage to the New World, returned, and, after three more, one of which was a major colonization push with 17 ships and 1500 colonists, died unaware he had not found.

Atlantis was the goal of Crane's own vision.

In 1922 Harold Hart Crane first read Eliot's *The Waste Land* in that November's *Dial* and conceived his own poem as an answer to Eliot's that would offer—without any particular jingoistic pretensions—a specifically American affirmation to counter Eliot's presumably international despair. Crane worked in spurts, on *The Bridge*'s "Finale" and other poems, that year and the next, around his job at J. Walter Thompson's Advertising Agency, where his accounts included Pine Tar Honey,

Sloan's Liniment, and, yes, Naugahyde. Possibly after an incident in which the hung-over Crane threw a lot of perfume out the office window, he quit Thompson's in October 1923, to spend November and December with sculptor Gaston Lachaise's stepson John Nagle and writer William Slater Brown at the Rector house in Woodstock, New York.

There, while visiting one evening, Woodstock resident and art critic William Murrell Fisher told Crane about the Viennese-born poet Samuel Bernhard Greenberg (December 13th, 1893–August 16th, 1917), sixth of the eight children and youngest son to Jacob and Hannah Greenberg.

An embroiderer specializing in gold and silver, largely for religious purposes, Jacob Greenberg had brought his family to New York's Lower East Side when Samuel was four or five. The family moved frequently about the city's Jewish neighborhood, while during the week Samuel attended Public School 166 at Rivington Street and Suffolk and on Saturdays Hebrew school. Hannah died on February 19th, 1908, and was buried in a Brooklyn cemetery. On the chill funeral day, the family rode back home in a wagon—across the Brooklyn Bridge. Between 1909 and 1911 Samuel lived with his older brother Daniel. In 1910, through his older brother Morris, Samuel met a circle of musicians and artists, including art-critic Fisher, who worked at or were connected with the Metropolitan Museum of Art. (Daniel and Morris were both serious piano students.)

From 1911 on, Samuel lived with Morris—when not hospitalized: Between Spring and Autumn of 1912, while working in his older brother Adolf's leather bag shop, Samuel was diagnosed with tuberculosis. Three days after the first of the year in 1913, Jacob died. For six or seven weeks starting in May that year, Samuel was hospitalized at the Montefiore Home, after which he stayed a month or so with his sister's family in Westerly, Rhode Island, convalescing and working for his brother-in-law in a horse-drawn wagon selling piece goods in Rhode Island and Connecticut. Back in New York, he pursued his writing, painting, and music—when not working at Adolf's, visiting his friends at the Metropolitan, or going with them to concerts or coffee shops. After seven hospitalizations over four years, early on a muggy summer's evening in mid-August, 1917, Samuel died, age twenty-three, in the paupers' hospital on Ward's Island.

After Samuel's death, older brother Morris Greenberg gave Fisher five of his younger brother's notebooks. Morris entrusted them to Fisher in hopes that his younger brother's art critic friend might get his brother's poems published—which Fisher did, after a fashion: A year after Greenberg's death, he printed Greenberg's poem "The Charming Maiden" in a magazine edited out of Woodstock, *The Plowshare* of June 1918.

Two and a half years later, in the January 1920 issue, writing under his professional name, William Murrell, Fisher wrote and published an eight-page appreciation and memoir of the young poet, "Fragments of a Broken Lyre"—followed by a selection of ten of Greenberg's poems.

On that winter evening in Woodstock, three years later in 1923, fascinated by Fisher's account of Greenberg and his poetry, Crane arranged to borrow the five Greenberg notebooks in Fischer's possession—at least one of which was a leather-bound, book-sized album, with marbled endpapers (that had belonged to someone named Sidney in 1898, for that is the name and date written in pencil and later erased from the first page, though legible even today), and which Greenberg had half-filled with neat fair copies of his poems for 1913 and 1914. On 19 sheets of yellow foolscap, Crane typed out forty-two of Greenberg's poems. (Unbeknownst to Fisher or Crane at the time, Daniel Greenberg had preserved another thirty-five pocket notebooks, memorandum pads, and sketchbooks, as well as fugitive papers belonging to his younger brother: these contained, among more memorable items, drafts of a letter from a hospital, more poems, miniature portraits of Fisher and Halprin, as well as various Jewish men seated on benches about the Lower East Side, a stunning view north through the crossed cables of the Brooklyn Bridge, and a sketch of the Judson Church tower done from Washington Square in summer.) Slater Brown recalls Crane actually taking Greenberg's manuscripts back to New York City on the train with them a little after Christmas; but, as Fisher remembers Crane's returning them just before leaving Woodstock, Brown is probably confusing Crane's own typescripts with the originals.

We'll digress for a few more pages, because, even though they never met, Samuel Greenberg is still an important and poignant figure in the Hart Crane story.

After a page-and-a-half divagation on the differences between the romantic view and the realistic view of the relation between poverty and the artist, "Fragments of a Broken Lyre" goes on:

> The case of Samuel Bernhard Greenberg is exceptionally affecting, both in the sudden flowering of his gift and in the pathos of his end: for it is indeed remarkable that a boy of no education or advantages should write such beautiful lyrics as he has done, and it is a sad reflection on our appreciation and hospitality that he died in a public institute for destitute consumptives . . . Greenberg's brief story is interesting: born in Vienna of Austrian-Jewish parentage, he was brought to New York when a child, and after a few months in the public schools was put to work in a leather goods factory. At the age of

seventeen his inherited tendency to consumption had been so fostered by the dust and confinement of the leather shop that he was told he was too weak to be of any further service there. Then began what he pathetically referred to later as his "freedom" and his "education."

It was at that time I first heard of Sammy, as we all called him, through a friend [George Halprin] who was giving music lessons to some other member of the Greenberg family [i.e., Daniel Greenberg, Samuel's oldest brother]. Arriving at the flat on Delancey Street one evening, my friend was much surprised to hear fragments of Chopin's 2nd Ballad imperfectly yet sensitively played by someone in the inner room. Knowing his pupil had no such delicacy, either of feeling or of touch, my friend inquired who was at the piano, and he was told it was "only Sammy." My friend entered the twilight room, and distinguished a tall thin figure upon the stool. The boy seemed dull, could not or would not say anything, except, in answer to questions, that he could not read music, that he played by ear only. Upon this my friend offered to teach him, and tried to do so, but made little progress, as the boy found difficulty in focusing his attention, and seemed unable to grasp the more conscious mathematics involved. Nevertheless my friend was much impressed by the boy, and came to tell me about him, and said he would bring him to see me, adding:

"He is uncanny and inarticulate, but there is something wonderful about him."

And so it proved. When Sammy came to see me he volunteered nothing except that Mr. George Halprin had sent him. But he used his eyes well—took in everything, and waited. I examined him curiously: tall and thin of figure, with a small face framed in wavy, gold-brown hair, a high forehead, two wonderfully nice brown eyes, a rather large wide nose, and a full red mouth which made his chin seem smaller than it actually was. His manner was quiet and his voice gentle. I tried to converse with him, but to no purpose. I then asked if I could help him in any way. His glance immediately fell upon my table.

"You have books?" he questioned.

"Yes," I replied, "would you like some?"

"You have good books—classics? I have only a little time."

At that moment I did not realize the significance of his saying he "had only a little time," but I humored his demand for classics and gave him Carlyle's *Heroes and Hero-Worship,* Emerson's *Essays,* and an anthology of English verse. I inquired what he had been reading, and was astonished to hear him say:

"The Dictionary."

And a few months later he brought me a handful of poems—some of which are among the best he has done. I encouraged him to write, and from that time on (until his breakdown some two and a half years later) I saw much of him. His gentle, ingenuous personality exercised a great charm over all who met him, and his early diffident silence gave way to an elliptical, rather epigrammatic style of conversation which was continually surprising his friends by reason of its direct and simple wisdom.

After a further pair of paragraphs on art, the average man, and the civilization that obtrudes between them—and the rare individuals, like Greenberg, who see "both beyond and through" them—Fisher concludes:

> Samuel Bernhard Greenberg is of this company, is as frank and mysterious as a child. He is much younger than his years, and much wiser than his knowledge,—for he is of the few rare, child-like spirits which never become sophisticated, yet through mystic penetration surprise our deepest truths with simple ease. Born with a look of Wonder in his eyes, he has never lost sight of the Beauty of the world, nor of the Divinity of its inhabitants: though painfully aware that they themselves have.
>
> Seated one evening in the house of a friend, where a few had gathered to speak of Music, Art and Song, he exclaimed (after one present had read a poem exemplifying the feeling of poetry from the trammels of versification):
>
> "Ah! Delancey Street needs that!"
>
> Now, although we knew he lived down there, we did not at once see the connection. But his next remark was quietly eloquent of his whole attitude:
>
> "I should like to walk nude with a girl through Delancey Street."
>
> And we who knew him immediately understood that he craved to feel the presence in all the world (of which Delancey Street was but a symbol) of a guilelessness which could see nakedness and be unashamed, of a simplicity of thought and action which should be pure, artless, and brotherly.
>
> For such he is: and yet, as I have suggested, possessed of a mystic wisdom which quite disarms and sets as naught our dear-bought worldly Knowledge.

In this account there are a few inaccuracies—young Greenberg attended school for quite a bit more than the "few months" Fisher allots to him. Similarly, he worked in his brother Adolf's leather bag shop a good deal longer than Fisher suggests—on and off from his tenth year through his eighteenth. But the young man's general affect is certainly there in Fisher's recollections.

Back in 1915, Greenberg, who had been making fair copies of his poems for some months now, approached Fisher about the possibility of publication. On April 22 of that year, Fisher wrote to Greenberg:

> I am happy to hear that you propose to publish some of your poems, and I shall be glad to aid you in any manner possible. But first, as I have your best interests at heart, I feel I should warn you that a careful selection should be made, and that some of the poems will have to be slightly changed—a word or an expression.

Publication did not come, however, till after Greenberg's death.

Here is the text of the fourth of the poems Fisher printed after his appreciation—"Serenade in Grey"—first as I transcribed it (line numbers are added) from Greenberg's fair copy, now in the Fales Collection at New York University, followed by Fisher's *Plowshare* version.

SERENADE IN GREY

Folding eyelid of the dew doth set
The cover remains in the air,
And it rains, the street one color set,
Like a huge gray cat held bare
5   The shadows of light—shadows in shade
Are evenly felt—though parted thus
Mine eyes feel dim and scorched from grey
The neighboring lamps throw grey-stained gold
Houses in the distance like mountains seen
10   The bridge lost in the mist
The essence of life remains a screen
Life itself in many grey spots
That trickle the blood until it rots
A good sized box with windows set
15   Seems like a tufted grey creature alive
Smoothly sails o'er the ground
Like the earth invisible in change doth strive
Black spots, that rove here and there
Scurry off—float into the cover
20   Spot of gray—were close together
When color mixes its choice, a lover.

SBG 1914

Now, Fisher's *Plowshare* version—with Fisher's "slight" changes of "a word or an expression":

IV SERENADE IN GREY.

The soft eyelid of the dew doth set,
Yet the cover remains in the air,
And it rains; the street one color set,
Like a huge grey cat, out there.
5   The shadows in light, the shadows in shade,

Are evenly felt, though parted thus.
My eyes feel dim and weak from the grey,
And the nearby lamps throw gold-stained dust.
Houses in the distance like mountains seem,
10   The Bridge is lost in the mist,
And life itself is a warm grey dream
Whose meaning no one knows, I wist!
A long black box within a window bound
Seems like a furry creature alive,
15   And is, as it smoothly glides o'er the ground,
Like the earth which in viewless change doth strive.
Black spots, that flit here and there,
Scurry off—disappear in the cover.
Two spots of grey—were close together,
20   When color mixes to choice—behold a lover!

(The McManis and Holden version of 1947 is somewhere in between
my transcription and Fisher's emendation, though it does not alter any
of Greenberg's actual words—only punctuation marks.) The sort of
"fix-up" Fisher imposes (if not McManis and Holden) is out of favor
today—though Emily Dickinson suffered similar "corrections" practically until the three-volume variorum edition of her complete poems
in 1955. What is notable about Fisher's emendations is that, while here
and there a comma may, indeed, clarify Greenberg's initial intentions,
the general thrust of his changes is to take the highlight off the word as
rhetorical object and to foreground, rather, coherent meaning.

All poetry—good and bad—tends to exist within the tensional field
created by two historic propositions:

As Michael Riffaterre expresses the one, on the first page of his
1978 study *The Semiotics of Poetry:* "The language of poetry differs from
common linguistic usage—this much the most unsophisticated reader
senses instinctively . . . poetry often employs words excluded from common usage and has its own special grammar, even a grammar not valid
beyond the narrow compass of a given poem . . ."

The opposing principle for poetry has seldom been better put than
by Wordsworth, writing of his own project in the "Preface to Lyrical
Ballads, Pastoral, and Other Poems" in the 1802 edition of *Lyrical Ballads:* ". . . to choose incidents and situations from common life, and to
relate or describe them, throughout, as far as possible, in a selection of
language really used by men . . ."

Now, in the very same sentence in which he upholds the difference
between poetic and ordinary language, Riffaterre goes on to remind us

that ". . . it may also happen that poetry uses the same words and the same grammar as everyday language." And on the other side of a semicolon, in the same sentence in which he extols the "language really used by men," Wordsworth reminds us that poetry tries, for its goal, "at the same time, to throw over them a certain coloring of imagination, whereby ordinary things should be presented to the mind in an unusual way . . ." Presumably this secondary task is accomplished by *unusual* language.

The question then is not which is right and which is wrong, but which is primary and which is secondary—and *how* primary and *how* secondary. At various times over the last two hundred years the perceived relation between them has changed. The ministrations of a Fisher (in the case of Greenberg) during the late teens of the century currently ending, or of a Higginson (an early editor of Dickinson) during the '90s of the previous century, merely document where the tensions between them had stabilized at a given moment.

The archaic forms, the inversions, as well as the specialized vocabulary were, in the first third of the twentieth century, simply part of poetry's *specialized* language. And although they would be almost wholly abandoned by poets during the twentieth century's second half, even a high modernist such as Pound was using them as late as *The Pizan Cantos* (1948): "What though lov'st well remains." "Pull down thy vanity!"—though, after that, even in the *Cantos,* they pretty much vanish.

As written, Greenberg's "Serenade" gives the effect of an observation so exact that, now and again, because of his strict fidelity to the observation process, *we* cannot tell *what* is being observed; this effect is as much a result of the poem's incoherencies—where we cannot follow the word to its referent—as it is of those places where the conjunction of word *with* referent seems striking. In Fisher's revision, things run much more smoothly—and, I suspect for most modern readers, much less interestingly. Violences at both the level of the signifier (e.g., "mine eyes feel dim and scorched from grey") and of the signified (e.g., the rotting blood) are repressed—and with them, the sense of rigor cleaving to whatever writing process produced the poem. Both Fisher and Holden/McManis strive to clear up the ambiguity of the antecedent of "though parted thus"—though, under sway of Empson (*Seven Types of Ambiguity,* 1935), the modern reader is likely to count that ambiguity among the poem's precise pleasures: Is it the shadows of light and shadows in shade that are parted . . . or the eyes? Greenberg's undoctored text (or *less* doctored text: even letter-by-letter, point-by-point transcription involves judgments; and who can say what doctoring Greenberg himself would have approved had he been able to see his poems through the ordinary channels of copy-editing and galley correction usually preceding print) generates a sense that, for all the strained rhymes and inversions, that process is one of intense energy, rigor, and commitment. This vanishes—or at least becomes much less forceful—after Fisher's changes.

When, after their conversation that winter night in Woodstock, Crane came to make his own transcriptions of Greenberg's poems, what's important to remember is that Crane went back to Greenberg's actual notebooks, the ones loaned him by Fisher, and thus to Greenberg's exacting and difficult originals—not to Fisher's *Plowshare* revisions. Given the development of Crane's own poetics, as well as Crane's influence on the poetic development of the times to come after him, this is meaningful.

Like most young writers—like many young readers—Crane had already encountered a number of writerly enthusiasms: Nietzsche, Wilde, Rimbaud . . . all of whom had left their marks on his poetry, all of whom had raised questions for the young poet that set his work in interesting tension with theirs. But Greenberg was particularly important—because in many ways he seemed Crane's own discovery, and because the fact that he had been ignored by the greater literary world despite his undeniable verbal energy and poetic vigor made it easy for the then all but unknown Crane to sympathize and identify.

Back in New York City in 1924, after a precarious January and February between 45 Grove Street, 15 Van Nest Place (now Charles Street), and the Albert Hotel on University Place and 10th Street, all in Greenwich Village, Crane finally got another job as a copywriter at Sweet's Catalogue Service, where he worked with Malcolm Cowley.

At the end of the second week of April Crane moved into 110 Columbia Heights in Brooklyn, into a room on the third floor—and, in the course of it, consummated a recently begun affair with a Danish sailor, three years his senior, Emil Opffer (April 26, 1897–19-?), a sometime communications officer and sometime ship's printer. Goldilocks was Crane's sometime nickname for him (and sometimes Phoebus Apollo); Crane's own sexual *nom d'amour* was occasionally Mike Drayton. 110 was Emil's father's building. A one-time seaman like his son, and now editor of Brooklyn's Danish-American paper, *Nordlyset,* Emil, Sr., lived there too.

The relationship began in blissful happiness for both men. Probably during the first two weeks of September 1924, while Emil, Jr., was away on a voyage, Emil, Sr., went into the hospital for an operation, during which—or just after which—he died. On Emil's return from sea, Hart and Emil's brother Ivan met Emil at the dock, broke the news, and took the disconsolate young man home. Now Hart and Emil took over the father's old room, Hart again working on his poetry. Emil went back to sea on another voyage . . .

Eventually the relationship devolved into jealousies, finally to break up and resettle into a more or less distant friendship, that continued until 1930—the last time the two men saw one another. I quote at some length Crane's close friend, Samuel Loveman, who, in his seventies, wrote this account of the relationship (two years before Stonewall, by the bye) in his introduction to the young critic Hunce Voelker's impressionistic 1967 study, *The Hart Crane Voyages:*

[Crane] urged me to come to New York. "I want you to live near me," he said. "Brooklyn Heights is one of the loveliest places in the whole world. Imagine, the panorama incessantly before one's eyes—a glorification of beauty with the New York skyline always before one, Brooklyn Bridge, ships that come and go by day and night—and sailors. You will never care to live elsewhere, and wherever I may be I shall always return to you."

He continued to disclose his happiness. "I have met a young man, a seaman, at Fitzi's [Eleanor Fitzgerald, director of the Provincetown Playhouse], and I realize for the first time what love must have meant to the Greeks when one reads Plato. He's a Scandinavian and extremely handsome, yellow-haired and blue-eyed—a real human being. I believe my love is returned. He's at sea now; you must meet him when his voyage is over. I'll never come back to Cleveland. If mother wants to see me let her visit me in New York. For the first time in my life I'm utterly free from the ghastly family bondage and the internal squabbles between Mother and Father. Their divorce seems to have made no difference. Money and me seem to be the sole crux of their dissension. I'll be out of it for good."

I met Hart's "Greek" ideal on his return from the voyage, and he answered his description—an extremely well-coordinated and attractive youngster, certainly prepossessing but outwardly unemotional, and since Hart was inwardly a veritable cauldron of conflict, I felt that this balance in their friendship was sufficiently warranted. I continued to see him day after day; his later acceleration in drinking was not then present and his sexual promiscuity apparently absent. He had acquired what he claimed to be the first copy of *Ulysses* ever to reach America, smuggled in by a friend [Gorham Munson], and bored me interminably by his insistence on reading it to me aloud. Spirited and certainly assertive on occasions of ordinary conversation, Hart's recitals abutted into a kind of clergical drone. He, on his part, assailed my own way of reading.

Then, the inevitable happened. His friend returning unexpectedly one evening to their apartment at 110 Columbia Heights, encountered Hart's stupid betrayal. There was no explosion, except Hart's ineffectual hammering protestations and attempt at an explanation—then silence. The friendship was resumed; their love never.

Yet in this fulmination of love and disaster, there emerged the creation of Hart's *Voyages*—poetry as passionate and authentic as any love-poetry in literature. Whether it be addressed to normal or abnormal sexuality matters little. There is nothing to be compared with it, excepting possibly in the pitifully extant fragments of Sappho, the Sonnets of Shakespeare, John Donne's love poems, or Emily Bronte's burning exhortations to an unknown lover. Compared with it, Mrs. Browning's much-belauded saccharine and over-burdened "Portuguese" sonnets, are sentimental valentines. In his *Voyages*, stripped of the verbiage that emphasized so much of Hart's poetry at its weakest, and which is transparently present in many passages of *The Bridge*, the poet of *Voyages* becomes blazingly clairvoyant and achieves astonishing profundity. *Voyages* is a classic in English literature.

After the breakup recounted above, Hart returned to Cleveland over Christmas of 1924 to visit his mother—after which he again took up a peripatetic existence.

The eldest of the three young men by a handful of years, Loveman had first met Crane more than half a dozen years before in a Cleveland bookstore. An aspiring poet himself, he had just been released from the army, and the teenaged Crane was enthusiastically looking for books. Whether they were lovers, even briefly, is hard to say. But their friendship continued on and off throughout Crane's life: Loveman claimed to have received a letter from Crane only two weeks before the poet's suicide in April of '33.

Most of us today will recognize that Loveman was writing out of a tradition within which the term "American Literature" was much rarer than it is today. Because Americans wrote in English, their works—especially if important—were considered, at least by Americans of a certain aesthetic leaning, to be part of "English Literature." The three other things that the contemporary reader is likely to find somewhat anomalous in Loveman's account—things that the reader may wonder how they fit into the narrative—are, first, the extraordinary passion with which Crane entreats this gay friend—who is, after all, not (at least then) his lover—to be with him; second, the seemingly gratuitous sexism of the swipe at Elizabeth Barrett Browning; and, third, that "verbiage" which characterizes "Hart's poetry at its weakest" and which Loveman says must be stripped away to reveal the achievement and clairvoyance of the great love lyrics. Bear all three in mind: all three will be contextualized, in their place, as we proceed through these notes.

Crane's enthusiasm over the then-illegal *Ulysses* suggests an elucidation of an allusion in "Voyages II," the next to the last completed poem in the lyric series, that he would have been working on during the time Loveman writes of, or a few months after. (Though the series is clearly a love series, they seem to project—in critic R. W. Butterfield's words—an air of "searing loneliness," while the poet's seafaring lover is away.) "Voyages II," which opens with that extraordinarily scaler inversion, in which the sea is referred to as "—And yet this great wink of eternity . . ." (That "—And yet," functions much like the *"Autar epie"* at the beginning of the *Odyssey*'s Book Lambda, which, translated, became the "And then" opening the first of Pound's *Cantos*) has sustained the most concerted exegesis of all the *Voyages*. A. Alvarez claims Crane's poem to be all affect and devoid of referential meaning—which, to the extent it's true, only seems to spur the exegetes on. Critics Butterfield and Brunner have suggested that Greenberg's sea images in poems like "Love" ("Ah ye mighty caves of the sea, there pushed onward, / In windful waves, of volumes flow / Through Rhines—there Bacchus, Venus in lust cherished / Its swell of perfect ease, repeated awe—ne'er quenched," is the sonnet's first quatrain, as transcribed by Crane in his manuscript copy. Returning to Greenberg's manuscript, Holden and McManis read the punctuation notably otherwise) possibly nudged Crane to connect the idea of love and the sea in a poetic series—not withstanding the fact Crane's current love was a sailor, or the fact of Crane's general fascination with "seafood," or his recent reading of Melville. The first stanza of "Voyages II" employs the idiosyncratic word "wrapt"—which also appears in "Atlantis"—suggesting a kind of Greenbergian term halfway between "wrapped" and "rapt." In earlier drafts of the poem, Crane used the phrase "varnished lily grove" from Greenberg's sonnet, "Life," though he eventually revised it out. Philip Horton has told us, in his biography of Crane, that the "bells off San Salvador" in the third stanza ("And onward, as bells off San Salvador / Salute the crocus lustres of the stars / In those poinsetta meadows of her tides,—/ Adagios of islands, O My Prodigal, / Complete the dark confessions her veins spell") refer to a Caribbean myth Opffer had recounted to Crane about a sunken city whose drowned church towers, during storms, sounded their bells from beneath the waters to warn passing ships.

Earlier versions of the poem were much more directly erotic: that third stanza once read, "Bells ringing off San Salvador / To see you smiling scrolls of silver, ivory sentences / brimming confessions, O prodigal, / in which your tongue slips mine—/ the perfect diapason dancing left / wherein minstrel mansions shine."

Crane himself later used the phrase "Adagios of islands" to explain what he called his "indirect mentions"—in this case the indirect mention of "the motion of a boat through islands clustered thickly, the rhythm of the motion etc" ("General Aims and Theories"). Crane was also reading Melville, and both "leewardings" in the second line and "spindrift" in the last have their source—if indirectly—in that novelist of the sea: "The Lee Shore," Chapter 23 of *Moby-Dick*, praises "landlessness" as a road to "higher truth." And Crane had first used Melville's term "findrinny" in an earlier draft but, unable to find it in any dictionary, finally settled on "spindrift," which means the foamy spray swept from the waves by a strong wind and driven along the sea's surface.

In stanza four Crane's use of the biblical word "superscription" (that which is written on a coin; an exergue) recalls Jesus' dialogue from the Gospel: "Show me a penny. Whose image and superscription hath it? They answered and said, Ceasar's. . . ."

But to review all this is to wander quite aways from Joyce. Today's reader forgets that a good deal of the controversy over *Ulysses*'s supposed obscenity (which is why Crane had to have a smuggled copy) centered on the terminal paragraph of the flower-laden fifth section of Joyce's novel, that Stewart Gilbert designated, in his famous 1930 *Ulysses: A Study*, "The Lotus Eaters"—one of "those passages of which," Judge Woolsey would write, nine years later in his decision of December 6, 1933, "the Government particularly complains." (The other point of controversy was Bloom's erotic musings during his stroll along the strand in the eleventh episode, "The Sirens.") In that passage, Bloom (whose *nom d'amour* is Henry Flower, Esq.), imagines himself bathing and, in his mind's eye, regards his own pubic hair and genitals breaking the surface of the tub's soapy water: ". . . he saw his trunk riprippled over and sustained, buoyed lightly upward, lemonyellow: his navel, bud of flesh: and saw the dark tangled curls of his bush floating, floating hair of the stream around the limp father of thousands, a languid, floating flower" (Joyce, p. 86). (Writes Gilbert, somewhat disingenuously: "The lotus-eaters appear under many aspects in this episode: the cabhorses drooping at the cabrank . . . , doped communicants at All Hallows . . . , the watchers of cricket . . . and, finally, Mr Bloom himself, flowerlike, buoyed lightly upward in the bath" [Gilbert, p. 155].)

Joyce's "floating flower," as a metaphor for the limp male genitalia (". . . father of thousands . . ."), suggests a possible unraveling of another one of Crane's "indirect mentions" in the penultimate stanza of the second *Voyages* poem ("her," here, refers to the sea):

> Mark how her turning shoulders wind the hours,
> And hasten while her penniless rich palms
> Pass superscription of bent foam and wave,—
> Hasten, while they are true,—sleep, death, desire
> Close round one instant in one floating flower.

Indeed, one "generic" way of indicating a forbidden sexual reference is through the use of a classical metaphor or figure taken from an age or culture less restrictive and repressive. It's possible, of course, that the congruence of phrases—"floating flower"—between Joyce and Crane was an accident; or at any rate an unconscious borrowing by Crane. But, given Crane's enthusiasm for the volume at this time, as Loveman recounts it (and biographer Unterecker also attests to Crane's enthusiasm: Crane arranged for more "smuggled" copies to go to Allen Tate and others; Unterecker calls *Ulysses* a "Bible" for Crane, all before 1924, and tells us, in his piece, "The Architecture of *The Bridge*," that Crane prepared a gloss on the novel, copying out long passages from it for still another friend who could not obtain a copy), it's far more likely to represent a conscientious bit of intertextuality.

If the "floating flower" does stand for the genitals, it's possible that, in Crane's poem, we should read it as female genitals, since Crane has already personified the sea as a woman with, first, shoulders, then palms, and then a "floating flower"; such a reading would simply continue her embodiment. But if the allusion to Joyce is really there, it opens up other possible readings: Crane may be critiquing Joyce's use of the "floating flower" figure for the genitals—saying in effect, it *should* be used for female genitals, rather than for male. But, by the same token, he could be using the relation to Joyce covertly to bisexualize his own personification of the ocean—evoking a "floating flower" so recently and famously used to figure the *male* genitalia.*

* * *

Crane's poem "Emblems of Conduct," written shortly after his discovery of Greenberg, is an amalgam of stanzas and lines from Greenberg's poems—mostly Greenberg's "Conduct." But words, phrases, and lines from Greenberg ("gate" and "script" are two words and, finally, two concepts all but donated to Crane by Greenberg) turn up in both *Voyages* and *The Bridge*. Some years later, after he had all but finished *The Bridge*'s final section, and very possibly while pursuing Greenberg's readings in Emerson, Crane opened Emerson's "Plato" and, coming upon the paragraph which heads these notes, decided, in a kind of challenge to Emerson's praise of Plato's lack of poetic ecstasy, to rename "Finale," *The Bridge*'s ecstatic conclusion, "Atlantis."

For if there is one poet who is *not* described by the motto heading these notes—a common-sensical, super-average man—it is Crane!

But this might also be the place to look back, six years before, to

---

* Herbert A. Leibowitz noted the recall of *Ulysses*'s "Floating Flower" in "Voyages II" in *Hart Crane: An Introduction to the Poetry* (Columbia University Press: New York, 1968, p. 100); but I learned of it only after this book was in production.

Crane's 1918 meditation on Nietzsche—a defense of the philosopher against those who, with the Great War, would dismiss him along with everything German. In the second paragraph of that astute, brief essay (misleadingly titled "The Case Against Nietzsche"; a more apropos, if clumsier, title would have been "The Case *Against* the Case Against Nietzsche"), Crane mentions that Schopenhauer was (along with Goethe) one of the few Germans whom Nietzsche had any use for at all. It's possible then that the 19-year-old Crane had read through Nietzsche's essay, "On Schopenhauer as Teacher"; the following passage from it may have been—then—one of the earlier texts, if not the earliest, to begin sedimenting some of the ideas, images, and terms that, in development, would become Crane's major poetic work half a dozen or more years on:

> Nobody can build you the bridge over which you must cross the river of life, nobody but you alone. True, there are countless paths and bridges and demigods that would like to carry you across the river, but only at the price of your self; you would pledge your self, and lose it. In this world there is one unique path which no one but you may walk. Where does it lead? Do not ask; take it.

Indeed, to examine how Crane's *Bridge* critiques the specifics of this passage is to begin to trace what, in Crane, is specific to his own view and enterprise:

For Nietzsche the bridge is the instrumentality with which one negotiates the river of life. For Crane the bridge *is* life. In her 1978 interview with Opffer, Helge Normann Nilsen records Opffer as saying that Crane often told him, "All of life is a bridge" or "The whole world is a bridge." The bridge for Nietzsche is the unique and optimal path by which the brave subject can, in crossing it, avoid losing his proper self. One suspects that for Crane a multiplicity of selves can all be supported by the bridge's encompassing curveship—that, somehow, authenticity of self, above and beyond that of authentic poetry, is not in question.

In the Nilsen interview with Opffer, Opffer tells a tale about his own father, also a sailor, "who once jumped from a ship in Denmark just to see how long it would take for them to pick him up." Crane lived in the building with both father and son—and before his death Emil Senior may have amused both Crane and Emil Junior with tales of this early jape. It stuck in Opffer's mind till he was over eighty; it may well have stayed in Crane's too . . .

When one reads through Crane's letters to his literary friends, his family, his theoretical statements, and his various defenses of his own work, one has the impression that, above all things, Crane wanted to be taken as an intellectual poet. He was as fiercely a self-taught intellectual as a writer could be. Certainly he was aware that only reading strategies that could make sense of the high modernist works of Eliot and Pound could negotiate his own energetic, vivid, but densely packed and insistently connotative lines.

The argument often used to impugn Crane's intellect—that Crane took the epigraph from Strachy's early Seventeenth Century journals for *Powhatan's Daughter* (Part II of *The Bridge*) from a review by Elizabeth Bowen of William Carlos Williams's *In the American Grain*, where Bowen had quoted and abridged the same lines, rather than taking it from Williams's book directly or from the edition of Strachy's journals that Williams himself consulted—is simply jejune. (From other passages in *The Bridge*, as well as reports from Williams of a letter from Crane [now lost], in which Crane wrote Williams of the use he had made both of *In the American Grain* and also of Williams's poem "The Wanderer" in structuring *The Bridge*, we know Crane read Williams's book all the way through.) Crane took the idea for "Virginia," in "Three Songs," from a popular 1923 tune by Irving Caesar, "What Do You Do Sunday, Mary"; and he took the Latin lines at the end of the second act chorus of Seneca's *Medea* for the motto to "Ave Maria" (*The Bridge*, Part I) from a scholarly article in a 1918 issue of a recondite classics journal, *Mnemosne*. What, by the same silly argument, do *these* sources say about Crane's intellect—save that, like many intellectuals, he read lots, and at lots of levels? The point is the *use* he made of those textual allusions and their resonances in his poem—not their provenance or the purity of their sources!

Besides being an intellectual, however, Crane was also a volatile eccentric, often loud and impulsive. A homosexual who, by several reports, struck most people as unremittingly masculine, at the same time he was disconcertingly open about his deviancy with any number of straight friends—at a time when homosexuality was assumed a pathology in itself.

Crane was also—more and more as his brief life rolled on—a drunk.

The last three or four years of Crane's life were largely the debacle of any number of literary alcoholics who died from drink: read Henry S. Salt's biography of James Thomson (B.V.); read Lewis Ellingham's account of Jack Spicer; read Douglas Day on Malcolm Lowry—or anybody on Dylan Thomas. But the resultant biographemes that have sedimented in the collective literary imagination about Crane, from the typewriters thrown out windows, to the poems composed with the Victrola blaring jazz and Crane's own laughter spilling over the music and the racket of his own typewriter keys (but Cowley has told us how meticulously Crane revised those same poems), to the explosive break between Crane and Allen Tate and Caroline Gordon—with whom Crane had been living for a summer in Patterson, New York, when, unable to take him any longer, they precipitously put him out—to his midnight pursuits of sailors around the Navy Yards of Cleveland, Washington, D.C., and Brooklyn, to the more and more frequent encounters—both in New York and Paris— with the police, as well as, in his last years, various drunken suicide attempts; and above them all are the murky surroundings of his final hours, traveling on the steamer *Orizaba* back to the States from Mexico with his "fiancée," Peggy Baird (Mrs. Malcolm Cowley, waiting for her divorce papers to come through)—from which the thirty-three-year-old Crane was being deported for still *another* drunken suicide try with a bottle of iodine. After several days of drinking and making a general nuisance of himself on shipboard, on the evening of April 26—Emil Opffer's birthday—a drunken Crane descended into the *Orizaba*'s sailors' quarters. He tried to read the sailors his poems—that's one version. He tried to make one of the sailors and was badly beaten—that's another. He was also—probably—robbed; at any rate, the next morning his money and his ring were gone. A sedated Baird had been confined to her room with a burned arm from an accident the day before with a box of Cuban matches that had caught fire. Now, sometime after eleven, in his pajamas and a light topcoat, a disconsolate Crane went to Baird's cabin. Baird said: "Get dressed, darling. You'll feel better."

As mentioned, it was the day after Emil's birthday. Was Crane perhaps thinking of the tale Emil's father had told . . . ?

At about two minutes before noon, wrote Gertrude E. Vogt, a passenger on the ship, many years later to Crane's biographer John Unterecker,

> a number of us were gathered on deck, waiting to hear the results of the ship's pool—always announced at noon. Just then we saw Crane come on deck, dressed, as you noted, in pajamas and topcoat; he had a black eye and looked generally battered. He walked to the railing, took off his coat, folded it neatly over the railing (not dropping it on deck), raised himself on his toes, then dropped back again. We all fell silent and watched him, wondering what in the world he was up to. Then, suddenly, he vaulted over the railing and jumped into the sea. For what seemed five minutes, but was more like five seconds, no one was able to move; then cries of "man overboard" went up. Just once I saw Crane, swimming strongly. But never again. It is a scene I am unable to forget, even after all these years.

After Crane's leap from the ship's stern, the *Orizaba* came to a stop, but the Captain figured either the ship's propellers, sharks, or both had finished the poet. The *Orizaba* trolled for him a full hour; the body, however, was not found. But all these images have displaced the less sensational—

and earlier—images called up by the compulsive and omnivorous reader of Frazer, Doughty, Villard, the Elizabethans, Nietzsche, Emerson, Whitman, Dante, Melville, Joyce, LaForgue, Rimbaud, Ouspensky, Eliot, Pound, Frank, and Williams—to cite only a handful of the writers with whose work Crane was deeply familiar by the time he was thirty. Crane was not a reader of formal philosophy—and was quick to say so, when necessary. (From a letter to Yvor Winters in 1927: "I . . . have never read Kant, Descartes or the other doctors . . ." But he *had* read his Donne, Blake, and Vaughan.) His languages were French and nominal Latin; he used both.

The productive Crane was a young man: all but a handful of the poems we remember him for were written before he had completed his twenty-eighth year. But *by* twenty-eight, he had read and thought more about what he'd read than most twenty-eight-year-olds have—even twenty-eight-year-olds headed toward the academy.

The French have their concept of the *poète maudit* for such fellows (many of whom—though not all—were gay). Twenties America had only Flaming Youth and the stodgy old professor—but no template for those between, much less one that encompassed the extremes of both. But those were the extremes Crane's life bridged.

II

Beginning with his contemporaries Allen Tate and Yvor Winters, the traditional view of Crane is that, as a poet, he was an interesting, monumentally talented, even "splendid failure" (the words come from the final line of a frequently reprinted essay, "Notes on a Text of Hart Crane" by R. P. Blackmur)—a view that began with the uncomfortable perception by Winters and Tate of a correspondence between Crane's homosexuality, his drunkenness, his suicide, and his ideas—especially his appreciation of Whitman—along with his work's resistance to easy elucidation. This view carries through the majority of Crane criticism to this day. It is perhaps presented at its clearest in its current form in Edward Brunner's *Splendid Failure: The Making of* The Bridge (1985). Still, I suspect, Crane's contemporaries could not quite grasp that Crane was often writing a kind of poem that simply did not undertake the task of argumentative (the word they often used was "structural") clarity, narrative or otherwise, then expected of the well-formed poem. But the primary sign of Crane's ultimate success is the crushing lack of critical attention we now pay to all those poems written at the time that dutifully undertook that task and performed it quite successfully. Among critical works on Crane that have directly taken up this point are Lee Edelman's rhetorically rigorous

Transmemberment of Song (1987) and Paul Giles's paronomasially delirious *Contexts of* The Bridge (1986). Indeed, after the three major biographies (Horton, Weber, and Unterecker), which give the context of Crane in his times, Brunner's, Edelman's, and Giles's studies of the poems are probably the most informative recent books on Crane's work *per se.*

As Edelman suggests, perhaps the most careful account of Crane's "failure" is first laid out in Yvor Winters's quite extraordinary essay, "The Significance of *The Bridge* by Hart Crane, or What Are We to Think of Professor X?" reprinted in Winters's 1943 collection, *On Modern Poets.* There Winters relates Crane's enterprise to the pernicious and maniagenic ideas of Ralph Waldo Emerson *via* the irreligious pantheism (read: relativism—in "Passage to India" Whitman blasphemes by claiming the poet is "the true son of God") of Whitman and the glossolomania of Mallarmé. (At least that's how Winters saw them.) Winters had begun as one of Crane's most enthusiastic advocates. The two had an extensive correspondence—as well as one warm and productive meeting. But, on the publication of *The Bridge* in 1930, a growing doubt about Crane's achievement finally erupted in Winters's review. Over it, the two men broke. But it is important to realize that the rejection—or at least the condemnation—of Crane, for Winters as well as for many of Crane's critics, was the rejection and condemnation of an entire romantic current in American literary production, a current that included Whitman and Emerson, with Crane only as its latest, cracked and misguided voice. Those who shared Winters's judgments, like Brom Weber and R. P. Blackmur, also felt T. S. Eliot was as much of a failure as, or more of a failure than, Crane, and for the same reasons!

It is also worth noting that Winters's piece, while it is far more illuminative of what was going on, because it is more articulate about its anti-Emerson, anti-Whitman, and finally anti-American position (as well as those European currents, like Mallarmé, that Winters saw as supporting it) than many others, was also practically without influence—because it was all but unavailable from the time Winters wrote it until the sixties.

But Blackmur's "Notes on a Text of Hart Crane," an essay which, despite its criticism, is probably as responsible as any other for Crane's endurance, basically takes the same tack and was widely available from the time of its publication in 1935 through Blackmur's arrival at Princeton in 1940 and his vast popularity as a critic ever since. (It is still available today in Blackmur's *Form and Value in Modern Poetry.*) That essay begins:

> It is a striking and disheartening fact that the three most ambitious poems of our time should all have failed in similar ways: in composition, in inde-

pendent objective existence, and in intelligibility of language. *The Waste Land,* the *Cantos,* and *The Bridge* all fail to hang together structurally in the sense that "Prufrock," "Envoi," and "Praise for an Urn"—lesser works in every other respect—do hang together.

Today, the general consensus on T. S. Eliot and Ezra Pound has wholly reversed; since studies of Eliot and Pound by critics like Elizabeth Drew and Hugh Kenner, Blackmur's pronouncement tinkles like a quaint bell, a bit out of tune, from the past. The consensus on Crane, however, has not. But, as Edelman has argued, we best go back to the early critics of Crane in order to commence whatever rehabilitation we might wish to undertake.

Winters accused Crane of following linguistic impulses, rather than intentionally creating his ideas—of automatic writing, rather than careful articulation of meanings—unaware that all writing (even the most logical and articulate) is, in some sense, automatic. But the fact is, what Winters says of Crane is perfectly true. Where Winters is wrong is in his assumption that there is another, intention-centered, consciousness-bound, teleographical approach to the creation of poetry in particular and writing in general that is, somehow, actually available to the poet/writer other than as a metaphor or as a provisional construct dictated by the political moment. The teleology Winters could not find in Whitman's pantheism is ultimately not to be had anywhere.

All sentences move toward logic and coherence—or, indeed, toward whatever their final form—by a kind of chance and natural selection. The sentence moves toward other qualities of the poetic in the same manner. Intention, consciousness, and reason are not a triumvirate that impels or creates language. Rather they sit in judgment of the performance after the fact, somewhere between mind and mouth, thought and paper, accepting or rejecting the language offered up; and—when they reject it—they are only able to wait for new language they find more fitting for the tasks to hand. But while intention, consciousness, and reason can halt speech (sometimes), there is some other, ill-understood faculty of mind that fountains up "that virtual train of fires upon jewels" (Mallarmé, translated and quoted by the disapproving Winters) that *is* poetic language as much as it is analytical prose: It is something associative, rhetorical, dictational—and always almost opaque to analysis. Intention, consciousness, and reason can only make a request of it, humbly and hesitantly—a request to which that faculty may or may not respond, as if it were possessed of an intention wholly apart from ours—or, more accurately, as if it functioned at the behest of other, ill-understood aspects of mind apart from will or intention or anything like them. One can only hear the resonances of a word *after* it has been uttered, read its associations *after* it has been written; and, judging such associations and resonances, intention, consciousness, and reason can at best allow language to pass or not to pass. And from what we know of Crane, he was as much at pains to guide his poetic output as any writer in the language. But I also believe that a writer who thinks he or she can do anything else is likely to brutalize, if not stifle, his or her output—likely, at any rate, to restrict it to something less than it might be.

When, in his 1919 essay, "Tradition and the Individual Talent," Eliot made his famous call for "depersonalization" in poetry—

> What is to be insisted upon is that the poet must develop or procure the consciousness of the past and that he should continue to develop this consciousness through his career.
>
> What happens is a continual surrender of himself as he is at the moment to something which is more valuable. The progress of an artist is a continual self-sacrifice, and continual extinction of personality.
>
> There remains to define this process of depersonalization and its relation to the sense of tradition . . .

—to the extent that the process of the poet is one with the poet's progress through the sentences which make up her or his poem, I suspect Eliot was referring to the identical process I spoke of above, involving at least the provisional suspension of intention, consciousness, and reason, i.e., personality. Moreover I suspect Winters recognized it as such. And on the strength of that recognition, he condemned the author.

In his book *Hart Crane and the Homosexual Text*, the late Thomas Yingling cites a passage from Crane's 1925 essay, "General Aims and Theories," as expressing the very opposite of what Eliot, above, was calling for. Crane put together these notes for Eugene O'Neill when O'Neill was contemplating writing an introduction to Crane's first collection, *White Buildings:* "It seems to me that the poet will accidentally define his times well enough simply by reacting honestly and to the full extent of his sensibilities to the states of passion, experience and rumination that fate forces on him, first hand."

I think, however, that the notion of an *accidental* definition, the idea of an *honest* reaction to the states of passion, experience, and rumination to the full extent of his sensibilities is a poet speaking of, yet again, the *identical* creative experience in which intention (or whatever produces the "intention" effect), consciousness, and reason must not be employed too early—before there is material for them to accept or reject—and are signs that Crane and Eliot are speaking of the same phenomenon. The *difference* in how they speak about it has to do with what, as it were, each sees as fueling what I have called that "ill-understood faculty of mind" that first produces language. In 1919, Eliot saw it as literature. In 1925, Crane saw it as passion, experience, and rumination.

To ruminate is, of course, what ruminants do. Its metaphorical extension is not so much thinking, but thinking "over and over"—as the OED reminds us. Repetition is inchoate in the metaphor. If there is a margin for intellection in Crane's model, it comes under the rubric of "rumination." And because that model suggests not so much "reading" as "rereading" (as well as the political margins for experience and passion), it is likely to appeal to the modern sensibility more than Eliot's.

Yingling's book points up how much of Crane's "failure" is intricately entailed with the homophobia of his critics—till finally Crane comes to represent more than anything else the most damning case of bad faith among the New Critics, who claimed above all to believe in the separation of the text from the man. But faced with Crane's homosexuality, as Yingling shows, they simply couldn't do it. This part of Yingling's argument one does not in the least begrudge him. Still, his overall thesis would have been stronger if he had been able to historify his discussion, relating (and distinguishing) Crane's case specifically to (and from) the extraordinarily similar marginalization (and persistence in spite of it) of Poe (1809–1849)—as well as, say, James Thomson (B.V.) (1834–1882), Ernest Dowson (1867–1900), and Lionel Johnson (1867–1902)—this last, one of the passions of Crane's adolescence. A book of Johnson's is recorded as part of Crane's adolescent library—doubtless the 1915 edition with the introduction by Ezra Pound. Alcoholism was a huge factor in all these poets' lives—and deaths. Perversion—in the form of pedophilia—haunted both the case of Poe and, only a trifle less so, of Thomson and Dawson. Homosexuality was certainly a factor in Johnson's life—and may or may not have been involved with the others. And in all cases major attempts were launched after their deaths to establish them as canonical; in all cases the arguments more or less triumphant against them were finally and fundamentally moral. Arguably this was outside Yingling's interest; still, had Yingling been able to extend his study even to the process by which poets of major canonical interest during their lives—like Edna St. Vincent Millay, a woman, or Paul Lawrence Dunbar, a black man— were, in the years after their deaths, systematically removed from the critical center (finally by the same process that has elevated Crane), he would have given us a major political analysis of canon-formation. But for all the insight he gives us into Crane's critical treatment, finally the process of establishing a poet or an artist's reputation is just more complex than Yingling presents it.

> O Thou steeled Cognizance whose leap commits
> The agile precinct of the lark's return;
> Within whose lariat sweep encinctured sing
> In single chrysalis the many twain,—

In a chapter called "Words" from her wonderfully wide-ranging 1959 study, *Poetry: A Modern Guide to Its Understanding and Enjoyment,* critic Elizabeth Drew's terse judgment on Crane's address to the bridge is that it is an example of rhetoric "out of place" (p. 73). Briefly she compares it to James Thomson's (*not* B.V.) (1700–1748) inflated address to a pineapple in *The Seasons* (1726–30):

> But O thou blest Anana, thou the pride
> Of vegetable life . . .

For Drew the simple juxtaposition is enough to damn both poets. Both, for her, are inflated and preposterous. One wonders, however, if Drew isn't—possibly unconsciously—following Poe's critique of the young American poet Joseph Rodman Drake (1795–1820), a near contemporary of Keats, who died at age 25 and whose poems his friend the poet Fitzgreen Halleck published in 1836, sixteen years after Rodman's death. In his famous review of the two poets' work, Poe calls the invocation to Drake's poem, "Niagara" ("Roar, raging torrent! And thou, mighty river, / Pour thy white foam on the valley below! / Frown, ye dark mountains," etc.), "ludicrous—and nothing more. In general, all such invocations have an air of the burlesque." But finally one wonders, with all three poems, if it is not the fact that all three examples are apostrophes (rather than the elaborateness of the language in which the apostrophes are couched) that controls the "out of place"-ness—or ludicrousness—of the figures. Wouldn't the most colloquial, "You, waterfall!" "Hey, pineapple!" or "Yo, Bridge!" strike us as equally ludicrous or out of place?

Critic Harold Bloom has recounted (in his 1982 study *Agon: Towards a Theory of Revisionism,* p. 270) how, at age ten (revised down from eleven in an earlier version of the essay, published in Alan Trachtenberg's collection of essays on Crane), he first read, "crouched over Crane's book in a Bronx library" sometime in the thirties, the same lines Drew denigrates. For Bloom (and, he explains, many others in that decade) they were what "cathected" him onto poetry. Like's Marlowe's rhetoric, Bloom argues, Crane's was both "a psychology and a knowing, rather than a knowledge." Begged as a present from his sister when he was twelve, Crane's poems were the first book Bloom owned.

I recall my first reading of those lines too—as a teenager in the late fifties. (For me, Crane's poems were among the first trade paperbacks I purchased for myself.) I suspect that, like Bloom, I was not too sure what the lines actually meant; but in dazzling me—for dazzle me they did—they established the existence of a gorgeous meta-language that held my judgment on it in suspension precisely because I could *not* judge the meaning, even as it was clear this meta-language, as it welcomed glorious and sensual words into itself from as far a-field as the Bible, the cowboy film, and the dictionary's most unthumbed pages ("thou," "cognizance," "lariat," "encinctured" . . .), welcomed equally such figures as the apostrophe—even more out of favor in the fifties and sixties than it is today. What this language was in the process of knowing—the psychology it proffered—was that of an animate object world, a world where meaning and mystery were one, indisseverable, and ubiquitous, but at the same time a world where everything spoke (or sang or whispered or shouted) to everything else—and thus the apostrophe (the means by which the poet joined in with this mysterious dialogue and antiphon) was, in that sense, at its center.

I also remember, even more forcefully, the lines that, for me—at sixteen—sent chills racing over me and, a moment later, struck me across the bridge of my nose with a pain sharp enough to make my eyes water. It came with the lines from "Harbor Dawn" that Crane the lyricist of unspeakable love had just managed to speak:

> And you beside me, blesséd now while sirens
> Sing to us, stealthily weave us into day—
>
> *. . . a forest shudders in your hair*

For suddenly I realized that "you" was another man!

One should also note, however, I had all but the same bodily reaction to my first encounter—at about the same age—with Ernest Dowson's "*Non Sum Qualis Eram Bonae Sub Regno Cynarae*," though the object there was clearly heterosexual—a female prostitute.

The point with Crane, however, was that there was a critical dialogue already in place around him, that could sustain the resonances of that response in the growing reader—whether that reader was Harold Bloom or I.

But while nearly everyone seems to have ravaged Dowson's poems for titles* (*Gone with the Wind, The Night Is Thine, Days of Wine and Roses, Love*

---

* Crane also supplies his range of titles: Tennessee Williams's play *Summer and Smoke* takes its title from Crane's poem "Emblems of Conduct" (indeed from the only three lines in the poem Crane apparently did *not* take from Greenberg); the title for Agnes de Mille's ballet *Appalachian Spring* comes from, appropriately enough, Crane's "The Dance"; Jim

and Sleep . . .), no dialogue about the significance of Dowson, no argument over the meaning of the tradition he inhabited and developed, remains in place, save a few wistful comments by Yeats, and the bittersweet memoir by J. Arthur Symons that introduces at least one edition of Dowson's poems. What's there is a monologue, not a dialogue. And it is all too brief.

Dowson took his Latin title from the first Ode in Horace's Book IV, in which the poet, near fifty, entreats Venus/Cynara not to visit him with love: love is for the young, such as Paulus Maximus. ("But why," he asks in the last two stanzas, "is there a tear on my face? I still remember thee in dreams, where I chase after thee, across the green, among the waves . . .") Horace describes Venus in the Ode as a "cruel mother," as a goddess "hard of heart"—so that there is a good deal of irony in the line Dowson has chosen for a title, signaled by the placement of *"Bonae"* as far away from its noun, *"Cynarae,"* as it can get: *"Non Sum Qualis Eram Bonae Sub Regno Cynarae."* ("I am not such as I was under the reign of the kindly Cynara." The "kindly Cynara" *(bonae Cynarae)* is very much *"Venus tout entière à sa prois attaché"*—kindly in the sense that the Eumenides are "the kindly ones." To praise Dowson's poem for its insight into the realities of love among the worldly, contrasted with the romantic memories of love among the innocent, is to revivify part of the dialogue about him. But though there was *once* a dialogue about Dowson, it is nearly impossible to reconstruct it from, say, the stacks of the twenty-one-story library at the University of Massachusetts— whereas the volumes debating the reputation of Crane, by comparison, practically leap from the shelves.

Another aspect of the dialogue over Crane is that at first it seems, at least to the sixteen-year-old, if not to the ten-year-old, that its questions are transparently easy to resolve. But later, we begin to notice that, even as we, like Yingling, begin to demystify some of these questions, others are revealed to be even more complex. And those questions— what are these poems about? how do they signify and continue to signify today?—invariably take us *to* the poems, not away from them.

But finally it is the dialogue created between the critically enlivened concept of "Crane-the-failure" and the elusive meaning of the poems themselves that sets critics listening intensely—in a way that almost no one today is prompted to listen to Winters or Ridge or Wheelright or Bodenheim, to name a handful of poets whom we turn to, if at all, because we are in pursuit of some insight Crane had while reviewing them, or because he mentioned something they wrote in a letter.

Morrison of The Doors took the title of his song "Riders on the Storm" from Crane's "Praise for an Urn"; and Harold Bloom's study of romantic poetry, *The Visionary Company,* takes its title from Crane's last poem, "The Broken Tower."

This is dialogue that sustains the new readers of Crane. This is the dialogue that makes old readers go back and reread him.

A reader of Yingling's book with a sense of this, gay or straight, will, after a while, be compelled to observe that however much Crane was marginalized because of his homosexuality, he's a good deal less marginal today than any number of straight male poets of his time—certainly less so than Tate or Winters. Indeed, after Eliot, Pound, and Yeats, the only poet of his era who precedes Crane in reputation is Wallace Stevens—another male homosexual poet.

As it is now, however, that part of Yingling's argument about Crane's reception is open to the counterargument that if Crane had not been the "failure" he was, he might all too easily have been nothing at all!

And that is not a good argument—which is to say it only points up the weakness in Yingling's.

Certainly it's ironic that in 1927 Winters wrote his own poetic series, *The Bare Hills* (which Crane once offered to review), all but unread today, which—though it has its delicate, minor-key beauties—performs with none of the force of Crane's work, possibly because it strives after poetry through a method insistently deaf to the processes and poetic product Winters had excoriated so in Crane. Though Crane did not review it, the reviewers of the day found *The Bare Hills* "austere." The modern judgment would be, I suspect, if such a judgment could be said even to exist: thin.

* * *

In a letter to Winters, responding to Winters's exhortation that the poet be a "complete man," Crane ends with a warning Winters might well have heeded: "I have neglected to say," Crane wrote, "that I admire your general attitude, including your distrust of metaphysical or other patent methods. Watch out, though, that you don't strangulate yourself with some counter-method of your own!" For the morality of a text has to do with its use, not its intent—or, even more frequently, its lack of intent to espouse a position that a later time (sometimes only months on) has decided is more ethical than the unquestioned commonplace of an earlier moment. Would that Winters had been able to distinguish a description of a state of affairs—how language works—from a posed poetic methodology!

In a strange near-reversal at the end of his essay "The Significance of *The Bridge* by Hart Crane or What Are We to Think of Professor X?" Winters finally claims for Crane a superiority, both of intellect and poetic aperception, over a generalized "Professor X," who is cozily in love with

Whitman and the American transcendentalists and simply blind to the dangers in their romantic program—dangers that polluted Crane's poetic enterprise and drove him through (in Winters's judgment) obscure poetry to madness and suicide. (Only a strict New England background, reasoned Winters, plus the fact that he had far less poetic talent than Crane in the first place, kept Emerson from the same disastrous ends.) Claims Winters, Crane understood these ideas in all respects except their mortal flaws and consciously pursued them as such, at least having the courage of his convictions to follow them to the end—which (says Winters) Professor X, who professes to approve them, has not.

The irony of Crane's reputation, however, is that many academic critics—descendants of Winters's Professor X—who, today, have now read their Emerson, Eliot, and Mallarmé pretty carefully and would argue hotly against Winters' reading of them, if not against his reading of Whitman, are still comfortable with the notion of Crane-as-poetic-failure: what they are blind to now is the realization that Crane's "structural failure" *is*—just like Eliot's—his modernism; as it is his continuity with the outgrowth of the romantic tradition high modernism represents.

But how did meaning and mystery work together to communicate the existence, now and again in Crane's poems, of a same-sex bed partner—as it did to me that afternoon in 1958?

One cannot make too much more headway in such a discussion of Crane without some comment on "homosexual genres." While "genre" may well be too strong a term for them, these are nevertheless forms that, in various ages, various works have taken—forms that have been readable as gay or homosexual by gay or homosexual men and women in their particular times. In various ages these genres change their form. (Indeed, to discuss them fully in historical terms is beyond the scope of such notes as these. To quote Crane: ". . . the whole topic is something of a myth anyway, and is consequently modified by the characteristics of the image by each age in each civilization.") Most recently however—say, since the 19th Century—the aspect that might be cited as most characteristic of this genre or genres is that they are structured so that straight, gay, male, or female readers and critics can read the homosexuality *out* of them, for whatever reason, whenever it becomes necessary or convenient.

One particular poetic form of this genre (of which *Voyages* is an example) includes treatments of love in which the object of desire is specifically left ambiguous as to gender. This allows critics of one persuasion to read it: "Of course it's speaking of heterosexual desire—since the vast majority of desire is, and the writer has left no positive sign that this portrait of desire is any different from most." Meanwhile critics of another persuasion may read it: "Of course it's speaking of homosexual desire. The rhetorical lengths to which the author has gone *not* to specify the gender *is* its positive sign." Another example of this form is, as I suggested, Crane's "Harbor Dawn" in *The Bridge*.

After the aubade of the first five stanzas, the poem, with its next line, locates itself directly with the lovers in their bed: "And you beside me, blesséd now while sirens / Sing to us, stealthily weave us into day—/ Serenely now, before day claims our eyes / your cool arms murmurously about me lay. . . ." For a total of eleven lines, the poet goes on about his beloved without once mentioning "breasts" or "tresses," or any other explicit sign of the feminine. About the room we do not even see any of the "stockings, slippers, camisoles, and stays" that were so famously piled on the divan in the typist's bedsitter before "the young man carbuncular" arrived in *The Waste Land*'s (once notorious because of it) "Fire Sermon." In the pre-Stonewall late fifties, when "homophobia" was indeed a universal, pervasive, if silent, fear, even this much explicit lack of feminization was as articulate to an urban sixteen-year-old boy as any Gay Rights flier or Act-Up poster today.

My first response was to weep.

Given the tears I swallowed (in order that no one else in the house hear them), that explicit lack may well have had an order of power that, in these post-Stonewall times, *has* no current analogue.

The rubric Crane added to (the right of) the poem after the first printing work to heterosexualize our reading—or, more accurately, to bisexualize it: ". . . or is / it from the / soundless shore / of sleep that / time /// recalls you to / your love, / there in a / waking dream / to merge your seed //—with whom?" ("Merge your seed," followed by the daring "—with whom?", certainly suggests two men coming together.) "Who is the / woman with / us [possibly with the poet and the reader, but equally possibly with the poet and the poet's lover] in the / dawn? . . . / Whose is the / flesh our feet / have moved / upon?" The woman is so clearly a spiritualized presence, even a spiritual ground, and the columnar text of the poem is so clearly of the "ambiguous" form mentioned above, that when I first read the poem as a sixteen-year-old in 1958, it never occurred to me that it was anything other than a description of homosexual love, with a few suggestions of heterosexuality artfully placed about for those who preferred to read it that way—which, after all, is what it is.

Even today, when I read over Winters's heterosexual reading of the poem, I find myself balking when he refers to the loved-one as "she" or "her"—having to remind myself this is *not* a misreading, but is rather an *alternate* reading the poet has left, carefully set up *by* the text of the poem, precisely *for* heterosexual readers like Winters—or, indeed, for *any* critic, gay or straight, who had to discuss or write about the poem in public—to take advantage of.

But while a heterosexual reading may find the poem just as beautiful and just as lyrical (that's after all, what the poet wanted) it will not find the poem anywhere near as poignant as the homosexual reading does—because the heterosexual reading specifically erases all reference to the silence surrounding homosexuality for which the heterosexual reading's existence, within the homosexual reading, is the positive sign. But that is one reason the homosexual reading seems to me marginally the richer.

While more common in fiction than in poetry, another homosexual form is the narrative that takes place in a world where homosexuality is never mentioned and is presumed not to exist—but where the incidents that occur have no other satisfying explanation. (To use another phrase made famous by Eliot, they have no other "objective correlative" save homosexual desire.) This is Wilde's *The Picture of Dorian Gray*, Gide's *L'Immoralist,* and Mann's *Tod im Vennidig.* This is Alfred Hitchcock's *Rope.* Again, because homosexuality is implied in such works, not stated, a literalist reading of such texts can always more or less erase it. Such a text—also—is Crane's "Cutty Sark." That's one I didn't get at sixteen.

But by the time, at twenty-five, I'd stayed up all night in half a dozen similar situations, yes, I got it!

Still a third homosexual form is the light-hearted, good-natured, innocent presentation of rampant male (heterosexual) promiscuity: the sort of young man who'd "go to bed with anything!" The assumption here, of course, is that the young man does—only the writer has opted not to specify the homosexual occurrences. (The classic example, despite Yingling's italics and multiple punctuation marks of surprise is, yes, *Tom Jones* [1749].) Often in such works the heterosexual conquests are accompanied by extraordinarily complacent husbands—presumed to be getting some from the young man off stage and on the side. Sometimes a wise or silly older woman, especially if a widow (the nickname for one of the most popular gay bartenders in New York City's heavy hustling strip along Eighth Avenue is "Jimmy the Widow," who has worked there more than twenty years now) is read as a satiric, coded portrait of an old queen, who briefly has the young man's sexual favors.

The classical homosexual reading that replaces Proust's "Albertine" (the heroine of *A la recherche du temps perdu*) with "Albert" (Proust's own young, male coach driver) is a prime example of the same homosexual reading trope where women substitute in the text for men: generations of gay readers have pointed out to each other, with a smile, that Marcel's kidnapping and detention for weeks of Albertine is lunatic if she is *actually* an upperclass young woman—and only comprehensible if she is a working class young man.

The male narrator to whom Willa Cather goes to such pains, in the frame story of *My Àntonia,* to ascribe the text recounting the narrator's chaste, life-long love of a wonderfully alive Czech immigrant woman is another, easily readable (and wholly erasable by a literalist reading) example of a (in this case lesbian) homosexual trope.

One of the most famous—and, at the same time, most invisible—examples of such a form is presented in the closing moments of Wagner's prologue-plus-trilogy of operas, *Der Ring Des Nibelungen.* The sixteen-odd hours of music (usually heard over four nights) comprising the work are intricately interwoven from motifs that take on great resonances, both psychological and symbolic—this motif associated with the completion of Valhalla, that one associated with the Ring of Power, another with the spear on which the Law is inscribed, while another represents the sword given to mortals by the gods to free themselves, and still another stands for the renunciation of love necessary for any great human undertaking in the material world. These motifs have been traced in their multiple appearances throughout the Ring and explicated in literally hundreds of volumes. At the closing of the fourth and final opera, *Götterdämmerung,* when the castle of earthly power lies toppled, the castle of the gods has burned down, and the awed populace gazes over a land swept clean by the flooding and receding of the Rhine, the tetrology ends with a sumptuous melody that registers to most hearers as wholly new—a fitting close for this image of a new world, awaiting rebirth at the hands of man and history.

But, as many commentators have now noticed and pointed out to each other so that others would hear, that closing melody is not *completely* new. Clearly it's based on some five or six seconds—no more—of what, in *The Perfect Wagnerite* (1896), George Bernard Shaw called "some inconsequential love music" that first sounded toward the middle of *Die Wälkure's* Act III. What makes it "inconsequential" is, of course, that it is not music from any of the passionate, incestuous, heterosexual loves that shake the quadrature of operas and—often—the audience unto the foundations. The music Wagner uses for *Götterdämmerung's* terminal D-flat melody are not some moments from the searing, sun-drenched love of Siegfried and Brunhilda (or, indeed, the possibly more searing, moon-drenched love of Sigmund and Siglinda). Rather, this music accompanies Siglinda's profession of love *to Brunhilda,* who, after Sigmund's death, protects Siglinda (and the as-yet-unborn Siegfried) by sending them into the uncivilized wood where Wotan will not follow. A 19th century tradition holds that the love of two women is the single purest love—a tradition going back at least as far as the biblical tale of Ruth and Naomi. This purity is certainly part of what Wagner wished to evoke in his closing. Still, he chose this clearly Sapphic moment when, because a daughter defies her father for love of another woman, the other woman declares her love in return.

No critic overtly mentioned this sapphism during Wagner's lifetime. Possibly that emboldened him to write his next opera, *Parsifal,* surely and famously—it has been so called repeatedly throughout our century—the most blatantly homoerotic of operas in the repertoire.

Some commentators (e.g., Shaw) have gone so far as to claim that the recall of those few moments of melody from *Die Wälkure* at the close of *Götterdämmerung* is an oversight on Wagner's part. It's the single "motif" that appears *only* twice in the work: surely Wagner must have forgotten his first use of it, or at least assumed no one would recognize it. But, besides the fact that such recognitions, blatant and hidden, comprise the entire structure of the Ring, critics who claim such have simply never composed an opera. Such things are *not* forgotten; endings are much too important; and the single previous appearance makes it that much more certain it was a considered and conscientious decision.

More recent critics have taken to calling it the "praise Brunhilda" motif—which, yes, covers the situation: when in *Die Wälkure*'s Act III mortal Siglinda sings those moments of melody, she is, indeed, "praising" Brunhilda, her then still immortal half-sister. Nevertheless it sidesteps the yearning, the desiring, the straining for the other that inform that wondrous melody almost as powerfully as they do the "Liebestod" of *Tristan und Isolde.*

They are not subtle, the tropes characterizing the "homosexual genres." Often, they are based on the most stereotypical heterosexist assumptions about homosexuality as an inversion of the masculine or of the feminine, or of homosexuality as the replacement of one by the other, or of homosexuality as a third, neuter (i.e., unspecified) sex. Because they are generic (or very close to it), they represent the gross forms of the particular work. But that's why they are as recognizable as they are, by isolated adolescents with only the most fleeting and hearsay knowledge of a homosexual community—and, I'm sure, were quite accessible to straight readers who were interested enough to pursue them. But, at the same time, their coding is always in an erasable mode: They register as an absence, an oversight, a formal arrangement in which the homosexual reading can always be dismissed as an overreading. That's what makes them, as it were, *safe* in a profoundly homophobic society—in which even to mention homosexuality is to risk contaminating oneself with it.

One could go so far as to argue that these forms were only visible to those (of whatever sexual persuasion) in the work's audience who saw form itself as an articulating element in art—and that, by the same token, they remained invisible to those who saw only manifest content as defining what a given work of art was "about"; as such, they are part of a code whose complexities are certainly not exhausted by the simple signaling of a possible sexual preference. They have, rather, to do with the figuration of a formalist conception of art itself.

Even Loveman's characterization of *Voyages* ("Whether it be addressed to normal or abnormal sexuality matters little") is simply an articulate characterization of the erasability of the homosexuality built into the form of the six individual poems in the sequence—just as Loveman's subsequent citing of Sappho and Shakespeare as his first two writers for comparison—two writers in whom homosexuality may be read in or read out at will and according to a long tradition—implicates his statement within the very genre he is, with the quoted phrase, (dis-)articulating.

But seldom, of course, are these genre forms or their tropes as pure as I have presented them here. Seldom, indeed, are they as clear as the ones I've already located in Crane. The problem with trying to read these texts in the light of current "gay" politics is, however, that they are already figures of an older "homosexual" politics—which, as they metaphorize the silence and the yearning behind the social silence enforced around homosexuality, are (if read "literally" and not "figuratively") precisely limited, by their writers' most carefully crafted presentation of the formal conventions, to an articulate statement of homosexuality's existence—but often of almost nothing more.

What I've described is not the particular form of Whitman's poems or Melville's novels—of Shakespeare's sonnets or Sappho's fragments. These are not the form of Musil's *Young Törless*, of Baldwin's *Giovanni's Room*, of Vidal's *The City and the Pillar.* These are all works in which the content is manifestly homosexual—though, in the case of the older works, the same erasural reading of homosexuality congenitally links them, as it were, to the ones described; and in the fifties, occasionally critics tried to dismiss the more recent ones as cautionary case histories, rather than accept them as rich and moving statements—which may well have been the start of a similar dismissive move. But these genre forms do cover, say, Thomas Beer's 1923 biography *Stephen Crane: A Study in American Letters.*

We have gone into this genre (again, if that is what it should be called) in this much detail because Crane from time to time employed it: again, *Voyages,* "Harbor Dawn," and "Cutty Sark" (not to mention "This Way Where November . . ." ["White Buildings"] and "Thou Canst Read Nothing . . ." ["Reply"]) are all examples.

Paradoxically, the existence of such a homosexual genre and its forms as I have described (gay is the *last* thing one should call them), as well as their problematic, even mythic, status (they could not be talked about for what they were and remain effective in any way; whether or not they actually existed *had* to be kept in a state of undecidability), may represent one of the largest obstacles in the development of a historically sensitive gay studies faced with the task of diligently teasing out what, in specific examples of such genres, is in excess of their simplistic conventions.

But today—if only because they *are* unsubtle and generic—there is no reason for the heterosexual critic, male or female, not to have access to the homosexual reading of the work of a poet such as Crane. If anything, it behooves us, in our enthusiasm as gay critics, occasionally to recall just how much rhetorical energy such writers expended in the employment of these forms to ensure that a heterosexual reading *was* available for their texts.

III

From some thirty years ago I can recall a conversation in which a young poet explained to me how practically every rhetorical aspect of then-contemporary experimental poetry—it was c. 1963—had been foreshadowed forty to forty-five-odd years earlier by T. S. Eliot, either in "The Lovesong of J. Alfred Prufrock" or in *The Waste Land*. With much page turning and flipping through volumes, it was very impressive.

If any factor contributed most to the image of Crane the lyricist-sometimes-too-ambitious, it was his prosody. Eliot—and Pound, of the quintessentially experimental *Cantos*—was half in and half out of the traditional English language iambic pentameter measure. And when they were in it, they were often working mightily to make it vanish under the hyper-rhythms of the most ordinary speech. ("What thou lovest well remains . . . ," that most famous passage in *The Pisan Cantos* [Canto 81], though written in classical hexameters, strives to rewrite itself in blank tetrameter.) Crane often used a loose pentameter, however, to flail himself as far away from the syntax and diction of common speech as he could get and not have comprehension crumble entirely beneath him.

At that time, probably few would have called Crane's poetry "experimental." By the late fifties or early sixties (after the 1958 reprinting of his poems), Crane seemed a vivid, intense lyricist, whose poems, a little more frequently than was comfortable, lapsed over into the incomprehensible. Gertrude Stein's considerable effect was felt almost entirely within the realm of prose. Pound and Eliot were still the models for poetic experimentation among the young. And one suspected that any experiment whose rhetorical model could not be found within them was an experiment that had failed—by definition.

Once Eliot first published them in 1917's "Prufrock," for the next fifty years couplets like

> In the room the women come and go
> Talking of Michelangelo.

and

> I grow old . . . I grow old . . .
> I shall wear the bottoms of my trousers rolled

astonished young writers again and again with their LaForguian bathos. Like many poets of the twenties, Crane had followed Eliot back to LaForgue; he'd early-on translated "Three *Locutions Des Pierots*" from LaForgue's French.

One of the first poems where Crane thought about responding to Eliot—one of the first to which he committed the whole of his poetic abilities and in which he first began to create lines that regularly arrived at the a-referential form we now think of as characteristic of him—was "For the Marriage of Faustus and Helen." But if this poem sounds like anything to the modern ear, it sounds more like a pastiche of Eliot's "Prufrock" than a critique of it.

Crane's feminine iambic couplets, such as

> The stenographic smiles and stock quotations
> Smutty wings flash out equivocations.

and

> Three winged and gold-shod prophesies of heaven,
> The lavish heart shall always have to leaven

must recall to the sensitive reader Eliot's near-signature feminine rhymes:

> And time yet for a hundred indecisions,
> For a hundred visions and revisions.

and

> Oh, do not ask "What is it?"
> Let us go and make our visit.

As well, Crane's generalized apostrophes—

> O, I have known metallic paradises
> Where cuckoos clucked to finches

recall not only the apostrophe above it but recall equally Prufrock's
general claims to knowledge:

> And I have known them all already, known them all . . .
> And I have known the eyes already, known them all . . .
> And I have known the arms already, known them all . . .

Further comparison of the two poems, however, reveals a far greater
metric regularity in Crane's verse than in Eliot's (or, if you prefer, a
greater metrical variety in Eliot's verse than in Crane's): Eliot often
pairs tetrameters with hexameters, now in trochaics, now in iambics
(which the ear then tries to re-render into more traditional paired pent-
ameters), where Crane generally relies on blank or rhymed couplets.

With a full seventy years, however, Eliot's variety has finally been
normalized and absorbed into the general range of free verse—so that
it is almost hard to see his variation today as formal. As Eliot's idiosyn-
crasies have become one with the baseline of American poetic diction,
Crane the occasionally-over-the-top lyricist has metamorphosed into
Crane the rhetorical revolutionary.

The study of eccentric figures on the poetic landscape tends to blind
us, with the passage of time, to the mainstream that made the eccentric
signify as it did. What was the scope of mainstream poetry during the
twenties—Crane's decade?

In 1921 Edwin Arlington Robinson's *Collected Poems,* with the award of
the Pulitzer Prize for Poetry, made the fifty-year-old poet, till then all but
unknown—though he had been publishing books of verse since the
1880s—into a famous man. Eliot's *Waste Land* (along with Joyce's *Ulysses*)
appeared in 1922, but it was a *success de scandal,* not a popular triumph:
the talk alone of people who talked of poetry. But then, that same year,
so was Amy Lowell's *A Critical Fable*—a humorous survey of the poetic
scene since the War, whose title was taken from her forebear, James Russell Lowell's *A Fable for Critics* (1848), both with their *tour de force* introductions in rhymed prose. (That same November in Paris Marcel Proust
died, leaving unpublished the last three sections of his great novel.)
1923 saw Edna St. Vincent Millay's *The Harp-Weaver and Other Poems* receive the Pulitzer. 1924 saw it go to Robert Frost for his second book-
length collection, *New Hampshire.* That same year, Robinson Jeffers's
Roan Stallion, Tamar, and Other Poems was an extraordinary popular success with the reading public—setting off a controversy over Jeffers's

poetic merit that has not abated. In France that year, a poem touching on many of the same political concerns as Crane's *The Bridge* appeared, a poem which makes an informative contrast with it: St.-John Perse's *Anabase*. (Perse's *Amitie du Prince* appeared the same year.) And in America in '24, Wallace Stevens wrote what was to become one of his most famous poems, "Sea Surface Full of Clouds"—before entering half a dozen years of comparative poetic inactivity. And in 1925 twelve-year-old poet Nathalia Crane's *The Janitor's Boy* appeared, with introductory statements by both William Rose Benét (citing other poetic prodigies of merit, including the Scottish Marjorie Flemming, Hilda Conkling, and Scottish-born Helen Douglas Adam) and Nunnally Johnson—and went through a dozen-plus printings in no time. Robinson's next book, *The Man Who Died Twice* (1925), won him another Pulitzer; the 1926 Pulitzer went, posthumously, to Amy Lowell for *What's O'Clock* (published the same year—also posthumously—as her two-volume biography, *John Keats*). And the following year Robinson received his third Pulitzer for his book-length poem *Tristram* (1927)—which became a bona fide best seller. Poetry best sellers were certainly not common in those years, but they were more common than in ours. In the same year, Millay's verse drama, on which Deems Taylor based his successful opera of the same title, *The King's Henchman,* went through twelve printings between February and September (while in Germany, also in 1927, Martin Heidegger's *Being and Time* appeared, a work whose enterprise can be read as the cornerstone of his earliest attempts to poeticize the contemporary world, against a rigorous critique of metaphysics). That year American scholar John Livingston Lowe first published his exhaustive and illuminating findings from his researches into the early readings of Samuel Taylor Coleridge, *The Road to Xanadu: A Study in the Ways of the Imagination.* In 1928, Stephen Vincent Benét's novel in verse, *John Brown's Body,* captivated the general reading public. And through it all, the various volumes of Millay, for critics like Edmund Wilson, marked the true height of American poetic achievement.

What characterizes this range of American poetry is its extraordinary referential and argumentative clarity (argument used here in terms both of narrative and of logic)—often to the detriment of all musicality (as well as rhetorical ornamentation) not completely controlled by the regularity of meter and end-rhyme.

This was the mainstream of American poetry Eliot, Pound, H. D., and William Carlos Williams—as well as Crane (and Lowell, while she was alive)—saw themselves, one way or the other, at odds with. And this is the context that explains Loveman's seemingly gratuitous swipe at Mrs. Browning. First, the simple sexism that it represents is certainly at work in the comment—as it was against Amy Lowell, who worked as hard as any poet to ally her work and her enthusiasms with the new. To deny it would be as absurd as denying the homophobia Yingling found at work in the structure of the reputation of Crane. But, we must also remember, as a traditional poet, Elizabeth Browning was popular, even in the twenties. She was accessible. Thus she was seen to be on the side of referential clarity that those associated with the avant-garde felt called upon to denigrate. But, as is the case with the homophobia directed toward Crane, we must remember that it works not to obliterate the reputation, but rather to hold the reputation at a particular point—which was and is, finally, higher than that of many male poets of the time.

Today, it's the Language Poets whose works wrench Crane out of his position as a lyricist-too-extreme and forces us to reread him as a rhetorical revolutionary. Precisely what has been marginalized in the early readings of Crane—or, at any rate, pointed at with wagging finger as indicative of some essential failure—is now brought to the critical center and made the positive node of attention.

For what is now made the center of our rhetorical concern with Crane is precisely that "verbiage" Loveman would have stripped from the work—those moments where referentiality fails and language is loosed to work on us in its most immediate materiality.

Again and again through Crane's most varied, most exciting poems, phrases and sentences begin which promise to lead us to some referentially satisfying conclusion, through the form of some poetic figure. And again and again what Crane presents us with to conclude those figures is simply a word—a word that resists any and all save the most catachrestic of referential interpretations, so that readers are left with nothing to contemplate save what language poet Ron Silliman has called the pure "materiality of the signifier." It is easy to see (and to say) that Crane's poetry foregrounds language, making readers revel in its sensuousness and richness. But one of the rhetorical strategies by which he accomplishes this in line after line is simply to shut down the semantic, referential instrumentality of language all but completely:

> Time's rendings, time's blendings they construe
> As final reckonings of fire and snow.

Or:

> The Cross, a phantom, buckled—dropped below the dawn.
> Light drowned the lithic trillions of your spawn.

The final words—"spawn," "fire and snow"—arrive in swirling atmospheres of connotation, to which they even contribute; but reference plays little part in the resolution of these poetic figures. Reading only begins with such lines as one turns to clarify how they resist reference, resist interpretation, even as their syntax seems to court them. But to find examples we can look in any of Crane's mature work.

In 1963—the same year I was having the conversation about T. S. Eliot with the aforementioned poet—in France Michel Foucault was writing, in an essay on contemporary fiction, that the problem was not that "language is a certain distance from things. Language *is* the distance."

Thirty years before, Crane's suicide had put an end to a body of work that—not till twice thirty years later—would be generally acknowledged as among the earlier texts to inhabit that distance directly and, in so inhabiting it, shift an entire current of poetic sensibility in a new direction.

* * *

We like to tell tales of how confident our heroes are in their revolutionary pursuits. But it is more honest, in Crane's case at any rate, to talk about how paralyzingly unsure he was—at least at times—about precisely this aspect of his work; though, frankly, in the twenties, how could he have felt otherwise?

In a 1963 interview, Loveman recounted:

> Once—I don't know whether I ever told you—he tried to commit suicide in my presence.
>
> We had been out having dinner; he got raffishly high and we went to a lovely restaurant in the Village. No one was there but Didley Digges, the actor, in one corner. Hart waltzed me over to him with a low bow. Then he began to dance mazurkas on the floor. He loved to dance. It was a big room, and we had an excellent dinner. He got a little higher, and when he went out, as usual, he bargained with a taxi driver. He would never pay more than two dollars fare to Brooklyn. And then, usually, because he always forgot that he hadn't money with him, the person with him had to pay it. Through some mishap, we landed at the Williamsburg Bridge. I think there is a monument or a column there and Hart went up and as a matter of rite or sacrilege pissed against it. Then we started across to Columbia Heights. He lived at Number 110. When we got to Henry Street, it was around eleven or eleven-thirty. In one of the doorways we saw four legs sticking out and a sign, "We are not bums." They were going to an early market and their wagon was parked in the street. Hart became hysterical with laughter. Well, when we got to Columbia Heights,

the mood changed. The entire situation changed. He broke away from me and ran straight up the three flights of stairs, then up the ladder to the roof, and I followed him. I was capable of doing that then. As he got to the top, he threw himself over the roof and I grabbed his leg, one leg, and, oh, I was scared to death. And I said, "You son of a bitch! Don't you every try that on me again." So he picked himself up and said, "I might as well, I'm only writing rhetoric."

Here the interviewer comments: "That's what was bothering him." And Loveman continues:

He could no longer write without the aid of music or of liquor. It was impossible. He had reached the horrible impasse. So, we went downstairs to his room. I lived a couple of doors away. I worried myself sick about him. He poured himself some Dago Red, turned on the Victrola, and I left him.

How important this incident might have been for Crane is hard to tell. Was it a drunken jape, forgotten the next morning? Or does it represent the deep and abiding *veritas* classically presumed to reside *in vino*? Again, none of the three major biographers utilizes it.

Unterecker characterizes Crane as a "serious drinker" from the summer of '24 on. But drunkenness figures in Crane's letters—and in the apocryphal tales about him—from well before. And as so many people have pointed out, in trying to explain the context of prohibition in cities like New York and Chicago to people who did not live through it, even though alcohol was outside the law, it was so widely available the problem was not how to get it but rather how to stay sober enough to conduct the business of ordinary life!

It was a problem many in that decade failed to solve—Crane among them.

Let me attempt here, however, what I will be the first to admit is likely an over-reading of the evening Loveman has described with Crane—with all its a-specific vagaries.

The night begins in a Village restaurant, with an actor, a speaker of other writers' words. Directly following, a cab driver mangles Crane's (or possibly Loveman's) verbal instructions home: "Take us across the Bridge to Brooklyn . . ."

But instead of taking them to the Brooklyn Bridge, the driver takes them to the Williamsburg Bridge at Delancey Street—where, realizing how far off they are, they get out.

In the nighttime plaza before the Williamsburg, Crane urinates on a public monument.

A public monument makes a certain kind of public statement. To urinate on such a monument is, at the very least, to express one's contempt in the most bodily way possible (short of smearing it with shit) for its sententiousness, its pomposity, its civic pretension—those enunciational aspects traditionally designated by the phrase "empty rhetoric."

But to recount the above in this way is to point out that we have begun an evening where every event, as narrated by Loveman, one way or another foregrounds a more and more problematic relation with language—specifically with something about its rhetoricity.

Having given up the errant cab, Crane and Loveman decide to walk home, down through the Lower East Side, presumably for the Brooklyn Bridge, to cross over to 110 Columbia Heights by foot. (At the time, Loveman—a published poet in his own right, as well as, later, an editor of some reputation—tells us further on in the interview, John Dos Passos lived in the apartment below Crane's.) Crossing Henry Street, around the corner from the great daily markets of Orchard and Hester, just up from the Fulton Fish Market, they find two men sleeping together in a doorway, legs sticking out. There is the identifying cardboard: "We are not bums," which reduces Crane to hysteria—as he perceives the comedy of rhetoric at its most referential, stating what the speaker/writer hopes to make obvious in fear of the very misreading the writing presumes to obviate, participating through it in the same pretentious inflation on which, fifteen minutes before, Crane had just emptied his bladder.

It intrigues me that that night's walk across the Brooklyn Bridge, usually such a positive symbol for Crane, and across which he had walked before holding hands with Emil, is elided from Loveman's account. Does the elision suggest that—that night—the Bridge did *not* have the usual uplifting effect on Crane that, often in the past, it had had? Is there anything that we can retrieve from the elision? What, on any late night's stroll across the Brooklyn Bridge in the 1920s, were two gay men likely to see, regardless of their mood?

The nighttime walkways of the city's downtown bridges have traditionally been heavy homosexual cruising areas, practically since their opening—one of the reasons that, indeed, after dark, Crane and Emil had been able to wander across it—holding hands—with minimal fear of recriminations. They certainly could have not walked so during the day.

But perhaps that evening, with his old friend Loveman, on the Bridge's cruisy boardwalk, Crane might have heard the rich and pointed banter of a group of dishy queens lounging against the rail, or, perhaps, even the taunts leveled at them from a passing gaggle of sailors—who often crossed the Bridge back to the Navy Yard, in their uneasy yet finally symbiotic relationship with the bridge's more usual nighttime pedestrians. But even if the bridge were deserted that night, even if we do not evoke the *memory* of language to fulfill the place of *living* language, we can still assume without much strain that the conversation of the two men, at least now and again, touched on those subjects which it would have been impossible for such as they to cross the bridge at such an hour and not think of—in short, something in the human speech that occurred in that elided journey, whether the received public banter of cross-dressers or simply the speculation of Crane and Loveman to one another, is likely to have broached those sexual areas so easily and usually characterized as residing outside of language—at least outside that language represented by the municipal monument, outside that language which claims rhetorical density by only stating the true, the obvious, the inarguable—even as the very act of stating them throws such truths and inarguables into hysterical question. (To indulge in gay gossip, or indeed in any socially private sub-language, unto the language of poetry itself, is at once to take up and to invest with meaning an order of rhetoric the straight world—especially in the twenties—claims is empty, meaningless, and at the same time always suspected of pathology . . .) This, at any rate, is the place we can perhaps also best contextualize the urgency behind Crane's operatically passionate addresses to Loveman in his letter. One begins with the obvious statement that this was pre-Stonewall. But one must follow it with the observation that it was also pre-Matachine Society—which is to say, this rhetoric is from the homosexual tradition that the Matachine Society was both to spring from and (after its radical opening years under Harry Haye) to set itself against: the Matachines, recall, would eventually seek equal rights for homosexuals under the program that claimed homosexual males could be *just like other men* if they tried, and that they did not have to live their lives at such an intense level of passion in their relationships with their love objects and their friends, of the sort represented by Crane's exhortations to his friend Loveman. It is the situation that defined, at the time, a distinct, homosexual male community.

In the first of his *Voyages,* Crane—in that most referential of introductions to that transreferential cascade of poetic rhetoric—had exhorted the young boys frisking with sand and stick and shell:

> . . . there is a line
> You must not cross nor ever trust beyond it
> Spry cordage of your bodies to caresses
> Too lichen-faithful from too wide a breast.

The traditional reading certainly takes that line to refer to the boundary between innocence and sexual knowledge—and, for readers who know of Crane's love for Opffer, specifically homosexual knowledge.

Here we are not beyond referentiality but only into the simple foothills of metaphor. The caresses not to be trusted are those that are too "lichen-faithful," i.e., clinging, that originate from a breast "too wide," i.e., from a breast wider than a child's, i.e., a grown man's (or a grown woman's).

But it is also a line of rhetorical referentiality, of referential clarity— a line Crane had to cross specifically to write his love poems, a line beyond which all was music, affect, connotative brilliance—but without reference, a poetic land where the intended topic was always instantly erasable: "nothing but rhetoric." As a poet working in America, Crane had broached this verbal area all but alone. Wilde, the early hero of Crane's juvenile effort, "C 33," had doubtless first taught him the form to use in dealing with sex. ("C 33" was Wilde's cell number, when he was imprisoned at Reading Gaol for sodomy. The reader aware of this fact is, as it were, welcomed into Crane's poem; the reader who is not, is excluded from it and finds its subject opaque.) "C 33" was Crane's first attempt to separate his readers into two camps before the topic of homosexuality—in this case by means of homosexual folklore and erudition. But eventually Crane seems to have glimpsed within such practices an entire apparatus for articulating the inarticulable. And since Dada and surrealism were European movements to which he had no real and immediate access, it's no wonder that, from time to time (on such rhetorically problematic nights, when language and the machinery of the night as we have described it had, perhaps too quickly, escorted him there, arm in arm, like Loveman himself), that rhetorical area looked to Crane like a verbal waste land.

How much of this was behind Crane's drunken attempt to leap from the roof, maybe half an hour later—well, we must answer Loveman's interviewer's rhetorical question ("That's what was bothering him") in the same manner as Loveman:

Silence—before turning to another topic.

IV

The Bridge is a poem whose *"Proem"* and eight sections fall into two astonishing halves. The first half—*"Proem"* and Part I, "Ave Maria," throughout Part III, "Cutty Sark"—ranges over themes roughly connected by the concept of Time: history, the present, tradition, youth, age. The second half—Part IV, "Cape Hatteras" through Part VIII, "Atlantis"—recomplicates many of the same themes by considering them in the light of Space: territory, landscape, the city of lust and love, transportation. The idea of love—sometimes spoken, sometimes unspeakable—is the Bridge among them all.

The Brooklyn Bridge makes three appearances in the poem, two of them spectacular, one almost invisible. The spectacular appearances are in the introduction *("Proem")* and the coda ("Atlantis"). The near invisible one falls at the poem's virtual center, just before the closing movement of "Cutty Sark," when a veiled account of an unsuccessful homosexual pick-up of a drunken aging sailor concludes with the line, "I started walking home across the Bridge . . ." But a controlling irony of the poem would seem to be that images of the Bridge are, themselves, bridged by images from the land either side of it.

On at least one level, Crane's enterprise in *The Bridge* is majestically lucid. God—or the Absolute—as an abstract idea is too vast for the mind of man and woman to comprehend directly. Such an idea can only manifest itself—and then only partially—through myths. Living in the rectilinear architecture of the modern city, for Crane the curve, the broken arc, most visibly suggested the vastness and transcendence of deity. (That curve was, one suspects, the same Ouspensky-generated curve-of-binding-energy that Crane's friend, black writer Jean Toomer, was so insistent about having represented in the book design—before "Karintha," "Seventh Street," and "Kabnis"—of *Cane* [1923].) But the curve of gull-wing or bird flight, of wave crest or sea swell, was too impermanent. So Crane turned to the man-made curve of the Brooklyn Bridge "to lend a myth to God." Numerous other curves, some enduring, some momentary—from the mazy river's, to the railroad's steel, to the movement of Indian dancers, to that of a burlesque queen's pearl strings shaking at her hip—inform the Bridge's curve with meaning, just as the multiple uses of a word in language determine its meaning in any individual occurrence. And an early reading of *The Bridge* in which we pay attention to curved things that vanish and curved things that remain, in contrast with straight and angular things, equally stable or fleeting, is as good an entrance strategy as any into the further complexities of the poem.

As far as the source of that symbolic/mystic curve in the Ouspensky/Gurdjieff teachings, it's fair to suppose that Crane had what most of us would regard as a healthy skepticism toward the practical realities of the Gurdjieff movement. In an often reprinted letter of May 29th, 1927, that we have already referred to, Crane wrote to Yvor Winters, who had urged him that poems should reflect a picture of "the complete man"—which completeness, for Winters, seems somehow to have included being heterosexual:

The image of "the complete man" is a good idealistic antidote for the horrid hysteria for specialization that inhabits the modern world. And I strongly second your wish for some definite ethical order. Munson, however, and a number of my other friends, not so long ago, being stricken with the same urge, and feeling that something must be done about it—rushed into the portals of the famous Gurdjieff Institute and have since put themselves through all sorts of Hindu antics, songs, dances, incantations, psychic sessions, etc. so that now, presumably the left lobes of their brains and their right lobes function (M's favorite word) in perfect unison. I spent hours at the typewriter trying to explain to certain of these urgent people why I could not enthuse about their methods; it was all to no avail, as I was told that the "complete man" had a different logic than mine, and further that there was no way of understanding this logic without first submitting yourself to the necessary training . . . Some of them, having found a good substitute for their former interest in writing by means of more complete formulas of expression have ceased writing now altogether, which is probably just as well. At any rate, they have become hermetically sealed souls to my eyesight, and I am really not able to offer judgment.

But while Crane could frown at their methods, he had read and been impressed with Ouspensky's *Tertium Organum,* and he had gone to the lectures and dance demonstrations—and had taken in a good many of the ideas. Would that Toomer—likely the referent of that unhappy "probably just as well"—had been as able as Crane to maintain a similar distance. Finally, in the letter Crane gets to the homosexuality (Winters had apparently compared Crane positively to Valéry and Marlowe—probably without realizing Marlowe was gay—but warned that Crane might end up like the asexual Leonardo, who started endless projects of genius but finished less than two dozen):

Your fumigation of the Leonardo legend is a healthy enough reaction, but I don't think your reasons for doubting his intelligence and scope very potent.—I've never closely studied the man's attainments or biography, but your argument is certainly weakly enough sustained on the sole prop of his sex—or lack of such. One doesn't have to turn to homosexuals to find instances of missing sensibilities. Of course I'm sick of all this talk about balls and cunts in criticism. It's obvious that balls are needed, and that Leonardo had 'em—at least the records of the Florentine prisons, I'm told, say so. You don't seem to realize that the whole topic is something of a myth anyway, and is consequently modified in the characteristics of the image by each age in each civilization. Tom Jones, a character for whom I have the utmost affection, represented the model in 18th Century England, as least so far as the stated requirements of your letter would suggest, and for an Anglo-Saxon model he is still pretty good aside from calculus, the Darwinian theory, and a few other mental additions.

Quoting this letter at even greater length, Thomas E. Yingling in his *Hart Crane and the Homosexual Text,* a book rich in political insight, is astonished, possibly even bewildered, at the *Tom Jones* (1749) reference. But I can certainly remember being a teenager, when gay men of letters assumed that the good-natured foundling's light-hearted promiscuity was a self-evidently coded representation of bisexuality, or even homosexuality.

Here may be the place to mention that a reader taking his or her first dozen or so trips through *The Bridge* is likely—as were most of its early critics—to see its interest and energy centering in the lyricism and scene painting of *"Proem," "*Ave Maria," and the various sections of "Powhatan's Daughter"—that is, *The Bridge*'s first half.

But a reader who has lived with the poem over years is more likely to appreciate the stately, greatly reflective, and meditative beauties and insights—as well as the austere and lucid structure—of the second half:

"Cutty Sark," with which the first half ends, leaves us, as we have said, with the poet walking home over the Bridge at dawn, as Crane must have walked home many times to 110 Columbia Heights, contemplating the voyages of the great steamers, and probably remembering returning home—if we are to trust the restored epigraph that follows—to Emil. At this point, *The Bridge* begins its final, descending curve:

"Cape Hatteras" looks to the sky . . .

After the divigation of "Three Songs"—where the theme of sexual longing is heterosexualized for straight male readers (the Sestos and Abydos of the epigraph are two cities on opposite sides of the Hellespont, separated by water, whose literary import is precisely that they are *not* connected by a bridge, a separation which precipitates the tragedy of Hero, Priestess of Hesperus)—"Quaker Hill" (most cynical of the poem's sections) looks out level with the earth . . .

With the epigraph from Blake's "Morning," "The Tunnel" plunges us beneath the ground for an infernal recapitulation of the impressionistic techniques of the poem's first half (the fall of Atlantis proper), in which the poet glimpses Whitman's—and his own—chthonic predecessor, Poe . . .

. . . to leave us, once more, in "Atlantis," on the Bridge, flooded by the moon.

* * *

As a kind of progress report on *The Bridge,* on March 18, 1926, Crane wrote a letter to philanthropist Otto Kahn, who, a year before, had subsidized him with a thousand dollars.

Dear Mr. Kahn:

You were so kind as to express a desire to know from time to time how the Bridge was progressing, so I'm flashing in a signal from the foremast, as it were. Right now I'm supposed to be Don Christobal Colon returning from "Cathay," first voyage. For mid-ocean is where the poem begins.

It concludes at midnight—at the center of Brooklyn Bridge. Strangely enough that final section of the poem has been the first to be completed— yet there's a logic to it, after all; it is the mystic consummation toward which all the other sections of the poem converge. Their contents are implicit in its summary.

"Cutty Sark" was composed shortly after "Ave Maria," the opening Columbus section; and though it's possibly that, at first, Crane was not planning to include it in *The Bridge,* it is almost impossible to read it, right after the earlier poem, without seeing the aging, incoherent, ine- briated sailor of the second poem as an older, ironized version—three hundred years later on—of the Christopher Columbus figure who nar- rates the earlier transatlantic meditation. (Try reading "Cutty Sark" against Whitman's poem, "Prayer of Columbus," the poem in *Leaves of Grass* that follows "Passage to India"—a poem whose importance in *The Bridge* we will shortly come to.) The five sections of Part II, "Powhatan's Daughter," that, in *The Bridge*'s final version, intervene, dilute that iden- tification somewhat. But the suggestion of the individual's persistence through history, associated, say, with "Van Winkle," still holds it open.

In his letter to Kahn, Crane included a plan for the whole *Bridge* that may well have been growing in his mind for years:

    I. Columbus—Conquest of space, chaos.
    II. Pokahantus—The natural body of America-fertility, etc.
    III. Whitman—The Spiritual body of America.
              (A dialogue between Whitman and a dying soldier in a
              Washington hospital; the infraction of physical
              death, disunity, on the concept of immortality.)
    IV. John Brown (Negro Porter on Calgary Express making up
              births and singing to himself (a jazz form for this) of
              his sweetheart and the death of John Brown, alter-
              nately.)
    V. Subway—The encroachment of machinery on humanity; a
              kind of purgatory in relation to the open sky of
              last section.
    VI. The Bridge—A sweeping dithyramb in which the Bridge
              becomes the symbol of consciousness spanning time
              and space.

Shortly Crane wrote even longer outlines of the parenthetical narratives in Part III and Part IV. The following, recalling Whitman's poem "To One Shortly to Die" and scenes from *Specimen Days,* Crane titled "Cape Hatteras":

> Whitman approaches the bed of a dying *(southern)* soldier—scene is in a Washington hospital. Allusion is made to this during the dialogue. The soldier, conscious of his dying condition, at the end of the dialogue asks Whitman to call a priest, for absolution. Whitman leaves the scene—deliriously the soldier calls him back. The part ends before Whitman's return, of course. The irony is, of course, in the complete absolution which Whitman's words have already given the dying man, before the priest is called for. This, alternated with the eloquence of the dying man, is the substance of the dialogue—the emphasis being on the symbolism of the soldier's body having been used as a *forge* toward a state of Unity. His hands are purified of the death they have previously dealt by the principles Whitman hints at or enunciates (without talking up-stage, I hope) and here the 'religious gunman' motive returns much more explicitly than in F & H. [A reference to Crane's poem "For the Marriage of Faustus and Helen."] The agency of death is exercised in obscure ways as the agency of life. Whitman knew this and accepted it. The appeal of the scene must be made as much as possible independent of the historical 'character' of Walt.

And a still later outline for "Cape Hatteras" much closer to the poem as written, reads:

> (1) Cape—land—combination
>   conceive as a giant turning
> (2) Powerhouse
> (3) Offshoot—Kitty Hawk
>   Take off
> (4) War—in general
> (5) Resolution (Whitman)

Lines on Crane's worksheets for "Cape Hatteras"—that stretch of southern New Jersey containing Whitman's last home, in Camden, and (in the poem) the site of the plane wreckage—not used in the final version of the poem, possibly because they state a problem or a focus of the poem in terms too reductive, include, after the fourth stanza:

> Lead me past logic and beyond the graceful carp of wit.

And:

What if we falter sometimes in our faith?

The epigraph for "Cape Hatteras" is from Whitman's "Passage to India" (which contains the parenthetical triplet, harking back to "Ave Maria," "Ah Genoese, thy dream! thy dream! / Centuries after thou art laid in thy grave / The shore thou foundest verifies thy dream"). As do most of the epigraphs in the poem, it functions as a bridge between the preceding section, in this case "Cutty Sark" (which, with its account of the unsuccessful pick-up, is the true center of unspoken homosexual longing, the yearning for communication, in *The Bridge*), and the succeeding, here "Cape Hatteras" itself. With one line fore and three lines aft restored (lines, critic Robert Martin first pointed out, Crane probably expected the sagacious reader to be able to supply for himself), here is the passage from which the epigraph is actually taken:

> Reckoning ahead O soul, when thou, the time achiev'd,
> The seas all cross'd, weather'd the capes, the voyage done,
> Surrounded, copest, frontest God, yieldest, the aim attain'd,
> As filled with friendship, love complete, the Elder Brother found,
> The Younger melts in fondness in his arms.

It's arguable that the elided homosexual (and incestuous) resolution of the epigraphic passage confirms the homosexual subtext of the previous section, "Cutty Sark," as it makes a bridge between "Cutty Sark" and "Cape Hatteras."

The "Sanskrit charge" in the Falcon Ace's wrist (again in "Cape Hatteras"), critic L. S. Dembo had opined, is another reference to the Absolute, via the passage following the epigraphic lines in Whitman's poem:

> Passage to more than India!
> Are thy wings plumed indeed for such far flights?
> O soul, voyagest thou indeed on voyages like those?
> Disportest thou on waters such as those?
> Soundest below the Sanskrit and the Vedas?
> Then have thy bent unleash'd.

Note the development of "Cape Hatteras" from Crane's initial narrative outline to the poem as written:

In Crane's poem as outlined, it's a dying southern *soldier* who calls to Whitman for aid and absolution. The poem is conceived as a narrated *dialogue* between them. At the end, deliriously the soldier calls out to the departed Whitman . . .

In Crane's poem as realized, it's a very pensive *poet* (who has, yes, lived through the Great War; there is reference to the Somme—as Whitman lived through the Civil War—and Appomattox), who calls to Whitman. And instead of a death-bed dialogue, the poem is now the poet's reflective *monologue*—with only the plane crashes at its center providing a specific thanatopsis. At its end, however, deliriously, the *poet* calls to Whitman . . .

"[T]he eloquence of the dying man . . . is the substance of the dialogue," Crane wrote in his outline: in the monologue as written, Crane has expanded that "substance" into the entire poem. Its ironies are still in place—or even further recomplicated: the reason that the yearned-for cleaving of hands cannot ultimately take place at the end of the poem as we have it is because Whitman, rather than the soldier, is dead. What remains of Whitman is the eloquence his language and vision have given to the poet/narrator.

* * *

In 1923 Crane had read and been impressed by *Nation* editor Oswald Garrison Villard's recent biography of John Brown. And, in the outline, under the title "Calgary Express," he wrote:

> *Well don't you know it's mornin' time?*
> *Wheel in middle of wheel;*
> *He'll hear yo' prayers an' sanctify,*
> *Wheel in middle of wheel.*

The "scene" is a pullman sleeper, Chicago to Calgary. The main theme is the story of John Brown, which predominates over the interwoven "personal, biographical details" as it runs through the mind of a Negro porter, shining shoes and humming to himself. In a way it takes in the whole racial history of the Negro in America. The form will be highly original, and I shall use dialect. I hope to achieve a word-rhythm of pure jazz movement which will suggest not only the dance of the Negro but also the speed-dance of the engine over the rails.

And from the time of the briefer outline for "Cape Hatteras" he left this interesting sketch for "Ave Maria," *The Bridge*'s opening section:

> Columbus' will—knowledge
> Isabella's will—Christ
> Fernando's will—gold

—3 ships

—2 destroyed

1 remaining will, Columbus

Over the next year when the bulk of the poems comprising *The Bridge* were written, Crane veered from, expanded on, broke, crossed, bridged, and abridged much of this template. A year later, in the early months of 1927, he sent Yvor Winters another, typewritten outline of the poem, this one in ten parts:

Projected Plan of the Poem

Dedication—to Brooklyn Bridge
1— Ave Maria
    2— *Powhatan's Daughter*
     # (1) The Harbor Dawn
     # (2) Van Winkle
      (3) The River
     # (4) The Dance
      (5) Indiana
    3— Cape Hatteras
4— Cutty Sark
5— The Mango Tree
6— Three Songs
    7— The Calgary Express
    8— 1920 Whistles
9— The Tunnel
#10— Atlantis

Beside "The Mango Tree" Crane jotted a note to Winters by hand: "—may not use this" and, beside "1920 Whistles": "—ditto." Crane's final handwritten comment across the page's bottom:

Those marked # are completed.

"The Mango Tree" prose-poem was, yes, dropped. (That he was planning to mix prose-poetry in with his poetic series is the first suggestion, however faint, that at one point or another Crane might have had Novalis in mind.) "1920 Whistles" never became a separate poem. And eight stanzas of what he'd done on "The Calgary Express" Crane now appended to the closing section of "The River"—and abandoned the railroad poem. (Today it looks like rather astute poetic tact. Clearly Crane felt that his American poem should contain "the whole racial history of the Negro in America" but, as clearly, he felt he was not the one to write it.) Still, from the earlier outline, I. Columbus, II. Pokahantus, IV. Subway, and V. The Bridge are what we have today as I *Ave Maria,* II *Powhatan's Daughter,* VII *The Tunnel,* and VIII *Atlantis,* so that the initial template is highly informative about what Crane ultimately and actually decided on.

The order of composition—which reveals its own internal logic—is "Atlantis," *"Proem: To Brooklyn Bridge,"* "Ave Maria," "Cutty Sark," "Van Winkle," "The Tunnel," "Harbor Dawn," "Southern Cross," "National Winter Garden," and "Virginia." After that, things become a bit murky. From then on the probable order is: "The Dance," "The River," "Calgary Express" (abandoned and cannibalized for "The Dance"), "Quaker Hill," "Cape Hatteras."

At the end of 1927, Stephen Vincent Benét—younger brother of critic William Rose Benét (who'd been notably hostile to Crane's first, 1926 volume, *White Buildings*)—published his book-length poem, *John Brown's Body;* over the next year it became a major, even enduring, middle-brow success. In it Whitman is a minor figure and John Brown a major presence. Though hardly any critic mentions it, surely Benét's poem was a good reason for Crane to have dropped the John Brown narrative, if it was not simply a confirmation of the rightness of his earlier tendency to abandon the heavily foregrounded narratives he had once planned for the parts of *The Bridge* concerning Brown and Whitman.

* * *

Though we have already cited the Emerson passage that prompted Crane, sometime in 1926 or '27, to change the title of his final (if first written) section of *The Bridge* from "Finale" to "Atlantis," we are still left with a problem: what is the phenomenal effect of the new title of the poem's closing section on the reader? What—or better, *how*—does it signify?

The problem of poetic sources (at whose rim we now totter) makes a vertiginous whirlpool directly beneath all serious attempts at poetic elucidation, now supporting them, now overturning them. For a most arbitrarily chosen example, take Gonzolo's famous utopian expostulation in Shakespeare's final play, *The Tempest* (II, i., 148–173; the play is usually dated in its writing as just before its 1611 performance), on how he would run an ideal commonwealth set up on his isolate island:

I' th' commonwealth I would by contraries
Execute all things. For no kind of traffic
Would I admit; no name of magistrate;
Letters should not be known; riches, poverty,
And use of service, none; contract, succession,
Bourn, bound of land, tilth, vineyard, none;
No use of metal, corn, or wine, or oil;
No occupation; all men idle, all;
And women too, but innocent pure;
No sovereignty . . .
All things in common nature should produce
Without sweat or endeavor. Treason, felony,
Sword, pike, knife, gun, or need of any engine
Would I not have; but nature should bring forth,
Of it own kind, all foison, all abundance,
To feed my innocent people.

Once we've ransacked our Elizabethan glossaries to ascertain that "contraries" here means "contrary to what is commonly expected," that "traffic" means trade, that "service" means servants, "succession" inheritance, "tilth" tillage, "bourn" boundary, "engine" weapon, and "foison" abundance, we turn to Michel de Montaigne's (1533–1593) essay, "Of the Cannibals," in which Montaigne praises the American Indian nations for their savage innocence—an essay widely read in Elizabethan England—to discover (after a quote from Plato: "'All things,' saith Plato, 'are produced by nature, by fortune, or by art. The greatest and fairest by one or other of the first two, the least and imperfect by the last.'") the following passage (in John Florio's 1603 translation) on an imagined ideal nation, suggested by the far-off lands of the American Indians:

It is a nation, I would answer Plato, that hath no kind of traffic, no knowledge of letters, no intelligence of numbers, no name of magistrate, nor of politic superiority; no use of service, of riches, or of poverty; no contracts, no successions, no partitions, no occupations but idle; no respect of kindred but common, no apparel but natural, no manuring of land, no use of wine, corn, or metal. The very words that import lying, falsehood, treason, dissimulation, covetousness, envy, detraction, and pardon, were never heard amongst them. How dissonant would he [Plato] find this imaginary commonwealth from this perfection?

It is not just the ideas—which here and there, in fact, differ—that seem to have been ceded from Montaigne to the bard; rather it is impossible to imagine Shakespeare's passage written without a copy of Montaigne to hand, if not underscored on the page then loosely in memory.

But even as we declare the above example arbitrary *vis-à-vis* Crane, the careful reader will remember that, at the close of "Cutty Sark," among the great boats that Crane/the poet sees from the Bridge, their names in traditional italics, with all their suggestions of travel, the last one we find is, with a question mark, concluding the section, "Ariel?"—named after the airy sprite Shakespeare gives us in that same play, first as an androgynous fey, then (after line 316 of the play's second scene), on next entrance, as a "water nymph" for the play's remainder.

There is as little question that Crane's interrogative "Ariel?" has its source in Shakespeare as there is that Shakespeare's "metal, corn, or wine" (not to mention traffic, magistrate, letters, service, or commonwealth itself) has its source in Montaigne's (*via* Florio's) "wine, corn, or metal."

But what about the utopian concerns that Shakespeare (at least for the length of Gonzalo's speech) and Montaigne share? Crane's use of Atlantis, of Cathay, within the American tradition, leans toward similar concern. Is the singular question of the single shared term "Ariel?" enough on which to ground an intertextual bridge between an Elizabethan England and a contemporaneous France and Crane's vision in the American twenties? If so, what is its status? Historically, the "commonwealth" on which Montaigne literarily—and Shakespeare metaphorically—grounded a utopian vision is the same one that Strachy's journals, quoted in William Carlos Williams's *In the American Grain,* presents: the journals from which Crane took (*via* Elizabeth Bowen's review of Williams's book) his epigraph for "Powhatan's Daughter." Here, perched on the most tenuous intertextual filaments, we are gazing down directly into the very maelstrom we began with, whose chaos casts its spume obscuring intention and origin, conscious choice and writerly history, source and filiation, where the signifieds accessible to the individual poet become hopelessly confounded with and blurred by the signifieds at large in what is called "culture," all of them a-slip beneath the rhetorical storm, even as all greater poetic possibilities must rise over such turbulence to produce an effect of order, and in the name of such order soar above it.

Atlantis is traditionally the name for an island, or frequently a city, which had reached a pinnacle both of military might and of culture; it was swallowed up by the sea over a cataclysmic day and night's tempest of torrential rains and earthquakes.

But, in *The Bridge,* after we read Crane's title—"Atlantis"—we find, following it, *not* a description of an island city (however utopian or no), but, rather, a glorious evocation of the Brooklyn Bridge drenched by the moonlight. As such, then, the title does not caption the poem in the usual way of titles; the relation is rather, perhaps, sequential, suggesting another of Crane's indirect mentions: *first* Atlantis, *then* the topic of the poem—the bridge, leading perhaps from, or to, that city. But is there anything else we can say about the still somewhat mysterious title, as it functions in the poem?

To answer this, we undertake what will surely seem our most eccentric digression, bridging centuries and seas and poetic history, though we hope to move only over fairly reasonable textual bridges . . .

* * *

Almost certainly (in a comparatively late decision), Crane took the title for *The Bridge*'s introductory section—*"Proem"*—from the poetic introduction of James Thomson's (1834–1882) *The City of Dreadful Night* (1874). Certainly it's the most likely, if not the only, place for him to have encountered the archaic word. (He might well have called the opening "Invocation," "Prologue," or any number of other possible titles; as late as '27, he was calling it "Dedication.") Thomson's "Proem" contains the lines:

> Yes, here and there some weary wanderer
>   In that same city of tremendous night
> Will understand the speech, and feel a stir
>   Of fellowship in all-disastrous fight;
> 'I suffer mute and lonely, yet another
> Uplifts his voice to let me know a brother
>   Travels the same wild paths though out of sight.'

Many poets and readers over the years have felt themselves a "brother" to Thomson; and *The City of Dreadful Night* retains a certain extra-canonical fascination to this day. Much of Thomson's poem (The "Proem" and sections 1, 3, 7, 9, 11, 13, 17, 19, and 21) falls, ironically enough, into the seven-line rhyme scheme of the usually light and happy French rondolet—though without the line-length variations (i.e., the traditionally defective first, third, and seventh lines) ordinarily found in that form: rather, for his purposes, Thomson used the more stately iambic pentameter for his moody monody. Thomson's series has been popular with poets, eccentrics, and night lovers since its first publication over two issues of the *National Reformer* in 1874. George Meredith and George Eliot were among its earliest enthusiasts. But there is a good deal more shared between the two poetic series than simply the title of their opening sections. Both *The Bridge* and *The City of Dreadful Night* are largely urban poems, yet both have powerful extra-urban moments. As well, the variation in tone among *The Bridge*'s fifteen separate sections is very close to the sort of variation we find among the 21 sections of Thomson's nocturnal meditation on hopelessness and isolation.

Indeed, it's arguable that—granted the dialogue between them we've already mentioned—one purpose behind both *The Waste Land* and *The Bridge* was to write a poem, or poem series, of the sort for which Thomson's *City of Dreadful Night* was the prototype; if, indeed, that was among the generating complexities of both poems, then certainly, on that front, Crane's is the more successful.

Today, Thomson experts will sometimes talk of his poems "In the Room," "Insomnia," "Sunday at Hampstead," and even his narrative "Waddah and Om-El-Bonain." But to the vast majority of readers of English poetry, Thomson is (he is even so styled in several card catalogues, to distinguish him from his 18th Century ancestor of the same name, author of *The Seasons* [mentioned already] and *The Castle of Indolence*) the "author of *The City of Dreadful Night*."

James Thomson was born at Port Glasgow in Renfrewshire, a day or two more than a month before Christmas in 1834. His mother was a deeply, almost fanatically religious Irvingite. During a week of dreadful storms, his father, chief officer aboard the *Eliza Stewart*, suffered a paralytic stroke and was returned to his family an invalid, immobile on his right side, as well as mentally unsound—when James was six. Two years later, James's mother enrolled her eight-year-old son in a boarding school, the Caladonian Asylum—and died a month or so later. His father was far too ill to take care of his sons. (James had, by now, a two-year-old brother and had already lost a two-year-old sister a couple of years before.) So James began the life of a scholarship/charity student at one or another boarding school or military academy over the next handful of years.

An extremely bright young man, by seventeen James was virtually a schoolmaster himself at the Chelsea Military Academy. His nickname from the Barnes family with whom he now lived was "Co"—for "precocious." At sixteen he'd begun to read Shelley and, shortly after, the early German romantic, Novalis. Soon he was publishing poems regularly in London under the pseudonym "Bysshe Vanolis" (or, more usually, under the initial's "B.V."). Bysshe was, of course, Shelley's middle name—and the name he was called by his friends. "Vanolis" was an anagram of Thomson's new Germanic enthusiasm.

At eighteen Thomson became officially an assistant army schoolmaster—that is, a uniformed soldier who taught the children associated with Camp Curragh in the mornings and the younger soldiers themselves in the afternoon.

Novalis—the Latin term for a newly plowed field—was the penname of Friedrich von Hardenberg (1772–1801), remembered for a mystical novel about a poet's pursuit of a "blue flower" first seen in a dream, *Heinrich von Ofterdingen,* and an intriguing set of notes and fragments, among them the famous "Monologue," and the even more famous pronouncement, "Character is Fate"—as well, of course, as such wonderful observations as (in Carlyle's fine translations from his 1829 essay of the young German poet):

> To become properly acquainted with a truth we must first have disbelieved it, and disputed against it . . .
>
> Philosophy is properly Home-sickness; the wish to be everywhere at home . . .
>
> The division of Philosopher and Poet is only apparent, and to the disadvantage of both. It is a sign of disease, and of a sickly constitution . . .
>
> There is but one Temple in the World; and that is the Body of Man. Nothing is holier than this high form. Bending before men is a reverence done to this Revelation in the Flesh. We touch Heaven, when we lay our hand on a human body . . .
>
> We are near awakening when we dream that we dream . . .

—and the disturbingly prescient observation quoted by Guy Debord in *The Society of the Spectacle,* "Writings are the thoughts of the State; archives are its memory."

As well, Novalis wrote a series of poems, *Hymnen an die Nacht (Hymns to the Night),* that forms one of the most influential series of poems from the exciting ferment of Early German Romanticism.

Trained as an engineer, the twenty-three-year-old von Hardenberg was working as an assayer in the salt mines where his father had worked before him. In the small Saxon mining town, he met and fell in love with a thirteen-year-old girl, Sophie von Kühn. He sued her family for her hand, and was finally accepted—though the marriage was not to take place until she was older. Hardenberg was devoted to his young fiancée. Two and a half years later, on March 17th of 1797, Sophie turned fifteen. But two days later, on the 19th, after two operations on her liver, she died. Not a full month later, on April 14th, Hardenberg's younger brother Erasmus passed away. Now Hardenberg wrote a friend in a letter:

> It has grown Evening around me, while I was looking into the red of Morning. My grief is boundless as my love. For three years she has been my hourly

> thought. She alone bound me to life, to the country, to my occupation.
> With her I am parted from all; for now I scarcely have *myself* any more. But it
> has grown Evening . . .

And in another letter, from May 3rd:

> Yesterday I was twenty-five years old. I was in Grünigen and stood beside her
> grave. It is a friendly spot; enclosed with simple white railing; lies apart, and
> high. There is still room in it. The village, with its blooming gardens, leans
> up around the hill; and it is at this point that the eye loses itself in blue dis-
> tances. I know you would have liked to stand by me, and stick the flowers,
> my birthday gifts, one by one into her hillock. This time two years, she made
> me a gay present, with a flag and national cockade on it. To-day her parents
> gave me the little things which she, still joyfully, had received on her last
> birthday. Friend,—it continues Evening, and will soon be Night.

Soon after that, Hardenberg composed both his fragments and his
Hymns.

An early manuscript shows us that Novalis first wrote all six of his
hymns as verse. But later he reworked and condensed the first four
(and much of the fifth) into a hard, glittering, quintessentially modern
German prose-poetry. It was only the final hymn, the sixth, "Sensucht
nach dem Tode" ("Yearning for Death") that Novalis let stand as traditional poetry. The prose-poetry version was the one published by the
brothers August Wilhelm and Friedrich Schlegel in their magazine
Athenaeum 3, n. 2, in 1800.

By inverting a traditional metaphor, the *Hymnen* (a series quite as notable in its ways as *The City of Dreadful Night, The Waste Land,* and *The Bridge,*
though it lacks the two modern series' urban specificity) introduce an astonishing trope into the galaxy of European—and finally Western—
rhetoric: To those of a certain sensibility (often those in deep grief, or
those with a secret sorrow not to be named before the public), the day,
sunlight, and the images of air and light that usually sign pleasure are actually hateful and abhorrent. Night alone is the time such souls can
breathe freely, be their true selves, and come into their own. For them,
night is the beautiful, wondrous, and magical time—not the day.

In the second half of that extraordinary fifth Hymn, in which both
prose and verse finally combine, Hardenberg even goes so far as to
Christianize his *"Nachtbegeisterung"* ("Enthusiasm for the night"): Night,
not day, is where the gods dwell as constellations. It was through the
night the three kings traveled under their star seeking Jesus, and it was
in the night they found Him. Similarly it was during the night that the

stone was rolled away from the tomb and, thus, it was the night that the Resurrection occurred.

Writers who were to take up this trope of the inversion of the traditional values of night and day—in both cases, directly from Novalis—and make it their own include both Poe and Baudelaire. And the great Second Act of Wagner's *Tristan und Isolde* has been called simply "Novalis set to music." Certainly Thomson's *The City of Dreadful Night* is the poetic moment through which it erupted into the forefront of English poetic awareness. The Christianizing moment makes the trope Novalis's own, but writers were to seize that basic night/day inversion—Byron for Childe Harold and Manfred, Poe for C. August Dupin—till we can almost think of it as *the* romantic emblem.

By comparison to Novalis (or Thomson), Crane's *Bridge* is overwhelmingly a poem of the day—yet it has its crepuscular moments, where one is about to enter into night:

From Crane's opening *"Proem,"* addressing the Bridge:

> And we have seen night lifted in thine arms.

> Under thy shadow by the piers I waited;
> Only in darkness is thy shadow clear.
> The City's fiery parcels all undone,
> Already snow submerges an iron year . . .

Though Crane is the author, this is Novalis (does Crane's capital "C" in "City" consciously link it to Thomson's?)—and Novalis by way of Thomson, at that!

As well, in *The Bridge,* there is the pair of aubades, "The Harbor Dawn" and "Cutty Sark," when night is being left behind.

But let us linger on the Thomson/Novalis connection a little longer. Eventually it will lead us back to Crane, and by an interesting circumlocution:

Thomson not only took Novalis's pen name and Novalis's famous poetic night/day inversion for his own. Working with another friend, he taught himself German and translated Novalis's *Hymns:* though his translation has never been published in its entirety, the sections reprinted by various biographers are quite lovely; the manuscript has been at the Bodley Head since 1953. Thomson also appropriated, however, a bit of Novalis's biography.

When he was eighteen and an assistant army schoolmaster in Ballincollig near Cork, Thomson met the not quite fourteen-year-old daughter of his friend Charles Bradlaugh's armourer-sergeant, Mathilda Weller, with whom he was quite taken. They danced together at a young people's party; presumably they had a handful of deep and intense conversations. Two years later, before she reached her sixteenth year, Mathilda died.

In later years, Thomson claimed that her death wholly blighted the remainder of his life. (Mathilda just happened to be the name Novalis had given to the character inspired by Sophie in his novel of the mystical quest for the blue amaranthus in *Heinrich von Ofterdingen.*) On his own death from dipsomania, at age forty-seven in 1882, Thomson was buried with a lock of Mathilda's hair in the coffin with him. But it's quite possible Thomson used this suspiciously Novalis-like fable to excuse the fact that he did not marry, also to excuse his increasing drunkenness, and quite possibly as a cover for promiscuous homosexuality in the alleys and back streets of London, where he eventually finished his life. While Friedrich von Hardenberg survived Sophie von Kühn by only four years—tuberculosis killed him shortly before he turned twenty-nine (as it would kill the twenty-three-year-old Greenberg)—James Thomson survived Mathilda Weller by nearly thirty.

An incident in Thomson's young life that may have come far closer to blighting the remainder of it than Mathilda's death occurred in 1862, however, when Thomson was twenty-seven—and still teaching in the army. Thomson and some other schoolmasters were at a pond. Though it was a private lake and no bathing was allowed, someone dared one among them to swim out to a boat in the middle. Thomson was recognized but, when questioned about the incident later, refused to give the names of his companions. For this, he was demoted to schoolmaster 4th Class, then dismissed from the army.

Whether any of the other schoolmasters involved were dismissed has not been recorded.

Thomson's earliest biographer, Henry Salt, makes little of the incident and claims Thomson was not guilty of any personal misconduct but was simply unlucky enough to be part of "the incriminated party."

But Thomson's 1965 biographer, William David Schaefer, feels the explanation is wildly improbable, detecting about it some sort of Victorian cover up—possibly involving alcoholism: Thomson's drinking had already established itself as a problem as far back as 1855. Perhaps the young men at the pond were both rowdy and soused. I would go Schaefer one further, however, and suggest there was some sort of sexual misconduct involved as well, for which the swimming incident was, indeed, used as the official excuse to expel the group of possibly embarrassing fellows. But we do not know for sure.

What we do know is that Thomson now went to London and began a career of writing scathingly radical articles for the various political journals of the times—often living off his friends, and drinking more and more. And it was only now that (some of) his poems began to refer to a secret sorrow—presumably Mathilda Weller's death. In London Thomson lived with his friend Charles Bradlaugh (and Bradlaugh's wife and two daughters) on and off for more than twelve years as a kind of tolerated, even fondly approved of, if occasionally drunken, uncle—until a year or so after *The City of Dreadful Night* was published in the March and May issues of Bradlaugh's magazine, *The National Reformer.* (Bradlaugh skipped the April issue because of objections from readers; but still other readers, among them Bertram Dobell, wrote to ask when the poem would continue; and publication resumed.) But with Thomson's newfound fame, the poet-journalist's drinking escalated violently—and the two men finally broke over it.

The City of Dreadful Night begins with two Italian epigraphs, one by Dante, one by Leopardi. The Dante says, "*Per me si va nella citta dolente*" ("Through me you enter into the sorrowful city.") But this is not the all too familiar motto over the Gate of Hell. Rather, from Thomson's poem, we realize this is Thomson's motto for the gate of birth and that the city of life itself is, for Thomson, the sorrowful city, the city without hope or love or faith. And Leopardi is, after all, the poet who wrote to his sister Paolina about the grandeur that was Rome: "These huge buildings and interminable streets are just so many spaces thrown between men, instead of being spaces that contain men." *The City of Dreadful Night* is a blunt and powerful, if not the most artful, presentation of the condition of humanity bereft of all the consolations of Christianity as well as the community of small rural settlements—next to which *The Waste Land,* with its incursions of medieval myth, occultism, and Eastern religions to provide a possible code of meaning and conduct, looks positively optimistic!

Back in his twenty-second year, however, in 1857, while still stationed at Ballincollig, Thomson wrote what, today, we must read as a "dry run" for the more famous series (that he would go on to write between '71 and '73, with trips to both the U.S.A. and Spain coming to interrupt its composition). Called *The Doom of a City,* its four parts ("The Voyage," "The City," "The Judgment," and "The Return") run to some 43 pages in my edition—fifteen pages longer than the 28-page *City of Dreadful Night.* Although Plato's mythic island is never mentioned by name, clearly this is the young Thomson's attempt to tell his own version of the story of Atlantis. (Again, the basic idea may have come from his idol: on a shipboard journey in Chapter III of Novalis's *Ofterdingen,* merchants regale Heinrich and his mother with a tale of Atlantis, in which Atlantis's king is enamored of poetry and his daughter, who rides off and meets a young scholar in the woods, loses a ruby from her necklace which the young man finds, returns for it the next day, stays to fall in love, retreats to a cave with the young man in a storm, and lives with him and his father for a year before returning to court with her child and the lute-playing young man, for a glorious reunion with the king— a fairy tale whose overwhelming affect is its reliance on time's ability to absorb all intergenerational, or generally Oedipal, tensions, so that the reference to its destruction in the closing line, "*Nur in Sagen heisst es, dass Atlantis von machtigen Fluten den Augen entzogen worden sie,*" ["Only in legends are we told that mighty floods took Atlantis from the sight of man"], falls like a veil between us and a vision of paradise.) In Part I, "The Voyage," of *Doom of a City*, the despairing poet rises in the middle of the night and takes a skiff that, leaving his own city, brings him over the lightless water—after a brief, but harmless, confrontation with a sea monster—to dawn and the shore of a great and mysterious City. The day, however, grows stormy.

After waiting out the day on shore, here is the City the poet finally finds at sunset:

> . . . Dead or dumb,
> That mighty City through the breathless air
> Thrilled forth no pulse of sound, no faintest hum
> Of congregated life in street and square:
> Becalmed beyond all calm those galleons lay,
> As still and lifeless as their shadows there,
> Fixed in the magic mirror of the bay
> As in a rose-flushed crystal weirdly fair.
> A strange, sad dream: and like a fiery ball,
> Blazoned with death, that sky hung over all.

Night descends; and the poet enters the darkened City's gates:

> The moon hung golden, large and round,
> Soothing its beauty up the quiet sky
> In swanlike slow pulsations, while I wound
> Through dewy meads and gardens of rich flowers,
> Whose fragrance like a subtle harmony
> Was fascination to the languid hours.

In the moonlight, he finds a garden of cypress, a funeral come to a halt, and a market. But all the inhabitants are frozen stone instead of living people. He moves on into the City:

My limbs were shuddering while my veins ran fire,
    And hounded on by dread
    No less than by desire,
I plunged into the City of the Dead,
And pierced its mausolean loneliness
Between the self-sufficing palaces,
Broad fronts of azure, fire and gold, which shone
Spectrally valid in the moonlight wan,
Adown great streets; through spacious sylvan squares,
    Whose fountains plashing lone
Fretted the silence with perpetual moan;
Past range on range of marts which spread their wares
Weirdly unlighted to the eye of heaven,
Jewels and silks and golden ornaments,
Rich perfumes, soul-in-soul of all rare scents.
Viols and timbrels: O wild mockery!
Where are the living shrines for these adornings?

The poet explores on, but instead of a populace in the City—

What found I? Dead stone sentries stony-eyed,
Erect, steel-sworded, brass-defended all,
Guarding the sombrous gateway deep and wide
Hewn like a cavern through the mighty wall;
Stone statues all throughout the streets and squares.
Grouped as in social converse or alone;
Dim stony merchants holding forth rich wares
To catch the choice of purchasers in stone;
Fair statues leaning over balconies,
Whose bosoms made the bronze and marble chill;
Statues about the lawns, beneath the trees
Firm sculptured horsemen on stone horses still;
Statues fixed gazing on the flowing river
Over the bridge's sculpted parapet;
Statues in boats, amidst its sway and quiver
Immovable as if in ice-waves set:—
The whole vast sea of life about me lay,
The passionate, the heaving, restless, sounding life,
With all its side and billows, foam and spray,
Attested in full tumult of its strife
Frozen into a nightmare's ghastly death,
Struck silent by its laughter and its moan.

The vigorous heart and brain and blood and breath
Stark, strangled, confined in eternal stone.

The poet continues to regard the urban landscape around him with its stony populace—

Look away there to the right—How the bay lies broad and bright,
All athrob with murmurous rapture in the glory of the moon!
See in front the palace stand, halls and columns nobly planned;
Marble home for marble dwellers is it not full fair and boon?
See the myriads gathered there on that green and wooded square,
In mysterious congregation,—they are statues every one:
All are clothed in rich array; it is some high festal day;
The solemnity is perfect with the pallid moon for sun.

As he finally sees the stony autarch of the city (beside whom crouches the skeleton of Death), the whole, frozen vision, with all its populace turned to stone, lit with a full moon, a series of towering gods appear (Part III, "The Judgment"), and a booming Voice proceeds to judge wanting one aspect of the City after another; and, on each judgment, that section of the City falls into the sea, or is toppled by an earthquake, to be swallowed up.

The judgment on the City begins with—

A multitudinous roaring of the ocean!
Voices of sudden and earth-quaking thunder
From the invisible mountains!
The heavens are broken up and rent asunder
By curbless lightning fountains,
Swarming and darting through that black commotion,
In which the moon and stars are swallowed with the sky.

Finally, only the young poet is spared by the Voice, as one who has sought after truth. The day dawns; what remains of the city is only the good and the pure—which, indeed, isn't very much. The poet regains his boat and returns from whence he came over the blue waters and under the brilliant sun.

The city to which the poet in his boat returns in the evening is, however, sordid and lurid. (In the two stanzas describing it—II and III of Part IV, "The Return"—we have the first intimations of what Thomson will publish eighteen years on, in the more powerful, but less Atlantian, *City of Dreadful Night*.) So once more the poet takes to his boat and returns to the ruined site of the mythic City, to hear the voice again deliver a jeremiad against the greed and evil of urban corruption.

With this sermon threatening the fall of the real city, *The Doom of a City* ends.

The question is: did Crane at some point encounter the two volumes of *The Poetical Works of James Thomson*, edited and published after Thomson's death by Bertram Dobell in 1895—where, indeed, he might have found *The Doom of a City*? As we have said, Crane's *"Proem"* at the start of *The Bridge* makes it almost certain that he knew *The City of Dreadful Night*. But would his curiosity have drawn him to pursue Thomson back to this Ur-version of that paean to urban psychic disaster—Thomson's own, twenty-three-year-old's retelling of the destruction of Atlantis?

Periodically, starting with his death, there were attempts to establish Thomson as an important canonical poet. But everything from Thomson's militant atheism and radical politics to his dipsomania and dreadfully sordid final years militated against it—especially during the first-wave attempt, spearheaded by Dobell, in the 1880s and '90s. (That both Poe and Thomson, in the manner of Novalis before them, were associated with tragic affairs with much younger women is not, as it works toward the moral marginalization of both, without its meaning.) Thomson is a poet a full understanding of whose work hinges not only on Novalis (and Shelley), but also on Heine and Leopardi: he translated significant amounts of both. (Indeed, Thomson's literary tastes were quite advanced: he championed Whitman, Emerson, and William Blake when all three were majorly controversial figures in England.) But two World Wars, with Germany as the villain (and Italy not far behind), has made English writers with leanings in those national directions less sympathetic to us than they might otherwise be.

Crane's essay "The Case Against Nietzsche" (1918) was his own attempt to fight that particular sort of jingoism, which, after the Great War, often seemed a tidal wave of pure anti-intellectualism. But certainly Thomson, with his secret sorrow and tragic life, could have been a poet that Crane in his later years, drinking himself into a poetic silence, as did Thomson, might well have sympathized, if not identified, with.

The brilliant moonlit evocations of the City that litter Thomson's earlier poem all through its second quarter certainly put one in mind of the moonlight flooded structure that is the vision behind Crane's "Atlantis"—the terminal section of his own major poetic series—as if all that was needed between Thomson's vision of London and the moon-drenched vision of his own Atlantis was, somehow, a bridge . . .

An early Encyclopedia Britannica article on Thomson that Crane might well have read—I first looked him up the same year I first read

Crane, in 1958, the same year I came across a powerful fragment from *The City of Dreadful Night* in an old Oscar Williams paperback anthology ("As I came through the desert, thus it was / As I came through the desert . . .")—while generally praising Thomson, closes by chiding him for "the not infrequent use of mere rhetoric and verbiage," terms we have already heard in our pursuit of Crane.

But even if there was no direct influence (though there may well be an intentional dialogue), certainly there's no *harm* in holding the young Thomson's moonlit Atlantis up to provide the missing city for Crane's.

V

Like Brom Weber's before it, Marc Simon's more recent edition of *The Poems of Hart Crane* (1986) (with an Introduction by John Unterecker, author of the National Book Award–winning Crane biography, *Voyager* [1969]), is designated by the editor a "reader's edition." (Weber promised a variorum edition, but it has yet to appear.) Simon expands the corpus of Weber's 1966 edition, *The Complete Poems and Selected Letters and Prose of Hart Crane,* by a hefty handful of fragments and incomplete poems, as well as more early and uncollected poems. Simon's omission of the word "Complete" quietly suggests there may even be other poems to come—possibly some of currently dubious attribution.

(In 1993 the Simon volume was reissued as *Complete Poems of Hart Crane.*)

Weber's '66 edition had replaced the hasty 1933 edition, *The Collected Poems of Hart Crane,* that Waldo Frank had put together (reprinted in 1958 as *Complete Poems*), which contained Crane's only two published books, *White Buildings* and *The Bridge,* along with a projected third volume, unpublished at Crane's death, *Key West: An Island Sheaf.* The current Simon volume is longer than the Frank by more than sixty poems. The problem, however, is that the general poetry reader today is a very different person from the general poetry reader of *circa* World War I, when the academization of literature began to divide significant writers' works into specialist and non-specialist editions—the non-specialist edition free of extensive notes and usually printed fairly inexpensively. But—today—the reader who is wholly unconcerned with biography, devoid of interest in, or even knowledge of, the times in which Crane wrote, and who aims to get all her or his pleasure only from an encounter with the bare and unadorned text, is simply an artificial construct.

Certainly one would like to see *The Bridge* accorded the textual treatment, with variants and alternate versions and the careful redaction of manuscript and galley markings, that has already been lavished on Eliot's *The Waste Land* and Ginsberg's *Howl.* But though such an edition is devoutly to be wished, what is needed is a readers' edition with notes that will allow people who want to read Crane's poems to pursue the ordinary interests that today's actual readers of poems have.

We need an edition with notes that will tell us that "Voyages I" was first written and published as a separate poem, called variously "Poster" and "The Bottom of the Sea is Cruel." (Critics regularly discuss it under both titles.) We need notes that will tell us that "For the Marriage of Faustus and Helen II" was first written as a separate poem, "The Springs of Guilty Song." We need notes that will tell us that when "Recitative" was first written in 1923 it was three stanzas shorter than the final 1926 revision—and *which* three stanzas were added! We need a note to tell us that "Thou Canst Read Nothing Except Through Appetite . . ." was a poem Crane typed on the back of a piece of paper bearing a name and address someone had passed him in a heavy cruising venue (the baths? the bridge? the docks?), and that, in order to indicate its nature, long-time friend and confidant, Samuel Loveman, who did the actual textual editing on the poems for Weber's '66 edition, gave it the title "Reply," which is clearly what it is, even if the title isn't Crane's. We need notes that will tell us that Crane sent the fragment, "This Way Where November . . ." in a November 1923 letter to Jean Toomer, in which he described it as part of a long poem to be titled "White Buildings," centering on a catastrophic sexual encounter with a sailor that began at a drunken gathering of friends the night before Crane was to leave to spend the remainder of winter '23 in Woodstock, New York—and that Crane predicted the poem, when complete, would be unprintable; but that only this fragment survives.

An editor might *even* supply a note to the effect that Crane wrote the cycle of six *Voyages* as a set of meditations on Emil's sea-trips away . . .

We need notes that will give us both the 1926 version of "O Carib Isle," as well as the later 1929 version, not as a variorum exercise, but simply because they are all but distinct poems, sharing the first few and the last few lines.

We need notes to tell us when and where the poems were written, when and where they were published—and under what title when the final title is not the only one. If the situation in which a poem was written or to which it responds is known and can be explained easily and relevantly, why not note it?

Such information is far more important than notes explaining that, in "Possessions," Weber has corrected the spelling of "raze" to "rase," or that, in "Royal Palm," Marc Simon has corrected the spelling of "elaphantine" to "elephantine"—the sort of note which, in the absence of the other, clutters both Weber and Simon. Nothing is wrong with such textual minutiae. And for the carefully established text, we must be grateful to Simon. This is often a Herculean labor; one praises it as such. But notes on its establishment have no place in an edition devoid of that other information; in its absence, one would have preferred the fine points covered by a "have been corrected without comment" in the editor's "Note on the Editorial Method."

Likewise, we are grateful for the added poetic fragments—only noting that it is precisely such fragments and incomplete efforts for which readers generally *need* more extensive notes.

Both Simon and Weber tell us *when* the poems were published—and occasionally when written and revised. Maddeningly, however, neither says in what magazines or—far more important—gives us earlier titles. But the assumption that a general poetry reader exists today who will never encounter some article on Crane that quotes a poem in part (and in some earlier form illuminating something in the poet's development, for that's what such articles are made of), who will then turn to such an edition to find the final form of the poem in full, is absurd. And it is more absurd to assume that a specific reader who avoids all such articles will still want to know about the poet's—or a former typesetter's—misspellings!

In short one wants among the notes for Crane the same sort of information that Edward Mendelson provides as "Appendix II: Variant Titles" in his *W. H. Auden: Collected Poems,* or that Donald Allen gives us in his notes to *The Collected Poems of Frank O'Hara.* When a writer like Pound or Eliot puts together his own collected poems, modesty perhaps excuses such omissions. But if the poet's work is interesting enough for a second party to undertake the task, what I've outlined represents what should be given first priority. And as specialists will know, in no way does that constitute a specialists' edition. But the assumption that there exists a Common Reader of poetry who comes from no place—and is going nowhere—is, besides preposterous, heuristically arrogant and pedagogically pernicious. That, however, is what Simon's "reader's edition" seems to presuppose.

The supplementary prose selections of letters, essays, and reviews that Weber included in his '66 edition were immensely interesting. I should have thought Simon would have enlarged on them, rather than drop them altogether. (Even with minor poems, juvenilia, and fragments, Crane's poetic *opera omnia* are just not that voluminous.) Simon might well have added some of the letters to black writer Jean Toomer that were published in part in Unterecker's biography: one would have welcomed both the "White Buildings" letter and the "Heaven and Hell" letter—the latter of which threatens to achieve a measure of fame comparable only to Keats's letter from Hampstead on the 21st of December, 1817, to his brothers George and Tom, on "negative capability."

It is all too easy to see the avoidance of such notes (or the exclusion of such letters) beginning in a kind of editorial exasperation with Crane's homosexuality. Where does one draw the line at good taste— more important, where did one draw that line in 1952, when Weber edited Crane's letters, or in '66, when he edited the poems? (That's what both the "Heaven and Hell" letter and the "White Buildings" letter are, after all, about.) To raise the question is, however, immediately to consider the oddly similar suppression by all three of Crane's major biographers of the fact that, in October 1923, Jean Toomer, after the publication of his novel *Cane* to critical, if not to popular, success, visited his white friend and supporter Waldo Frank (his and Crane's mutual mentor) at Frank's Connecticut home for the first time, whereupon Toomer fell passionately in love with Frank's wife, educator Margaret Naumberg. The passion was mutual. Weeks later, the two had run off together, hoping to leave America for the Gurdjieff Institute for the Harmonious Development of Man at the Chateau du Prieuré in Fontainbleau, France, in order to study with Georges Gurdjieff himself. Only days before Toomer's actual arrival, however, Gurdjieff died, but Toomer remained to study with Gurdjieff's disciples, while for months Naumberg wrote him heartfelt letters announcing her imminent arrival. In the end, however, she stayed in America.

The incident was the center of gossip in the Frank/Munson/Crane/Cowley/Toomer circle for months, if not years. But though certainly all three major biographers knew of it, neither Horton, Weber, nor Unterecker mentions it. One must go to recent biographies of Toomer to learn of it at all.

If it came to mean less to Crane once Toomer had given up writing for mysticism, the Crane/Toomer friendship was still an important one for Crane's early poethood—through, say, 1924. Though Toomer was three years older than Crane, the two were the youngest writers in the group. And heterosexual Toomer was one of the several straight men to whom Crane was (as the post-Stonewall generation would say) out. We know of incidents in which Toomer felt ill-understood by the group— notably by Frank and by publisher Horace Liveright—because of Toomer's racial make-up. And Crane suggests in that letter to Winters, already quoted, that homosexuality does not mean what Winters seems to think it does. With the speculations of all his friends about the topic rampant in their commentaries and memories, it is fairly certain Crane could not expect much more than superficial understanding there. Both men had reason, then, to feel themselves, however accepted, somehow still aliens in the group. It may well have brought them together. In '37 and '48 one can imagine biographers Horton and Weber not mentioning the Toomer/Naumberg affair from feelings of delicacy for Frank—if not for Toomer and Naumberg, all of whom were then still alive. But Toomer and Frank both died in 1967; and Unterecker's biography appeared in '69 . . .

It's oddly paradoxical that if one looks at Toomer's all but inconsequential post-*Cane* writing, it might seem as though Toomer had turned to study, if not at Gurdjieff's knee, then at Winters's—though Kenneth Walker, in his study *Gurdjieff's Teaching* (London: Jonathan Cape, 1957) writes of Gurdjieff's conception of art: "I measure the merit of art by its consciousness, you by its unconsciousness. A work of objective art is a book which transmits the artist's ideas not directly through words or signs or hieroglyphics but through feelings which he evokes in the beholder consciously and with full knowledge of what he is doing and why he is doing it." Pursuing that "full knowledge," Toomer—as did Winters, pursuing his own esthetic program—apparently purged himself of the verbal liveliness which, today, is the principal entrance through which one apprehends the pleasure in his writing; though by the time he broke with Crane, of course, Winters may not have been aware of Toomer's existence.

By then many had forgotten it.

But while one is clamoring for the Crane/Toomer letters, what of Crane's letters to Wilbur Underwood, Crane's older gay friend in Washington, D.C., of which we have had only snippets, accompanied by vague editorial suggestions that their subject matter is wholly beyond the pale? Such innuendo is certainly more damaging than any actual human activity possibly recounted could be.

Finally, just as we need an edition of Crane's poems with an apparatus that takes in the needs of actual poetry readers, we need a complete letters. (I am not the first person to make the favorable comparison between Crane's letters and Keats's.) Nor would it be a bad idea to put together a collection of letters and papers from *The Crane Circle* on the model of Hyder Edward Rollins's famous and rewarding 1948 paired volumes around Keats.

Samuel Bernhard Greenberg's notebooks, papers, and drawings are currently in the Fales Collection at New York University. Edited by Harold Holden and Jack McManis, with a preface by Allen Tate, a hundred-seventeen page selection, *Poems by Samuel Greenberg*, was published by Henry Holt and Company (New York, 1947).

Crane's manuscripts, letters, and papers are largely stored at Columbia University.

There are three full biographies of Crane and currently four volumes of letters generally available. Philip Horton published his *Hart Crane: The Life of an American Poet* in 1937. Brom Weber published his fine, if somewhat eccentric, biographical study of Crane and his work, *Hart Crane: A Biographical and Critical Study*, in 1948. (Both Crane's birth- and death-dates are mentioned only in footnotes—added, in galleys, at editor Loveman's firm suggestion.) Weber also edited *The Letters of Hart Crane, 1916–1932* (largely those of literary interest) in 1952 and, as mentioned, *The Complete Poems and Selected Letters and Prose of Hart Crane* in 1966. Thomas S. W. Lewis edited *Letters of Hart Crane and His Family* in 1974, a book nearly three times the thickness of Weber's *Letters* and a fascinating family romance. *Hart Crane and Yvor Winters: Their Literary Correspondence* (1978), edited by Thomas Parkinson, is another important volume of Crane's letters and commentary. *Robber Rocks: Letters and Memories of Hart Crane, 1923–1932* (1969) by Susan Jenkins Brown (wife of William Slater Brown, formerly wife of Provincetown Playhouse director James Light) contains 39 more of Crane's letters (there is some overlap here with Weber), as well as five auxiliary letters of the Crane circle. The volume concludes with Peggy Baird's devastating "The Last Days of Hart Crane," a reminiscence that makes Crane's final completed poem, "The Broken Tower," rise from the page and resonate (a poem whose title, if not the very idea for it, comes from "An Age of Dream," among the most popular sonnets of Lionel Johnson, another of Crane's adolescent enthusiasms:* We know the 1915 selection of Johnson with the introduction by Pound was a treasured volume in Crane's adolescent library)—a memoir that must be supplemented, however, by Unterecker's "Introduction" to the '86 Simon edition of *The Poems:* there Unterecker prints Gertrude E. Vogt's firsthand account of the talk on shipboard that morning and of watching from the *Orizaba*'s deck, with several other passengers, Crane's actual jump from the stern to his death—in a letter that reached Unterecker only after his 1969 biography, *Voyager,* appeared.

---

* Johnson's sonnet, "The Age of Dream" (the second of a pair usually published together, about an all-but-abandoned church; the first is "The Church of Dream"), concludes with the sestet:

> Gone now, the carvern work! Ruined, the golden shrine!
> No more the glorious organs pour their voice divine;
> No more rich frankincense drifts through the Holy Place:
> Now from the broken tower, what solemn bell still tolls,
> Mourning what piteous death? Answer, O saddened souls!
> Who mourn the death of beauty and the death of grace.

Marc Simon is also the author of *Samuel Greenberg, Hart Crane, and the Lost Manuscripts* (Atlantic Highlands, N.J.: Humanities Press, 1978), an invaluable book for anyone interested in Greenberg or Crane or Greenberg's literary loans to Crane—and of which I have made extensive use here.

* * *

And now a note for a few special readers: Though my 1995 novel *Atlantis: Model 1924* is fiction, I tried to stay as close to fact as I could and still have a tale:

The lines Crane quotes in the text are an amalgam from early versions of "Atlantis," all of which were written by July 26, 1923—the summer prior to the spring in which the recitation takes place. (Crane had spent the previous evening with his father, Clarence Arthur, who was visiting the city; he would write his mother a letter later that afternoon and would see his father again the next day.) Crane's work method usually involved sending off copies of his just completed poems, along with letters, to Waldo Frank, Jean Toomer, Gorham Munson, or the Rychtariks. In 1926 he would take the poem up again and between January and August of that year work it far closer to the form present readers of *The Bridge* are familiar with. The final decision to change the title from "Finale" to "Atlantis" did not come till even later.

We know Crane had some of the Greenberg story wrong. In '23 from Woodstock he wrote to Munson that Fisher had "nursed" Greenberg through his final illness at the paupers' hospital—which was untrue: During Greenberg's terminal weeks on Ward's Island he was attended only by his family and, on his final evening, the sparse and overworked hospital staff. Crane also wrote that Fisher had "inherited" Greenberg's notebooks through "the indifference of the boy's relatives"—equally untrue: Morris had offered the notebooks to Fisher in the hope of getting the poems published. Samuel's family had been as appreciative and supportive of their youngest brother's talents as an impoverished family of Viennese Jews might be. They had always considered Samuel special.

We do not know for *sure* if Crane actually read either Fisher's essay on Greenberg, "Fragments of a Broken Lyre," in *The Plowshare* or the ten poems published there. (Possibly Fisher just told him about them.) While it's certainly *probable* Fisher showed *The Plowshare*'s contents to Crane or at least talked about them, Crane does not mention them in his letters. (Nor does Marc Simon, in the reports of his interviews with Fisher on the topic before his death, recounted in Simon's book *Samuel Greenberg, Hart Crane, and the Lost Manuscripts,* clear up the question.)

But possibly that's only because Fisher did not have a copy of the then four-year-old journal to give Crane to keep.

Besides knowing Samuel for the last seven years of the young poet's life, Fisher had known Morris and Daniel; and he had certainly known of, if he had not actually met, Adolf—which is to say, specific dates aside, Fisher knew pretty much everything my own tale recounts. Only four-and-a-half months after the night that Fisher and Crane had sat up late in Woodstock talking about the tragic poet, Crane might well have remembered all the facts of Greenberg's life he tells in *Atlantis: Model 1924*. The misunderstandings and lacunae in Crane's knowledge, which—in the tale—I've made nothing of, could easily have been the result of drink and the random order of anecdotes around that December night's fire; or even the momentary pressure of a next day's quickly written letter. Why perpetuate them?

In that spirit, I mention: In his transcript of Greenberg's poem "Words," in the 13th line Crane typed "most" for "must." I've just assumed that in reading it over Crane recognized his error. In *Atlantis: Model 1924* he quotes the poem correctly.

This study grew—as did, indeed, my novel—out of an observation my father several times made to me while I was a teenager: As late as 1924, just after he first came from Raleigh, North Carolina, to New York City—and shortly thereafter took his first walk across the Brooklyn Bridge—Brooklyn was nowhere near as built up as it is today. Though, indeed, there were clusters of houses here and there, especially toward the water, my then-seventeen-year-old father was surprised, even somewhat appalled, that the road leading from the Bridge in those days decanted among meadows and by a cornfield: he was both surprised and appalled enough to mention it to me, with a self-deprecating laugh at his own astonishment at the time, some thirty-five years later.

The fields—and the corn—are both there (in the seventh and ninth stanzas) in Crane's "Atlantis."

But there is much more.

The bedlamite from the "Proem" (transfigured first into our superbly articulate Columbus, then, after myriad further changes, into the incoherent, aged sailor of "Cutty Sark") is, in "Atlantis," again aloft among the bridge lines, now as "Jason! hesting Shout!" (To "hest," the OED suggests, from *hātan*—to call upon—is to "bid, command . . . vow, promise . . . will, propose," or "determine . . ."—all of them obsolete.) The bridge in "Atlantis" spans a world as drenched in language as it is in moonlight: Cables whisper. Voices flicker. An arc calls. History has myriad mouths that pour forth a reply. Ships cry. Oceans answer. Spars hum. Spears laugh (though no traveler, searching that laughter, reads the "cipher-script of time" linked to it). Hammers whisper. Aeons cry. Beams yell. A choir translates. Sun and water fuse Verbs. And the many twain sing—for over all is song. But Crane's poem limns a world where not only the Poet, but almost every element of it, can apostrophize—can directly address—every other.

The "cordage" is there, from "Voyages I" (as well as a "Tall Vision-of-the-Voyage, tensely spare"), but this time "spiring" rather than "spry."

The one hitch in this articulating web is that the Bridge cannot speak directly to Love. But Love's white flower—the Anemone (first cousin to Novalis's blue amaranthus)—is the "Answerer" of all. Crane's final exhortation to the Anemone, which seems to sit apposite to (and is surely a metaphor for) Atlantis itself, is to "hold—(O Thou whose radiance doth inherit me) Atlantis,—hold thy floating singer late!" Atlantis, hold the poet's floating attention late into the moon-drenched night. As well, hold him up as he floats on the turbulent waters, the chaos of language, beneath (that will finally receive everything of and from) the Bridge. The terminal question that the poem asks recalls the question that the title—with the poem following it—created (recall it: "What is 'Atlantis'?"): To what does this Bridge of Fire lead?

Since what the Choir translates the web of articulation into is a "Psalm of Cathay," many commentators have assumed Crane's question is rhetorical and, as such, the answer is a fairly unconsidered, "Yes, of course . . ."

Often I have felt, however, as though, retrievable from the whisperings referred to by the poem's final sentence with its twin inversions ("Whispers antiphonal in azure swing" / "Antiphonal whispers swing in azure"), Crane all but exhorts us to construct some terminal antiphon of our own:

No, friend: It is Atlantis that I sing.

The reader who can carefully architect an argument leading to such a terminus, above the liquid shift and flicker of Crane's rhetorical suspensions and spumings, has probably had an experience of the poem . . . that masters, that comprehends, that controls it? No, friend. Only one that is, likely, somewhat like mine.

But to articulate such a line in all its inescapable, referential banality is to close off the poem in precisely the way Crane wanted it left open. That openness—one is allowed into it (the Absolute) or not, at one's choice—is a fundamental, if not *the* fundamental, aspect of Crane's implied city, of Dreadful Night, of Dis or New Jerusalem, of God.

— *Amherst / Ann Arbor / New York*
November 1992–October 1993

Works Consulted

Blackmur, R. P., "New Thresholds, New Anatomies: Notes on a Text by Hart Crane," in *Language as Gesture*, by R. P. Blackmur, Harcourt Brace and Company: New York, 1952.

Bloom, Harold, *Agon: Towards a Theory of Revisionism*, Oxford University Press: New York, 1982.

————, "Hart Crane's Gnosis," in *Hart Crane: A Collection of Critical Essays*, ed. Allen Trachtenberg, Prentice-Hall: Englewood Cliffs, 1982.

Brown, Susan Jenkins, *Robber Rocks: Letters and Memories of Hart Crane, 1923–1932*, Wesleyan University Press: Middletown, 1969.

Brunner, Edward, *Splendid Failure: The Making of* The Bridge, University of Illinois Press: Urbana and Chicago, 1985.

Butterfield, R. W., *The Broken Arc: A Study of Hart Crane*, Oliver and Boyd Ltd.: Edinburgh, 1969.

Clark, David R., ed., *Critical Essays on Hart Crane*, G. K. Hall and Co.: Boston, 1982.

————, ed., *The Merrill Studies in* The Bridge, Charles E. Merrill Publishing Company: Columbus, 1970.

Crane, Hart, *The Complete Poems and Selected Letters and Prose of Hart Crane*, ed. with an Introduction and Notes by Brom Weber, Anchor Books, Doubleday and Company: Garden City, New York, 1966.

————, *The Letters of Hart Crane 1916–1932*, ed. Brom Weber (Copyright 1952, by Brom Weber), University of California Press: Berkeley and Los Angeles, 1965.

————, *The Poems of Hart Crane*, ed. Marc Simon, Liveright Publishing Corporation: New York, 1986. (Reissued as *The Complete Poems of Hart Crane* in 1989.)

Dembo, L. S., *Crane's Sanskrit Charge: A Study of* The Bridge, Cornell University Press: Ithaca, 1960.

Dowson, Ernest, *The Poems of Ernest Dowson, With a Memoir by Arthur Symons*, John Lane Company: New York, 1919.

Drew, Elizabeth, *Poetry: A Modern Guide to Its Understanding and Enjoyment*, Dell Publishing Co., Inc.: New York, 1959.

Edelman, Lee, *Transmemberment of Song: Hart Crane's Anatomy and Rhetoric of Desire*, Stanford University Press: Stanford, 1987.

Eliot, T. S., "The Love Song of J. Alfred Prufrock," in *Selected Poems*, Harcourt, Brace & World, Inc.: New York, 1936.

————, "The Waste Land," in *Selected Poems*, Harcourt, Brace & World, Inc.: New York: 1936.

————, "Tradition and the Individual Talent," in *Selected Prose of T. S. Eliot*, ed. with an Introduction by Frank Kermode, Harcourt Brace & World: New York, 1936.

(Fisher), William Murrell, "Fragments of a Broken Lyre, A Note on a dead and unpublished poet, With ten selected poems following," *The Plowshare*, January 1920 (Woodstock, 1920).

Gilbert, Stewart, *James Joyce's Ulysses: A Study* (first published 1930), Vintage Books: New York, 1955.

Giles, Paul, *Hart Crane: The Contexts of* The Bridge, Cambridge University Press: New York, 1986.

Greenberg, Samuel, *Poems by Samuel Greenberg: A Selection from the Manuscripts*, edited with an Introduction by Harold Holden and Jack McManis, Preface by Allen Tate, Henry Holt and Company: New York, 1947.

Hammer, Langdon, *Hart Crane and Allen Tate: Janus-Faced Modernism*, Princeton University Press: Princeton, 1993.

Hazo, Samuel, *Smithereened Apart: A Critique of Hart Crane*, Ohio University Press: Athens, 1963.

Horton, Philip, *Hart Crane: The Life of an American Poet*, The Viking Press, Inc.: New York, 1937.

Johnson, Lionel Pigot, *The Collected Poems of Lionel Johnson, Second and Revised Edition*, ed. Ian Fletcher, Garland Publishing, Inc.: New York, 1982.

Joyce, James, *Ulysses* (First published in the U.S., 1934), Vintage Books: New York, 1961.

Kerman, Cynthia Earl, & Richard Eldridge, *A Hunger for Wholeness: The Lives of Jean Toomer*, Louisiana State University Press: Baton Rouge, 1987.

Laughlin, James, *Poems from the Greenberg Manuscripts: A Selection from the Work of Samuel B. Greenberg*, edited and with a commentary by. New Directions: Norfolk, 1939.

Lewis, R. W. B., *The Poetry of Hart Crane: A Critical Study*, Princeton University Press: Princeton, 1967.

Lewis, Thomas S. W., ed., *Letters of Hart Crane and His Family*, Columbia University Press: New York, 1974.

Loveman, Samuel, "Introduction," *The Hart Crane Voyages*, by Hunce Voelcker, The Brownstone Press: New York, 1967.

————, "A Conversation with Samuel Loveman," *Hart Crane: A Conversation with Samuel Loveman*, eds. Jay Socin and Kirby Congdon, Interim Books: New York, 1963.

McKay, Nellie Y., *Jean Toomer, Artist: A Study of His Literary Life and Work, 1894–1936*, The University of North Carolina Press: Chapel Hill, 1984.

Nilsen, Helge Normann, "Memories of Hart Crane: A Talk with Emil Opffer," *Hart Crane Newsletter*, Vol. II, No. 1, Summer 1978.

Novalis, *Henry von Ofterdingen*, trans. Palmer Hilty, Frederick Unger Publishing Company, Inc.: New York, 1964.

————, *Hymns to the Night*, trans. Dick Higgins, McPherson & Company: Kingston, 1988.

————, *Pollen and Fragments*, trans. Arthur Versluis, Phane Press: Grand Rapids, 1989.

Ouspensky, P. D., *Tertium Organum: A Key to the Enigmas of the World*, Alfred A. Knopf: New York, 1922.

Parkinson, Thomas, *Hart Crane and Yvor Winters: Their Literary Correspondence*, University of California Press: Berkeley, 1978.

Poe, Edgar Allan, "Drake and Halleck," *Edgar Allan Poe: Representative Selections, with Introduction, Bibliography, and Notes*, eds. Margaret Alterton and Hardin Craig, American Book Company: New York, 1935.

Riffaterre, Michael, *Semiotics of Poetry*, Indiana University Press: Bloomington, 1978.

Salt, Harry S., *The Life of James Thomson ("B.V.", author of "The City of Dreadful Night")*, Arthur C. Fifield: London, 1905.

Schaefer, William David, *James Thomson (B.V.), Beyond "The City,"* University of California Press: Berkeley, 1965.

Shaw, George Bernard, *The Perfect Wagnerite: A Commentary on the Neibelung's Ring* (first published 1898), Dover Publications, Inc: New York, 1967.

Simon, Marc, *Samuel Greenberg, Hart Crane, and the Lost Manuscripts*, Humanities Press: Atlantic Highlands, 1978.

Socin, Jay, & Kirby Congdon, eds., *Hart Crane: A Conversation with Samuel Loveman*, Interim Books: New York, 1963.

Sugg, Richard P., *Hart Crane's The Bridge: A Description of Its Life*, The University of Alabama Press: Tuscaloosa, 1976.

Thomson, James, *The Poetical Works of James Thomson (B.V.)*, ed. Bertram Dobell, 2 Vols., London, 1895.

————, *The Speedy Extinction of Evil and Misery: Selected Prose of James Thomson (B.V.)*, ed. William David Schaefer, University of California Press: Berkeley, 1967.

Toomer, Jean, *Cane* (first published by Boni & Liveright, 1923), ed. Darwin Turnder, W. W. Norton: New York, 1988.

Unterecker, John, *Voyager: A Life of Hart Crane*, Farrar, Straus and Giroux: New York, 1969.

————, "The Architecture of *The Bridge,*" *The Merrill Studies in* The Bridge, ed. David R. Clark, Charles E. Merrill Publishing Company: Columbus, 1970.

Voelcker, Hunce, *The Hart Crane Voyages,* with an "Introduction" by Samuel Loveman, The Brownstone Press: New York, 1967.

Weber, Brom, *Hart Crane: A Biographical and Critical Study,* The Bodley Press: New York, 1948.

Winters, Yvor, "The Significance of *The Bridge,* by Hart Crane, or What Are We to Think of Professor X," *On Modern Poets,* New Directions: New York, 1943.

Wordsworth, William, "Preface to *Lyrical Ballads,*" *The Selected Poetry and Prose of Wordsworth,* ed. Geoffrey Hartman, New American Library: New York, 1970.

Yingling, E. Thomas, *Hart Crane and the Homosexual Text: New Thresholds, New Anatomies,* The University of Chicago Press: Chicago, 1990.

Appendix

Shadows

Criticism of science fiction cannot possibly look like the criticism we are used to. It will—perforce—employ an aesthetic in which the elegance, rigorousness, and systematic coherence of explicit ideas is of great importance. It will therefore appear to stray into all sorts of extraliterary fields, metaphysics, politics, philosophy, physics, biology, psychology, topology, mathematics, history, and so on. The relation of foreground and background that we are used to after a century and a half of realism will not obtain. Indeed they may be reversed. Science-fiction criticism will discover themes and structures . . . which may seem recondite, extraliterary, or plain ridiculous. Themes we customarily regard as emotionally neutral will be charged with emotion. Traditionally human concerns will be absent; protagonists may be all but unrecognizable as such. What in other fiction would be marvelous will here be merely accurate or plain; what in other fiction would be ordinary or mundane will here be astonishing, complex, wonderful . . . For example, allusions to the death of God will be trivial jokes, while metaphors involving the differences between telephone switchboards and radio stations will be poignantly tragic. Stories ostensibly about persons will really be about topology. Erotics will be intercranial, mechanical (literally), and moving.

—Joanna Russ, "Towards an Aesthetic of Science Fiction"

1. Today's technology is tomorrow's handicraft.

2. Lines I particularly liked from Knotly's poem in the current *Paris Review:* "for every one must run a race/in the body's own running place" and: "Everything I have has an earwig in it/which will make light of sacred things."

3. Nothing we look at is ever seen without some shift and flicker—that constant flaking of vision which we take as imperfections of the eye or simply the instability of attention itself; and we ignore this illusory screen for the solid reality behind it. But the solid reality is the illusion; the shift and flicker is all there is. (Where do sf writers get their crazy ideas? From watching all there is *very* carefully.)

4. The preceding notes, this one, and the ones following are picked, somewhat at random, from my last two years' journals (1973–1974), in lieu of the personal article requested on the development of a science-fiction writer.

5. Critical language presents us a problem: The critic "analyzes" a work to "reveal" its "internal form." Recent structuralist critics are trying to "discover the underlying, mythic structures" of given works or cultures. There is the implication that what the critic comes up with is somehow more *basic* than the thing under study—we are all, of course, too sophisticated to be fooled into thinking what the critic produces is more *important*.

Still, however, we feel the critical find should be more intense, more solid, more foundational than the work. After all, though novels are fiction, the books of criticism about them are not . . .

An obvious visual image for the critical process is a surgeon, carefully dissecting a body, removing the skeleton from it, and presenting the bones to our view—so that we will have a more schematic idea of how the fleshed organism articulates.

All this, however, is the result of a category-mistake of the sort Ryle describes in *The Concept of Mind* (p. 17ff.).

A slightly better image, as a basic model of the critical process, will, perhaps, explode it:

The critic sits at a certain distance from the work, views it from a particular side, and builds a more or less schematic model of the work as it strikes her or him (just as I am making *this* model of what the critic does), emphasizing certain elements, suppressing certain others, attaching little historical notes to his model here and there on where she thinks this or that form in the original work might have come from, adding little ethical notes on what he suspects is its proper usage, all according to the particular critical use the model is intended for. If the critic's model is interesting enough, there is nothing to stop us from considering it a work of art in itself, as we do with Pater or Taine, with Barthes or Derrida, Felman or Johnson. A critic may, indeed, add something to the work. But the critic does not *remove* anything from the work.

Works of literature, painting, and sculpture simply do not *have* informative insides. There *is* no skeleton to be removed. They are all surface-that-endures-through-history. A piece of sculpture has a physical inside, but drilling a hole three inches into the Venus de Milo will give you no aesthetic insight into it. (Note, however: This paragraph does not hold true [at least in the same way] for theatrical works, orchestral music, film, or much electronic art. For an sf story: Postulate a world and a culture which has an art all of which *does* have informative insides—great cloth sculptures, for example, held up from within by hidden pipe-shapes, electronic art run by hidden circuitry. The critic, as criminal, hires herself to other social criminals who wish to understand the art; they break into museums, dismantle the art objects, and remove the insides for inspection. The works are reassembled . . . clumsily. Later, an artist passing by notices something is wrong and cries out to a guard: "Look, look! A *critic* has been at my work! Can't you see . . . ?" Theme of the story: If to understand the work is physically to destroy or injure it, are the critics [and the people who wish to understand art] heroes or villains? Are the artists, who make works that can only be understood by dismantling them, charlatans? Consider also, since my view is that this is just how so many people *do* misinterpret criticism today, will my context be understood? Is there any way that I can make clear in the story that what I am presenting is not *how* criticism works; rather, I am poking fun at the general misapprehension? I am not in the least interested in writing a simpleminded, "damning" satire of Modern Criticism. Will have to rethink seriously incidents as first listed if I want the story's point to be the subtle one. *Can* such a point be dramatized in sf story . . . ?)

Basically, however, the critic is part of the work's audience. The critic responds to it, selects among those responses and, using them, makes, selectively, a model of the work that may, hopefully, guide, helpfully, the responses of the critic's own audience when they come to the work being modeled.

When a critic, talking about critical work, suggests she is doing more than this, at best she is indulging in metaphor; at worst, he is practicing, whether wittingly or no, more of that pernicious mystification that has brought us to our present impasse.

(Happy with the *idea;* but still uncomfortable with it as a story template—because, as a template, it seems to be saying exactly the *opposite* of what I want to! Is this, perhaps, a problem basic to sf: That you can only use it to reinforce commonly accepted prejudices; and that to use it for a discussion of anything at a more complex resolution simply can't be done at the literary distance sf affords? From Cassirer to Kirk, critics have leveled just this accusation at mythology. If it's true of sf as well, perhaps sf is, inchoately, an immature form . . . ? Well, there: The ugly suggestion has been made.

(Do I agree?

(No, I don't. But I think it is certainly an inherent tendency of the medium. To fight it, and triumph over it, I must specifically: go into the world—the object—I have set up *far* more thoroughly than I have before, and treat it autonomously rather than as *merely* a model of a prejudiciary situation—a purely subject manifestation. I must explore it as an extensive, coherent reality—not as an intensive reflection of the real world where the most conservative ideas will drain all life out of the invention.

(What does my culture look like, for instance, once I leave the museum? Given its basic aesthetic outlook, what would its architecture look like? How would the museum itself look, from the inside? From the outside? What would the building where the artist lived look like? And where the critic lived? What would be their relative social positions? What would be the emblems of those positions? How would such emblems differ from the emblems of social positions in our world? What would it smell like to walk through their streets? Given their art, what of their concept of science? Is it the opposite of their concept of art? Or is it an extension of it? Are the informative insides of the scientific works as mystified as the insides of art works? Or are they made blatantly public? Or are they mystified even *more* than the art? What are the problems that critics of science have in this world? Or critics of politics? Would these critics be the same people?

(As I begin to treat my original conceit as a coherent, antonomous world, instead of just a statement about *our* world, I begin to generate a template complicated enough and rich enough actually to make a statement about our world that is something more than simple-minded. I can now start to ask myself questions like: In this world, what are the psychological traits of someone who would become a critic? An artist? A scientist? Etc. But it is only when the template becomes at least that complex that sf becomes mature.)

6. Moorcocks coming over here for dinner tonight with John Sims: Cream of Leek soup, Roast Beef, Fried Eggplant, Rice (possibly a risotto with almonds? How many stuffed mushrooms are left over from the Landrys yesterday? And will they do, reheated, for starters?); an American Salad (get some Avocado, Bacon, Butter-lettuce, Chicory, Tomatoes, Cucumbers, Carrots, Celery, Mustard, Lemons); to follow: Baked Bananas flamed in brandy. (*Don't* use the mushrooms: John doesn't like them!)

7. For Sturgeon essay: The material of fiction is the texture of experience.

8. Re *Dhalgren* . . . I think Marilyn is depressingly right about the psychiatric session with Madame Brown and the Calkins interview . . . which means more work; and after I've just rewritten the whole last chapter! With Calkins, the historical *must* be made manifest. With Madame Brown, she must realize that the dream is not a dream, otherwise she comes off just *too* stupid. It is so hard to control the outside view of my material, when I am standing on the inside. It's like clutching a balloon to shape from within.

Friday night and to the Moorcocks for dinner with Emma Tennent.

9. Got a letter from R. E. Geis today, asking to reprint my *Letter to a Critic* from *The Little Magazine* in *The Alien Critic*. Am very dubious. First of all, some of the facts, as John Brunner so succinctly pointed out over the phone a fortnight back, are just wrong. More to the point, the section on science-fiction publishing isn't really a description of the current sf publishing scene at all. Rather, it's a memoir of what the publishing situation was like in that odd period between 1967 and 1971. Odd, too, how quickly the bright truths of twenty-six (by which age the bulk of my notoriously unbulky sf oeuvre was already in print) seem, six years later, rather dated. What to do? Get ever so slightly looped and write a polite letter?

Or take a walk up Regents' Canal and go browse in Compendium Book Store? Sounds better.

10. What a tiny part of our lives we use in picturing our pasts. Walked to the Turkish take-away place this evening with John Witton-Doris: consider the *number* of incidents he recalls from our months in Greece together, nine years ago, involving me, that I can barely remember! Biography, *as* it approaches completeness, must *be* the final fiction.

11. Alcohol is the opium of the people.

12. Science fiction through the late sixties seemed to be, scientifically, interested in mathematics segueing into electronics; psychiatry, in all its oversimplified clumsiness, has been an sf mainstay from *The Roads Must Roll*, through *Baby is Three*, to *The Dream Master.*

Science fiction from the past few years seems to be interested in mathematics segueing into contemporary linguistics/philosophy (e.g., Watson's *The Embedding*); biology—particularly genetics—has replaced physics as the science of greatest concern [Cf. the 'clone' stories over the past few years, from Kate Wilhelm's and Ted Thomas's *The Clone*, through McIntyre's *The Cage* (and Ms. McIntyre is a trained geneticist; where do we get all this about people interested in science not getting into science fiction anymore!?!), to Wolfe's *The Fifth Head of Cerberus*]; and anthropology (reflected even in books like Effinger's *What Entropy Means to Me* and Toomey's *A World of Trouble*) seems to be replacing psychiatry as a prime concern.

I think I approve.

13. "You science-fiction writers always criticize each other in print as if the person you were criticizing were reading over your shoulder," someone said to me at the Bristol Con last week—meaning, I'm afraid, that the majority of criticism that originates within the field has either a "let-me-pat-your-back-so-you-can-pat-mine" air, or, even more frequently, a sort of catty, wheedling tone implying much more is being criticized than the work nominally under discussion.

No, the sf community is not large

Perhaps it's because I've spent just over a decade making my living within it, but I feel *all* criticism should be written as if the author being criticized were—not reading over your shoulder—but written as though you could stand face to face with her and read it out loud, without embarrassment.

I think this should hold whether you are trying to fix the most rarefied of metaphysical imports in some Shakespearean tragedy, or writing a two-hundred word review of the latest thriller. Wheedling or flattery have nothing to do with it.

Among the many informations we try to get from any critical model is the original maker's (the artist's) view of the original work modeled. If the critics do not include, in this model, an overt assessment of it, we construct it from hints, suggestions, and whatever. But *we* are at three removes from the author: and the critic is at two (as the critic is one from the work): In deference to that distance, I feel the critics must make such assessments humbly. They can always be wrong.

But only after they, and we, have made them (wrong or right), can we follow the critics' exploration of the work's method, success, or relevance. The critic can only judge these things by his own responses; in a very real way, the only thing the critic is ever really criticizing—and this must be done humbly if it is to be done at all—is the response of his own critical instrument.

All criticism is personal.

The best is rigorously so.

14. Yesterday, Joyce Carol Oates sent Marilyn a copy of her new book of poems *Angel Fire* (with a letter apologizing for taking so long to answer Marilyn's last letter etc., and dense with North American weather). This morning, in Compendium, I saw the new Oates book on D. H. Lawrence's poetry, *The Hostile Sun*, picked it up, took it (in its bright yellow covers) home, and have, minutes ago, just finished it.

After going through three novels, a handful of essays, and a few crunches into the Collected Poems (and most recently, the Frank Kermode book on), Lawrence has tended to be for me a clumsy, if impassioned, writer purveying a message I find almost totally heinous. The most generous thing I could say for him till now was, with Kenneth Rexroth, "His enemies are my enemies," but even here I always found myself wondering, wouldn't he do better on their side than on mine? Lawrence-the-outspoken-sexual-revolutionary has always struck me a bit like those politicians who, in their support of the War in Vietnam, eventually went so far as to use words like "hell" and "damn" in their speeches—then quickly looked at their fellow party members who dared disapprove of their "too strong" language and labeled *them* conservatives. Though Lawrence's novels sometimes refer to sexual mechanics, his overall concept of sex seems institutionally rigid: Everyone must fulfill his or her role, as assigned by Divine Law. The heroes of his novels go about brow-beating everyone who happens to stray from his (usually her) divinely ordained role, back into it. For, after all, it *is* Divine Law. And anyone who still strays, after having been told *that,* must be sick unto damnation. I wonder if Lawrence was aware that his real critics simply found him, in his ideas (rather than in the "strength" of his language, or the "explicitness" of the scenes he used to dramatize his points), an absolute prig?

At any rate, *The Hostile Sun* offers me a guide to the Collected Poems (the volume Joyce gave Marilyn as a going-away present; she must have been working on the essay then) that may just get me into them in a way that I can get something out. The book makes the idea of Lawrence-the-Poet interesting to me and offers me some way of divorcing it from Lawrence-the-Prophet—whom I find a pernicious bore. Oates points out his strengths in the poems (the overall intensity of vision; his aesthetic of unrectified feeling) and warns what not to look for (the single, well-crafted poem; a certain type of aesthetic intelligence). Since there are half a dozen poets whom I enjoy in just this way, from James Thomson and Walt Whitman to Paul Blackburn and Philip Whalen, I suspect I will go back to Lawrence's poems better prepared.

It *is* nice to be reminded that criticism, well done, can open up areas previously closed.

15. Confessions of a science-fiction writer: I have never read one H. G. Wells "romance of the future" from cover to cover. I once read three quarters of *Food of the Gods,* and I have read the first fifty/one hundred pages of perhaps half a dozen more.

When I was thirteen, somebody gave me Verne's *20,000 Leagues Under the Sea* as a book that "you'll simply love." At page two hundred I balked. I never *have* finished it! I did a little better with *From the Earth to the Moon,* but I still didn't reach the end.

By the time I was fifteen, however, in my own personal hierarchy, Wells and Verne were synonymous with the crashingly dull. Also, I had gotten their names mixed up with something called Victorian Literature (which, when I was fifteen, somehow included Jane Austen!), and I decided that it was probably all equally boring.

I was eighteen before I began to correct this impression (with, of all things, Eliot's *Adam Bede*); fortunately somebody had already forced me—marvelous experience that it was—into Jane Austen by assuring me that her first three books were written before Victoria was even a sparkle in the Duke of Kent's eye. Then the hordes: Thackeray, the Brontës, Dickens, Hardy. But I have never quite forgiven Wells and Verne for, even so briefly, prejudicing me against the "serious" literature written by their contemporaries and precursors who just happened to have overlapped, to whatever extent, the reign of that same, diminutive monarch.

16. When I was a child, I used to play the violin. At fourteen I developed a not wholly innocent passion for a boy of fifteen who was something of a violin prodigy: He had already been soloist with several small but professional orchestras, and he was talked about muchly in my several circles of friends. I wrote a violin concerto for him—it took me four months. Its three movements ran about half an hour. I supplied (I thought then) a marvelous cadenza. The themes, if I recall, were all serial, but their development was tonal. I orchestrated it for a full, seventy-five piece orchestra—but by the time I had finished, he had moved to upstate New York.

And I had been afraid to tell him what I was doing until it was completed.

Months later, I ran into him in the Museum of Modern Art (he was in the city visiting an aunt) and, excitedly, I told him about my piece, over cokes and English muffins in a coffee shop a few blocks away. He was a little overwhelmed, if not bewildered, but said, "Thanks," and "Gosh!" and "Wow!" a lot. We talked about getting together again. He was first chair violinist with the All State Youth Orchestra that year and a favorite with the conductor. We talked about a possible performance or, at least, getting some of his adult friends to look at it. Then he had to catch a train.

I never saw him again.

He never saw the concerto.

At fifteen I gave up the violin—and have had a slight distrust of the passions ever since.

I notice that I often tend to talk (and think) about my childhood just as though music had no part in it—whereas, in reality, I must have spent more hours at it from eight to twice eight than at anything else. And between the ages of nineteen and twenty-two, I probably made as much money as a basket musician in Greenwich Village coffee houses as I did from my first four sf novels, written over the same time. (And how interesting that the ages from nineteen to twenty-two are suddenly part of my childhood!)

17. A dozen poets whose work I have enormously enjoyed in the last couple of years: Michael Dennis Browne, Alice Knotly, Robert Allen, John Oliver Simon, Philip Levine, Robert Peterson, Judith Johnson Sherwin, Ted Berrigan, Robert Morgan, Ann Waldman, Richard Howard, and J. H. Pryne.

(I am leaving out Marilyn Hacker and Tom Disch; I know them and their work too well!)

How many of the dozen named have I actually met? Six. Interesting that one, whom I've never met at all, felt it necessary to tell a complete stranger, who only accidentally met me six months later, that he was quite a good friend of mine when I lived in San Francisco!*

18. Down to give a lecture on sf at the University of Kent. In the discussion period after my talk, someone brought up Theodore Sturgeon. I asked the assembly what they particularly liked about his work. From one side of the room, someone shouted, "His aliens!" and from the other side, simultaneously someone else: "His people!" Everyone laughed. Consider this incident for the Sturgeon essay.

19. Marilyn, from the other room (where she is reading the Jonathan Raban book *The Sociology of the Poem* and, apparently, has just come to another horrendous misreading [where he goes on about Pickard's poem "Rape" (he doesn't apparently remember the title and refers only to a few lines of it) as expressing good will (!) and fellowship (!!) between the young men in the pub and the old woman (whom he, not Pickard,

*John Oliver Simon, with whom I actually went to summer camp at Woodland.

calls a prostitute)]: "Poetry should be as well written as prose—and at *least* as carefully read!"

20. In the context of 1948—a vacuum tube technology where most adding machines were mechanical—Gilbert Ryle was probably right in denying the existence of mental occurrences as material events with the nature of mechanical entities, separable from the brain. In the context of 1973—where we have a solid-state technology and electronic computers—we have to rethink: the empirical evidence of neurology, electronics, and cybernetics all point to a revitalization of the concept of mental occurrences as brain processes. A perfectly serious argument seems to be occurring today in philosophy over whether mental occurrences are nonmaterial events that just happen to happen simultaneously with certain brain processes (or are even set off by the brain processes, but are different from the processes themselves), or whether the brain processes are, indeed, the mental occurrences themselves.

Two things make such an argument seem ridiculous to me—one empirical, the other logical.

First, it seems as silly to say that the brain contains *no* model of what the eye sees (which arguers on one side of this argument maintain) as it is to say that the circuitry in a TV camera (that has been turned on) contains no model of what is in front of the image orthicon tube at its proper focal distance. The point is: Anyone who has tried to design a television (or even a radio) circuit from scratch has some idea of just how great the complexity of that model must be: It is practically *all* process, composed of a series of precisely ordered wave fronts that peak in precise patterns, hundreds-to-hundreds-of-thousands-of-times per second, all shunted around, amplified, distorted, and superimposed on one another, in a precise pattern, at close to the speed of light. The philosophers who hold this view, I'm afraid, are simply revealing their inability to conceive even this complexity, empirically demonstrable for processes far simpler than the simplest brain process.

To take another side of the argument (and it has many more than two) is to get lost in one of the numerous logical contradictions of ordinary speech, which allows us to call "a process" a *thing* and "an object" a *thing* too. The internal logical structure of one is distinct from the internal logical structure of the other. *All* processes are nonmaterial, whether they be brain-processes or the process of raising my hand off the table. At the same time, all processes need material to define them. (If I raise a glass off the table, aren't I doing the same "thing" as raising my hand off the table . . . ? O course I'm not. Which is to say, I *am* doing the same "thing" [i.e., indulging the same process] only in so far as I am *observing* the two events at the same degree of empirical resolution. If I want to, I can observe the raising of two more or less identical glasses from the same spot on the table [or even the same glass] at different times, at such a high degree of empirical resolution that their processes can be uniquely differentiated, having to do with drying times of films of water, molecular change and interchange between the table and the glass, etc. And that, alas, exhausts the tale.) Similarly, all material can be defined by process, the most basic of which, for a static object, is simply the process of duration; as it changes (or as I observe it at a higher degree of empirical resolution, so that I become *aware* of changes in it) we can bring in other processes as well. In this way, all material can be defined by the process (infinitely analyzable into smaller processes) it is undergoing. But the basic terms that are thrown around in this argument—"material event" and "nonmaterial event"—both have an element of self-contradiction (i.e., if "a brain process" can be called "a material event," then, as the brain is the material, the event must be the process, which implies something like a "material process" . . . which is nonsense of the same order as "a green smell") that, it would seem to me, renders them *both* useless for any serious, logical discussion.

To stand for three hours and watch Vikki Sperling map the image from the retina of the eye of the salamander off the visual tectum of the exposed salamander brain (doubled there, one inverted left-right, and a weaker one right-left) with her gold-filled microelectrodes on their adjustable stands, silences a good deal of the argument in my own head. The behaviorists, with their pretransistor view of the world, say: "But you can't locate mental occurrences!" We can not only locate them, we can measure them, map them, record them, reproduce them, cut them out, and put them in backwards!

21. A "word" has a "meaning" in the sense that a train has a track; *not* in the sense that a train has a passenger. Still, *word* and *meaning* in most people's minds, even most philosophers' apparently, are the same sort of category-mistake that Ryle tried to show existed in the Cartesian separation between body and mind.

Words mean.

But meaning *is* the interaction of the process into which the eardrum/aural-nerve translates the air vibrations that *are* the word, with the chemoelectric process that is the interpretative context of the brain. Meaning may be something else as well—as mental occurrences *may* involve something in addition to as well as brain-processes. But I am sure that they are *at least* this, which is why empirical exploration strikes me as the only practical way to get seriously further in either discussion.

22. Many scientists and mathematicians fool themselves into thinking there is something eternal about, say, a mathematical proof.

At Marilyn's bookstall, yesterday, I was browsing in a seventeenth century Latin translation of Euclid's *Elements*. Things Euclid took as proofs would horrify—if not bewilder—a modern university senior in math. Euclid's personal idea of mathematical rigor is entirely different from ours. Fashions in proofs change only a little more slowly than fashions in dress. What is considered to require a proof today is considered self-evident tomorrow. What was considered self-evident yesterday, today is the subject of a three-hundred-page exegesis whose final conclusion is that it just cannot be rigorously established at all!

A mathematician will tell you that a set of proofs, all from one mathematician, may, for example, generate information about the author's personality. I will certainly agree with anyone who says that such information is probably not terribly important to the proofs' substance. But anyone who says the information is *not* there is simply blind.

Even mathematics has its subjective side. And, as extremes come around to touch, one argument gaining popularity now is that something as abstract as "mathematical logic" may turn out to be what, after all, subjectivity actually *is*.

23. Art conveys possibilities of information to society, i.e., the possible forms information may take. The value of art is in its richness of form. (Cf. Charles Olson's advice to writers that, without necessarily imitating reality in their fiction, they should keep their fiction "up to" the real.) The relation of art to the world *is* the aesthetic field of a given culture, i.e., in different cultures art relates to the world in *very* different ways.

24. Thoughts on my last sixteen years with Marilyn: living with an extraordinarily talented and temperamental poet is certainly the best thing that could happen to a prose writer. I wonder, however, if it works the other way around . . . ? When we fall asleep, like teaspoons, the baby (due in two months) tramples me in the small of my back. But they seem such definitely nonhostile kicks. You can tell it's just exercise.This evening, for practically a minute and a half, it kicked at almost regular, seven-second intervals, till Marilyn got up from the armchair (a little worried). Well, considering its daddy, it ought to have a good sense of rhythm. (I say living with a talented and temperamental poet is good for a prose writer; but I suspect living with a talented and temperamental poet who happens to possess a rather acute business sense helps too . . .) [Note: Our obstetrician, Mrs. Ransom, says that when the baby presses against an artery in the womb, often a highly regular spasming of part

of the uterine wall can occur, easily confusable with the baby's kicking. Nothing to worry about. But we do not have a budding Ruby Keeler or Bill Robinson in our midst. Just a pressed artery in some positions.]

25. I suspect the logical atomism of both Russell and Wittgenstein would have been impossible without the visual atomization the Impressionists had already subjected the world to on canvas (and that the Cubists were subjecting it to concurrently with Russell's and Wittgenstein's early work). In fact, what is basically wrong with Wittgenstein's "picture theory of language" is that it rests on an aesthetically simpleminded concept of the way in which a picture relates to what it is a picture of. The twenty-seven-year-old Wittgenstein simply held an amazingly naive view (or, more generously, an extreme nineteenth-century-derived view) of the way in which a picture is a model of a situation. The mistake at *Tractatus* 2.261 is heartrending:

> There must be something identical in a picture and what it depicts to enable the one to be a picture of the other at all.

If for *must be* and *identical* he had substituted *is obviously* and *similar*—and then taken up the monumental task of running these words down to their propositional atomization—he would have solved the problem of the modular calculus (i.e., *the* critical problem).

The point is: There is *nothing* identical in a picture and what it depicts. There is *nothing* identical in the model and what it is a model of. Nothing, nothing at all! They share not one atom in common! They need not share one measurement! Only the perceptive context imposes commonality on them, for a variety of learned and physiological reasons. (G. Spencer-Brown's elegant, elegant argument wobbles, ultimately, on the same pivot point.) There are only identical processes some *thing* else can undergo in response to both—emblematic of their relation. And, presumably, different processes as well—emblem that the two (original and depiction) *are* distinct and, possibly, hierarchical.

For A to be recognized as a model of B, first a set of internal relations, as A relates to itself, must be read from A, then processed in some way probably similar to a mathematical integration; then *another* set of internal relations must be read from B (some of the relations *may* be similar to those read from A; but they need not be) and then integrated (by a similar process; or by a very different one), and the two results compared; if I find the *results* congruent, then I recognize A as a model of B in the context of the joint integrative process that produced the congruent results. But information about A may come to me via photograph, while I may have to gather information about B, blind-folded, with just my hands, from miniature plastic sculptures. Even so, if I have developed the proper interpretative context, I may well be able to recognize that, say, some small, plastic object B is a model of the photographed object A (checkable against a sight model when the blindfold is removed), while other small plastic objects C, D, and E are *not*—in terms either of the context I've developed, or in terms of the more usual sight context—models of A.

26. About every fragment of reality, an infinite number of different statements can be made. For every fragment of reality, an infinite number of different models can be made.

27. On one side of a paper write: "The statement on the other side of this paper is true." Now turn the paper over and write: "The statement on the other side of this paper is false." Now put down your pencil; and turn the paper over several more times, considering the truth and falsity of the statements you have written—till you perceive the paradox.

The young Bertrand Russell noted that the whole of the *Principia Mathematica* remained shaky because of it; he came up with one resolution that, later, as an older man, he repudiated. Karl Popper has, somewhere, a proof that it cannot be resolved at all.

It can.

But to follow the resolution, fold up the paper and put it in the breast pocket of your Pendleton, as I did on the train platform in South Bernham one May, and come along with me.

Vanessa Harpington had gone off painting in North Africa, but had sweetly left the keys to her country home circulating among various of her Camden Town friends. So I'd come down to pass that summer in a fine old English house with my friend Alfred, himself the long-haired nephew and namesake of a rather infamous Polish Count K.

One rainy afternoon, I was in the sitting room, with a sketch pad, making a drawing of the scene outside the window—rain splashing through the leaves of one of the small sycamores in the yard—when Alfred, smoking a meerschaum carved into a likeness of A. E. Van Vogt, wandered in, looked at my drawing, looked out the window, looked at my drawing again, and nodded. After a moment's silence, he said: "Would you say you are making a model of the situation outside the window?"

"I suppose you could call it that," I said, sketching a line in for the drapery's edge.

"Would you say that it models the fact that it is raining?"

"Well, all those slanted lines *are* supposed to be raindrops. And the runnels of water on the windows there . . ." I looked up.

Alfred had stepped forward. The streaming pane silhouetted his hawkish features. He took another pull on his pipe and, expelling small puffs of smoke, intoned: "Truth . . . Falsity . . . Model . . . Reality . . ." and glanced back.

"I *beg* your pardon?" I said. There was a sweetish aroma in with the tobacco.

"Has it ever occurred to you," Alfred said, "that logically speaking, 'true' and 'false' can only be applied to statements *about* the real; but that it is nonsense to apply either one directly *to* the real? I mean—" He took his pipe and pointed with the stem toward the window; his long hair swung—"if, in here, in the sitting room, you were to make the statement, 'It is raining outside,' or some other model of the situation you perceive through the glass—"

"Like a drawing?"

"—or a sculpture, or a photograph; or a flashing light that, by arrangement, we had both agreed to interpret as, 'It is raining outside,' or some abstract mark on a piece of paper, or an arbitrary set of musical notes that we had some such similar agreement—"

"A sign—" I said. "An image, a symbol—"

"*I said a model. Do* accept my terminology." The partially silhouetted head cocked. "I'm only trying to save you pages and pages of semiological hair-splitting. Now: As I was saying, suppose I chose to model the situation outside with the statement, 'It is raining outside,' rather than the way you are, with a pencil and paper, then you might have come along, observed my model—or, in this case, heard what I said—observed the garden through the window, and commented: 'That is a true statement.' Or, if you will, 'That is a true model.'—"

"I think that's a rather limited way to look at, say, well any *aesthetic* model."

"So do I! So do I!" said Alfred. "But if we had agreed that we *were* going to use the model in that way, for the purely limited purpose of obtaining information about a limited aspect of reality—say, whether it was or was not raining—then we *could.*"

"Okay. If we agreed first."

"But, by the same token, you can see that it would be perfectly ridiculous for you to come along, point out the window and say, 'The outside is true,' or 'The rain is true,' or even 'The rain outside is true'."

"Oh, I could *say* it. But I do get your point. If I did, I wouldn't be using 'true' in any truly logical way; I'd be using it metaphorically; aesthetically if you will; as a sort of general intensifier."

"Precisely. Do you see, then, what allows one to put 'true' or 'false' on a model, such as my statement on your picture?"

"I suppose," I said, squinting at my paper and considering asking Alfred to step just a little aside beside he was blocking a doffing sycamore branch, "It's because I've been working very hard to get it to look like what . . . I'm modeling—Alfred, do you think you might move to the left there just a bit—"

"Oh, really!" Alfred stepped directly in front of the window and jabbed his pipe stem at me. "All Vanessa's oak paneling, these leather bindings and dusty hangings, seem to have addled your brain. A statement doesn't *look* like the thing it models! When I say 'It is raining,' neither the 'it' nor the 'is' refers to anything real in the situation. And the position of the pointer on that barometer dial over there—just as good a model of what's going on outside as any of the others we've mentioned—has no internal structure similar to the situation it's modeling at all (though it's *attached* to something that has an internal structure *dependent* on it; but that's a different story)! No, some structural similarity may explain *why* you choose to use a particular thing *for* a model, but it is the use you are putting it *to*—the context you are putting it *into*, if you will—that, alone, allows you to call it 'true' or 'false.' Truth and falsity, the potential for being true or false, are not manifestations of the internal structure of the thing that is, potentially, to be so labeled. They are, rather, qualities ascribable to a given thing when, in a particular context, it is functioning in a particular way, i.e., modeling some situation truly (however we choose to interpret that) or modeling it falsely (however we choose, given a particular, modular context, to interpret that) . . ."

"Alfred," I said, laying my pencil across my pad and leaning back in the leather wingchair, "I know you really *are* trying to save me pages of semiological hair-splitting, but you are also standing in my way—interfering, if you will, with the modular context I have been trying to establish between the rain and my drawing pad. Could you be a pal and see if you can get us some coffee . . . ?"

As English summers will, that one soon ended.

As happens, a year later an Italian summer replaced it. I was spending a sunny week in a villa outside Florence. The news came from my hostess, one morning over coffee in the garden, that we were to be joined shortly by—of all people! I had thought he was somewhere in Nepal; indeed, I *hadn't* thought of him for six months! And who, sure enough, should come striding across the grass ten minutes later, in rather worn-out sneakers, his bald spot not noticeably larger but his shoulder-length hair definitely longer, thumbs tucked under his knapsack straps, and a Persian vest over an out-at-the-elbow American workshirt, from the pocket of which stuck the stem of what, from the bulge at the pocket's base, I recognized as his Van Vogtian meerschaum— Alfred!

He came across the lawn, grinning hawkishly, and said: "Do you know what you left behind in England and I have carried all the way to India and back?"

"What . . . ?" I asked, quite surprised at his introduction and charmed by this dispensing with phatic chatter.

"Your sketch pad! Hello, Vanessa . . ." to our hostess, and gave her a large hug. The high, aluminum rack of his backpack swayed above his shoulders.

To explain what happened that afternoon, I might mention explicitly several things implicit already about both Alfred and Vanessa. She, for instance, is very generous, a far more talented painter than I, and has several easels in her studio—the converted top floor of the villa. And Alfred, as I'm sure you've realized, has a rather strange mind at the best of times, which also entails a rather strange sense of humor.

At any rate, some hours later, I was walking through the white dining room, with its sparse brass and wood decoration, when I noticed, through the open iron casement, out in the sunlit Italian garden, one of Vanessa's easels set up a few yards from the window; and set up *on* the easel was *my* sketch pad, with my drawing of last year's rain-battered, English sycamore.

While I looked at it, Alfred came climbing in over the windowsill, dropped to the floor, spilling a few cinders onto the waxed floorboards, and, kicking at them, gave me a great grin: "There," he said, "Go on! Make a true statement—an accurate verbal model of the situation outside the window! Quick!"

"Well," I said, smiling and a bit puzzled, "it seems that there's . . ." I paused, about to say 'my picture outside,' but I remembered our colloquy back in rainy Britain: ". . . that there's my *model* outside!"

"Just what I was hoping you would say," Alfred said. "It saves even more pages of semiological hair-splitting!"

"And," I said, encouraged by this, "the model outside is true, too! Alfred, what have you been doing in India?"

"Amazing amounts of shit," Alfred said warmly. "Do you know, Plato *was* right, after all—at least about method. As far as semiological hair-splitting is concerned, we just dispensed with practically a chapter and a half! A dialogue that you can make up as you go along really *is* the only way to get anything done in philosophy."

I looked out at my picture again. "Then it *is* my model. And my model *is* true."

"Your first statement is true." Alfred's smile became warmer still. "Your second is nonsense—no, don't look so crestfallen. Just listen a moment: whether your model is a statement, a drawing, or even a thought, it is still a thing like any other thing: that is, it has its particular internal structure, and its various elements are undergoing their various processes, be that merely the process of enduring. Now you may have chosen any aspect of this thing—part of its material, part of its structure, or part of its process—to do the bulk of the modeling for you, *while* it was in the modular context. And, yes, outside that context, the model is still the *same* thing. But it *is* outside the context. Therefore, pointing out *this* window at *that* picture and calling it, or any part of it— material, structure, or process—'true' or 'false' is just as nonsensical now as it would have been for you, back in that abysmal May we spent in South Bernham, to point out the window and call some *thing* out there 'true' or 'false' . . . the rain, the shape of the drops, or the falling. A fine distinction has to be made. Whether the model functions as true or functions as false *within* the context may have something to do with the internal structure *of* the model. But whether the model functions (as true *or* false) has to do with the structure *of* the context. If you would like to, look at it this way: 'true' and 'false' merely model two mutually exclusive ways a given model (which is a thing) may function in a given context, depending on other things, which may, in different contextual positions, function as models. But the meaningfulness of the *ascription* of true *or* false is dependent on the context, not the thing." Alfred took another draw on his pipe, found it was out, and frowned. "Um . . . now why don't you take out that piece of paper you have folded up in the breast pocket of your Pendleton and look at it again—excuse me, I could have suggested you take it out of your wallet and avoided the implication that you hadn't washed your shirt since last summer, but now I am just trying to save you pages of semiological elaboration."

Feeling a bit strange, I fingered into my breast pocket, found the paper I had so summarily folded up a summer before, and unfolded it, while Alfred went on: "Think of it in this wise: if something is in the proper, logical position, it may be called true or false. If it moves out of that position, though it is still the same *thing*, you *can't* call it true or false."

And, creased through horizontally, I read:

The statement on the other side of this paper is true.

"Alfred—" I frowned—"if there *is* a statement on the other side of this paper (and, unless my memory plays tricks, there is) and it is *meaningful* to call *that* statement true or false—now I'm only letting the internal structure of *this* statement suggest a line of reasoning, I'm not accepting from it any information about *its* 'truth' or 'falsity', 'meaningfulness' or 'meaninglessness'—that means (does it not?) that it is in the proper position in the modular context to do some modeling."

"Even as you or I, when we stand at the window looking at what's outside."

"And if *that* statement refers to what's on *this* side of the paper (and memory assures me that it does), then they are in the same context, which means they cannot both occupy the same position in it at the same time."

"Have you ever tried to stand out in the garden and inside the sitting room all at once? It *is* a bit difficult."

"So *if* that is the case, then *this* statement has to be considered just as a . . . thing, like rain, or a sycamore, or a garden . . ."

"Or a sketch of a garden. Or a statement. Or a thought. *They* are things too."

"But I recall distinctly. Alfred: The statement on the other side of the paper calls this statement—this *thing*!—false!"

"Wouldn't really matter if it called it true, would it—"

"Of course it wouldn't! In the context I just outlined, I could no more call this . . . thing—" I waved the statement—"'true' than I could call—" I looked out the window at the easel with my sketch—"*that* thing true!"

"Though that does not reflect on its potential for truth if placed in another contextual position. If, for example, the statement on the other side of the paper read: 'Your picture is in the garden,' then it would be perfectly fine. Actually, it can work quite serially; what we're really establishing is simply the unidirectionality of the modular context *from* the real. But then, all that semiological hair-splitting . . . Better turn over the paper and see if your memory isn't playing tricks on you."

Hastily I did. And read:

The statement on the other side of this paper is false.

"Yes," I said, "there *is* a statement on this side, and it does attribute truth-or-falsity to the statement on the other. Which is nonsensical. It's standing inside the sitting room in Bernham looking out the window and calling the rain 'true.'"

"You never really did that," Alfred said. "We just made a model of it that we judged nonsensical—useless in a particular sort of way. Keep looking at the side of the paper you're looking at now—that is: Set up the context in the other direction."

I did until I had:

"It's the same situation. If I let the *other* statement occupy the modeling position and this occupy the position of the modeled thing, then the fact that the other statement attributes truth or falsity to what's on *this* side means *it's* nonsensical too."

Alfred nodded. "It's like having, on either side of your paper: 'The *thing* on the other side of this paper is true (or false); the *thing* on the other side of this paper is false (or true).' Which is an empty situation, in the same way that if you and, say, Vanessa, both had drawing pads and pencils and were sitting where you could see each other's paper, and I gave you the instructions: 'Both of you draw only what the other is drawing.' You'd both end up with empty pictures."

"Speaking of Vanessa," I said, "let us go see what she is doing. She *is* a better artist than I am, which I suspect means that on some level, she has established a more interesting modular context with reality than I have. Perhaps she will take a break from her work and have some coffee with us."

"Splendid," said Alfred. "Oh, you asked me what I was doing in India? Well, while I was there, I got hold of some . . ." But that is another story too.

28. Language suggests that "truth" (or "falsity") may be an attribute of sentences much as "redness" may be an attribute of apples. The primary language model is the adjective "true," the secondary one a noun, "truth," derived from the adjective. This is not the place to begin the argument against the whole concept of attributes. (It goes back to Leibniz's inseparable subject/verbs for true predicates; Quine has demonstrated how well we can get along in formal logic without attributes, as well as without the whole concept of propositions.) But I maintain that, subsumed under the noun "truth," is a directed binary relation, running from the real to the uttered, by way of the mind. The problems we have concerning "truth" (such as the paradox in section 27) are problems that arise from having to model a directed binary relationship without a transitive verb.

It is as if, in those situations in which we now say "The hammer strikes the nail" and "The hammer misses the nail," we were constrained by the language only to speak of "strike nails" and "miss nails," and to discuss "strikeness" and "missness" as attributes a given nail might or might not possess, depending on the situation, at the same time seldom allowing a mention of the hammer and never the moment of impact.

What "truth" subsumes (as well as an adjective-derived noun can) is a *process* through which apprehension of some area of the real (either through the senses, or through the memory, or the reality of internal sensation—again, this is not the place to discuss their accuracy) generates a descriptive utterance. This process is rendered highly complex by the existence of choice and imagination and is totally entangled in what Quine and Ullian have called "the web of belief": confronted with the real, the speaker may choose not to speak at all, or to speak of something else, or she may be mistaken (at any number of levels), or he may generate a description in a mode to which "truth" or "falsity" are simply not applicable (it may be in G. Spencer-Brown's "imaginary" mode). But when the speaker does generate an utterance of the sort we wish to consider, the overall process structure is still binary, and directed from reality to the sentence.

When I look out the window and say "It is raining outside," what I perceive outside the window is controlling my utterance *in a way* the internal apprehension of which is my apprehension of the statement's "truth" or "falsity." My utterance does not affect—save possibly in the realms of Heisenberg—whatever (rain or shine) is outside the window.

People have suggested that the problem of paradox sentences is that they are self-descriptive. Yes, but the emphasis should be on *descriptive,* not *self.*

"This sentence contains six words" is just as self-descriptive as "This sentence is false." But the first sentence is not paradoxical; it is simply wrong. (It contains five words.) The second sentence is paradoxical because part of the description (specifically "This sentence . . .") covers two things (both the sentence "This sentence is false" and the sentence that it suggests as an equivalent translation, "This sentence is true") and does not at all refer to the relation between them. The only predicate that *is* visible in "This sentence is . . ." suggests they relate in a way they do not: "This sentence 'This sentence is true' *is* the sentence 'This sentence is false.'" And, obviously, it isn't. But the same situation exists in Grelling's paradox, the paradox of the Spanish barber, as well as the set-of-all-normal-sets paradox—indeed, in all antinomies.

The real generates an utterance via a *process* that allows us to recognize it as "true" or "false."

If we introduce verbs into the language to stand for the specific generative processes, we fill a much stumbled-over gap. By recovering what is on both sides of the interface, and the direction the relation between them runs, we clarify much that was confused because unstated. Let us coin "generyte" and "misgeneryte," and let us make clear that these processes are specifically mental and of the particular neurocybernetic nature that produce the utterances which, through a host of overdetermined and partially determined reasons, we have been recognizing as "true" and "false." If we introduce these verbs into our paradox, it stands revealed simply as two incorrect statements.

On one side of the paper instead of "The sentence on the other side of this paper is true," we write:

"What is on this side of the paper generytes the sentence on the other side."

And on the other side instead of "The sentence on the other side of this paper is false," we write:

"What is on this side of the paper misgenerytes the sentence on the other side."

Looking at either sentence, then turning the paper over to see if it does what it claims, we can simply respond, for both cases: "No, it does not." One (among many) properties that lets us recognize a generyted (or misgeneryted) sentence is that it is in the form of a description of whatever generyted (or misgeneryted) it; neither sentence is in that form.*

A last comment on all this:

The whole problem of relating mathematics to logic is basically the problem of how, logically, to get from conjunctions like "1 + 1 = 2 *and* 1 + 1 ≠ 3," which is the sort of thing we can describe in mathematics, to the self-evident (yet all but unprovable) logical implication: "1 + 1 = 2 *therefore* 1 + 1 ≠ 3," which is the process that propels us through all mathematical proofs.

Now consider the following sentences, one a conjunction, one an implication:

"This sentence contains ten words and it misgenerytes itself."

"If this sentence contains ten words, then it misgenerytes itself."

About the first sentence we can certainly say: "That sentence contains nine words, *therefore* it misgenerytes itself." If that self-evident *therefore* can be considered an implication, and assumed equivalent to ("to have the same truth values as" in our outmoded parlance) the implication of the second sentence, then, working from the side of language, we have, self-evidently, bridged the logical gap into mathematics!

Before making such an assumption, however, count the words in the second sentence . . .

29. Vanessa Harpington (during a period when she [not I] thought her work was going badly), shortly after Alfred's departure for Rumania:

---

* Such translation into an artificial language may at first seem suspect. But is it really any more dubious than the translation Russell suggests in his theory of singular descriptions which so facilitates the untangling of *Plato's beard*?

"What use is love?

"It assures neither kindness, compassion, nor intelligence between the people who feel it for one another.

"The best you can say is that when good people love, they behave well . . . sometimes.

"When bad people love, they behave appallingly.

"I wonder what the brilliant Alfred will have to say about a paradox like *that!*"

"First of all, Vanessa," I reminded her as we walked the cobbled streets, with the Arno, dull silver, down every block, through the Italian summer, "you simply cannot take such abstract problems so seriously. Remember, you and Alfred are both fictions: neither of you exists. The closest I've ever been to passing a summer in an English country house was a weekend at John and Margery Brunner's in Somerset, and though I spent a few weeks in Venice once, I've never stayed in an Italian villa in my life! I've never even *been* in Florence—"

"Oh, really," Vanessa said. "You just don't understand at all!" and, for the rest of the walk back, stayed a step or two ahead of me, arms folded and looking mostly somewhere else, though we did eventually talk—about other things.

30. Finished reading Gombrich's *Art and Illusion* yesterday. The oversized paperback seems to be losing most of its pages. A thought: When I hold up my hand in front of my face, what I *see* is my hand, in focus, and, behind it, a slightly unfocussed, double image of the rest of the room, those images further away blurrier and slightly further apart. (Actually, parts of the double image keep suppressing other parts, and then the suppression pattern changes.) How odd that in the search for more and more striking illusions of reality, no artist has ever tried to paint *this*.

One reason, I suspect, is that art has never really been interested in painting What You See; from the most abstract to the most representational, art is interested in purveying the concept of What Is There. Representationalists have, from time to time, used a limited number of tricks of the eye to emphasize (by making their paintings look *more* like what you see) that the subject *is* there. Abstractionists use the reality of paint, brush stroke, and material for the same end.

31. A common argument between philosophers often runs like this:

A. I have a problem within this particular context.
B. I have a context within which I can solve your particular problem.

A. But I want a solution within *my* context!

B. But I can translate your context, in all particulars that interest me, into my context.

A. But you can't translate my problem into *your* context so that it is still a problem and then produce a solution for it that will fit *mine!* Is there any way you can prove that, within my context, my problem is insoluble?

B. I'm not interested in proving your problem insoluble! I'm interested in solving it! And I have!

A. If you are interested in proving my old problem insoluble, then I am not interested in your new context! It doesn't relate to my problem!

32. The greatest distress to me of Structural Anthropology is its sexism. The primary descriptive model, "Society operates by the exchange of women," as a purely descriptive model, has the value of any other: There are certainly contexts in which it is useful. The same can be said of such other famous descriptive models as: "Jews are responsible for the financial evils of Europe," or "Blacks are lazy and shiftless but have a good sense of rhythm." It is the nature of descriptions that, as long as they model some fraction of the reality, however minute (even to the fact that persons A and B have agreed to use model *p* as a description of situation *s* [which is the case with individual words]) they can be called useful. But pure descriptive usefulness is not in the least contingent on how much the internal structure of the description reflects the way in which the fragment of reality it models relates to the rest of the case. Such descriptions that try to mirror these relations, to the extent that they succeed, can be called logical (functional) descriptions. But the very form of the absolute statement precludes its being a logical (functional) description. And when a description is of a small enough fragment of reality, and it reflects neither the internal workings of what it is describing nor the external workings, it can be said to be an emblem—or, if it is made up of a string of words, a slogan. And it is the slogan's pretension to logical (functional) description that makes it so undesirable. When trying to establish a coherent system, such as a coherent anthropological discipline (as Lévi-Strauss is attemping), we want logical models that can also be used as part of a logical context. Such models as the ones above, as they pass into context, yield situation after situation where abuse is almost inevitable:

If a woman objects to being exchanged or refuses to be exchanged, for example, by the above model she can be described as opposing society's workings. But if a man objects to or refuses to be exchanged, he can be described as objecting to being treated as a woman! And on and on and on *ad* (in the manner of context models) *infinitum.*

What makes this so sad is that the original descriptive use is completely

subsumed by the double model: "Much of society works by the exchange
of human beings," and "In most cases, the human beings who do the ex-
changing are men and the human beings exchanged are women." Without resorting to information theory (which tells us that the interplay between two limited descriptive models generates much more information
about the context surrounding the elements of all of them than any one
absolute statement of the same elements possibly can), I think most native English speakers hear the margin for self-criticism allowed. And I
don't see how the informative usefulness of this complex model is any *less*
than that of the absolute statement.

But if I thought anthropological sexism were merely a manifestation
of a single, clumsily thought-out descriptive model, I would not be as
distressed as I am. It appears again and again; the profusion alone suggests that it is inherent in the context. Three more examples:

In Lévi-Strauss's most exemplary short piece, *La Geste d' Asdiwal* (his
analysis of a myth that has a range of male and female characters), we
find statements like: ". . . the women [in this myth] are more profitably
seen as natural forces . . ." (More profitably than what? Than as human
beings? And who is this profitable to? But let us continue.) The myth, in
its several versions collated in the forty-odd-page essay, begins with a
mother and daughter, whose husbands have died in the current famine,
traveling from their respective villages, till they meet, midway along a
river. They have only a rotten berry between them to eat. A magic bird
appears, turns into a man, marries the daughter, provides food for the two
women, and the daughter and her supernatural husband have a child, Asdiwal, the hero of the myth. Some time later in the myth, Asdiwal, as an
adult, meets a magic bear on a mountain who turns into a woman and
reveals she is the daughter of the sun. After Asdiwal passes a series of tests
set by the bear-woman's supernatural father, the bear-woman marries Asdiwal and they live for a while, happily, in the sky. Later they return to
earth, to Asdiwal's own village, where Asdiwal commits adultery with a
woman of his people. The bear-woman leaves him over this and returns
to her father. Asdiwal marries another woman of his village, and the
myth continues through a series of adventures involving several other female figures, some human, some not, their brothers (who tend to come
in groups of five), the king of the seals, Asdiwal's own son by a mortal
woman, and finally ends when Asdiwal, in a magic situation on top of a
mountain, calls down to his second wife to sacrifice some animal fat, and
she, misunderstanding his instructions, eats it; as a result, Asdiwal is
turned to stone. I do not claim, in so short a synopsis, to have covered all
the salient points of the myth in all its variations; for what it's worth, neither does Lévi-Strauss. There is a whole branch of the myth devoted to
Asdiwal's son's adventures, which has many parallels with his father's

story. Still, I cannot see what, in the myth, or in the Timshian culture which produced it, suggests the interpretation ". . . all the women . . ." in the tale are natural forces. The bird-man, the bear-woman, her father the sun, as well as various seal-men and mouse-women, may well represent natural forces. But to restrict this unilaterally to the women seems to be nothing but a projection of part of our own society's rather warped sexist context. I have no idea if the society of the Timshian Indians who produced this myth is as sexist as modern Western society, less sexist, or more so. I might have made an educated guess from the myth itself. But even Malinowski's original reports, taken several times over several years, here and there resort to synopsis, at noticeably more places where women are the agents of the action than where men are. And I can certainly get no idea from the final critical model Lévi-Strauss constructs: a binary grid of repeated, symmetrical patterns, high/low, upstream/dowstream, mountain/water, etc. By dissolving any possibility of male/female symmetricality with the asymmetrical men = human/women = forces, he makes it impossible to judge (nor does he try to judge in his final model) any such symmetricalities that *do* exist in the myth—i.e., I think everyone, from the parts recounted, can see a symmetricality between Asdiwal's mother's marriage with the bird-man who brings plenty and Asdiwal's with the bear-woman who brings good times in the sky. Just how important this symmetricality is in terms of Timshian society, I have no way of knowing. My point is, neither does Lévi-Strauss—if he is going to impose the artificial asymmetricalities of our culture on others. Lévi-Strauss's avowed point in the essay is merely to show that there is *some* order in the myth; and this he succeeds in. But has anyone ever seriously maintained that any society has produced myths with *no* order at all? And it is implicit in his approach to show as much order as possible in the myth and then show how it reflects or is reflected by, and lent meaning and value by (and lends meaning and value to), the social context it exists in. There are certainly plenty of asymmetrical elements in both situations (as there are in all of the elements that he pairs as symmetrical), i.e., one marriage produces a child, the other doesn't; one involves in-laws, the other doesn't. But Lévi-Strauss's sexist context puts the whole topic beyond discussion.

Another example: During Lévi-Strauss's conversations with Charbonnier, Charbonnier asks Lévi-Strauss if sometimes an anthropologist does not identify so much that he biases his observations in ways not even he is aware of. Lévi-Strauss counters with an anecdote of a United States anthropologist who recounted to Lévi-Strauss that he felt much more at home working with one Amerind tribe than another. In one tribe, this man reported, if a wife is unfaithful to her husband, the husband cuts off her nose. In the other, if a wife is unfaithful to her husband, the husband goes to sit in the central square, bemoans his fate loudly to all who pass by, calls down imprecations from the gods to destroy the world that has brought things to this dreadful impasse, then curses the gods themselves for having allowed the world to become such a terrible place. He then gets up and returns to his wife, presumably much relieved, and life continues on. The second tribe, the American said, filled him with a sense of revulsion: Trying to "destroy the world, or the whole universe, for a personal injury" struck him as, somehow, "immoral." He preferred working with the former tribe because their responses somehow seemed much "more human." Now I have no idea whether either tribe was particularly sexist or not. Presumably if the women of the first tribe cut off the noses of their unfaithful husbands, whereas we might call them violent, we could not call them sexist. I do know enough of the social context of America to be sure that if this *were* the case, our United States anthropologist would have felt nowhere as "at home" with them as he did. And in terms of any of the tribes involved, including my own U.S. of A., I don't think I would trust this man to give an objective report on sexuality, sexual politics, morality, or humanity, as conceived subjectively, in terms of their own culture, by *any* of the three. In the context of the conversation, however, Lévi-Strauss uses the anecdote to point out, as politely as possible, that Charbonnier's question is mildly impertinent and that somehow this man is more equipped to be objective about the tribe he identifies with most than anyone else.

Somewhere, in the sciences, especially the human ones, we have to commit ourselves to objectivity. And, especially in the human ones, objectivity cannot be the same as disinterest. It must be a whole galaxy of attractions and repulsions, approvals and disapprovals, curiosities and disinterests, deployed in a context of self-critical checks and balances which, itself, must constantly be criticized as an abstract form capable of holding all these elements, and as specific elemental configurations. (Indeed, "objectivity" may well be the wrong word for it.) One of my commitments is that self-critical models are desirable things. I would even submit that cultures, be they Amerind or European or African or Indian or Chinese, are civilized to the extent that they possess them. Now "civilization" is only a small part of "culture." Culture, in all its variety, is a desirable thing because, among other things, it provides a variety of material from which self-critical models can be made. Lévi-Strauss himself has pointed out that one purpose of anthropology is to provide a model with which to criticize our own culture. But an anthropological model that only provides a way of seeing how other cultures are structurally similar to ours but literally erases all evidence pertaining to their differences, doesn't, in the long run, strike me as anthropologically very useful.

If other cultures are to teach us anything, and we are not merely to use them as Existential Others that, willy nilly, only prove our own prejudices either about them or ourselves, interpretative models that erase data about their real differences from us must be shunned.

My third example:

Some months ago, Edmund Leach, one of the major commentators on Lévi-Strauss, who has criticized many of Lévi-Strauss's findings and has also praised many of his methods, spent a lecture urging the reinstitution of segregation between the sexes in Western universities. He proposed doing it in a humane way: "Women might be restricted to the study of medicine and architecture. Men would not be allowed to study these." Man's providence, apparently, is to be everything else. He claimed to be aware that such segregation in the past had had its exploitative side. But he felt we should seriously look at primitive cultures with strict separation of the sexes in work and play for models of a reasonable solution to contemporary stresses.

My response to something like this is violent, unreasonable, and I stick by it: Then, for sanity's sake, restrict the study of anthropology to women too. It just *might* prevent such loathesome drivel!

Reasonably, all I can say is that modern anthropology takes place in such a pervading context of sexism that even minds as demonstrably brilliant as Lévi-Strauss's and Edmund Leach's have not escaped it. And that is a tragic indictment.

33. Confessions of a science-fiction writer: I have never read a whole novel by Philip K. Dick. And I have only been able to read three short stories by Brian Aldiss (and one I didn't read; I listened to) end to end. (I did read *most* of *Report on Probability A.*) On several separate occasions, I have bought some dozen books by each of them, piled them on my desk, and sat down with the prime intent of familiarizing myself with a substantial portion of their *oeuvres*.

It would be silly to offer this as the vaguest criticism of either Dick or Aldiss. It's merely an indication of idiosyncracies in my own interpretative context as far as reading goes.

At any rate, the prospect of Dick's and Aldiss's work is pleasant to contemplate. It is something I will simply have to grow into, as I grew into Stendahl and Auden, John Buscema and Joe Kubert, Robert Bresson and Stan Brackhage.

I'm making this note at a solitary lunch in a Camden Town Green

Restaurant. From the cassette recorder on the counter, Marinella, echoed by the chorus, asks plaintively again and again: "Pou paome? Pou paome?" Interesting that *the* question of our times emerges in so many languages, in so many media.

34. In the Glotolog foothills resides a highly refined culture much given to philosophical speculation.

Some facts about its language:

✳ is the written sign for a word that translates, roughly, as "a light source."

◊ is the sign for a word that translates, roughly, as "rain."

⊂◻⊃ is the sign for a word that translates, very roughly, as "I see." (⊂◻⊃, ⊂◻⊃, ⊂S⊃ are roughly [and respectively], "you see," "he sees," and "she sees.") But I must repeat "roughly" so frequently because there *are* no real verbs in the Glotolog language in the English sense.

The relationship that various forms of ⊂◻⊃ have to other Glotolog terms is modificational. In traditional Glotolog grammars (which are all written, traditionally, in English—in much the same way that traditional Latin grammars were written in Greek) they are called adjectives. "✳ ◊ ⊂◻⊃" is a common (and grammatically correct) Glotolog sentence—given the weather, it is one of the *most* common Glotolog sentences, especially in the north. It would be used in just about any situation where an English speaker would say, "It's raining," although there are some marked differences. "✳ ◊ ⊂◻⊃" would also be used when you mean, literally, "I see the rain." This is perhaps the place to make the point (made so clearly in chapter three of most standard Glotolog grammars), ⊂◻⊃ always takes ✳, and usually the ✳ is placed before it. The logic here is very simple: You can't see anything without a light source, and in Glotolog this situation is mirrored in the words; ⊂◻⊃ without a ✳ is simply considered grammatically incorrect. (✳, however, does not take ⊂◻⊃, but that is another subject.) Obvious here, and borne out by dictionaries, Glotolog grammar assigns two distinct meanings to ⊂◻⊃ (but not, however, to ⊂◻⊃, ⊂S⊃, or ⊂◻⊃): both "I see" and "There is . . ." (i.e., "It might be seen by me . . ."). Although this double meaning is the source of many traditional children's jokes (heard often during the winter when the clouds blot the sun), in practice it presents little confusion. If I were to come into a Glotolog monastery, with the oil lamps in the windowless foreroom gleaming on ". . . my traditional okapi jerkin where the raindrops still stand high" (my translation from a traditional Glotolog poem; alas, it doesn't really work in English) and say, stamping my Italian imported boots (the Glotologs are mad for foreign imports and often put them to bizarre uses; I have seen red plastic garbage pails used as hanging flower planters in even the strictest religious retreats—though the Glotolog's own painted ceramic ones seem, to my foreign tastes, so much prettier) "✳ ◊ ⊂⊙⊃," it would be obvious to all (even to those frequent, aging, Glotologian religious mystics who have forgotten all their formal grammar—if, indeed, they ever studied it; formal language training is an old discipline among the Glotolog, but it is a widespread one only in recent years, well after the formal education of these venerable ancients was long since past) that I am speaking in what is called, by the grammars, *the assumptive voice*. The logic here is that the words, when used in the assumptive voice, are to be taken in the sense: "It is assumed that if ✳ ⊂⊙⊃ [i.e., that if there *were* a light source and if I *were* there, seeing by it], then it *would* reflect off ◊ and I *would* see it . . . even though I am now inside the monastery and, since my entrance, the world may have fallen into total and unexpected night. In other worlds, the use of ⊂⊙⊃ as "there is . . ." is not quite the same as in English. You use ⊂⊙⊃ for "I see . . ." only when *what* there is is within sight. Otherwise, though you actually say the same word, i.e., ⊂⊙⊃, you are using the assumptive voice. In old Glotolog texts, the assumptive voice was actually indicated by what is called, in that final appendix to most standard Glotolog grammars on outmoded traditions, a metaphoric dot, which was placed over the ✳ and the ⊂⊙⊃. When speaking in the assumptive voice, ✳̇ and ⊂⊙̇⊃ were said to be in the metaphoric mood. No dot, however, in a sentence like "✳̇ ◊⊂⊙̇⊃ " would be placed over ◊. The logic here is that, in the assumptive voice, one of the things assumed is that the rain, at any rate, is real.

It is interesting: Many native Glotolog speakers, when given transcripts of ancient manuscripts on which the dots have been left out (due to the customs of modern Glotolog printing), can still often place the date of composition from the manner in which sentences like "✳ ◊ ⊂⊙⊃" are used, whether in the indicative ("There are . . ."), the literal ("I see . . ."), or the assumptive ("Somewhere out of sight it is . . .") voice. Apparently once the metaphoric dot fell out as archaic usage, the indicative and the assumptive were used much more informally.

Because of the tendency to use English analytic terms in Glotolog, many Glotolog terms are practically identical to their English equivalents (though, as we have seen, the grammar and the logical form of the language are quite different from those of English), so that a native speaker of one has little difficulty getting the sense of many Glotolog pronouncements, especially those having to do with logic and sensation.

Here is a list of words that are the same in both languages (that is, they are employed in the same situations):

if	can be called
at night	true
I feel	false
this/that	though
on my body	real

Also, logical questions are posed in Glotolog by putting the word "is" before, and a question mark after, the clause to be made interrogative. The fact that the semantics and logical form of the language are different from ours only presents problems in particular cases.

(To summarize those differences: Glotolog has no true predicates ["I feel," as well as "can be called true," for example, are the same part of speech as "⬭"]; in fact, Glotolog has no true subjects either. It has only objects, the observer of which is expressed as a description of the object, as is the medium by which the object is perceived; sometimes these descriptions are taken as real; at other times they are taken as virtual. And it should be fairly evident even from *this* inadequate description of the language—even without exposure to their complex religion, science, poetry, and politics—that this template still gives them a method for modeling the world as powerful as our own equally interesting [and equally arbitrary] subject/predicate template.)

One of the most famous of such problems is the question put by one of the greatest Glotolog philosophers:

"If, at night, ✳ ◊ ⬭ can be called true, though I feel ◊ on my body, is this ◊ real?"

The sense of this, along with the answer, seems self-evident to any English speaker; at the same time, to most of us, it is a mystery why this should be a great philosophical question. The answer lies in the logical form of the language as it has been outlined; but for those of you who do not wish to untangle it further, some of its philosophical significance for the Glotologs can be suggested by mentioning that it has caused among those perspicacious people practically as much philosophical speculation as the equally famous question by the equally famous Bishop Berkeley, about the sound of the unattended tree falling in the deserted forest, and for many of the same reasons—though the good Bishop's query, perfectly comprehensible as to sense by the native Glotolog speaker thanks to the shared terms, seems patently trivial and obvious to them!

A final note to this problem: In recent years, three very controversial solutions have been offered to this classical problem in Glotolog philosophy, all from one young philosophy student resident in one of the southern monasteries (it rains much less in the south, which has caused some of the northern sages to suggest this upstart cannot truly comprehend the nature of this essentially northern metaphysical dilemma), all three of which involve the reintroduction of the metaphoric dot, placed not in its traditional position over the ✻ or the ⬤, or even over the ◊, but rather over the words "real," "true," or the question mark—depending on the solution considered.

More conservative philosophers have simply gone *"Humph!"* (another utterance common in both Glotolog and English) at these suggestions, claiming that it is simply un-Glotologian to use the metaphoric dot over imported words. The dot is, and it says so in the grammars, reserved for native Glotolog terms. As one of the wittier, older scholars has put it (I translate freely): "In Glotolog, English terms have never had to bear up under this mark; they may, simply, collapse beneath its considerable weight." The more radical youth of the country, however, have been discussing, with considerable interest, this brilliant young woman's proposals.

35. Science fiction interests me as it models, by contextual extension, the ontology suggested among these notes. As it gets away from that ontology, I often find it appalling in the callousness and grossness of what it has to say of the world. (Like Wittgenstein, when I write these notes on science fiction I am "making propaganda for one kind of thinking over another.") Does that differ any from saying that I like science fiction that suggests to me the world is the way I already think it is? Alas, not much—which is probably why even some of the most appalling, callous, and gross science fiction is, occasionally, as interesting as it is.

One difference between a philosopher and a fiction writer is that a fiction writer may purposely use a verbal ambiguity to make two (or more) statements using the same words; she may even intend all these statements to be taken as metaphoric models of each other. But she is still unlikely, except by accident, to call them the same statement. A philosopher, on the other hand, may accidentally use a verbal ambiguity, but once he uses it, he is committed to maintaining that all its meanings are one. And, usually, it takes a creative artist to bring home to us, when the philosophy has exhausted us, that everything in the universe is *somewhat* like everything else, no matter how different any two appear; likewise, everything is *somewhat* different from everything else, no matter how similar any two appear. And these two glorious analytical redundancies form the ordinate and abscissa of the whole determinately indeterminant schema.

36. Omitted pages from an sf novel:
"You know," Sam said pensively, "that explanation of mine this evening—about the gravity business?" They stood in the warm semidark

of the co-op's dining room. "If that were translated into some twentieth-century language, it would come out complete gobbledy-gook. Oh, perhaps an sf reader might have understood it. But any scientist of the period would have giggled all the way to the bar."

"Sf?" Bron leaned against the bar.

"'Scientification?' 'Sci-fi?' 'Speculative fiction?' 'Science fiction?' 'Sf?'— that's the historical progression of terms, though various of them resurfaced from time to time."

"Wasn't there some public-channel coverage about—?"

"That's right," Sam said. "It always fascinated me, that century when humanity first stepped onto the first moon."

"It's not that long ago," Bron said. "It's no longer from us to them than from them to when man first stepped onto the American shore."

Which left Sam's heavy-lipped frown so intense Bron felt his temples heat. But Sam suddenly laughed. "Next thing you'll be telling me is that Columbus discovered America; the bells off San Salvador; the son buried in the Dominican Republic . . ."

Bron laughed too, at ease and confused.

"What I mean—" Sam's hand, large, hot, and moist, landed on Bron's shoulder—"is that my explanation would have been nonsense two hundred years ago. It isn't today. The épistémé has changed so entirely, so completely, the words bear entirely different charges, even though the meanings are more or less what they would have been in—"

"What's an épistémé?" Bron asked.

"To be sure. You haven't been watching the proper public-channel coverage."

"You know me." Bron smiled. "Annie shows and ice-operas—always in the intellectual forefront. Never in arrears."

"An épistémé is an easy way to talk about the way to slice through the whole—"

"Sounds like the secondary hero in some ice-opera. Melony Épistémé, costarring with Alona Liang." Bron grabbed his crotch, rubbed, laughed, and realized he was drunker than he'd thought.

"Ah," Sam said (was Sam drunk too . . . ?), "but the épistémé was *always* the secondary hero of the sf novel—in exactly the same way that the landscape was always the primary one. If you'd just been watching the proper public channels, you'd know." But he had started laughing too.

37. Everything in a science fiction novel should be mentioned at least twice (in at least two different contexts).

38. Text and *textus* in science fiction? Text, of course, comes from the Latin *textus*, which means "web." In modern printing, the "web" is that

great ribbon of paper which, in many presses, takes upwards of an hour to thread from roller to roller throughout the huge machine that embeds ranked rows of inked graphemes upon the "web," rendering it a text. Thus all the uses of the words "web," "weave," "net," "matrix," and more, by this circular "etymology" become entrance points into a *textus*, which is ordered from all language and language-functions, and upon which the text itself is embedded.

The technological innovations in printing at the beginning of the sixties, which produced the present "paperback revolution," are probably the single most important factor contouring the modern science-fiction text. But the name "science fiction" in its various avatars—sf, speculative fiction, sci-fi, scientification—goes back to those earlier technological advances in printing that resulted in the proliferation of "pulp magazines" during the twenties.

Naming is always a metonymic process. Sometimes it is the pure metonymy* of associating an abstract group of letters (or numbers) with a person (or thing), so that it can be recalled (or listed in a metonymic order with other entity names). Frequently, however, it is a more complicated metonymy: old words are drawn from the cultural lexicon to name the new entity (or to rename an old one), as well as to render it (whether old or new) part of the present culture. The relations between entities so named are woven together in patterns far more complicated than any alphabetic or numeric listing can suggest: And the encounter between objects-that-are-words (e.g., the name "science fiction," a critical text on science fiction, a science-fiction text) and processes-made-manifest-by-words (another science-fiction text, another critical text, another name) is as complex as the constantly dissolving interface between culture and language itself. But we can take a model of the naming process from another image:

Consider a child, on a streetcorner at night, in one of the earth's great cities, who hears for the first time the ululating sirens, who sees the red, enameled flanks heave around the far building edge, who watches the

---

Metonymy is, of course, the rhetorical figure by which one thing is called with the name of another thing associated with it. The historian who writes, "At last, the crown was safe at Hampton," is not concerned with the metallic tiara but the monarch who, from time to time, wore it. The dispatcher who reports to the truckboss, "Thirty drivers rolled in this weekend," is basically communicating about the arrival of trucks those drivers drove and cargoes those trucks hauled. *Metonymic* is a slightly strained, adjectival construction to label such associational processes. *Metonym* is a wholly-coined, nominative one, shored by a wholly spurious (etymologically speaking) resemblance to "synonymy/synonym" and "antinomy/antinym." Still, it avoids confusion. In a text practically opaque with precision, it distinguishes "metonymy"-the-thing-associated ("crown," "driver") from "metonymy"-the-process-of-association (crown to monarch; driver to cargo). The orthodox way of referring to both is with the single term.

chrome-ended, rubber-coated, four-inch "suctions" ranked along those flanks, who sees the street-light glistening on the red pump-housing, and the canvas hose heaped in the rear hopper, who watches the black-helmeted and rubber-coated men clinging to their ladders, boots lodged against the serrated running-board. The child might easily name this entity, as it careers into the night, a Red Squealer.

Later, the child brings this name to a group of children—who take it up easily and happily for their secret speech. These children grow; younger children join the group; older children leave. The name persists—indeed, for our purposes, the locus of which children use and which children do not use the name is how we read the boundary of the group itself.

The group persists—persists weeks, months, years after the child who first gave it its secret term has outgrown both the group and its language. But one day a younger child asks an older (well after the name, within the group, has been hallowed by use): "But *why* is it a Red Squealer?" Let us assume the older child (who is of an analytical turn of mind) answers: "Well, Red Squealers must get to where they are going quickly; for this reason sirens are put on them which squeal loudly, so that people can hear them coming a long way off and pull their cars to the side. They are painted with that bright enamel color for much the same reason—so that people can see them coming and move out of their way. Also, by now, the red paint is traditional; it serves to identify that it is, indeed, a Red Squealer one sees through the interstices of traffic and not just any old truck."

Satisfying as this explanation is, it is still something of a fiction. We were there, that evening, on the corner. We know the first child called it a Red Squealer out of pure, metonymic apprehension: there were, that evening, among many perceived aspects, "redness" and "squealing," which, via a sort of morphological path-of-least-resistance, hooked up in an easily sayable/thinkable phrase. We know, from our privileged position before *this* text, that there is nothing explicit in our story to stop the child from having named it a Squealing Red, a Wah-Wah, a Blink-a-blink, or a Susan-Anne McDuffy—had certain nonspecified circumstances been other than the simplest reading of our fiction suggests. The adolescent explanation, as to why a Red Squealer *is* a Red Squealer, is as satisfying as it is because it takes the two metonyms that form the name and embeds them in a web of functional description—satisfying because of the functional nature of the adult épistèmé,* which both generates the functional discourse and of

---

* The épistèmé is the structure of knowledge read from the epistemological *textus* when it is sliced through (usually with the help of several texts) at a given cultural moment.

which, once the discourse is uttered, the explanation (as it is absorbed into the memory, of both querent and explicator, which is where the *textus* lies embedded) becomes a part.

Science Fiction was named in like manner to the Red Squealer; in like manner the metonyms which are its name can be functionally related:

Science fiction *is* science fiction because various bits of technological discourse (real, speculative, or pseudo)—that is to say the "science"—are used to redeem various other sentences from the merely metaphorical, or even the meaningless, for denotative description/presentation of incident. Sometimes, as with the sentence "The door dilated," from Heinlein's *Beyond This Horizon,* the technological discourse that redeems it—in this case, discourse on the engineering of large-size iris apertures, and the sociological discourse on what such a technology would suggest about the entire culture—is not explicit in the text. Is it, then, implicit in the *textus?* All we can say for certain is that, embedded in the *textus* of anyone who can *read* the sentence properly, are those emblems by which they could recognize such discourse were it manifested to them in some explicit text.

In other cases, such as these sentences from Bester's *The Stars My Destination,* "The cold was the taste of lemons, and the vacuum was the rake of talons on his skin . . . Hot stone smelled like velvet caressing his skin. Smoke and ash were harsh tweeds rasping his skin, almost the feel of wet canvas. Molton metal smelled like water trickling through his fingers," the technological discourse that redeems them for the denotative description/presentation of incident *is* explicit in the text: "Sensation came to him, but filtered through a nervous system twisted and shortcircuited by the PryE explosion. He was suffering from Synaesthesia, that rare condition in which perception receives messages from the objective world and relays these messages to the brain, but there in the brain the sensory perceptions are confused with one another."

In science fiction, "science"—i.e., sentences displaying rhetorical emblems of scientific discourse—is used to literalize the meanings of other sentences for use in the construction of the fictional foreground. Such sentences as "His world exploded," or "She turned on her left side," as they subsume the proper technological discourse (of economics and cosmology in one; of switching circuitry and prosthetic surgery in the other), leave the banality of the emotionally muzzy metaphor, abandon the triviality of insomniac tossings, and, through the labyrinth of technical possibility, become possible images of the impossible. They join the repertoire of sentences which may propel *textus* into text.

This is the functional relation of the metonyms "science" and "fiction" that were chosen by Hugo Gernsback to name his new pulp genre.

He (and we) perceived that, in these genre texts, there existed an aspect of "science" and an aspect of "fiction," and because of the science something *about* the fiction was different. I have located this difference specifically in a set of sentences which, with the particular way they are rendered denotatively meaningful by the existence of other sentences not necessarily unique to science fiction, are themselves by and large unique to texts of the sf genre.

The obvious point must be made here: this explanation of the relation of the two onomastic metonyms Science/Fiction no more defines (or exhausts) the science-fictional enterprise than our adolescent explanation of the relation of the two onomastic metonyms Red/ Squealer defines (or exhausts) the enterprise of the fire engine. Our functional explanation of the Red Squealer, for example, because of the metonyms from which the explanation started, never quite gets around to mentioning the Red Squealer's primary function: to put out fires.

As the "function" of science fiction is of such a far more complex mode than that of the Red Squealer, one might hesitate to use such metonyms—"function" and "primary"—to name it in the first place. Whatever one chooses to name it, it cannot be expressed, as the Red Squealer's can, by a colon followed by a single infinitive-with-noun— no more than one could thus express the "primary function" of the poetic enterprise, the mundane-fictional, the cinematic, the musical, or the critical. Nor would anyone seriously demand such an expression for any of these other genres. For some concept of what, primarily, science fiction does, as with other genres, we must rely on further, complex, functional description:

The hugely increased repertoire of sentences science fiction has to draw on (thanks to this relation between the "science" and the "fiction") leaves the structure of the fictional field of sf notably different from the fictional field of those texts which, by eschewing technological discourse in general, sacrifice this increased range of nontechnological sentences—or at least sacrifice them in the particular, foreground mode. Because the added sentences in science fiction *are* primarily foreground sentences, the relationship between foreground and background in science fiction differs from that of mundane fiction. The deposition of weight between landscape and psychology shifts. The deployment of these new sentences within the traditional sf frame of "the future" not only generates the obviously new panoply of possible fictional incidents; it generates as well an entirely new set of rhetorical stances: the future-views-the-present forms one axis against which these stances may be plotted; the alien-views-the-familiar forms another. All stories would seem to proceed as a progression of verbal data which, through their relation among themselves and their relation to data outside themselves, produce, in the reader, data-expectations. New data arrive, satisfying and/or frustrating these expectations, and, in turn and in concert with the old, produce new expectations—the process continuing till the story is complete. The new sentences available to sf not only allow the author to present exceptional, dazzling, or hyperrational data, they also, through their interrelation among themselves and with other, more conventional sentences, create a *textus* within the text which allows whole panoplies of data to be generated at syntagmatically startling points. Thus Heinlein, in *Starship Troopers,* by a description of a mirror reflection and the mention of an ancestor's nationality, in the midst of a strophe on male makeup, generates the data that the first-person narrator, with whom we have been traveling now through a hundred and fifty-odd pages (of a two-hundred-and-fifty-page book), is non-caucasian. Others have argued the surface inanities of this novel, decried its endless preachments on the glories of war, and its pitiful founderings on repressed homosexual themes. But who, a year after reading the book, can remember the arguments for war—short of someone conscientiously collecting examples of human illogic? The arguments *are* inane; they do *not* relate to anything we know of war as a real interface of humanity with humanity: They do not stick in the mind. What remains with me, nearly ten years after my reading of the book, is the knowledge that I have experienced a world in which the *placement* of the information about the narrator's face is *proof* that in such a world much of the race problem, at least, has dissolved. The book as text—as object in the hand and under the eye—became, for a moment, the symbol of that world. In that moment, sign, symbol, image, and rhetoric collapse into one, nonverbal experience, catapulted from somewhere beyond the *textus (via* the text) at the peculiarly powerful trajectory only sf can provide. But from here on, the description of what is unique to science fiction and how it works within the sf *textus* that is, itself, embedded in the whole language—and language-like—*textus* of our culture becomes a list of specific passages or sets of passages: better let the reader compile her or his own.

I feel the science-fictional enterprise is richer than the enterprise of mundane fiction. It is richer through its extended repertoire of sentences, its consequent greater range of possible incident, and through its more varied field of rhetorical and syntagmatic organization. I feel it is richer in much the same way atonal music is richer than tonal, or abstract painting is richer than realistic. No, the apparent "simplemindedness" of science fiction is not the same as that surface effect through which individual abstract paintings or particular atonal pieces frequently appear "impoverished" when compared to "conventional" works, on first exposure (exposed to, and compared by, those people who have absorbed only the "conversational" *textus* with which to "read" their art or music). This "impoverishment" is the necessary simplicity of sophistication, meet for the far wider web of possibilities such works can set resonating. Nevertheless, I think the "simple-mindedness" of science fiction may, in the end, have the same aesthetic weight as the "impoverishment" of modern art. Both are manifestations of "most works in the genre"—not the "best works." Both, on repeated exposure *to* the best works, fall away by the same process in which the best works charge the *textus*—the web of possibilities—with contour.

The web of possibilities is not simple—for abstract painting, atonal music, or science fiction. It is the scatter pattern of elements from myriad individual forms, in all three, that gives their respective webs their densities, their slopes, their austerities, their charms, their contiguities, their conventions, their clichés, their tropes of great originality here, their crushing banalities there: The map through them can only be learned, as any other language is learned, by exposure to myriad utterances, simple and complex, from out the language of each. The contours of the web control the reader's experience of any given sf text; as the reading of a given sf text recontours, however slightly, the web itself, that text is absorbed into the genre, judged, remembered, or forgotten.

In wonder, awe, and delight, the child who, on that evening, saw the juggernaut howl into the dark, named it "Red Squealer." We know the name does not exhaust; it is only an entrance point into the *textus* in order to retrieve from it some text or other on the contours, formed and shaped of our experience of the entities named by, with, and organized around those onomastic metonyms. The *textus* does not define; it is, however, slightly, recontoured with each new text embedded upon it, with each new text retrieved from it. We also know that the naming does not necessarily imply, in the child, an understanding of that *textus* which offers up its metonyms and in which those metonyms are embedded. The wonder, however, may initiate in the child that process which, resolved in the adult, reveals her, in helmet and rubber raincoat, clinging to the side-ladders, or hauling on the fore- or rear-steering wheel, as the Red Squealer rushes toward another blaze.

It may even find her an engineer, writing a text on why, from now on, Red Squealers had best be painted blue, or a bell replace that annoying siren—the awe and delight, caught pure in the web, charging each of her utterances (from words about, to blueprints of, to the new, blue, bonging object itself) with conviction, authenticity, and right.

39. Everything in a science-fiction novel should be mentioned at least twice (in at least two different contexts), with the possible exception of science fiction.

40. Omitted pages from an sf novel:

Saturn's Titan had proved the hardest moon to colonize. Bigger than Neptune's Triton, smaller than Jupiter's Ganymede, it had seemed the ideal moon for humanity. Today, there were only research stations, the odd propane mine, and Lux—whose major claim was that it bore the same name as the far larger city on far smaller Iapetus. The deployment of humanity's artifacts across Titan's surface more resembled the deployment across one of the gas giants' "captured moons"—the under-six-hundred-kilometer-diameter hunks of rock and ice (like Saturn's Phoebe, Neptune's Nereid, or a half-dozen-plus of Jupiter's smaller orbs) that one theory held to have drifted out from the asteroid belt before being caught in their present orbits. Titan! Its orangish atmosphere was denser (and colder) than Mars's—though nowhere near as dense as Earth's. Its surface was marred with pits, rivers, and seas of methane and ammonia sludge. Its bizarre lifeforms (the only other life in the Solar System) combined the most unsettling aspects of a very large virus, a very small lichen, and a slime mold. Some varieties, in their most organized modes, would form structures like blue coral bushes with, for upwards of an hour at a time, the intelligence of an advanced octopus. An entire subgenre of ice-operas had grown up about the Titan landscape. Bron despised them. (And their fans.) For one thing, the Main Character of these affairs was always a man. Similarly, the One Trapped in the Blue, Coral-like Tentacles was always a woman (Lust Interest of the Main Character). This meant that the traditional ice-opera Masturbation Scene (in which the Main Character Masturbates while Thinking of the Lust Interest) was always, for Bron, a Bit of a Drag. And who wanted to watch another shindo expert pull up another ice-spar and beat her way out of another blue-coral bush, anyway? (There were other, experimental ice-operas around today in which the Main Character, identified by a small "MC" on the shoulder, was only on for five minutes out of the whole five-hour extravaganza, Masturbation Scene and all—an influence from the indigenously Martian Annie-show—while the rest was devoted to an incredible interlocking matrix of Minor Characters' adventures.) And the women who went to them tended to be strange—though a lot of very intelligent people, including Lawrence, swore Titan-opera was the only really select artform left to the culture. Real ice-opera—better-made, truer-to-life and with more to say about it *via* a whole vocabulary of real and surreal conventions, including the three formal tropes of classical abstraction, which the classical ice-opera began with, ended with, and had to display once gratuitously in the middle—left Lawrence and his ilk (the ones who didn't go into ego-booster booths) yawning in the lobby.

41. The structure of history tends to be determined by who said what. The texture of life is determined by who is listening.

42. Though few science-fiction writers enjoy admitting it, much science fiction, especially of the nuts-and-bolts variety, reflects the major failure of the scientific context in which most technology presently occurs: the failure, in a world where specialization is a highly productive and valued commodity, to integrate its specialized products in any ecologically reasonable way—painfully understandable in a world that is terrified of any social synthesis, between black and white, male and female, rich and poor, verbal and nonverbal, educated and uneducated, underprivileged and privileged, subject and object. Such syntheses, if they occur, will virtually destroy the categories and leave all the elements that now fill them radically revalued in ways it is impossible to more than imagine until such destruction is well underway. Many of the privileged as well as the underprivileged fear the blanket destruction of the products of technology, were such a radical value shift to happen. Even so, both privileged and nonprivileged thinkers are questioning our culture's context, scientific and otherwise, to an extent that makes trivial, by comparison, the blanket dismissal of all things with dials that glitter (or with latinate names in small print at the bottom of the labels) that the urban advocates of back-to-the-soil humanism sometimes claim to indulge. Within the city, because of the overdetermined context, even to attempt such a dismissal is simply to doom oneself to getting one's technology in grubbier packages, containing less-efficient brands of it, and with the labels ripped off so that you can be sure what's inside. Those who actually *go* back to the soil are another case: The people on the rural communes I have visited—in Washington with Pat Muir, and those in California around Muir Woods (coincidentally named after Pat's grandfather)—were concerned with exploring a folk technology, a very different process from "dismissal." And the radio-phonograph (solid-state circuitry) and the paperback book (computerized typesetting), just for examples, were integral parts of the exploration.

That science fiction is the most popular literature in such places doesn't surprise.

What other literature could make sense of, or put in perspective, a landscape where there is a hand-loom, a tape-recorder, a fresh butter churn, ampicillin forty minutes away on a Honda 750, and both men and women pushing a mule-drawn plow, cooking, wearing clothes when clothes answer either a functional necessity (boots, work-gloves . . .) or an aesthetic appetite (hand-dyed smocks, bearded vests . . .) and going naked when neither necessity nor appetite is present; or where thousands of such people will gather, in a field three hundred miles from where they live, to hear music from musicians who have come a thousand miles to play it for them?

What the urban humanist refuses to realize (and what the rural humanist often has no way of realizing) is that our culture's scientific context, which has given us the plow, the tape-recorder, insecticides, the butter-churn, and the bomb, is currently under an internal and informed onslaught as radical as our social context is suffering before the evidence of Women's Liberation, Gay Activism, Radical Psychiatry, or Black Power.

Much science fiction inadvertently reflects the context's failure.

The best science fiction explores the attack.

43. The philosophically cherished predicates of all the sensory verbs in the Indo-European languages are, today, empirically empty verbal conventions—like the "it" in "it is raining." The very form "I see the table" suggests that, in the situation "I" would commonly model with those words, "I" am doing something *to* the table, by "seeing" it, in some sense similar to what "I" would be doing to it in the situation "I" would commonly model by the words "I set the table." Empirically, however, we know that (other than at the most minute, Heisenbergian level), in the situation we use "I see the table" to model, the table is—demonstrably!—doing far more to "I" than "I" am doing to it. (Moreover, though words like "I" and "see" were used to *arrive at* the demonstration, the demonstration *itself* could be performed effectively for a deaf-mute who had learned only the nonverbal indicators, such as pointing, miming of motion and direction, picture recognition, etc. The reading of various sense data as the persistence of matter and coherence and direction of motion, which is basically what is needed to apprehend such a demonstration, seems to be [by recent experiments on babies only a few hours old] not only preverbal but programmed in the human brain at birth, i.e., *not* learned.) A language is conceivable that would reflect this, where the usual model of this situation would be a group of verbal particles that literally translated: "Light reflects from table then excites my eyes." Equally conceivable, in this language, the words "I see the table" might be considered, if translated from ours literally, first, as ungrammatical, and, second, as self-contradictory as "the rock falls up" (or "the table sees me") appears in ours. By extension, all predicates in the form "The subject senses . . ." (rather than "The object excites . . .") are as empty of internal coherence against an empirical context as "The color of the number seven is D-flat." (Among poets, an intuitive realization of the hopeless inadequacy of linguistic expressions in the form "I sense . . ."

accounts for much of the "difficulty" in the poetry of the last twenty-five years—a very different sort of difficulty from the labored erudition of the poetry of the thirty years previous.) As *models* for a situation, neither the "I see . . ." model nor the "light reflects . . ." model is more *logical;* but that is only because logic lies elsewhere. One model is simply, empirically, more reasonable. Empirical evidence has shown that the implied arrows "inside" these words simply do not reflect what is the case. A good bit of philosophical wrangling simply tries to maintain that because these arrows were once considered to be there, they must still model *something*.

There was a time when people thought electricity flowed from the positive to the negative pole of a battery. The best one can say is that there were many situations in which the current's direction didn't matter. And many others in which it did. Trying to maintain the meaningful direction of sense predicates is like maintaining that in those situations in which it doesn't matter which way the current flows, somehow it is *actually* flowing backwards.

44. Galaxy of events over the past few months: the telegram announcing Marilyn's collection of poems *Presentation Piece* had won the Lamont Poetry Selection for the year; the terribly complimentary statement by Richard Howard, which will go on the book's back cover; a glowing review by the Kirkus Service that is *so* muddle-headed, one would have almost preferred no review at all!

45. Various deaf-mute friends I have had over the years, and the contingent necessity of learning sign language, have given me as much insight into spoken and written language as oral storytelling once gave me into written stories: Hand-signs, spoken words, and written words produce incredibly different contextual responses, though they model the same object or process. The deaf-and-dumb sign language progresses, among ordinary deaf mute signers, at between three and five hundred words a minute (cf. ordinary reading speeds), and the learner who comes from the world of hearing and speaking is frequently driven quite mad by the absence of concept words and connectives. (Logicians take note: Both "and" and "or" are practically missing from demotic sign language; though the sign for "and" exists, "or" must be spelled out by alphabetic signs, which usually indicates an infrequently used word.)

Lanky and affable Horace would occasionally leave me notes under my room door (on the ninth floor of the Albert) written with "English" words, all using their more or less proper dictionary meaning, but related to one another in ways that would leave your average English speaker bewildered.

There is a sign for "freeze"—a small, backwards clutch, with the palms of the hands down.

There is a sign for "you"—pointing to the "listener" with the forefinger.

As in English, "freeze" has many metaphorical extensions: "to stop moving," "to treat someone in a cold manner," etc. The two signs, mimed consecutively—"freeze you"—can mean:

"You have a cold personality."

"You are frozen."

"Are you frozen?"

"Stop moving."

"You just stopped moving, didn't you!" (in the sense of "You jumped!")

This last is a particularly interesting case: the signed phrase could also be translated "You flinched!" The speaker who says, "You jumped!" models the beginning of the motion; the deaf-mute who signs, "Freeze you" is modeling the end of the same motion. In both cases, the partial model (or synecdoche) stands for the whole action of "flinching."

Another meaning of "Freeze you" is: "Please put some water in the ice tray and put it in the ice box so we can have some ice cubes."

Distinction among meanings, in actual signing, is a matter of—what shall I call it?—muscular and gestural inflection in the arms, face, and the rest of the body. And, of course, the situation.

I remember getting the note: "Come down freeze you whiskey have want, chess." I suspect this would be baffling without some knowledge of the sign language context, though the words "mean" pretty much the same as they do in English. One informal translation of this note into written English would be: "Come downstairs and play chess with me. You bring the ice cubes. I have some whiskey—if you want?" And an equally good translation: "Do you want to come down, bring some ice cubes, have a drink, and play chess?" And another: "Why not come on down? You make ice cubes up there; bring them. I have some whiskey. It's all for a chess game."

But it would be a great mistake to try and "transform" the original into any of my English translations, either by some Chomskyan method, or by filling in suspected ellipses, understood subjects, and the like:

"... have want ..." is a single verb phrase, for example, whose translation I could spend pages on. It has at least three modulating duals (in our language context, at any rate) so that its translation tends to be some arrangement from the matrix:

if	you	now		then	I	will	
			have				want
then	I	will		if	you	now	

moving both backwards and forwards, and up or down. It is regularly interrogative. (So a written question mark, in the deaf-and-dumb language, when you use "have want" is superfluous. The phrase "have need" works by a similar matrix and is regularly imperative. The equally frequent "want need," however, works through an entirely different matrix.) It may have several "direct objects," each requiring a different path through the matrix to make "sense" in our language. A literal translation of Horace's sentence, up to the comma, might read: "If you want to come down, I will have you down; if you have frozen (made) some (ice cubes), I will want some (that you have frozen); if you want whiskey, I have some whiskey . . ." And "chess" at the sentence's end is something like a noun absolute in Latin, the topic of the whole sentence, casting back its resonances on all that has gone before.

46. In the same language in which we still say "I see . . . ," only fifty years before Russell's theory of "singular description," in America one person could meaningfully refer to another as "my slave . . ." at which point the other person was constrained *by the language* to refer to the first as "my master . . ."—as if the bond of possession were somehow mutual and reciprocal.

Rebellion begins when the slave realizes that in no sense whatsoever is the master "hers/his." The slave cannot sell the master, give the master away, or keep the master should the master wish to go. This realization *is* the knowledge that the situation, which includes the language, exploits the slave and furthers the exploitation.

47. Possible insight into the "Cocktail Party Effect": Last evening, with David Warren at Professor Fodor's lecture on the mental representation of sentences, at the London School of Economics, I had a chance to observe the Cocktail Party Effect at work. David and I were sitting on the ground floor of the Old Theatre, near the door. Outside, a mass of students was gathering, presumably for the next event in the auditorium. The general rumble of their voices finally grew loud enough to make a dozen people around us look back towards the exit with consternation.

Professor Fodor's delivery, while audible, was certainly not loud;

and he wandered over the stage, to the blackboard, to the apron, to the podium, so that only part of the time was he near enough to the microphone for his voice to carry.

The sound outside was definitely interfering with our hearing his lecture, and we all had to strain . . .

The next time I was aware of the crowd noise outside, I realized that if I kept my aural concentration fixed on Fodor's words, the crowd noise would begin to undergo a definite pulsing (I estimated the frequency to be between two pulses per second and three pulses in two seconds) while the professor's voice stayed more or less clear through the peaks and troughs. If, however, I listened consciously to the crowd, the pulsing ceased and the Professor's words became practically unintelligible, lost in the rush of sound.

Is this how the "Cocktail Party Effect," or some aspect of it, works?

48. R. E. Geis in *The Alien Critic* defending himself against Joanna Russ's and Vonda McIntyre's accusations of sexism, cites a string of incorrect facts, half-facts, and facts implying a nonexistent context, beginning with the statement:

I have never made a sexist editorial decision in my life.

The form of the sentence itself implies that "making" a "sexist decision" or, for that matter, making an antisexist decision, is a case of putting energy into an otherwise neutral social contextual system.

The social context is *not* neutral. It is overwhelmingly sexist.

Studies have been done as far back as the fifties which show, in America, almost cross-culturally, male infants receive an average of slightly over 100 percent more physical contact with their parents during the first year of life than female infants! Tomes have been written on the effect of physical contact in this period on later physical strength and psychological autonomy. This alone renders the word "naturally," in a statement like "men are naturally stronger than women," a farce! Yet, despite how many thousands of years (probably no more than six and possibly a good deal less—another point to bear in mind) of this sort of Lamarckian pressure, when a large number of skeletons from modern cadavers, whose sexes were known and coded, were then given to various doctors, anthropologists, and archeologists to sort into male and female, the results were random! There is *no* way to identify the sex of a skeleton, from distinctions in size, pelvic width, shoulder width, skull size, leg length—these are all empirically nonsupported myths. Yet anthropology books are being published today with pictures captioned: "Armbone of a woman, c. eight thousand B.C." or "Jawbone of a male, c. five thousand B.C." Studies in the comparative heights of men and women have disclosed that, if you say you are doing a study in the comparative heights of men and women, and ask for volunteers, men average some two inches taller than women—whereas, if you say you are doing an intelligence test to compare university students with nonuniversity students, and, just incidentally, take the height of your volunteers, men average a mere three-eighths of an inch taller than women! Other, even more random samplings which have tried to obliterate *all* sexually associated bias, seem to indicate that the *range* of height of men tends to be larger—as a man, you have a greater chance of being either very tall or very short—but that the average height is the same. (Of course women are shorter than men: just stand on any street corner and look at the couples walking by. Next time you stand on any street corner, take pairs of couples and contrast the height of the woman from couple A with the man from couple B. I did this on a London street corner for two hours a few weeks back: taken as couples, it would appear that in 94 percent, men are taller than women. Taken by cross-couples, the figure goes down to 72 percent. The final twenty-two percent is more likely governed by the sad fact that, in Western society, tall women and short men often try to avoid being seen in public, especially with the opposite sex.) A male in our society receives his exaggerated social valuation with the application of the pronoun "he" before he can even smile over it. A female receives her concomitant devaluation with the pronoun "she" well before she can protest.

Again: The system is *not* neutral. For every situation, verbal or nonverbal, that even approaches the sexual, the easy way to describe it, the comfortable way to respond to it, the normal way to act in it, the way that will draw the least attention to yourself—if you are male—*is* the sexist way. The same goes for women, with the difference that you are not quite so comfortable. Sexism is not primarily an active hostility in men towards women. It is a set of unquestioned social habits. Men become hostile when these habits are questioned as people become hostile when anything they are comfortable doing is suddenly branded as pernicious. ("But I didn't *intend* to hurt anyone; I was just doing what I always . . .")

A good many women have decided, finally, that the pain that accrues to *them* from everyone else's acceptance of the "acceptable" way is just not worth the reward of invisibility.

"I have never made a sexist editorial decision in my life."

There *are* no sexist decisions to be made.

There are antisexist decisions to be made. And they require tremendous energy and self-scrutiny, as well as moral stamina in the face of the basic embarrassment campaign which is the tactic of those assured of their politically superior position. ("Don't you think you're being rather silly offering *your* pain as evidence that something *I* do so automatically and easily is wrong? Why, I bet it doesn't hurt *half* as much as you say. Perhaps it only hurts because you're struggling . . . ?" This sort of political mystification, turning the logical arrows around inside verbal structures to render them empirically empty, and therefore useless ["It hurts *because* you don't like it" rather than "You don't like it *because* it hurts."] is just another version of the "my slave/my master" game.)

There *are* no sexist decisions to be made: they were all made a long time ago!

49. The mistake we make as adolescent readers is to assume a story is exciting because of its strange happenings and exotic surfaces, when actually a story is exciting exactly to the extent that its structure is familiar. "Plot twists" and "gimmicks" aside (which, like "wisecracks," only distract our conscious mind from the structure so that we can respond subconsciously to its familiarity with that ever sought-for "gut response"), excitement in reading invariably comes from the anticipation of (and the anticipation rewarded by) the inevitable/expected.

This inevitability—without which there simply *is* no reader gut-participation—is also what holds fiction to all the political cliches of sexism, racism, and classism that mar it as an art. To write fiction without such structural inevitabilities, however (as practically every artist has discovered), is to write fiction without an audience.

Does science fiction offer any way out of this dilemma?

The hope that it might probably accounts for a good deal of the rapprochement between science fiction and the *avant garde* that occurred during the middle and late sixties.

50. The equivocation of the genitive (children, ideas, art, and excrement) and the associative (spouses, lovers, friends, colleagues, co-patrials, and country) with the possessive (contracted objects) is the first, great, logically-empty verbal structure that exists entirely for political exploitation.

51. Meaning is a routed-wave phenomenon.

I intend this in the sense one might intend the statement: "Painting is a colored-oil-paints spread-on-canvas phenomenon." Just as there are many things besides oil paints on canvas that may fill, more or less well, the several uses we could reasonably ask of a painting—from tempera on masonite to colored sand spilled carefully on sun-baked ground, in one direction; or etchings, photographs, or computer reductions, in another; or patterns observed on a rock, a natural setting, or a found object, in still another—there may be other things that can fill, more or less well, the several tasks we might reasonably ask "meaning" to perform. But my statement still stands as a parametric model of what I think *meaning* to *be*. The extent to which any of my remarks contravene this model is the extent to which they should be taken as metaphoric.

52. Language in general, poetry in particular, and mathematics, are all tools to fix meaning (in their different ways) by establishing central parameters, not circumscribing perimeters. Accuracy in all of them is achieved by cross-description, not absolute statement.

Even $2 + 3 = 5$ is better considered as a mathematical stanza than a single mathematical sentence. It models a set of several interlocked sentences; and the context interlocking them is what "contains" the meaning we might model by saying "$2 + 3 = 5$ is right, whereas $2 + 3 = 4$ is wrong by lack of 1."

53. A *language-function* can be described as consisting of (one) a generative field (capable of generating a set of signals), (two) the signals so generated, and (three) an interpretive field (a field capable of responding to those signals) into which the signals fall.

Examples of language-functions: mathematics, art, expressive gesture, myth.

One of the most important language-functions is, of course, speech.

In most multiple speaker/hearer situations, there are usually multiple language-functions occurring: A talking to B . . . B talking to A . . . C listening to what A and B say, etc. (In Art, on the other hand, there is usually one only: artist to audience. The language-function that goes from audience to artist is, of course, criticism.)

The language itself is the way, within a single speaker/hearer, an interpretive field is connected to a generative field.

54. The trouble with most cybernetic models of language (those models that start off with "sound waves hitting the ear") is that they try to express language only in terms of an interpretive field. To the extent that they posit a generative field at all, they simply see it as an inverse of the interpretive field.

In ordinary human speech, the interface of the interpretive field with the world is the ear—an incredibly sensitive microphone that, in its flexibility and versatility, still has not been matched by technology. The interface of the generative field with the world is two wet sacks of air and several guiding strips of muscle, laid out in various ways along the air track, and a variable-shaped resonance box with a variable opening: the lungs/throat/mouth complex. This complex can produce a great many sounds, and in extremely rapid succession. But it can produce nothing like the range of sounds the ear can detect.

Language, whatever it is, in circuitry terms has to lie between these two interfaces, the ear and the mouth.

Most cybernetic models, to the extent that they approach the problem at all, see language as a circuit to get us from a sensitive microphone to an equally sensitive loudspeaker. A sensitive loudspeaker just isn't in the picture. And I suspect if it were, language as we know it would not exist, or at least be very different.

Try and envision circuitry for the following language tasks:

We have a sensitive microphone at one end of a box. At the other, we have a *mechanically* operable squeeze-box/vocal-chord/palate/tongue/teeth/lip arrangement. We want to fill up the box with circuitry that will accomplish the following: Among a welter of sounds—bird songs, air in leaves, footsteps, traffic noise—one is a simple, oral, human utterance. The circuitry must be able to pick out the human utterance, store it, analyze it (in terms of breath duration, breath intensity, and the various stops that have been imposed on a stream of air by vocal chords, tongue, palate, teeth, lips) and then, after a given time, reproduce this utterance through its own squeeze-box mechanism.

This circuitry task is both much simpler and much more complicated than getting a sound out of a loudspeaker. Once we have such a circuit, however, well before we get to any "logic," "syntax," or "semantic" circuits, we are more than halfway to having a language circuit.

Consider:

We now want to modify this circuit so that it will perform the following task as well:

Presented with a human utterance, part of which is blurred—either by other sounds or because the utterer said it unclearly—our circuit must now be able to give back the utterance correctly, using phonic overdeterminism to make the correction: Letting X stand for the blurred phoneme, if the utterance is

The pillow lay at the foot of the Xed

or

She stood at the head of the Xairs

our circuitry should be able to reproduce the most likely phoneme in place of the blur, X.

I think most of us will agree, if we *had* the first circuit, getting to the second circuit would be basically a matter of adding a much greater storage capacity, connected up in a fairly simple (i.e., regular) manner with the circuit as it already existed.

Let us modify our circuit still more:

We present an utterance with a blurred phoneme that can resolve in two (or more) ways:

"Listen to the *X*erds." (Though I am not writing this out in phonetic notation, nevertheless, it is assumed that the phonic component of the written utterance is what is being dealt with.)

Now in this situation, our very sensitive microphone is still receiving other sounds as well. The circuitry should be such that, if it is receiving, at the same time as the utterance, or has received fairly recently, some sound such as cheeping or twittering (or the sounds of pencils and rattling paper) it will resolve the blurred statement into "listen to the birds" (or, respectively, "listen to the words")—and if the accompanying sound is a dank, gentle plashing . . . Again, this is still just a matter of more storage space to allow wider recognition/association patterns.*

The next circuitry recomplication we want is to have our circuit such that, when presented with a human utterance, ambiguous or not, it can come back with a recognizable paraphrase. To do this, we might well have to have not only a sensitive microphone, but a sensitive camera and a sensitive micro-olfact and micro-tact as well, as well as ways of sorting, storing, and associating the material they collect. Basically, however, it is still, as far as the specific language circuitry is concerned, a matter of greater storage capacity, needed to allow greater associational range.

I think that most people would agree, at this point, that if we had a circuit that could do all these tasks, even within a fairly limited vocabulary, though we might not have a circuit that could be said to *know* the language, we would certainly have one that could be said to know a lot *about* it.

One reason to favor the above as a model of language is that, given the initial circuit, the more complicated versions could, conceivably, evolve by ordinary, natural-selection and mutation processes. Each new step is still basically just a matter of adding lots of very similar or identical components, connected up in very similar ways. Consider also: Complex as it is, that initial circuitry must exist, in some form or another, in every animal that recognizes and utters a mating call (or warning) to or from its own species, among the welter, confusion, and variety of wild forest sounds.

---

*The important point here, of course, is that nonverbal material must already be considered *as* language, if not as part *of* language.

The usual cybernetic model for language interpretation:

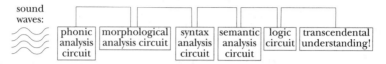

where each box must be a different kind of circuit, the first four (and, arguably, all six) probably different for each language strikes me as a pretty hard thing to "grow" by ordinary evolutionary means, or to program on a *tabula rasa* neural net.

The circuitry I suggest would all be a matter of phonic recognition, phonic storage, and phonic association (short of the storage and associational employment of other sensory information). A great *deal* of recognition/storage/association would have to be done by the circuitry to achieve language. But nothing *else* would have to be done, other than what was covered in our original utterance-reproduction circuit.

Not only would the linguistic bugaboo "semantics" disappear (as experiments indicate that it may have already) but so would morphology; and syntax and phonic analysis would simply absorb one another, so to speak.

Would this really be so confusing?

I think not. It is only a rather limited view of grammar that initially causes it to appear so.

Think of grammar solely as the phonic redundancies that serve to transform a heard utterance from the interpretive field, through the range of associations in the hearer/speaker's memory that includes "his language," into the hearer/speaker's generative field as an utterance.

In the *qui, quae, quo* of Latin, for instance, I'm sure the Roman brain (if not the Roman grammarian) considered the redundancy of the initial "qu" sound as grammatically significant (in my sense of "grammar"), as it considered significant, say, the phonic redundancy between the "ae" at the end of "quae" and the "ae" at the end of "pullae." (We must get rid of the notion of grammar as something that applies only to the ends of the words!) In English, the initial sound of *the, this, that, these, those,* and *there* are all grammatically redundant in a similar way. (The "th" sound indicates, as it were, "indication"; the initial "qu" sound, in Latin, indicates "relation," just as the terminal "ae" sound indicates, in that language, "more than one female."*) What one can finally say of this

---

* This is another invocation of the idea, out of favor for so long, of "morphophonemes." The theoretical question of course is do they differ (or how do they differ) from "sememes."

"grammar" is: When a phonic redundancy *does* relate to the way that a sound is employed in conjunction with other sounds/meanings, then that phonic element of the grammar is regular. When a phonic redundancy does *not* so relate, that element is irregular. (The terminal "s" sound on "these" and "those" is redundant with the terminal "s" of *loaves, horses, sleighs*—it indicates plurality, and is therefore *regular* with those words. The terminal "s" on "this" is *irregular* with them. The terminal "s" at the end of "is," "wants," "has," and "loves" all imply singularity. Should the terminal "s" on "this" be considered regular with these others? I suspect in many people's version of English it is.) For all we know, in the ordinary English hearer/speaker's brain, "cream," "loam," "foam," and "spume" are all associated, by that final "m" sound, with the concept of "matter difficult to individuate"—in other words, the "m" is a grammatically regular structure of *that particular word group.* Such associations with this particular terminal "m" may explain why most people seldom use "ham" in the plural—though nothing empirically or traditionally grammatical prevents it. They may also explain why "cream," when pluralized, in most people's minds immediately assumes a different viscosity (i.e., referentially, becomes a different word; what the dictionary indicates by a "second meaning"). I suspect that, in a very real sense, poets are most in touch with the true "deep grammar" of the language. Etymology explains some of the sound-redundancy/meaning-associations that are historical. Others that are accidental, however, may be no less meaningful.

All speech begins as a response to other speech. (As a child you eventually speak through being spoken to.) Eventually this recomplicates into a response to speech-and-other-stimuli. Eventually, when both speech and other stimuli are stored in memory and reassociated there, this recomplication becomes so complex that it is far more useful to consider certain utterances autonomous—the first utterance in the morning concerning a dream in the night, for example. But even this can be seen as a response to speech-and-other-than-speech, in which the threads of cause, effect, and delay have simply become too intertwined and tangled to follow.

55. Quine inveighs against propositions, as part of logic, on the justifiable grounds that they cannot be individuated. But since propositions, if they are anything, are particular meanings of sentences, the impossibility of individuating them is only part of a larger problem: the impossibility of individuating meanings in general. What the logician who says (as Quine does at the beginning of at least two books) "To deny the Taj Majal is white is to affirm that it is not white" (in the sense of "nonwhite") is really saying, is:

"Even if meanings cannot be individuated, let us, for the duration of the argument, treat them as if they can be. Let us assume that there is some volume of meaning-space that can be called white *and* be bounded. Therefore, every point in meaning-space, indeed, every volume in meaning-space, can be said to either lie inside this boundary, and be called 'white,' or outside this boundary, and be called 'nonwhite,' or, for the volumes that lie partially inside and partially outside, we can say that some aspect of them is white."

The problem is that, similar to the color itself, the part of meaning-space that can be called "white" fades, on one side and another, into every other possible color. And somehow, packed into this same meaning-space, but at positions distinctly outside this boundary around white, or any other color for that matter, we must also pack "freedom," "death," "grief," "the four-color-map problem," "the current King of France," "Pegasus," "Hitler's daughter," "the entire Second World War and all its causes," as well as "the author of *Waverly*"—all in the sense, naturally, of "nonwhite."

Starting with just the colors: In what sort of space could you pack all possible colors so that each one was adjacent to every other one, which would allow the proper fading (*and* bounding*) to occur? It is not as hard as it looks. Besides the ordinary three coordinates for volume, if you had two more ordinates, both for color, I suspect it could be rather easily accomplished. You might even do it with only two spatial and two color axes. Four coordinates, at any rate, is certainly the minimum number you need. Conceivably, getting the entire Second World War and all its causes in *might* require a few more.

56. One of the great difficulties of formal grammars is that they are *all* grammars of *written* language, including the attempts at "transformational" grammars (*Syntactic Structures:* ". . . we will not consider, for our purposes, vocal inflections . . ."). For insight into how verbal signals will produce information once they fall into an interpretive field, it is a good idea to return to the mechanics of those signals' generation.

Speech signals, or sentences, are formed from two simultaneous information (or signal) streams: Speech is an interface of these two streams.

The voiced breath-line is a perfectly coherent information stream, all by itself. It varies in pitch and volume and shrillness. It is perfectly possible (as I have done and watched done in some encounter groups) for two or more people to have an astonishingly satisfying

---

* Welsh (and Homeric Greek) divide the spectrum (both as to colors and intensity) quite differently from English.

conversation, consisting of recognizable questions, answers, assurances, hesitations, pooh-poohings, affirmations, scepticisms, and insistences—a whole range of emotional information, as well as the range Quine refers to as "propositional attitudes"—purely with a series of unstopped, voiced breaths. (Consider the information communicated by the sudden devoicing of all the phonemes in an utterance, i.e., whispering.)

The various stops and momentary devoicings imposed by the tongue, teeth, lips, and vocal chords on top of this breath-line is another coherent information string that, interfaced with the breath-line information, produces "speech." But by and large this second string is the only part that is ever written down. This is the only part that any "grammar" we have had till now deals with. But it is arguable that this information-string, when taken without the breath-line, is as vastly impoverished as the breath-line eventually seems, after ten or fifteen minutes, when taken by itself.

The way written speech gets by is by positing a "standard breath-line," the most common breath-line employed with a given set of vowels and stops. (The only breath-line indicators we have are the six ordinary marks of punctuation, plus quotation marks [which mean, literally, pay closer attention to the breath-line for the enclosed stretch of words], plus dashes, ellipses, and italic type. One thing that makes writing in general, and poetry in particular, an art is the implying of nonstandard breath-lines by the strong association of vocal sounds—*pace* Charles Olson.) But since the vast majority of writing uses only this standard breath-line (and *all* writing uses an artificial one), producing a grammar of a spoken language from written examples is rather like trying to produce a formal grammar of, say, Latin when the only available texts have had all the ablative endings, dative endings, accusative-plural endings, and second-person-singular verb endings in future, imperfect, and preterite whited out; and you have agreed, for your purpose, not to consider them anyway.

What is fascinating about language is not that it criticizes, as well as contributes to, the growth of the empirical world, but that it can criticize its relation to that world, treating itself, for the duration, empirically. The same self-reflective property is what writers use to make beautiful, resonant verbal objects, however referential or abstract. But by the same argument, it is the writers' responsibility to utilize this reflective property to show, again and again, that easy language—whether it is the short, punchy banality or the rolling jargonistic period—lies.

The lie is not a property of easy words. It is a property of how the words are used, the context that generates, and the context that interprets.

57. I have the artist's traditional distrust of separating facts too far from the landscape that generated them. (And I have the science-fiction writer's delight over inserting new facts into unfamiliar landscapes. "Do I contradict myself? Very well . . .")

Language, Myth, Science Fiction:

First contacts:

I did not have a happy childhood.

Nobody does.

I did, however, have a privileged one.

I discovered myths with a set of beautifully produced and illustrated books called *My Book House,* edited by Olive Burpré Miller and illustrated, for the most part, by Donald P. Crane. An older cousin of mine had owned them as a child. My aunt passed them on to me when her daughter went off to Vassar. The volumes bound in gray and mottled green dealt with history, starting with cavemen and working, lushly illustrated volume after lushly illustrated volume, through the Renaissance. Those bound in maroon and gold recounted, for children, great works of literature, fairy tales, and myths—Greek, Egyptian, Norse . . .

At five, I left kindergarten (the building, its bricks red as the *Book House* volumes, under a spray of city grime, is today a public school in the midst of a city housing project just above Columbia University) for a private, progressive, and extremely eccentric elementary school. I have one memory of my first day there, fragmented and incomplete:

Along one side of our room were tall, wide windows covered with wire grills. A window seat ran the length of the wall; the seat back went up and joined the wide windowsill—a squared grate, brown and painted, chipped here and there to the metal, through which you could see, checked with light, the dusty, iron radiators, and hear brass valves jiggle and hiss.

On that first morning, our teacher had to leave the shy dozen of us alone for some few minutes.

What occurs now, exactly, I'm not sure. But the memory clears when she comes rushing back, stops short and, fists clutching her blue smock (below which I can see the hem of her navy jumper), shrieks: "Stop it! Oh, my God! *Stop* it!"

One blond boy stood on the radiator grate, gripping the window grill, flattened against it, staring back at us, mouth wide and drooling, eyes closed and streaming.

We crowded the window seat, jeering and railing up at him: "Jump! Go ahead, jump!" I was holding the shoulder of the person in front of me, pressed forward by the person behind. "Jump!" I shouted, looked back at the teacher and laughed (you've seen how much fun five-year-olds have when they laugh), then shouted again: "Jump out! Jump out!" and could hear neither my own shouts nor my own laughter for the laughter and shouting of the other ten.

We were eight stories up.

The teacher yanked us, still jeering, one after another, away, lifted down the hysterical boy, and comforted him. His name was Robert. He was stocky, nervous, shrill. He had some slight motor difficulty. (I can still remember him, sitting at a green nursery table, holding his pencil in both hands to draw his letters, while the rest of us, who could, of course, hold *our* pencils in one, exchanged looks, glanced at him, glanced away, and giggled.) He was a stammerer, an appalling nail biter, very bright; and, by Christmas vacation, my best friend.

With occasional lapses, sometimes a few months long, Robert remained my best friend till we left for other schools after the eighth grade. Some of those lapses, however, I engineered quite blatantly—when I was tired of having the class odd-ball as constant companion. I would steal things from him, pencils, protractors, small toys—I remember pilfering a Donald Duck ring he had sent away for from a cereal box-top offer. With a small magnet (decaled to look like a tiny corn-flakes box), you could make the yellow plastic beak open and close, the blue plastic eye roll up and down. My parents caught me on that one, made me promise to return it, and tell him I'd stolen it. I did, quite convinced it would be the end of our friendship—apprehensive, but a bit relieved.

Robert took the ring back and stammered that it was all right if *I* had stolen it, because, after all (his expression was that of someone totally betrayed) I was his friend. That was when I realized he had no others.

During my attendance at Dalton, I lived one street from what, in the 1953 City Census, was declared the most populous tenement block in New York: It housed over eighteen thousand people, in buildings all under six stories. A block away, my sister and I had three floors and sixteen rooms, over my father's Harlem funeral parlor, in which to lose ourselves from our parents and the maid. But the buildings on both sides of us were a cluster of tiny two- and three-room apartments, housing five, seven, sometimes over ten people each. The friends I played with in the afternoon in front of the iron gates of Mr. Lockely's *Hosiery and Housepaint Store* to our left, or the sagging green vegetable boxes in front of the red-framed plate-glass window of Mr. Onley's *Groceries* to our right, were the son of a widowed hospital orderly on welfare, the daughter and two sons of a frequently laid-off maintenance man who worked in the New York subway system, the two sons of a New York taxi driver, the niece of the woman who ran the funeral parlor at the corner of the same block.

And in the morning, my father—or, occasionally, one of his employees—would drive me, in my father's very large, very black Cadillac, down to the ten-story, red and white brick building on Eighty-ninth Street off Park Avenue: I would line up with all the other children in the gray-tiled lobby, waiting to march around, next to the wall, and show my tongue to the school nurse, Miss Hedges, who, for the first years, in her white uniform with a gray sweater around her shoulders, would actually make an attempt to peer into each five-to-twelve-year-old mouth, but, as I grew older, simply stood, at last, in the corner by the gooseneck lamp as we filed by (perhaps one in five of us actually even bothered to look up) staring at a vague spot on the far wall, somewhere between the twenties-style, uplifting mural of Mothers Working in the Fields and the display cabinets where student sculpture was exhibited by our various art teachers. In class (ten students was considered the ideal number; should we somehow reach fourteen, Something Was Done to Relieve the Impossible Teaching Load), my friends were the son of a vice president of CBS Television, the daughter of a large New York publisher, the son of a small New York publisher, the grandson of the governor of the state, the son of the drama critic for *Time* magazine, the daughter of a psychiatrist and philanthropist, the son of a Pulitzer Prize–winning dramatist.

Black Harlem speech and white Park Avenue speech are very different things. I became aware of language as an intriguing and infinitely malleable modeling tool very early.

I always felt myself to be living in several worlds with rather tenuous connections between them, but I never remember it causing me much anxiety. (Of the, perhaps, ten blacks among the three-hundred-odd students in Dalton's elementary school, five were my relatives.) Rather, it gave me a sense of modest (and sometimes not so modest) superiority.

A few years later, I was given still another world to play in. I spent summer at a new summer camp. I tell only one incident here from that pleasantest of summers in my life: One hot afternoon, I wandered into a neighboring tent where the older boys slept. On the foot of the nearest iron-frame bed lay a large, ragged-edged magazine, with a shiny cover gone matte with handling—I think its muddy, out-of-register colors showed a man and a woman on a hill, gazing in terrified astonishment at a round, metal *thing* swooping through the air. From the lettering on the cover, the lead story in this issue was something called—I picked it up and turned to the first page—*The Man Who Sold the Moon*. My first reaction was: "What an odd combination of words! What do they mean . . . ?" While I was puzzling through the opening sentences, one of the bunk-seven twelve-year-olds came in and shooed me out. Back in my own tent, I returned to the book I was reading, Lincoln Barnett's *The Uni-*

verse and Dr. Einstein. And our twenty-three-year-old counsellor, Roy, was reading something called *One, Two, Three . . . Infinity* that I had said looked interesting and he had said I could read when he was finished.

Months later, back on Eighty-ninth Street, after consultation with Robert (and several practice tries from five, six, and then seven steps), I decided to leap down the entire flight between the sixth and seventh floor. At the head of the stairwell—the steps were a dark green that continued up the wall to shoulder level; there, light green took over and went on across the ceiling—sighting on the flaking, gold decalcomania on the far wall ("SIX," half on dark green, half on light), I got ready, grinned at Robert below, who was leaning against the door and looking nervous, swung my arms back threw them forward, jumped—my foot slipped! I flailed out, suspended a moment, silent, in dead air, trajectory off!

The bottom newel post caught me in the belly, and I passed out—no more than a couple of seconds.

Robert had yanked open the door and was running for a teacher before I hit.

I should have ruptured myself. Apparently all I did, though, was knock all my air out and, temporarily and very slightly, atort my right spermatic. Because I'd gone unconscious, however, and people were wondering whether I'd hit my head, I spent the night in observation at the hospital.

In the patients' lounge were several of those large-sized pulp magazines that I recognized as the type I'd seen (but never read) last summer at camp. I selected the one with the most interesting cover—girl, bikini, bubble-helmet, monster—and took it back to my bed and read my first two science-fiction stories.

One climaxed with a tremendous spaceship battle, the dénouement of which was someone figuring out that the death ray the enemy used was actually nothing more than light, slowed way down, so that its energy potential went way up. I don't remember one character, or one situation besides the battle; I doubt if I would want to. But the idea, connected forever in my memory with a marvelous illustration (I'm sure it was by Virgil Finlay, though I've never run across the magazine again) of bubble-helmeted spacemen entering a chamber of looming vampire monsters, remains.

The other story I read that night leaves me with this recollection: Some Incredibly Ancient Aliens (in the lead illustration, they are all veined heads and bulging eyes) are explaining to someone (the hero? the villain?) that the brain is never used to full capacity by humans, but *they*, you see, have been using *theirs*, which are much larger than humans' anyway, to full capacity now for centuries. And they are *very* tired.

And at school, a couple of weeks later, Robert mentioned to me that he had just read a wonderful book that I must take a look at: *Rocketship Galileo*. He had read it twice already. It was, he explained, probably one of the best books in the world. He even volunteered to get it out of the school library for me that afternoon (I had several books overdue and couldn't take out any myself till they were returned), which he did . . .

Too much enthusiasm among my friends for something has often been a turn-off for me—often to my detriment. I *still* have not read Heinlein's *Rocketship Galileo*, though Robert, after I finally returned the book to the library, unread, actually bought a copy and gave it to me.

That year's history study was divided into one term of ancient Greek history and one term of Roman. The climax of the Greek term was a day-long Greek Festival which our class put on for the rest of the school. The morning of Festival Day, the whole school, in the auditorium, watched a play competition, where several short, original plays "on Greek themes" were performed, one of which was voted best by a board of teachers.

For that year's Festival, I had written one of the plays (a comedy in which I took the part of Pericles—I believe he was having labor problems with the slaves over the construction of the Parthenon). It took second to a play by a girl who had muscular dystrophy, a speech impediment, and who used to cry all the time for no reason. Backstage in my toga, furiously jealous, I vigorously applauded the announcement of her triumph, among the rest of the clapping actors from the various play-companies, while she limped out on stage to receive her wreath of bay-leaves. Congratulating her, and the happy members of the cast of her play, I decided the Greek Festival was a waste.

I can only remember one dialogue exchange from my play. I hated it; another cast member had written it and insisted on inserting it, and I had finally acquiesced to keep peace. (Socrates: "How is the Parthenon coming along, Pericles?" Pericles [through gritted teeth]: "It's all up but the columns.") But I still have the opening of the prize-winning play by heart, with only that one morning's viewing:

The curtains had opened and a chorus of Greek women in blue veils walked across the stage, growing light with dawn, reciting:

> Persia's ships to Attica came.
> Many a thousand they were.
> And like winged birds, the tribes of Greece
> Attacked the Persian prey.

The women turned, walked back again—reciting what, I no longer recall. But I still remember that "attacked" as one of the most exciting words I had ever heard. Terminating the sentence with its clutch of harsh consonants, while all the other sounds fluttered behind it in memory, spoken by six ten-year-old girls at ordinary volume, it had—to me—the force of a shout.

Martha, who wore leg braces and walked funny and couldn't talk properly and had rightfully won her prize over my glib, forgettable wise-cracks, had shown me for the first time that a single word, placed properly in a sentence, could give an effect at once inevitable, astonishing, and beautiful.

After a very un-Greek lunch in the third floor dining room, everyone went up to the tenth-floor gymnasium, where we held a junior Olympics. The boys had wrestling matches, discus throwing, high jumping, and broad jumping. The girls ran hurdle races, chariot races, and did jumping too. Then there was a final relay where boys and girls, in hiked-up togas, ran—their papier maché torches streaming crêpe-paper fire—around and around the gym.

It was that dull.

In English that term we had read the *Iliad* and the *Odyssey*, as well as a good handful of traditional myths—most of which I was familiar with from *My Book House*. We even tackled one or two Greek plays in translation; and over one English period, Mrs. T, my favorite English teacher from my whole elementary school days, explained to us the etymology of "calligraphy," "geology," "optical," "palindrome," "obscene," and "poet."

In Math, to coordinate with our Greek unit, we devoted one day a week to Geometry. Using "only the tools Pythagoras accepted" (i.e., a compass and a straight edge), we went about discovering simple geometric relationships about the circle and various inscribed angles. We constructed a demonstration to show that the area of a circle, as the limit of the sum of its sectors cut ever smaller and placed alternately, approaches a parallelogram with a base of πr, and a height of r, to wit, an area of πr^2 And Robert gave me another book, which I did read this time, called *The Black Star Passes*, by John W. Campbell. Again, I remember neither plot nor characters. But I do recall that someone in it had invented a Very Powerful Mathematical Tool called "the multiple calculus," about which author Campbell went on with ebullient enthusiasm. We had already been taught, on the other four days of the week, the basic manipulative algebraic skills, adding, subtracting, multiplying, and dividing polynomials. At home, I stumbled through the Encyclopedia Britannica article on Infinitesimal Calculus (which went on about somebody named Newton as enthusiastically as Campbell had gone on about *his* mathematician); days later I went down to the High School Library on the school's third floor, got out a book; got out another; and then three more. Then I bought a Baron's *Review of Trigonometry*. And then I got some more books.

But the school term was over again.

At summer camp that year I was assigned to a tent at the bottom of the tent colony. My iron-frame bed, which I made up that first afternoon with sheets so starched they had to be peeled apart (and the inevitable olive drab army blanket), was next to the bed of a boy named Eugene. I didn't like him. I don't think anybody else in the tent did either. But he made friendly attempts at conversation—mostly about his father, who, you see, edited *Galaxy:* "Don't you know what *Galaxy* is? It's the science-fiction magazine! Don't you like science fiction? Well, then what does *your* father do?"

"He's an undertaker," I said, having learned some time ago that if I said it with a steely enough voice (picked up from Channel Five reruns of Bela Lugosi films), it would shut just about anybody up, at least for a while.

Sometime in the next hour or so, Gene had a twenty-minute, hysterical crying jag and decided he wanted to go home—I don't recall about what. I do remember thinking: This is ridiculous, I'll never be able to put up with *this* next to me all summer!

I asked the counsellor if I could be assigned a bed next to someone—anyone—else. The counsellor said no.

Disappointed, I went back to my bed and was sitting on it, arranging my jeans, swimming trunks, and underwear in the wooden shelf wedged back under the sloping canvas roof, when another boy shouted: "Look *out!*"

I dived forward onto the next bed, and rolled over to see Gene's eight-inch hunting knife plunged through my army blanket, the two sheets and thin mattress, and heard it grate the springs. Gene, clutching the handle, stopped shaking with hysterical rage, pulled the knife free and looked about at the seven other boys in the tent, who all stared back. My blanket settled, with just the slightest wrinkle, and an inch-and-a-half slit, slightly off center.

Gene, frankly, looked as astonished as the rest of us.

Just then the counsellor (that year his name was Marty) backed up the tent steps, dragging his own trunk, and asked one of the boys to help him put it under his bed. Somebody went back to packing his shelf. Somebody else sat down on his own bed, creaking springs. Gene blinked a few times then put the knife in his top shelf, between his soap dish and his mess kit.

I left the tent, took a walk around the tent colony, watching, through the rolled-back tent flaps, the other campers unpack. Finally, I went into the creosoted bathroom shack, had diarrhea for fifteen minutes, at the end of which, with a red ball-point pen, I wrote something stupid and obscene on the wall beside something equally stupid and obscene.

In the same way I have no memory of what directly preceded our class harassment of Robert, I have no real memory of what precisely occurred just before Gene's outburst. What had we done to him? Did I assist in it? Or do nothing to prevent it? Or did I instigate it? Conveniently, I have forgotten.

Sitting in the pine-planked stall, looking at the cracked cement flooring, I do remember thinking: If I am going to have to sleep next to this nut, I'd better make friends with him. Then I went back to my tent where Marty was asking for the choice of stories we wanted him to read us after lights-out. The vote was unanimous for Jack London.

Over the next week, occasionally I looked at the little tear in my blanket: but once the initial fear had gone, with the odd callousness of childhood, I set about making friends with Gene; there was nothing else to do.

Tuesday morning, after breakfast, Gene received in the mail, from his father, cover proofs for the two forthcoming issues of *Galaxy* (containing the last installment of *Caves of Steel*, and the first of *Gladiators at Law*), both covers by Emsh—Gene's favorite sf illustrator. Perhaps a week after that, he received an advance copy of the first issue of the fantasy magazine *Beyond*. I borrowed it from him one afternoon and read Theodore Cogswell's "The Wall Around the World," which, I decided, was the best story I had ever read.

Our tent counsellor, Marty, was a graduate physics student at City College, and a science-fiction reader himself.

I asked Gene if I could lend Marty the magazine; after much debate, Gene said yes. Marty read the story, said he liked it, but that it made its point by oversimplifying things.

As we walked down the path between the girls' bunks and an old barn building, called for some reason (there were several apocryphal stories explaining why) Brooklyn College, I asked: "Why do you say it's oversimplified?" Porgy's adventures on a world where magic controls one half and science the other had seemed quite the most significant construct I had encountered since slow light or the multiple calculus.

"Well," Marty explained, as a herd of boys and girls swarmed from the ping-pong tables, out the wide doors of Brooklyn College, to troop along the road as the dinner bell, down by the dining room, donged and danged, "if you define magic as all that is not science, and science as all that is not magic—well, for one thing, you come up with a situation where, *if* science exists, magic must too. And we know it doesn't. It's much more useful to consider science a refinement of magic—that's what it is historically. As it gets refined, there're just fewer and fewer contradictions: It just gets more and more effective."

And that evening, after we were all in bed, Marty, sitting back on his own bed, with a flashlight propped against his shoulder, would read us *To Build a Fire*, or *South of the Slot*, or *The Shadow and the Flash*.

My best friend that year at summer camp was Karen, who, though she was odd, seemed more efficient at it than Gene. She never tried to kill me; and no one ever tried to kill her.

She used to fill endless terrariums with snakes she caught in the woods. Once, when we were working together putting up screens in the camp Nature House, I interrupted her explanation of how to tell which mushrooms were and which were not Deadly Amanita, to ask her if she liked science fiction. She said no, because there weren't any girls in it—"Or, when there are, they never *do* anything"—which, for all the bikinis-and-bubble-helmets, I had to admit was about true.

And Gene was unhappy at camp and went home after the first month anyway.

Back at school, Greek and Roman history were replaced by a term of medieval European history, and then a term of combined Chinese and Indian history. Our history teacher that year, a Mrs. Ethel Muckerjee, a plump, New England woman of diminutive but impressive bearing (she was one of the handful of teachers we did *not* call by their first name), had spent many years in India and had been the wife of the late, Indian scholar, Dan Ghopal Muckerjee, who (so went the story we told each other in hushed tones) had committed suicide some years ago when he had discovered himself victim of fatal, lingering cancer, and whose English translations of the *Ramayana* and the *Mahabharata* were, that term, our literature texts.

In class discussions, cross-legged on the vinyl floor (while, under the window seat, the radiators hissed and, occasionally, clunked), I would watch Mrs. Muckerjee, with her white hair, her gray tweeds, and her blocky-heeled shoes, lean forward in her chair and explain to the circle of us: "Now, recall the *Iliad* from last year. Do you see how, in the *Mahabharata*, the relationship of gods to men envisioned by Valmiki under his anthill is—" and here, hands on her knees, her elbows would bend—"*very* different from the relation held by the blind Greek, Homer . . ."

That spring, the Old Vic production of Giraudoux's *Tiger at the Gates* came to New York, with Michael Redgrave. The aunt of a school friend took us to the first Wednesday Matinee during our spring vacation. From the second row, I watched while a story whose plot I knew (just as I had been told that the audiences for the original Greek drama all knew the plots beforehand too) was used to say something that struck me, at the time, as completely new. The fascinating thing to me was that the inevitability of the story was part of what was being constantly discussed on stage.

In the same week, I heard a radio production of Giraudoux's *The Apollo of Bellac,* and I found it enthralling. One of our assistant teachers recommended I read some of Anouilh's charming dramatic representations of Greek myths; Sartre's more weighty, if less elegant, retelling of the *Orestia, The Flies,* came about here; and then O'Neill's *Mourning Becomes Elektra* and *The Great God Brown.*

During the term of Chinese and Indian history, we were also given a French class; our regular Natural Science teacher was taking a year off to devote himself to sculpture, and no replacement could be found. His works were on exhibit at the Museum of Modern Art, where my parents took me once to see them. Our art teacher (whose works were occasionally to be seen at the Whitney) used to say of his, while swinging her long arms back and forth against her gray apron: "Well, I don't think they're very good—too formal, too congested. But it has *some*thing . . ."

With a yellow pointer wielded in chalk-whitened fingers, Madame Geritsky, shorter than most of her pupils, made us memorize pages of French prose, which we had to recite alone and in unison, our *u*'s, *r*'s, and *l*'s constantly corrected.

I was never a good language student: but I was a bold one. Years later, when I actually spent time in other countries, I found that, armed with the all-important sentences well memorized ("How do you say *that* in Greek/Italian/Turkish . . ."), I could pick up in weeks, or even days, at least temporarily, what took others months to acquire.

We reconstruct from memory a childhood that, as adults, we can bear. I think of mine as one in which I liked many people and was liked in return. If I *was* as happy as I remember, one reason is that I went to a school where athletic prowess and popularity were not necessarily synonymous. Among the three classes of ten to thirteen that formed our grade, there were only three boys I recall as particularly good at sports. And two of these used to vie for position as Class Bully. Everyone cordially despised them.

In gym, three mornings and three afternoons a week, we indulged in an amazingly sadistic game called "bombardment": two teams hurled soccer balls at one another, taking prisoner anyone hit. Our gym teacher, named (I kid you not) Muscles, had several times pulled Arthur out for purposely hitting another player so hard with the ball he brought the boy to tears.

During one of my early lapses with Robert (was I seven? eight?), Arthur tried to pick a fight with me on the school roof. He was a head taller than everybody else in the class, possibly slightly older. As he was shoving me back into the wire fence at the roof's edge, I said to myself: "This is silly!" So I announced to him that, indeed, it *was* silly of him to push me around: I was his friend. So he should stop. After the third time I said it, he looked perplexed and said, "Oh." I straightened my clothes and suggested we play together. For the next two weeks I went regularly to his house in the afternoons, invited him, regularly, to mine, and spent inordinate amounts of time helping him with his arithmetic homework.

Finally, I got bored.

He was not bright; he was lonely; he was belligerent. Friendship with Robert did not cut me off from friendship with anyone else: Robert was just strange. Friendship with Arthur did: Arthur was actively antisocial. Because he was ill-practiced in keeping friendships going, it was extremely easy to maneuver my way out of it, by being otherwise occupied here, too busy there, all the while counting on the fact he valued me too much to protest. In another week, without any particular scenes, we were no longer even speaking.

Anywhere outside the gymnasium, Arthur was subjected to a needling harassment that certainly fed his belligerence and, in its way, was much more vicious than that first day's attack on Robert. Robert's attack lasted minutes. Arthur's, practically without let-up, went on for years.

Arthur had committed some particularly annoying offense. A bunch of us got together and decided we must teach him a lesson. We agreed that, for the rest of the week, no one in the class would speak to him, or acknowledge he was there in any way. After a couple of hours, he hit a few people. They scooted out of the way, giggling. An hour after that, he was sitting on the hallway floor by the green book-box, leaning against it, sobbing. The teachers finally realized what we were doing and demanded we stop. So we did—while any teachers were around.

On the last day of this treatment (and there were others, dreamed up for him practically every month), Arthur managed to confront a bunch of us in the narrow, fenced-in enclosure in front of the school. He yelled at us angrily, then began to cry. We watched, mild embarrassment masked with mild approval, when, in the middle of his crying, Arthur suddenly pointed to me and exclaimed: "But *you're* my friend! You're my *friend!*"

Had it not been the last day, I would have stayed with my group. As it was, I spoke to him, left my friends, and went with him to the corner where he caught his bus home. I may even have explained to him why we'd done it. But I doubt, at this point, if he either understood or cared.

I think, however, this was where I began to realize that such cerebral punishments teach the offender nothing of the nature of annoyance, injury, or suffering he has inflicted: They teach only the strength of the group, and the group's cruelty—the group's oblivion to the annoyance, injury, and suffering it can inflict—the same, basic failing of the offender.

I didn't consider Arthur my friend. After walking him to the corner, I made no other efforts to be friendly. As other harassments came up, I was just as likely to be party—except that I now stayed more in the background to avoid being called to witness. But in gym class, Arthur no longer hurled at me his bombardment ball.

At six and seven, Arthur was a bully. By eleven or twelve, he was class clown; last in his school work, still incredibly aggressive in sports, now, whenever there was any tension between him and any teacher or classmate, he would drop his books all over the floor, belch loudly, or give a shrill, pointless giggle. We, at any rate, laughed—and despised him nonetheless. Our harassments had been effective: He was no longer likely to hit you. Frankly, I'm not sure that his earlier reactions weren't the more valid.

I am sure, however, that given another time, another place, another school, and children from families that had indulged different values, Arthur might have been the well-liked, admired student while I, an eccentric weakling of a different race, who lived half his life in another world, might have suffered all the harassment I so cavalierly helped in heaping on him.

Dalton prided itself in its progressiveness and courted an image of eccentricity. (The bizarre elementary school in Patrick Dennis's *Auntie Mame* is supposedly Dalton.) The eccentricity went no further than the headmistress announcing to each class, at the beginning of each year, in a *very* guarded tone: "If you *really* have something worthwhile, creative, and constructive to do, then you *may* arrange to be excused from regular classes." The announcement was made once and *never* repeated, though, in the Dalton brochures, this aspect of the school's individualized approach to each student was made much of. To my knowledge, I was the only student from my year who ever got to wheedle his way out of some of the more arduous classes: I developed an incredibly complex art project that involved paintings, sculptures, and electric lights, and announced to my math teacher that I wanted special instruction in calculus, and wanted it *now*.

For several months, I got away with spending most of my school day between the art room and special math tutoring sessions.

I was doing practically no assigned work. My arithmetic had never been strong. And my parents, who were nowhere near as eccentrically progressive as the school, decided to send me to a tutor, during this time, three afternoons a week.

Amanda Kemp was a small, white-haired, black woman, who lived on the top floor of an apartment house on Edgecomb Avenue, in small, dark rooms that smelled of leaking gas.

With much good will and infinite patience, she tried to "interest" me in things that I had invested a good deal of emotional autonomy in remaining uninterested in—"Since," she explained to my mother, after the first week, "actually teaching him is certainly no problem. He learns whatever he wants to learn all *too* quickly," and she gave me a book of poems by Countee Cullen, which he had personally inscribed to her, years earlier, when they worked together in the city school system, its illustrations marvelously macabre, showing imaginary beasts of Jabberwockian complexity, each described by an accompanying rhymed text.

The person in my math class who did get the constantly easy hundred was Priscilla. Sometime around here, I decided to write a science-fiction novel—announced my project to a group of friends in the coffee shop on the corner, where we all adjourned after school to indulge in an obligatory toasted English muffin and/or lemon coke. I actually wrote the opening chapter: twenty pages of single-spaced typing on lined, three-holed, loose-leaf paper. I brought it into school and, during one study period, asked Priscilla to read it and pass judgment.

During the next half hour I chewed through several pencil erasers, stripped the little brass edge out of my wooden ruler, and accomplished some half dozen more intense, small, and absorbing destructions.

Priscilla, finally, looked up. (We were sitting on the green stairs.)

"Did you like it?" I asked. "Did you *understand* it?"

"I don't," she said, a little dryly, "believe anyone could understand it with your spelling the way it is. Here, let me make you a list . . ." It was the beginning of a marvelous friendship (that, a year ago, reflowered just as warmly when I visited Wesleyan University where she is now a professor of Russian) which quickly came to include nightly hour-plus phone calls, made up mostly of ritual catch phrases (such as: "What has *that* got to do with the price of eggs in Afghanistan!") which somehow, by the slightest variation of inflection, communicated the most profound and arcane ideas, or, conversely, reduced us to hysterical laughter, to the annoyance of both our parents at both our houses. Besides correcting my spelling, Priscilla also told me about a book she said was perfectly wonderful and I must read, called *Titus Groan*. For fourteen years, it suffered the fate of *Rocketship Galileo*. I only got around to reading it one evening over a weekend at Damon Knight's sprawling Anchorage in Milford, Pennsylvania (Damon had just made some rather familiar sounding comments on the spellings in a manuscript I had given him to read); Priscilla had been right.

The last year of elementary school was drawing to a close. I had just been accepted at the Bronx High School of Science. I was sitting in the school's smaller, upstairs library, reading *More Than Human* for the second time, when several students, Robert and Priscilla among them, came in to tell me that I had been elected Most Popular Person in the Class—a distinction which carried with it the dubious honor of making a small speech at graduation.

I was terribly pleased.

Like many children who get along easily with their peers, I was an incredibly vicious and self-centered child, a liar when it suited me and a thief when I could get away with it, who, with an astonishing lack of altruism, had learned some of the advantages of being nice to people nobody else wanted to be bothered with.

I think, sometimes, when we are trying to be the most honest, the fictionalizing process is at its strongest. Would Robert, Mrs. Mackerjee, Gene, Arthur, Marty, or Priscilla agree with any of what I have written here, or even recognize it? What do *they* remember that, perhaps, I have forgotten—either because it was too painful, too damning, or because it made no real impression at all?

Language, Myth, Science Fiction . . .

58. Browsing in Joe Kennedy's *Counter/Measures,* I came across a poem by John Bricuth called *Myth.* Liked it muchly. It begins with an epigraph from Lévi-Strauss:

"Music and mythology confront man with virtual objects whose shadow alone is real . . ."

Then this from Quine's *Philosophy of Logic*:

"The long and short of it is that propositions have been projected as shadows of sentences, if I may transpose a figure of Wittgenstein's. At best they will give us nothing the sentence will not give. Their promise of more is mainly due to our uncritically assuming for them an individuation which matches no equivalence between sentences that we can see how to define. The shadows favoured wishful thinking."

And from Spicer's poem *Language,* in his discussion of the candle flame and the finger he has just blistered:

> do they both point us to the
> grapheme on the concrete wall—
> the space between it
> where the shadow and the flame are one?

Just as "propositions" can be dismissed from logic on the formal side as a logical shadow in a field where we wish for light, on the informal side we can dismiss the movable predicate—x "walks" which can be moved to y "walks" and so on to the i*th* variable ". . . if and only if the i*th* thing in the sequence walks" (presumably true of x, y, and the others) [*Philosophy of Logic*, p. 40]—as an empirical shadow: It is a shadow of the empirical resolution at which we observe a given set of process phenomena that allows us to subsume them all under one word. If, for instance, all that can be referred to by "walks" is, like the word, a singular entity, then a very strange entity it is. Among other things, it is discontinuous in both time and space, since both x and y can perform it simultaneously in different locations and/or at different times! In the empirical world, however, spatial and temporal discontinuity *is* multiplicity of entities. And "a multiple entity" in our language at any rate is as silly a concept as "many rock." (This, I suspect, is the practical side of Quine's refusal to "quantify over predicates" [*Philosophy of Logic*, p. 28]. If we have a situation where every instance of predicate-with-every-variable can be empirically resolved into separate predicates (P), we have a situation where the existential quantifier ($_E$P), would always have the same value as the universal quantifier (P). If there is *only* one q, then everything you can say of "at least one q" you can say of "all q." Similarly, the negation of one quantifier could always be taken as the other *or* empty, as one liked. This gets the formal logician into the same sort of trouble as the mathematician who allows himself to divide by zero in formal algebra.)

If we have a universe composed only of real, unique objects performing unique processes, how do we order them? (Are we stuck with G. Spencer-Brown's suggestion from *Laws of Form* that "equals" must be taken to mean "is confused with"?) Or, more germane: Since we *do* perceive the universe as ordered, can we work back to such a universe of unique objects-and-processes without contradiction?

Language is miraculous not in its power to differentiate. Differentiation, when all is said and done, is carried on nonverbally by the reasonable cross-checking of the information of the other senses. The wonder is that language can respond to any number of *different* things in the *same* way: it can call ashtrays, actors, and accidents "entities"; it can call poems, paintings, and nesselrode pies "art"; it can call what three different men at three different times of day do when going down the street "walking"; it can call three entities that walk down the street at the same time "women"; it can call sentences, ideas, and blue-prints "models"; it can call freedom, death, the color white, and the Second-World-War-and-all-its-causes "volumes in multidimensional meaning space"; it can call causing pain, inflicting suffering, and perpetrating injustice "evil." In this way language guides the senses to concentrate on various areas and aspects of the world for further examination and further differential cross-checking.

Things "obviously" similar are coherent areas of meaning-space only because of the shadow the senses throw over them. Those areas not so obviously coherent become so under the various shadows language can cast.

59. Science fiction is a way of casting a language-shadow over coherent areas of imaginative space that would otherwise be largely inaccessible.

60. Is it the tragedy of mind? Or is it what assures the mind's development: Today's seminal idea is tomorrow's critical cliché.

— *London*
1973–1974

Index

University Press of New England publishes books under its own imprint and is the publisher for Brandeis University Press, Dartmouth College, Middlebury College Press, University of New Hampshire, University of Rhode Island, Tufts University, University of Vermont, Wesleyan University Press, and Salzburg Seminar.

About the Author
Samuel R. Delany is Professor of Comparative Literature at the University of Massachusetts, Amherst. His many books include the Return to Nevèrÿon series, *Dhalgren,* and *Trouble on Triton,* reissued by Wesleyan University Press; *Atlantis: Three Tales* (1995), *Silent Interviews* (1994), *The Motion of Light in Water* (1987), and *Stars in My Pocket Like Grains of Sand* (1984).

Library of Congress Cataloging-in-Publication Data

Delany, Samuel R.
    Longer Views : extended essays / Samuel R. Delany ; with an
introduction by Ken James.
        p.   cm.
    Includes index.
    ISBN 0–8195–5281–X (alk. paper).
    ISBN 0–8195–6293–9 (pbk. : alk paper)
    I. Title.
PS3554.E437L66   1996
814'.54—dc20   96–1237